He leaned toward me and said, "I might as well tell you, Dolphy, that my big book, my *Meisterwerk*, will deal solely with my theory of historical cusps." His voice grew grave—"I will venture to mention the most crucial and yet the most disputable of them all."

"Go ahead," I told him indulgently.

"Very well. In November of 1918, when the British had broken the Hindenburg Line, and just before the Allies had launched the final crushing drive which cut a devastating swath through the heartland to Berlin, there existed the strong possibility that an immediate armistice would be offered and signed. There would inevitably have been a secret recrudescence of pan-German militarism. German scientific humanism would not have won its total victory over the Germany of the Huns."

I let out a gusty sigh. His interpretation was completely valid. I raised my glass and said, "Let us drink to your amazing cusps." We drank, and I brushed to either side with a thumbnail the short horizontal black mustache which decorates my upper lip, and I automatically swept back into place the errant lock of black hair which tends to fall down across my forehead. . . .

From the award-winning story, *Catch That Zeppelin!*

Other ACE Books by Fritz Leiber you will enjoy:

THE BIG TIME
THE GREEN MILLENNIUM
THE MIND SPIDER
SHIPS TO THE STARS
SWORDS AGAINST DEATH
SWORDS AND DEVILTRY
SWORDS AGAINST WIZARDRY
SWORDS IN THE MIST
THE SWORDS OF LANKHMAR
YOU'RE ALL ALONE

THE WORLDS OF FRITZ LEIBER

by
Fritz Leiber

ace books
A Division of Charter Communications Inc.
A GROSSET & DUNLAP COMPANY
1120 Avenue of the Americas
New York, New York 10036

THE WORLDS OF FRITZ LEIBER

Copyright © 1976 by Fritz Leiber

All rights reserved. No part of this book may be reproduced in any form or by any means, except for the inclusion of brief quotations in a review, without permission in writing from the publisher.

All characters in this book are fictitious. Any resemblance to actual persons, living or dead, is purely coincidental.

An ACE Book

First ACE printing: November, 1976

Printed in U.S.A.

ACKNOWLEDGEMENTS

"The Hatchery of Dreams," copyright 1961 by Ziff-Davis Publishing Company

"The Goggles of Dr. Dragonet," copyright 1961 by Ziff-Davis Publishing Company

"Far Reach to Cygnus," copyright 1964 by Ziff-Davis Publishing Company

"Night Passage," copyright 1975 by Llewellyn Publications

"The Nice Girl With Five Husbands," copyright 1951 by World Editions, Inc.

"When the Change-Winds Blow," copyright 1964 by Mercury Press, Inc.

"237 Talking Statues, Etc.," copyright 1963 by Mercury Press, Inc.

"The Improper Authorities," copyright 1959 by Ziff-Davis Publishing Company

"Our Saucer Vacation," copyright 1959 by Great American Publications, Inc.

"Pipe Dream," copyright 1958 by Quinn Publishing Co., Inc.

"What's He Doing In There?" copyright 1957 by Galaxy Publishing Corporation

"Friends and Enemies," copyright 1957 by Royal Publications, Inc.

"The Last Letter," copyright 1958 by Galaxy Publishing Corporation

"Endfray of the Ofay," copyright 1969 by Galaxy Publishing Corporation

"Cyclops," copyright 1965 by Galaxy Publishing Corporation

"Mysterious Doings in the Metropolitan Museum," copyright 1974 by Terry Carr

"The Bait," copyright 1973 by Stuart Schiff

"The Lotus Eaters," copyright 1972 by Mercury Press, Inc.

"Waif," copyright 1974 by Roger Elwood

"Myths My Great-Granddaughter Taught Me," copyright 1963 by Mercury Press, Inc.

"Catch That Zeppelin!," copyright 1975 by Mercury Press, Inc.

"Last," copyright 1957 by Fantasy House, Inc.

TABLE OF CONTENTS

Page

Introduction .... ix & x
The Hatchery of Dreams 1
The Goggles of Dr. Dragonet 17
Far Reach to Cygnus 41
Night Passage 71
The Nice Girl With Five Husbands 95
When the Change-Winds Blow 111
237 Talking Statues, Etc. 123
The Improper Authorities 135
Our Saucer Vacation 151
Pipe Dream 175
What's He Doing in There? 191
Friends and Enemies 199
The Last Letter 219
Endfray of the Ofay 233
Cyclops 251
Mysterious Doings in the Metropolitan Museum 261
The Bait 271
The Lotus Eaters 275
Waif 281
Myths My Great-Granddaughter Taught Me 307
Catch That Zeppelin! 315
Last 339

INTRODUCTION

I believe this collection represents me more completely, provides a fuller measure of the range of my fictional efforts, than any other. I've tried to make it that way, without repeating stories from other collections, especially the ones currently in print. There's no overlap with *those* whatever. (Overlapping collections are an annoyance to readers and author alike.)

Rather to my surprise, it's a light-hearted collection. The terrors are there, but they're seasoned with humor— at least I hope so; even the atomic dooms have escape clauses and the lonely people generally find comfort. It's also a *personal* collection—I didn't expect to find so many first-person narratives. It's very much concerned with *vision,* whether into the future or the heights and depths of the mind: Dr. Hugo Dragonet (stories two and three) lives in Hollywood and invents things for the films, and there are peerings into (and *from*) the realms of insects, actors, cats, robots and witches—we even take an Earth man for a ride in our flying saucer. Finally, from the first to the antepenultimate story, there are *girl*s (forgive me that sweet sexist word, O Liberated Women) growing younger all the way.

The first three stories were written for Cele Goldsmith, the lovely and brilliant editor of *Fantastic* in the 1960's. "Night Passage" I wrote only last year, for Isaac Bonewits and his charming wife, Rusty, who plays a wicked game of chess; it grew from a nightlong drive I made myself.

"The Nice Girl With Five Husbands" and "When the Change-Winds Blow" skirt the edges of my Change-War stories, while "237 Talking Statues, Etc.," explores my theatrical background and exemplifies my psychological tales. (My, there's a lot of "my" in this preface!)

"Our Saucer Vacation" ought to be dedicated to Robert Heinlein, for it certainly owes a great deal to his matchless juvenile novels, even if I do reverse the formula.

The next four stories after that one dip back into the 1950's: Greenwich Village, Martians, the atomic bomb, and robots played for comedy, not to say farce. The bomb story ("Friends and Enemies") originally had a Christ-character, but I realized I was taking myself too seriously and put in a girl instead, fresh out of high school, and it went better.

"Endfray of the Ofay" was originally contemporaneous and set in Chicago's south side, but *it* went better after I'd enthroned a Black empress over America and put all the Whites in Indian reservations.

"The Lotus Eaters" and "The Bait" sample my cat stories and lifelong saga (five books so far) of the sword-and-sorcery characters Fafhrd and the Gray Mouser.

The girls return, getting very young indeed, in "Waif" and "Myths my Great-Granddaughter Taught Me," while last year's "Catch That Zeppelin!" was awarded the Nebula to comfort my old age—old people *do* have an advantage in such competitions, if they can manage to function at all.

Welcome to my worlds!

HATCHERY OF DREAMS

When Giles Wardwell woke up Saturday morning and Joan wasn't beside him in bed or anywhere in the house and there was no message on the slate in the kitchen or any response when he banged on the door of her lab, and when a glance showed their blue car sitting on the drive, his first impulse was to report the matter to CAMZ at once. Grim old Mr. Copps himself had warned the whole CAMZ staff that all their lives and those of their loved ones were in slight but definite danger from America's enemies now that Copps, Arbuthnot, Mather, and Zim were doing public relations work for the Secondman Missiles Project. Mr. Zim, looking almost equally a dour Puritan father despite his Turkish background, had filled them in with some excruciating first-hand details on Russian espionage methods.

Just before they'd gone to sleep last night Joan had asked Giles, "Do the Russians have hypnosis beams? I have the feeling someone's trying to get control of my mind." And he had replied in a joking way that made him sick to remember, "Only in science-fiction magazines," to her first remark and "Probably your mother-in-law, God help us," to her second.

Giles decided to put on his glasses and have a closer look around before calling CAMZ. He didn't find the red nightgown Joan had been wearing, but he did find the little penned note on the bedside table.

"Dear Giles (it read), I'm taking a vacation from our marriage, maybe for a month, maybe forever. In case it's the latter I'll let you know. You know I don't fit in. Anyhow, I can't stick your stodgy conformity—or your mother's!—any longer. Maybe being with other humans will give me perspective. You can be respectable to the hilt and tell people I'm visiting Mable in Wisconsin, but that's not where I'm going. Good luck. Joan."

When Giles Wardwell had read that, Russia was a name in the geography books, CAMZ were eccentric wheels, and an old fear of his had become an active torment: the knowledge that he was fifteen years older than Joan and a proper Bostonian, and that being bald as an egg from thirty-five on was not at all the same thing as being romantically shaven-headed like Yul Brynner.

He'd been afraid once or twice before that Joan was unhappy, though that was by no means his deepest fear about her. He'd known she couldn't stand his mother, though they only saw the old lady two or three times a week. He'd thought Joan was restless lately, in spite of her bridge and cosmetics hobbies. And certainly she didn't exactly fit in—she had no real friends he knew of in the Boston area except for the three amusing but socially off-trail women who made up her bridge foursome.

He wondered where she could have gone. Mr. and Mrs. Bishop—Joan's parents—were both dead and there were no uncles, aunts, or close cousins. Mable was just a college roommate, rarely mentioned. Joan did have a little money in an account of her own.

While he was thinking these things, Giles' feet had been carrying him, still in his dull olive pullover pyjamas, on another circuit of the house and now brought him up short at the door to Joan's lab. He hesitated—he'd always sensed (though Joan had never told him in so many words) that she didn't like him to barge into her perfume distillery and he had made a point of never offending, and besides the place was associated in his mind

HATCHERY OF DREAMS

with his deepest fear about her.

Then he opened the door and went in.

His first impression was of gloom—the shades were tightly drawn—and an unnatural heat.

The small flasks and jars, the electric mixer for cold cream, and the elaborate distilling setups all seemed to be in their usual places.

He switched on the overhead light.

Then he saw it: a silver-sided platform with heavy cables leading from it and resting on it on its side a huge white egg almost exactly the size of his own head—in fact, his instant fantastic thought was that it was a horrid tableau set up to ridicule his baldness.

He went up to it. The heat was coming from the platform, all right—the humpy soft reddish fabric on which the egg rested was almost too hot to touch. And there seemed to be a faint vibration in the stuff, barely perceptible to the fingertips.

The egg looked astonishingly genuine. Minute pores dimpled its surface.

But it was far too large for an ostrich egg or any other Giles could conceive. And it was being kept at a far higher temperature, he was quite sure, than that used for any normal hatching. He started to turn the heat down, then wondered if he could figure out how, then decided not to try. He put his ear near the shell but couldn't hear anything moving inside.

Beside the platform was a deep cardboard box big enough to have held the egg. It was silvered on the outside, half full of cotton wool, and silver ribbons were strewn around.

Giles recognized the box. Joan had brought it back from her last Bridge Wednesday, explaining it contained a china atrocity she'd won but never wanted to look at again and which she intended to gives Giles' mother for her birthday.

Vastly confused, Giles clamped onto one valid-seeming train of thought with just two cars: one—no woman with a fabulous egg hatching in her laboratory would willingly go away for a day, let alone a month or forever, no matter how much she loathed her husband; two—if anyone knew anything about Joan or the egg, it would be one or more of her three bridge partners: Mary Nurse, Margo Cory, and Alice Something-or-other—Greene? No, Redd!

Thirty minutes later Giles had hurriedly dressed, sketchily shaved, swallowed a cup of coffee with a tablespoon of the powdered milk in it, and was piloting the blue, sedately chromeless car from the Wardwell home "back of Back Bay," as he liked to describe it, to Margo Cory's improbable address on Prince Street in Boston's crooked, crowded North End.

None of the three women had been in the phone books and Joan didn't keep an address book Giles could find. Margo Cory's address had only turned up on an empty envelope that had slipped down behind Joan's desk.

Giles never liked visiting the North End and he didn't want to think about the egg because it was, to put it mildly, impossible. He spent the drive totting up how stodgily conformist he could be accused of being. He was at least par for the Boston course, he decided. For instance, he had recently given up chess and concentrated on bird-watching because Mr. Mather had pointed out that too many Slavic and Baltic types played chess. "Semites, too, of course," Mather had finished primly. "I think we must look on it as purely a Russian game."

Could his Sunday bird-watching have anything to do with the egg? More fantastic ridicule? Giles doubted if he had ever trained his binoculars on a bird that had an egg much bigger than a gumdrop.

Margo Cory's address turned out to be a brand-new narrow tall glass-walled apartment building. As he went up to the twelfth floor in the newfangled glass-backed elevator, the Old North Church became visible across the roofs and then the green square of Copps Hill Burying Ground over toward the Inner Harbor.

HATCHERY OF DREAMS

Margo Cory's apartment was furnished in pale Swedish modern that went oddly with the dark tone in the glass. Margo herself wore bare feet, a gray linen robe and her short hair was tousled like a boy's. It gave Giles a pang to see how young she was, remembering Joan was no older. He must seem an old fogey to them all, he told himself.

He thought she was carrying hugged to her chest a motionless pale tan kitten, then he saw it had overbuilt shoulders, canine teeth like great daggers, and forepaws that suggested hands.

Margo noted his gaze and giggled. "Kitty's just a Steiff toy, made of plush," she said. "Did you know teddy bears were Steiff toys named after Teddy Roosevelt? This one's a kind of sabertooth tiger. Here, look."

She thrust it briefly toward him. With the same movement the top of her robe fell apart, showing she was not at all boyish in that area and dressed solely for showering. She seemed unconscious of the exposure.

"No, I haven't seen Joan since Wednesday," she told Giles. She swung nervously toward the view-wall with a flash of legs. "Why don't you come over here beside me," she said with an odd chuckle, "and enjoy my view?"

Another time Giles might have been tempted, proper Bostonian or no. Now he said, "Miss Cory, I *am* looking for my wife."

She faced him. "You really are worried about Joan, aren't you?"

"Of course!" He grimaced at her and rapidly waved his fingers together at chest level. She scowled back at him and at last pulled her robe tight around her.

"I'm an exhibitionist, Mr. Wardwell, *and* a nymphomaniac," she announced defiantly. "It's a very rare combination."

"Really, Miss Cory, you don't have to tell me these things," he countered.

"I certainly do," she retorted. "If I tell them I don't have to do them. Think what I'm sparing you. But if I can't do them I have to tell them."

He might have reacted stuffily to this frankness. Instead he felt something open inside himself that he had kept carefully closed all day in spite of the egg and other shocks.

"Miss Cory," he said, "do you think my wife dabbles in witchcraft?"

"*Dabbles?*" the girl yelled. "Why, what a weird question. There's no such thing as witchcraft."

"I know," Giles said, pouring it off his chest, "but she has this lab where she concocts things, and I've heard her mutter gibberish that might be incantations and spells, and she has a lonely bitter attitude toward life, and then she could be descended from the first witch hanger at Salem in 1692—even if Bridget Bishop isn't known to have had children. And then we've got the tradition of witchcraft all around us here in New England and Boston and especially right here in the North End." He gestured at the smoky window. "Why right over there in Copps Hill the Mathers are buried who did so much to fight it and—"

"Excuse me, Mr. Wardwell, but I can't listen to you any longer," the girl interrupted. "I'm a bit psychotic, as I've told you, some days more than others, and today is one of the real bad ones—I'd fall apart if it weren't for Kitty here." She clutched the plush sabertooth to her. "I'll give you Alice Redd's address—maybe she can tell you something about Joan."

She called brightly after him down the corridor, incidentally letting her robe fall open again, "Remember, Mr. Wardwell, there's no such thing as witchcraft!"

Alice Redd lived in a dignified old apartment on Louisburg Square back across the Common and she seemed in other ways the antithesis of Margo Cory—a china-delicate young woman with pale reddish hair and wearing a robe of thick brocaded white silk that was conspicuously buttoned from neck to hem.

She spoiled the effect somewhat by moaning immediately, "Come in quickly, Mr. Wardwell, so I can collapse again. Ooh, what a fuzzy black head I've got inside, this morning. I know I shouldn't mix barbiturates with alcohol, but there must be more to it than that."

She pointed vaguely at a chair and let herself down onto a spindle-legged couch, to the head of which was hanging by one paw a small dark brown stiff monkey made of what Giles decided must be the finest basket weave— the texture suggested tiny scales.

Alice Redd reached out feebly and put a finger in the other paw. "Pongo's such a help on mornings like this," she told Giles. "I don't know what I'd do without him. He keeps off the black megrims and things. He's supposed to come from Hong Kong or maybe Malaya.

"Yes, Mr. Wardwell, I do so much enjoy the bridge with Joan and the other girls. Do you know, we're hoping eventually to get together three tables, so there'd be twelve of us, and have duplicate tournaments. Then we'd need a man to be tournament director, a woman would be much too flighty. Has Joan said anything to you—? Ooh, my head!

"No, I haven't seen Joan since Wednesday. Mary Nurse might be able to tell you something. I'll give you her address, though the's been laid up with flu the last two days. There seems to be something wrong with all of us, doesn't there? Oooh!

"No, I don't think Joan was unhappy, Mr. Wardwell. I'll tell you one thing, though—she didn't like those CAMZ people you work for, she thought they were too restrictive and inquiring and dictatorial. Certainly we have to worry about the Russians, but Joan says those CAMZ people enjoy worrying, they must bathe in black megrims. I know they're fine old Boston men, most of them, but didn't Mr. Arbuthnot work for Senator McCarthy and isn't Mr. Mather descended from the witchhunting Mathers—Cotton, Increase, and—Oooh! Pongo, come here, comfort Mother."

"Speaking of witches, Miss Redd," Giles said on impulse, "I've just had an amusing thought. You know how each witch is supposed to have a familiar?—a little animal given her by Satan to protect her and help her work magic? Well, if old Cotton Mather could have been with me this morning and seen Margo Cory with Kitty and you with Pongo—"

"Ha-ha-ha, very funny. And Mary Nurse with Pounce. He'd have called them poppets, because they aren't alive, but he'd have claimed they come alive when people's backs were turned—Oooh! Pongo, make it stop!

"But Mr. Wardwell, if you were seriously thinking about witchcraft, surely you'd have asked Joan herself —No, I can see you're the Boston type who never asks crucial questions until it's much too late or something—Ooh!"

"I wonder," Giles said softly, "in what *form* Satan would give familiars to witches? Not in a brown paper bag, surely, or just handing them over by the scruff of the neck—you'd think there'd be a little more ceremony to it."

"Ha-ha-ha— Ooooh! Mr. Wardwell, I'm sorry, but Pongo and I are going to have to curl up and go to sleep—it's the only way we'll ever get through this. But first I'll write you Mary Nurse's address."

Giles didn't look at it until he was outside, standing beside the black iron pickets fencing the private park that occupied Louisburg Square. It turned out to be on Salem Street and he shrank from going back into the North End, so he drove home, relieved to find the house wasn't burning down, and sat watching the egg and thinking a great variety of mad disturbing thoughts.

He reread Joan's note several times. As far as he could tell, it was her handwriting or a good imitation, but he noticed now that there were three expressions in it which she detested: "In case," "Anyhow," and "humans" for "human beings." If someone had wanted to convince him that Joan had run away and keep him from making inquiries, he might have concocted a note like this.

Once he got a tack hammer and poised it above the egg . . . and after a few seconds carried the hammer back to the kitchen.

And once he thought he heard something stir inside the egg. He bent his ear to it until his cheek was burning hot, but heard nothing more.

After three hours of that he drove back to the North End. He passed the CAMZ headquarters in the new building in Sewall Court, recalling that it was named for Judge Sam Sewall, who had presided over the Salem witch trials. He passed the Paul Revere house with its strange nail-studded door exactly like that in the house of the hanged Salem witch Rebecca Nurse.

Nurse.

Salem Street was noisy with pushcarts and the evening air seemed to carry as much Italian as English.

Mary Nurse's address was a dreary walk-up over a fish store with windows smeary-tracked by live snails and tiny climbing squid. He remembered Joan telling him Mary Nurse was an artist keen on local color.

But she'd made some changes. Her door at the end of the corridor wasn't like the others, but unpainted oak studded with rows of nail-heads.

In answer to his knock a deep voice called to him to come in.

The room was stuffy and crowded, easels elbowing chairs and bookcases—studio and living room combined.

And bedroom. The light of two thick candles showed Mary Nurse lying on a wide studio couch under a quilt of diamond patches. She was a big girl—five foot ten, he'd judged—but now she lay like a log, looking really sick, pale, her thick black hair streaming across the pillow.

But her deep voice was steady enough. "I've been expecting you, Giles Wardwell. Margo Cory dropped in this afternoon."

"I'm sorry about your 'flu," Giles said.

"This isn't 'flu," Mary Nurse said with a deep unhumorous chuckle. "Someone's put a curse on me. On all of us, I'd say. What are you looking around for?"

"Pounce," Giles admitted.

Again the big blonde chuckled. She beckoned to Giles and lifted the quilt a little. Giles looked—and almost jumped out of the room.

Crouched on the sheet beside her, just under her arm, was a jet-black spider with a body big as a flattened grapefruit and furry black legs that would have spanned a platter. Around the body were wedges of bright green, while two ruby-red eyes glared up at him.

It couldn't be real, Giles told himself. It must be—

"Black velvet." For a third time Mary Nurse chuckled. She dropped the quilt. "Just the same, I'd probably be dead without Pounce. You've surely noticed by now how neurotically dependent we are on our little . . . toys. That's why Joan's in trouble—she doesn't have one . . . yet."

Giles was staring at the top of a bookcase back in the shadows. It seemed to have an egg on it as big as that in Joan's lab.

"Surely you've noticed other things about us too," Mary Nurse was saying.

"Your door, your name," Giles said, edging between an easel and a chair toward the bookcase.

"All our names are witch names. Even your name, Giles Wardwell. Samuel Wardwell was one of the five wizards hung in Salem. Giles Cory was pressed to death with rocks on his chest for refusing to testify."

Giles saw that the egg was an empty shell, cracked across and with a huge hole in one side. "What's that?" he asked sharply.

"That's the shell of a spider—I mean, dinosaur . . ." Mary Nurse broke off and looked at him burningly. "I don't think we need to fence any longer, Giles Wardwell. You've found Joan's egg? Unbroken?"

"Yes. Yes."

"Then if you love your wife, be there when it hatches. I think there's time. I'd go but I'm too cursed to move. I'd send the Black Man, but we haven't one. Joan's only hope and safety are in the egg. Follow the signs. Call it Grizzle. Don't ask questions. Hurry!"

"I will."

"The Horned God go with you, Giles Wardwell."

The lab seemed hotter than before when Giles got back to it, but that may have been because he was sweating. At first the egg seemed intact, then he saw there was a tiny triple crack radiating from a point near the top. As he watched, one of the branches lengthened abruptly by the width of a finger. There was a faint scratching and rustling inside.

He settled down to watch, gripping his knees with shaking hands. The heat alone was making him feel faint. He stripped off his coat and shirt, noting without much surprise that he was still wearing his pyjama top under the latter.

The cracks lengthened. Others appeared. Suddenly bits of shell flew and a tiny blue arm with a jagged crest on it like a lizard's shot out, groped around wildly, and then jerked in.

Trembling, Giles moved around the egg, trying to peer in but staying at arm's length.

Two tiny blue hands were methodically breaking away small fragments of shell, enlarging the hole. He couldn't see more of the creature, it was too dark inside.

The room began to swim. Giles dragged at the collar of his pyjamas, then staggered to the window and heaved it up, sucked in three breaths of cool air. The room steadied. He saw that the hole in the egg was now big as a spread hand.

He was halfway back to it when something blue shot out, scurried in a circle across the floor three times, too fast to be seen definitely, and dove out the open window.

Giles grabbed up his coat and went out the front door and looked around in the dark. He couldn't see anything on the lawn or drive. He walked around the front of his car and froze.

A stocky jewel-blue lizard was crouched down on the hood of his car exactly as if it were a moderately ornate radiator ornament. It seemed to grip into the blue-painted metal with its hind claws and left forepaw or arm. The right arm, extended beside its hideously crested face, was pointed straight ahead.

"Grizzle!" Giles ejaculated.

The blue creature shivered and stretched its arm still further forward.

Giles climbed in and started the car, his eyes on Grizzle. As he neared the street, the foreward-pointing arm swung abruptly to the right. Giles obeyed, his heart pounding.

Follow the signs!

They were near the Common when Giles began to guess where they were going. As they neared Sewall Court, Grizzle raised its foreward-pointing arm as if to say, "Go slow," and then suddenly pointed downward as if for "Stop."

Fred, the CAMZ garageman, came up to the window. He was looking at the hood. Then, "Take her for you, Mr. Wardwell?" They traded places. As Giles was walking away, Fred called excitedly, "Mr. Wardwell!" Giles turned back. "I'd have sworn," Fred said from behind the wheel, "that you'd put a blue radiator ornament on your car, a sort of wild dinosaur. But now it's gone."

Giles said, a bit stuffily, "Blue? Wild? Now, Fred, would anyone be apt to do a thing like that to his car, in Boston?"

Inside the lobby Grizzle was playing unseen around the feet of George, the night guard and elevator-man. Giles kept his eyes away from the familiar.

"Fifth floor, Mr. Wardwell?" George volunteered. "All

HATCHERY OF DREAMS

our big ones are up there." He stared at Giles' pyjama top under his coat. "They sure pulled you out of bed in a hurry, Mr. Wardwell. Must be something real emergency, though I haven't taken up any army men."

Giles maintained a dignified mysterious silence.

On the fifth floor the drapes were drawn tight behind the heavy glass wall of the main office. A little light shone through the drapes toward one end, not much. As the elevator door closed, Giles headed down the hall toward the office he shared, but there was a tug at his trouser leg. Grizzle led him to Mr. Arbuthnot's office, which was next to the end of the main office away from the light.

Arbuthnot's office was empty and dark, but the door from it to the main office was open. Giles walked to it and stopped.

Mr. Copps, Mr. Arbuthnot, Mr. Mather, and Mr. Zim were all standing toward the other end of the main office, looking very serious and dignified and business-like in their dark suits, except that Mr. Zim was holding a small golden wand and wearing a tall conical black hat covered with golden stars and moons, and Mr. Arbuthnot was cradling in his arms a submachinegun.

And Joan was there, facing Giles' end of the office, the single light glaring full in her face. She was sitting up straight and defiant-faced on a stool with her arms stretched out straight to either side of her by thin white ropes anchored to filing cabinets.

She was wearing her red nightgown. A bit of Giles' mind jumped back to 1692 Salem, where Bridget Bishop had worn "a red paragon bodice" before her grim sober judges.

Joan flirted her black hair away from her eyes with a shake of her head and said loudly, "But this is ridiculous, I keep telling you. My husband has never told me a word about the Secondman Missiles Project. I have no Communist connections. Presumably I was cleared by the F.B.I. at the same time Giles was. The rest is nonsense—or insanity."

"Must I take you over that ground again?" Mr. Mather said in his soft voice that was so clear and far-carrying. "Mrs. Wardwell, America has older and more formidable enemies than Communism. Unfortunately, the F.B.I. does not clear for witchcraft. But CAMZ, which embodies the finest traditions of Old New England, does. And somehow advertising is more sensitive to the occult than is the military." He tapped a sheaf of papers in his hand. "Confess yourself a witch, Joan Wardwell, tell where and how you bound yourself to Satan, detail for us your spells and magics, above all name the other witches of your coven—or you will force us to prove these facts upon your body! Mr. Copps, is the needle ready?"

"You can't make me testify against myself," Joan countered. "I plead the Fifth Amendment!"

"*Our* Massachusetts never ratified it," Mr. Mather told her. "Remember what happened to Giles Cory, Mr. Copps?"

Giles surged forward, then stopped. Four men and a submachinegun! His hands turned icy cold. Then something hot stroked his cheek, his face turned as cold as if a mask of ice had been slipped over it, and he almost shrieked.

Grizzle had climbed the front of his suit, was clinging to his left lapel as a sailor might to a sail, and had just finished licking his cheek with his long black tongue.

Mr. Arbuthnot turned and stared straight at the door of his office, leveling the gun. Giles froze, hoping the gloom would hide him though afraid his white hands and face were bound to stand out. But after a searching glance, Arbuthnot turned back toward Joan.

Mr. Mather was saying, "Joan Bishop Wardwell, consider well the helplessness of your situation. Your poor foolish husband, deceived by the note you wrote at our hypnotic dictation when we summoned you, believes you have deserted him. Your sister witches, who and where-ever they may be, are held in check by Mr. Zim's helpful little spells. Confess yourself, redeem your wickedness, salvage what you can of the good American girl who yielded to the blandishments of Satan."

"I won't!" Joan cried ringingly. "Compared to your brand of Americanism, witchcraft is the soul of decency."

"The needle!"

Grizzle, still clinging to Giles with hind claws and one forepaw, tweaked Giles' arm painfully with the other, then pointed commandingly at Arbuthnot.

Follow the signs!
Going behind Joan, Mr. Copps ripped her nightgown down the back and poised something that was glittering, long, and terribly slim.

Giles walked out into the main office, raising his right hand and pointing straight at Mr. Arbuthnot—though he almost dropped it when he saw that his hand was no longer flesh-colored but dead black.

Arbuthnot froze in mid-whirl. His flesh turned a faint gray. The submachinegun thudded on the thick-piled carpet.

The finger with which Giles had pointed at him was flesh-colored again and the rest of his hand was no longer dead black but charcoal gray.

Successively, copying Grizzle's gestures, Giles pointed his second finger, ring finger, and thumb at Mr. Zim, Mr. Copps, and Mr. Mather.

With each pointing, the man indicated froze and faintly grayed, while Giles' flesh lightened by stages until at the end he was no darker than they were.

For once in his life Giles Wardwell was seething with anger.

"You persecuting, smug, self-satisfied, hypocritical fiends!" he shouted. "You're worse than the Russians with your brainwashing. Now listen to me—you're going to forget this witchhunting obsession forever, I command it! *Silentium, silentium, mutus, mutus, mutus*. I'm letting you off easy—if you'd actually injured my wife, I'd make you really suffer. But believe me, after this you're never going to browbeat me, any of you. And I'm going to start playing chess again and seeing my mother as often as I please!"

He stopped because Joan was laughing delightedly.

"Darling, they can't hear you," she called to him happily. "The Black Man's spell works a lot faster than barbiturates. For hours at least they'll be dead asleep. Now cut me loose and let's get out of here. I think your charm's certain to work, but to make sure we'll take Mr. Mather's papers and Mr. Zim's wand and cap and Mr. Arbuthnot's submachinegun and drop them in the Charles. You've got your little finger to put the night guard asleep and your left hand for emergencies. Is that Grizzle? He's a dear!"

A half hour later they were driving slowly home through Back Bay. Joan sat close to Giles, her head resting on his shoulder. Grizzle was curled on Joan's shoulder, holding her ripped red nightgown together with his hind claws. The car's heater flooded them with pleasant warmth.

"Giles," Joan said sleepily, "there's one more question I want to ask you. When you visited Margo and Alice and Mary today, did you find them . . . attractive?"

"Rather," he admitted. "I must say they're very weird women, but then it looks as if I'm going to have to get used to a great many extremely strange things. Pounce, for instance. Yes, to tell the truth I found all three girls quite attractive."

Joan nodded without opening her eyes. "I was afraid of that," she said. "You see, as Black Man of our little coven you will have certain duties and privileges. Oh well, I suppose I'll simply have to accept it."

Then, with a sleepy chuckle, she added, "but don't forget, Giles Wardwell, now and forever, that I'm your First Witch."

THE GOGGLES OF DR. DRAGONET

"HAVE YOU EVER thought what it would be like if we could see *minds*?" Dr. Hugo Dragonet asked.

"You've got something will do *that*?" I demanded.

Dr. Hugo Dragonet indicated the four pairs of black goggles scattered across the center of the gleaming gray table and sat back grinning at us like a genial old condor.

Marty, Alice and I eyed them suspiciously. The last time we had ventured to wear a gadget of the Doctor's —an innocuous-seeming sort of hearing aid—it had been to hear a nervous jungle murmur which the Doctor had asserted was the sounds of the subconscious mind. Just a jungle murmur, a little like the background music for a darkest Africa movie, but after five minutes of it Alice had become hysterical, Marty had growled out a senseless accusation of murder against me, and I had a terrifyingly vivid vision of the great city around us choked with vines, a-crawl with huge snakes, a-rustle with giant spiders, and a-creep with great black panthers. Hypnotic suggestion, we had told ourselves afterwards, not very confidently. Although Southern California is a land of fakers, and Los Angeles a city of illusion, Marty, Alice and I find it difficult to write off Dr. Hugo Dragonet simply as a charlatan.

Now we looked at four pairs of black goggles. Each pair had a fine wire connecting one of the massive bows to a black-enameled power pack or control device about as big as a package of kingsize cigarettes and reminiscent of the subconscious hearing aids.

"You say these gadgets will let you see thoughts?" Marty asked. The Doctor shook his head. "I didn't say thoughts I said *minds*." I don't know that I like the idea," Alice said.

I didn't exactly like the four white canes hooked over the back of the Doctor's big chair. Taken together with the goggles they looked much too much like equipment for three blind men and one blind girl.

Nevertheless I reached out and gingerly drew the nearest pair of goggles to me along with its trailing flat black box. So did Alice and Marty. Dr. Dragonet's gadgets are always a shade more fascinating by the fact that they are frightening. He had the charlatan's gift of always arousing interest, sometimes by fabulous hints, sometimes as now by silence.

But he was grinning at me and the grin had a fatherly-sardonic twist to it, as if he had read my suspicious thoughts and were amused. Alice, Marty and I like to think of ourselves as reasonably mature—a fairly successful sculptress-actress, newspaperman, and writer—but Hugo Dragonet has a way of treating us as if we were a trio of bright children, whom it pleases him occasionally to provide with wonderful toys. None of us can decide whether he is really a charlatan or a brilliant physicist-physiologist who works completely freelance and has not chosen (at least as yet) to share his important discoveries with the world of academic and industrial science. So far as we know, the Doctor supports himself solely—though quite lavishly—by specialized and little-known inventions in the realms of film and TV effects and by his occasional services as technical advisor to the studios on psychiatric and anthropological movies. If he cashes in on his important inventions (or his charlatanism, if it's that), we haven't an inkling of it and his patrons (or his victims) move in lofty circles quite unknown to us. What we are agreed upon, all three of us, is that we look forward to and are wholly fascinated by our little meetings with him—even if we always do feel a bit uneasy as we approach them.

As I uncertainly fingered my pair of goggles and carefully drew the companion box to me by the fine connecting wire, I wondered if this was one of the important inventions and if so how it would work. Four pairs of black goggles . . . four gleaming black kingsize boxes, each with two tiny switches on it, one gray and rough, the other white and smooth . . . four white canes . . . I was still bothered by the implications.

Not that there was anything sinister about our surroundings, though they would have given a sensitive person a touch of vertigo. The cantilevered, black-flagged, magnesium-roofed terrace thrust out like the flying bridge of a futuristic ship from Dr. Dragonet's house, which lifted from an easterly crest of the Santa Monica Mountains, as if the house in turn were the figurehead of a ship of hills, with Hollywood below us to the south, the San Fernando Valley below us to the north, while before us to the southeast, sprouting white skyscrapers and slashed by freeways and only faintly hazed today by smog, stretched the central sections of sprawlingly spacious Los Angeles. Behind us were the mountains, the westering sun, and the invisible Pacific.

The inevitable Hollywood note of the fabulous and fake was provided by a white-walled gilt-domed group of small buildings on the hillside just below. Even at this distance, looking across the intervening lawn and flowerbeds, we could read the neat black-on-white sign: GREATER COSMIC FELLOWSHIP.

The mildly exotic atmosphere of the terrace itself was pointed up by a few earthenware oriental figures and a remarkably realistic ceramic of a kinkajou, which looked as though the thick-tailed, dark yellow Asiatic carnivore had been frozen in mid-scamper along a dead branch.

Karl, the Doctor's squarely built chauffeur and precision machinist, sat on the northern verge of the terrace, where steps go down to the garage and the magnificent machine shop where he fabricates the Doctor's inventions, presumably including these goggles.

Karl was methodically turning the pages of *The Los Angeles Times*. Impet, the Doctor's slim black cat, snoozed in the sun on the southern edge. Otherwise we were completely alone.

The round gray-topped table was poker size. Alice sat to my left, Marty, to my right, the Doctor across. The only things on the table were the four gogglesets and a square of dull whitish sheet-metal about a foot wide.

Marty touched a goggle set. "See *minds*, you said?" The Doctor just nodded.

I began to inspect closely the black instruments in my hands. I saw that I had been right in thinking of them as goggles rather than glasses, for although they had bows like glasses there was a wide spongy black flange going back from each lens that I could see would fit against the skin of cheek and orbit, shutting out all light from the sides.

Then I looked at the lenses themselves, first from the front, then from the back—without putting them on—in growing perplexity. All I could think of for a moment was a demonstration the Doctor had once put on for us of a girl who told colors blindfolded and read books through heavy cardboard. Alice made my point first.

"You can't see through them," she said. "They seem to be made of a black metal." She hadn't put hers on either.

Hugo Dragonet smiled and nodded.

Marty carried his own pair over into the sunlight. Impet looked up resentfully. Marty turned the glasses front to back toward the sun and looked through one lens cautiously.

GOGGLES OF DR. DRAGONET

"No, they're not like eclipse glasses," the Doctor called after him. "You couldn't see even an atomic blast through them. They're opaque to X rays too, probably to *all* electric light—using the term to mean the whole electromagnetic spectrum."

Marty returned excitedly. "But if that's true, it's amazing, Doctor! This black metal would be the perfect material to shield atomic reactors! Might work for bomb shelters too!"

Hugo Dragonet yawned. Impet cradled his head between his paws and went back to sleep.

Marty flushed and chewed his lip. Besides being an incurable enthusiast, Marty is quite an idealist and patriot, and what he calls the Doctor's cynical and frivolous impracticality gets under his skin.

"To return to matters of real interest," the Doctor said, "these goggles *are* transparent to rays of both the gravitoelectric and magnetogravitic spectra and, when properly excited, will translate bands of those spectra into visible colors."

"But Doctor," Marty burst out, irrepressibly, "those other two spectra are just an obscure possibility from field theory. There's absolutely no evidence for their existence."

"Are you sure of that?" Hugo Dragonet asked softly, weighing the fourth pair of goggles in his palm. "However I don't insist that you accept my explanations," he added with a smile. "Explanations are never the most interesting part of science."

"Doctor, how do the goggles help to see minds?" Alice put in hurriedly.

"Why, my dear," he said, "they translate into electric or visible light two narrow bands of gravitic and magnetic light—if, purely for convenience, I may use those terms," he added elaborately with a sardonic little bow toward Marty. The Doctor likes to needle our young science reporter.

Marty blushed.

Keeping it simple like Alice, I asked, "How do minds show up in the gravitic and magnetic light?"

The Doctor did not answer my question. Instead he put on his pair of black goggles and tucked the attached black box into the top of his outside breast pocket with the two switches facing front.

It made him look like a blind man.

After a bit he reached his right hand across his chest and pushed the gray switch, then sat back stolidly. I got the impression he was counting under his breath.

Paper rustled faintly as Karl turned another page. Impet sat up and stared intently at the Doctor, seeming to study the change the goggles had made in his face. The sunlight struck bronze tints from the cat's black fur.

Time stretched out. Karl swatted something with his newspaper—he has a thing about insects—and took up the next section.

Then the Doctor touched the white switch. Immediately he sat forward in his chair and looked long and carefully at each of us in turn—first me, then Marty then Alice.

His goggles were more opaque-seeming than ever—round flats of dull black metal—but I never in my life had such an intense sensation of someone looking through me or rather *into* me.

He frowned at me—at least the vertical furrows deepened above the bridge of his goggles—and he gave a faint grunt of what sounded like surprise.

When he looked at Marty his grunt seemed to say "Just as I thought," but when he turned to Alice there was a rising note to his "Umm," as though he had found something that tickled his imagination.

"What *is* it, Doctor?" Alice asked nervously, shrinking back in her seat. "You're buzzing like an X-ray machine."

Hugo Dragonet smiled. "Why don't you try the goggles?" he said. "Why don't you all try them? And see for yourself? Just put them on and then follow my directions. Only one thing: once you're wearing them, don't take them off until I tell you."

Suddenly I was no longer reluctant but fumblingly eager to get the goggles on. I judged from my last jumbled glimpse that Marty and Alice were the same. But as the thick black flanges settled down against my skull, I had a flurry of unexpected panic. The rubbery material seemed not so much to touch my skin as to kiss it suckingly and for a moment I had the gruesome fear of suction applied to my eyeballs. I started to snatch the things off, then told myself not to be a nervous fool.

"Take it easy," I heard the Doctor say as if from a considerable distance. "Make sure they're comfortable. But remember, no peeking. And don't throw the little switches until I tell you."

I realized that in my rush I'd forgotten about the control box—if that was what it was—so I ghosted my fingertips down the wire from the left bow until they felt the box, which I slid halfway down into my breast pocket as I'd seen the Doctor do.

"Don't be in a hurry," he was saying. "Just as at the planetarium, if we wait a bit our eyes get more sensitive to the darkness."

But this was more than darkness, I realized with another spurt of inward panic, it was blackness complete and absolute. You know how when you close your eyes in no matter how dark a room, you always see churning specks of light and faint washes of color—even if you don't apply pressure with your fingertips to your lidded eyeballs, which can bring on blue flashes and all sorts of things. Well, now there wasn't anything of that sort at all, just velvety limitless darkness—*black* black, if I may call it that. It didn't make sense to me, because I'd always thought that the churning specks weren't due to light at all but just a random automatic discharge of a few of the retinal cells, which would go on whether there was an atom of light or not. Unless, I suggested to myself, the goggles had some sort of general inhibiting effect? It really seemed quite incredible that I should still be sitting on a bright terrace with dazzling golden sunlight striking a few yards away and not getting one hint of it—not even a reddish glow transmitted through the flesh of my cheeks—just because of a pair of goggles, and for a moment I had the thought of Dr. Dragonet rearing up leanly and blotting out the sun like some Old Testament prophet or medieval sorcerer. Or suppose these goggles literally blinded their wearer? Suppose—

I was about to disobey instructions and take the things off when I heard the Doctor say, "Now you might each of you gently depress the gray switch, as you saw me do. It's the rough-surfaced one.

"Don't expect to see anything startling, or even much of anything at all," he added. "This part is merely preliminary and doesn't work too well for everyone. But it creates a *framework*."

At first I thought I must be one of the ones for whom this part didn't work, whatever it was, then I became aware that the absolute blackness had been invaded by large shapes of dark gray faintly edged with silver. At first I thought they made only an arbitrary geometrical pattern, but then I realized that they added up to an extremely dark picture of the table in front of me and the terrace around us—with this important difference, that my companions had vanished; I could see only the three empty chairs. But it was all extremely faint—maybe it was just my imagination, it occurred to me; or maybe the Doctor was using suggestion on me—some sort of hypnotic deal, as we'd tried to tell ourselves about the subconscious hearing aids.

"But I can't see *us*," I heard Alice say excitedly. "I can't even see my own hand."

"It's like a very overdeveloped negative of the terrace

GOGGLES OF DR. DRAGONET

with the people left out," I heard Marty add in puzzled tones.

"You are now seeing by gravitic light," came the cool but heavier voice of Hugo Dragonet. "Gravitic light is reflected by most inorganic materials—metals, minerals and so on—though not all—for instance, you can't see each other's goggles. But *all* organic materials—animals, plants, the clothing made from plant fiber or animal wool or simply any carbon-based material—are transparent to gravitic light and so don't show up."

I looked around. Sure enough, Karl and Impet were both invisible, assuming they were still sitting where I'd seen them last. Much more startling to me, the ceramic kinkajou was also gone, although the earthenware figures remained, suggesting that the kinkajou wasn't ceramic at all but some sort of literally frozen amimal flesh. I started to ask the Doctor about it, then remembered that it usually doesn't do to ask Hugo Dragonet about extraneous mysteries glimpsed while exploring a main one. There are some parts of his life, such as his years in Vietnam—old Indochina then—that he doesn't talk about.

One of the many odd things about my present vision of my surroundings was that the sun-drenched outside looked no brighter than the shaded terrace. And it was a frighteningly *empty* world.

"Of course you are not seeing by gravitic light direcly," the Doctor's voice cut in, "but by the electric light your goggles translate it into. The goggles are adjusted to keep it very dim. It's just a framework or background for what you'll be seeing next—by magnetic light. Which reminds me, it's time for you to throw the white switch— the smooth one."

This time I hesitated on the brink. Alice gave an involuntary cry in which there was more wonder than fear. I depressed my switch.

Over each of the three chairs, exactly where my friends'

heads would be, hung a ghostly globe of colored light.

Marty's and Alice's were identical shades of green. Hugo Dragonet's was blue shot with streaks of dark red —and much brighter, though none of the globes was very bright: they were like compact clouds of phosphorescent mist.

And they weren't perfect globes either. Marty's almost was, at least it had very sharp boundaries, but its shape was that of a large egg tipped forward—the shape of Marty's brain if the skull were removed. Its green glow was brightest to the front.

By contrast the Doctor's globe was misty-edged. The dark red streaks that banded the bright blue kept fading, changing, reappearing.

Alice's globe tapered down into a ghostly but recognizable replica of her face. It was as if a gossamer mask hung from the green globe. And that was all. No, not quite. On the table in front of Alice alone were very faint folded curves of light, like fingers.

Then the Doctor spoke. His voice seemed to me to be coming out of the globe of blue light. Natural enough, I suppose—just normal sound-localization—but the effect was monstrously eerie.

"You are now seeing by magnetic light," the blue globe (I mean the Doctor) said. "Magnetic light is generated solely by mental activity—specifically by consciousness or awareness. I sometimes call it mind light. In fact, you're seeing minds."

"You mean we're seeing each other thinking?" the mask-trailing green globe on my left (Alice, of course) asked wonderingly.

"In a way, yes."

"We're seeing each other's thoughts?" she pressed.

"Alas, no. Perhaps some day we will find a prism, a lens, some way of refocussing mind light, so that we can actually see the little inner world of form and color and feeling that is another person's consciousness. But not yet. Now all we are seeing is the diffuse outward glow of inward awareness—the envelope or aura of thought. It's possible that throughout history a few individuals have been sporadically sensitive to mind light without translating goggles—accounting for persistent mystical beliefs about human auras and the halos of saints."

It hit me all of a sudden what a terrific gimmick for spiritualism these goggles would be. Believers would pay limitlessly to see auras, to see their own minds glowing like spheres of pure incorruptible light. But right away I ran into the snag of the Doctor's apparent disinterest in my con money or build-up. In any case my vague suspicions couldn't compete for long with the amazement I was feeling. The simple awe of the thing began to take hold of me.

"We're seeing brain waves," Alice said huskily.

"I don't believe so, my dear," the Doctor told her. "So-called brain waves are simply tiny rhythmic changes of electric potential in the flesh around the skull."

"But we *are* seeing nervous activity," Marty suddenly put in sharply.

"If that were true," the Doctor replied, "we'd see the spine, the whole nerve-tree, as sharply as the brain. No, we're seeing the glow of *consciousness*—that inward world of awareness that means life and identity, that little cosmos locked inside the skull that is all of reality to each of us. As I've said before, we're seeing *minds*."

None of us said anything for a while then, as it sank in. The awe of the thing gripped me completely. Mind Light!

"I'm not all locked inside my skull," Alice nervously broke the silence at last. "I can see my hands." And as she said that, the ghostly fingers became a little more definitely outlined.

"That's because you're a sculptress." the Doctor answered. "You send your awareness into your fingers—molding, shaping. You literally see and think with your hands—like some blind men I've watched by magnetic light. By contrast Marty and Arthur show a sharply delimited consciousness, as if it actually were skull-bounded—they're word-and-idea men, rationalists.

"Whereas you're an artist," he continued to Alice, "and an actress too, highly conscious of your appearance. That's why you project your consciousness into your face as well as your hands."

"I do?" Alice sounded both ashamed and excited. "Doctor, is there some way for me to see myself?"

The Doctor chuckled. A dark grey rectangle lifted from the table. I remembered the square of whitish metal that had been lying there.

"Here's a mirror for mind light," he said to Alice. Her ghostly fingers gripped it, the filmy mask of her face a trace brighter as she stared at it, then it began to fluctuate as (I suppose) delight and embarrassment struggled together.

"What's the mirror made of?" Marty asked eagerly.

"Something quite unsuitable for reactor shielding or for wrapping gum," the Doctor told him sourly, then continued, "Projected awareness is rather common. Occasional unaided glimpses of it, due to magnetic sensitivity, may account for spiritualists' claims about ectoplasm."

Marty and I looked in turn at the reflections of our mind globes. Mine was sharply bounded like his but more toward the blue.

"Green and blue are the normal range," the Doctor explained. "Blue seems to link with introversion and contemplation, green with extroversion and action. The other colors come in when the *feelings* are involved. Yellow goes with joy, red with savage passions, orange with sensuousness, misery is gray. Violet I've almost never seen."

"Doctor," Alice asked, "why did you say 'Umm' that way when you first saw my mind? Because it was in my face?"

He chucked. "No," he said, "more because it was exactly the same shade as Martin's—something I've seldom seen except in identical twins and long-married couples."

Alice said, "Hmm." Marty mumbled vaguely.

"Happily married couples," the Doctor added encouragingly. Then, "*I'm* a strange mixture, as you can see," he went on. "Blue, the philosopher's color, shot through with sudden animal impulses—the dark red. The old orang at the zoo has a mind that's *all* that second color."

"You've been out with these goggles?" I asked.

"Of course, Arthur. You wouldn't expect me to pass up a new way to pry into people, would you? I carry a white cane and pose as a blind man, mostly to justify the glasses. Karl always goes with me, pretending to guide me. Actually I do need his help from time to time—the dim gravitic background-light is not very useful in fast traffic. Besides, there are some people who don't have visible minds at all—blacked-out drunks, for one thing—and I don't want to go bumping into them."

"Will *we* be able to go out?" Alice asked.

"You counted the canes behind my chair, didn't you? First, though, we'll have a look at the mind-map. Come on."

The banded blue globe rose and the doctor's chair pushed back. I got up cautiously, feeling at the table edge. It was very strange to feel it and to see it by gravitic light, but not see my hands that were doing the feeling—ghosts must have such sensations, I thought. Just then a very faint globe of yellowish light about as big as a tennis ball flashed up onto the table (or bounced up, it seemed to me) and moved toward the Doctor. The word *Poltergeist* jumped into my mind at the same instant, and I felt the back of my neck crawl, but just then the Doctor said, "Come on, Impet, you too," and the pale little globe was lifted close to the bright blue one.

"Cats do have minds, you see," he said. "All the higher animals appear to have consciousness and awareness."

I had a strong inpulse to take off my goggles and

check for myself that the weird sight was only the Doctor carrying his cat, but I remembered his warning and refrained.

"What's this mind-map and where do you keep it?" Marty asked.

"I'll show you," the Doctor said and led us toward the southern edge of the terrace. Although it was well-defined in gravitic light I felt uneasy about the edge because it's unrailed and at that point the drop to the flower beds is considerable. But the Doctor stopped short of it, and I noticed that an olive globe had appeared beside us—Karl, I supposed. Once more I suppressed the impulse to check.

"Look," said Dr. Dragonet.

The lights of Los Angeles seen from the hills behind Hollywood can be a most spectacular sight. Now it seemed to me as if I were seeing them on a very smoggy night, or—more precisely—seeing them as they would be if a giant rheostat dimmed all of them greatly though leaving hints of their neon coloring.

Gravitic light showed little of the city's structure and barely distinguished dark land from darker sky. It was almost a plane of solid black that backgrounded the faint glow of mind light that faded off toward the horizon in faint patches and rivulets.

We watched silently for some time. The Doctor said, "Notice how it keeps getting a little brighter? When you first switched on the magnetic light, you wouldn't have noticed any of this distant stuff at all. You'll go on getting more sensitive the longer you wear the goggles—up to three hours. But just one flash of ordinary light will cancel your sensitivity—that's why I warned you against peeking."

I asked, "What's the brighter glow due south? Downtown? And the one far off to the west?"

"You mean *that* and *th*at?" the Doctor asked. A pale yellow blob moved to indicate the two directions—I realized he was using Impet for a pointer. "No, that's not downtown, that's the University of Southern California, while the one to the west is UCLA, though it may run into RAND. While that one off to the east over the hills—you missed that—is Cal Tech." He chuckled. "It amused me greatly to discover that more thinking actually does go on at universities."

He gestured again with Impet. "But many of those bright patches I can't interpret at all. I haven't explored them yet, or they keep shifting. And I can't explain that violet glow just below us. With one exception I've never seen violet anywhere else."

Alice said, "If your blue and red would mix, it might make violet."

Meanwhile I studied the glow he'd just pointed out and asked, "Doesn't that come from the Greater Cosmic Fellowship? But why should a bunch of crackpots have a rare color?"

Alice laughed nervously. "Maybe they're Martians. Great planet-hoppers, the Martians, especially in cartoons."

"What made you say Martians?" the Doctor demanded with a sharpness that startled me.

"I don't know—I guess I always call anything from off the earth Martians," Alice explained fumbingly. "Doctor, I was only joking. I didn't really think you'd take me seriously."

"I know you didn't," he told her. "But you know me, I take everything seriously—except practical matters."

"What's the one violet exception?" I wanted to know.

"I may show you later, Arthur."

Marty now spoke up at last, his voice sighing with wonder. "Doctor, I've just been thinking what a terrific advantage mind light would be for espionage, or military patrolling, or even simple police work. Doctor, in this instance wouldn't you be willing to let the government in on—"

Dr. Dragonet yawned audibly, then tossed Impet to the floor and said briskly, "How about that outing I promised all of you? Good! Just remember to keep your goggles on at all times—one peek ruins the sensitivity. Karl, get the car—but first bring us the canes!

The rest of that afternoon and night we saw Los Angeles as black canyons and caves through which minds streamed like globes of undissolving mist driven by random winds.

Karl not only chauffeured and shepherded us, but also quietly interpreted the passing scenes. Otherwise we would not always have been sure what we were watching, for a mind shows neither sex nor race nor (generally) age and certainly carries no signs of class or station, poverty or wealth.

We saw freeways racing with wraithlike gravitic-sketched cars, in each of which poised one or a few of the phosphorescent spheres.

We saw a silver-gray cemetery where minds floated like ghosts among the tombstones—unutterably eerie even after Karl had described to us the funeral party he saw by ordinary light.

We saw dim minds, murky orange mostly, behind the bars at the Griffith Park Zoo. The old orang's was dark red, just as the Doctor had said. Even the snakes had shadowy minds, though Karl would not accompany us into the reptile house. Karl classes snakes with insects and arachnids.

We saw the golden minds of a jazz band. We saw a projected orange mind twinkling in the feet of a dancer.

In a church we saw a scattering of dim indigo minds, like patches of light from deep blue stained glass.

In a skid row bar we saw smoky amber minds winking on and off like fireflies.

We saw red minds in a gang rumble.

We saw a mind vanish suddenly in a crimson burst when a driver was thrown and killed in a freeway accident. That made us ask the Doctor a question. He answered softly, "Wearing the goggles, I have watched death in hospitals. The light only faded and then winked out."

We saw minds sun-hued with joy at the beach, glowing minds in a schoolroom, and (so Alice insisted) the silver-rosy minds of lovers.

Once we saw a violet mind in the rear of a car driven by an ordinary green mind, and remembering what the Doctor had said, we instantly asked Karl for a description. But our curiosity was thwarted in this instance—the car was a small panel truck. We asked the Doctor if this was the violet mind he'd promised to show us, but he denied it.

Many times I was tempted to take off my goggles—more for the kick of verifying the incredible than because of fatigue or any lingering suspicions of trickery on the Doctor's part—but I hated to lose my ever-growing sensitivity to mind light. You see, by now I was becoming convinced that there was much more to be seen by mind light than I'd observed so far—faint things that hovered on the edge of vision. There was the suggestion that some minds had tenuous *tentacles* of mind light and that sometimes the tips of these tentacles plunged into other minds—I'll swear that once I saw one mind leading five or six others, like dogs on leashes.

There were hints, too, that some brains held more minds than one—shadowy splits and mergers, dominations, possessions, vampirisms, clashes, battles. Once I seemed to see a mind flow around another, engulfing or perhaps dissolving it. I kept peering—I admit it—for minds without bodies.

Also I occasionally seemed to see a trace of color in the cold gravitic gray of some material objects—as if some minds were projecting themselves into things, or even the inanimate itself struggling toward awareness.

I asked the Doctor about these things, whether they were reality or imagination, but he would only say, "Keep watching."

Finally he told Karl to drive us back to his home. We sped out of the mind-dazzle of the city into the blackness of the hills.

The Doctor said, "I'm glad you've all followed my suggestion about keeping the goggles on without intermission. At least I hope you have. By now your eyes should be about sensitive enough for something rather special I want to show you. The desert or the mountains or the open sea would be better, but this local outback will have to do. Slide back the top of the car, Karl."

A moment later, "Look up," said Hugo Dragonet.

Desert nights have taught me the shape of the Milky Way. Smog blots it out in Los Angeles or any other city.

But tonight, very faintly but definitely, I saw the unmistakable shape of our galaxy a-glow over Los Angeles with muted rainbow light.

"Mind," Alice whispered, "all over the universe, beating on us in tiny waves."

As she said that, I could almost feel it on my skin— incredibly delicate flakes sifting down.

"How can something faint as mind light travel so far?" I wondered.

Dr. Dragonet said: "Who can say how dim minds are on other worlds? Or how bright? There may be minds like novas."

"What's that point of violet light near the horizon to the south?" Marty asked suddenly.

"You should know," the Doctor told him. "I thought you kept track of the planets."

Marty said: "Mars."

The Doctor commented, "So you see why I was struck by Alice associating violet with Martians." He laughed thinly. "An interesting coincidence."

At that moment the car was climbing past the small, gravitic-etched domes of the Greater Cosmic Fellowship— making another coincidence, I told myself.

"I'm going to regret taking these goggles off," Alice

said, "and seeing things by ordinary electric light." I realized I felt reluctant about it too and I found myself recalling the German psychologist who wore glasses that turned everything upside-down for so long that upside-down became normal and when he finally took the glasses off, everything seemed to be standing on its head.

As Karl was putting the car away, we started up the stairs to the terrace, the doctor just ahead of me, Marty and Alice lagging behind. In a few hours I'd got so used to gravitic light that the steep steps were no great challenge.

There was a sudden hissing ahead of us, then a single enraged or terrified squall. A small pale globe came streaking down past us from the terrace, not pausing at the Doctor's "Impet!"

I was beside him as we mounted the last steps. Marty and Alice were just behind.

I became aware of a wholly unfamiliar odor—acrid, nauseating.

A glowing sphere, the brightest mind I had seen yet, was on the other side of the terrace.

It hung only inches above the flagging.

Its color was violet.

Footsteps pounded on the steps behind us and I heard Karl call, "I'm coming, Doctor!" The olive sphere of his mind appeared beside me.

With a dry rustling like light bony plates or metallic feathers scraping together, the violet mind across the terrace swiftly reared up to a height of eight or nine feet.

There was a clucking gasp of horror beside me, a swallowed scream. Simultaneously Karl's mind flared and winked out and I heard his body slump to the flagging.

"Keep your goggles on!" the Doctor cried.

The next voice I heard came from the violet mind towering across the room. It spoke English, but it was the mechanical English of a talking machine, or voder, that is operated by a keyboard and puts words together like snippets of magnetized wire. Yet in spite of its mechanical quality it conveyed an impression of power, intellectual and otherwise, that made me cringe.

VODER: Dr. Hugo Dragonet, I presume?

DR. D: What do you mean, sir, by this unheralded intrusion?

VODER: Really, Dr. Dragonet, I think you have little cause for surprise.

As the conversation between the Doctor and the violet mind went on, I was several times tempted to take off my goggles. Along with my terror I felt an agonizing curiosity, a gnawing desire to know if I could bear to see what had made Karl faint—if that was all that had happened to him. Truthfully, I was grateful that the Doctor had ordered us all to keep them on. I was even more grateful for the courage and poise he showed as he answered the voder voice.

DR. D: It is true that I have been half expecting someone? At least I have considered the possibility. (*Then to us*) Keep the goggles on!

VODER: And you too, Doctor. It will be wiser if we do not see each other in the... I am not sure if "flesh" is the word I want, at least for myself.

DR. D: May I ask what attracted your attention to my dwelling?

VODER: Can't you guess, Doctor? We recently became aware that there were instruments in it sensitive to the magnetic light of consciousness. *Our* instruments detected *your* instruments.

DR. D: That seems reasonable enough.

VODER: Doctor Dragonet, are you aware of where I come from?

DR. D: I believe so. The Greater Cosmic Fellowship?

VODER: You are tactful, perhaps even elusive. I mean are you aware of where I come from—originally?

DR. D: If I must hazard a guess, the planet Mars.

VODER: That is correct.

DR. D: (to us) Keep the goggles on!

GOGGLES OF DR. DRAGONET

VODER: And now I must ask you, Dr. Dragonet, what you intend to do with your knowledge.

DR. D: Nothing. Nothing at all.

VODER: Excuse me, Dr. Dragonet, but I find that difficult to believe.

DR. D: Why, sir? What would you expect me to do?

VODER: Well, sir, I would expect you to inform your government, your police and military authorities, of the presence of Martians in the city of Los Angeles. Since most of your fellows have not been educated to an acceptance of intelligence in physical shapes different from their own, this information, once confirmed, would lead to raids, riots, panic, and a general demand for the immediate extermination of all the extraterrestrials. Attempts would be made to root out our innocent little observation post. Such attempts would encounter resistance, since we Martians are burdened with the same self-preservatory instincts as you are and have besides a certain dignity to maintain as peaceful observers from a senior planet. The result would be a brisk skirmish—more likely, as Mars is rather stuffy about protecting her own, a full-scale interplanetary war.

DR. D: Exactly.

VODER: Excuse me, I do not quite understand.

DR. D: I think you do. What I mean is that you have described exactly what would be likely to happen if I should inform Terran authorities about your presence on earth. And so, as I have already told you, I propose to do nothing. Nothing at all.

VODER: Ah! I must confess I did not expect such a civilized decision from an earthling.

DR. D: Come, come! Earthmen aren't absolute idiots!

VODER: I am beginning to appreciate that, Doctor. I must say I am greatly relieved that this is your decision. It excuses me from taking certain steps, unpleasant to you and your companions, which I would otherwise have been obliged to carry out.

DR. D: Or attempt to.

VODER: Yes, sir, attempt to. Though I fancy that with our greater destructive powers—

DR. D: *We* are not altogether powerless you know.

VODER: That too, I suppose, is possible. Excuse me for bringing up such unpleasant matters.

DR. D: Certainly, certainly.

VODER: Dr. Dragonet, can you offer us assurance that your companions will be properly secretive?

DR. D: I vouch for them. You have my word.

VODER: That is sufficient.

DR. D: Thank you. And now, I don't wish to seem inhospitable, but . . .

VODER: (The violet globe bowed with a repetition of the dry, rustling sound.) Of course. I will depart immediately. I can understand that this interview must be something of a strain to junior minds. I trust, however, Dr. Dragonet, that there will be opportunities for you and me to discuss in private matters of interest to two philosophical denizens of the cosmos?

DR. D: Surely. Come back at any time I'm alone.

VODER: Thank you, Dr. Dragonet. Farewell, friends.

Dipping close to the flagging again, the violet globe rapidly headed toward the edge of the terrace. Although I still found the accompanying rustling or heavy scuttling sound detestable, my earlier fears had been stilled enough by the strange urbane conversation I'd just heard so I thought I might risk a look.

I lifted my hands to my temples, but, "Keep the goggles on!" commanded Dr. Dragonet.

The violet globe went over the edge. Not long afterwards the Doctor said, "It's all right now, I imagine, to take them off."

Normal vision was something of an anticlimax. The terrace was very dark. And chilly. The first thing I did was turn on some lights.

The Doctor was kneeling by Karl, who came out of his faint quickly now and seemed almost embarrassed by it. Yet when asked what he had seen, he almost fainted again. Then he said firmly, "What I saw was some sort of black centipede four yards long with eyes big as saucers. It reared and swayed like a cobra. In its upper claws it had a black box with a keyboard on it."

At that point Marty, Alice and I all started to talk at once, but the Doctor, pleading weariness, refused to enter into a discussion of any sort. However, while scanning the flowerbeds below for evidence of the creature's trail between the terrace and the Fellowship, he did say, almost apologetically, to Marty, "I'm sure you can see why it's the better part of wisdom to keep the authorities out of cases like this. The CIA might be able to deal with humanoid Martians, but giant black centipedal longhairs—I don't know."

Then gazing thoughtfully at the white walls looming faintly through the dark, he said, shaking his head, "You certainly never know whom you have for neighbors in Hollywood. Good night, children—I'm beat."

Impet appeared at the top of the steps, crossed the terrace very gingerly, and sniffed the spot where the creature had gone over the edge. Then, backing away with a hiss that seemed her last word on the subject, she went into the house.

"Good night," the Doctor repeated to us, following her.

Driving down from the hills with Marty and Alice I had a try at convincing them that the whole business could have been a hoax—at least the Martian episode (perhaps the Doctor simply had an earth friend with a violet mind and a stepladder)—but I didn't begin to convince even myself.

FAR REACH TO CYGNUS

I SHIFTED my borrowed Hillman Minx into double low to help the brave but under-engined little dear scrabble up the last steep-shooting stretch of asphalted road to Dr. Hugo Dragonet's house, perched like an angular flying saucer about to take off from one of the highest pinnacles in the eastern end of the Santa Monica Mountains—a pinnacle overlooking Hollywood, downtown Los Angeles, Griffith Park, Forest Lawn Cemetery, and North Hollywood in the San Fernando Valley.

My heart was thudding like the engine of the Minx—not with overexertion, but excitement. Nineteen minutes ago the Enigmatic Engineer—of psychology and everything else, including wealth-winning cinematic devices—had said to me, "Arthur, I've discovered a drug that is to mescalin and LSD as they are to weak coffee. Come up and try it." Then Dr. Dragonet's voice, dry as Rhine wine, had broken off and bang had gone down his phone.

Sirens silent, an LA police car and black-and-white truck hurtled past me by all of three inches, almost scaring my Minx into the ditch. At first I thought their target was the Greater Cosmic Fellowship, and I shuddered to think what *that* might let loose on the world—if one could believe Dr. Dragonet's assertions about the GCF, which would have frightened a Communist or Birchite pea-green alike.

But the two police vehicles shot past the gilded gate

in the Fellowship's white wall. Drawing up in the turn-around by the Doctor's house, they spewed out bluecoats and also brown-britches, who poured into the shrubbery beyond the house.

My thoughts whizzed: *My phone tapped . . . the Doctor's brazen invitation . . . a raid by LA's unsleeping Narcotics Squad, which has no respect for any secret scientists or any other kind.*

My Minx wouldn't whizz. In the nearest view window of Dr. Dragonet's cantilevered dwelling, in front of the tightly drawn pale drapes, I made out the Doctor's black cat peering down at the police.

I thought: *I hope you're playing lookout, Impet, and doing a right job of it. Snarl the alarm, girl! Fizz, "Fuzz!"*

The last two cops carried great nets trailing from iron hoops five feet across. I wondered dismally how Dr. Dragonet's erect lank silver-topped form would look hanging acutely bent in the mesh of one of them. Very dignified and intensely menacing, I decided impartially.

Unaided by the redoubling of my heartbeat, my Minx painfully crawled to the foot of the steps leading up to the cantilevered terrace-porch. Setting the brakes with a swipe of one hand and snatching up with the other my innocent-looking cane—which I have taken to carrying ever since my adventures with Dr. Dragonet began to go deep—I jumped out and raced up the steep steps toward a cloud-flecked blue sky, blown clear of smog for once by a steady west wind, and—here I slowed a bit, I couldn't help it—toward a very pretty pair of slim black-stockinged legs swinging coquettishly from the edge of the terrace still well above me.

I'd never met legs like *that* an any previous session with Dr. Dragonet. But then I'd never known much about his private affairs. In fact, I'd never thought of the old boy as having any.

I resumed speed and soon, three steps from the top, I was looking straight into the dark eyes of the most delicious girl I've ever encountered. She had a slim pale face, humorous sensuous lips, and long black hair hanging sleekly yet unconfined. She was wearing black leotards and a black velvet cape which draped casually from her shoulders across the dull black flagstones of the terrace.

"Why the haste, my hearty?" she asked me tranquilly, sitting there and swinging her legs.

I pictured *her* in a net—or rather explaining to one of LA's hanging judges how she had been cajoled into smoking super-marijuana by a lewd and sinister pseudoscientist old enough to be her grandfather, almost.

"I'm Arthur Gary," I informed her somewhat breathlessly, eager to create a sensation with my police raid news.

"And I'm Eduina Capasombrio."

Just then I saw it approaching her stealthily yet ripple-swift across the half-roofed, sunbright, shadow-dark terrace—and wondered for a split second if I'd already been somehow dosed, maybe by spray, with the Doctor's new drug. Then for another split instant I thought it was Impet, magnified by some illusion to thrice Impet's height at the shoulder and thirty times the housecat's mass. But *this* narrow black feline had eyes of blue fire and fangs with a steely glitter and its black pelt alternately shimmered and blurred as it moved.

I whipped my sword out of its cane-sheath and thrust it fast over Eduina's shoulder, at least an inch outside her close-fitting ear, just as the creature pounced.

The blade hit something and jarred, an electric shock traveled up my sword-arm, then everything went black before my eyes as if I were about to faint from excitement or fear.

I squinted my eyes and shook my head sharply. My power of sight came back. I stared around the terrace wildly, numb arm posing the sword for another lunge. But the black leopard was gone.

"Arthur, that was very uncool," Eduina informed me

severely, "to go stab at a poor panting animal after the police and every idiot he-man with a gun have been hunting him across the hills for a week or more.

"Except coming so near my ear with your skimevitch," she added with a note of consolation. "That was cool, Arthur." She'd still not moved, though her legs were still swinging.

At once the memory came back to me, making sense of the police nets, of the black leopard that had escaped from a private zoo near Tarzana and been pacing back and forth across the bottom of the front page of the *LA Times* for ten days, far below the black jungle treetops of the second-coming headlines about the illegal Soviet bomb-test.

"It didn't look one bit worn and weary to me," I said, still scanning shiveringly for the beast, which had really reminded me of one I'd read about in a science-fiction story—a lordly creature of evil with electricity for blood. "It looked all spruced up, as if it had come to take you to dinner—to be the meat course."

Eduina lightly shook her head. "Probably just wanted sympathy—or his horoscope cast. I'd want my Cat Stars read in his situation."

"Are there Cat Stars?" I asked.

"There are Dog Stars, aren't there?" she responded wide-eyed. I didn't quite know how to take some of her remarks and reactions. Kids change so fast these days that a ten-year age-gap sometimes seems like ten generations. With Eduina, I felt as though I was blundering in the dark. Delightful dark, though, even better than iced Irish coffee.

There came low shouts, two gunshots, then a thrashing of underbrush from the other side of the terrace. I gave Eduina my free hand as she scrambled up. We ran across and looked down from the unrailed edge.

Twenty feet below, the police were tramping back to their cars. Two of them carried, in a doubled-over net between them, a sad sweaty-looking black leopard. Its fur was dusty too, but its chest was heaving and I could see no sign of blood. Evidently my sword, if it had ever really hit that leopard, had done no great damage and the police gunshots had been only for scare-effect. The Los Angeles police are good efficient guys, really—the amateurs wouldn't have been satisfied until they'd blown the creature to bits.

I noticed that the police had left behind them in the shrubs a small black suitcase. Or perhaps someone else had dropped it there first.

Alone I wouldn't have been noticed, but girls like Eduina are stare-o-magnetic.

"We got him safe and sound, miss," one of them called up. "You can quit worrying now."

Although my attention was still wholly on the netted leopard, I was tempted to call back, "I do not think worrying is one of the young lady's skills," but just then the same cop called up, "What's that weapon you got there, fellow?"

"A long shish-kebab skewer," I assured him, guiltily making sure my hand hid the silver-knobbed grip. Sword canes are decidedly illegal and although the LA police are often good guys, they are always sticklers. I was still studying the captured leopard, very doubtfully now.

There was a loud *hist*! behind us. I spun around. It was only Karl, the Doctor's sturdy butler and precision machinist, beckoning us from the porch door.

But I had already made up my mind. The black leopard the police had netted was not *my* black leopard and never had been.

Little Impet, peering around Karl's thick ankles, seemed to agree with me, for the black house-cat scanned about fiercely, then sprang back with a spitting *hiss* of her own.

I was glad myself we were leaving the terrace. Now that the sun was dropping out of sight and the west wind humming higher, the place had turned eerie.

Protectively—well, that was a bit of my reason—I

shifted my free arm to Eduina's waist. Even through the velvet cape it felt remarkably slim and supple.

The big living room with its thick tight-drawn drapes was so dark I couldn't see anything clearly. I was annoyed at Karl for closing the door tightly behind us, then remembered what might be lurking outside and stopped feeling irked. Realizing other advantages of the darkness, I shifted my arm to the same position under Eduina's cloak. She didn't mind or maybe didn't notice. She was a very cool girl, truly.

There was a pale shape stretched above the center of the floor—on a low dark couch, I guessed. Or maybe floating there. Around it was a circle of eight motionless, weirdly hunched forms. I wondered if they were having drugged visions and perhaps drugged shape-changes, supposing the Doctor's experiment had already begun.

I started to ask, but Eduina breathed at my ear a *shh* that was almost a kiss, while from the pale shape there came a sweet monotonous voice saying:

"It's a blue blue planet, not from oceans, but from great prairies of blue grass reaching almost to the poles and dotted here and there with tiny lakes. Dipping closer, I can see herds of unicorns and tricorns cropping the blue savannas. Now, closer still, I see bands of slim elvish folk. Their naked skins are pale blue. They ride the unicorn, they pound a bluish grain to flour, they study the stars through telescopes with lenses of water and mirrors of liquid mercury curved by force fields. They dance to pipes and sleep or they meditate alone under their fiery moon ..."

For a moment I could *see* the blue scene hovering before my eyes—so sharply that I wondered if there could be visions contagious like diseases and delusions—although the edges of my mind and feelings were still busy with my rather loony guesses about a drug-orgy and with *my* black leopard, the deadly one . . . and with Eduina, of course.

As the sweet voice died away, the living room lights came up softly. I looked at the pale figure lying in the center of the room—on a low couch, as I'd guessed—and my heart jumped about a yard away from Eduina and hung there for several seconds.

The pale figure was a long girl in an unbelted white flannel dress that covered her from neck to pink toes. Her tranced face had the lines but not the fullness of that of a Greek goddess. Her long hair outspread was a pale golden sunburst.

The eight weirdly hunched forms dissolved into eight of the Doctor's angularly asymmetric but comfortably cushioned chairs with five superficially normal-looking occupants. The three chairs to my left were empty. The next two held grasshopper-thin restless Professor Seibold and, clerical collar indenting his jowls, plump Father Minturn—two highly intelligent men I'd met before at the Doctor's sessions on those occasions when he'd wanted a thorough materialistic scientist and a thoughtful Man of God among his observers.

Next to the priest reclined a very tall, very thin nun in black flowing habit and a visored and veiled wimple which completely concealed her features. Not so normal-looking, that one, I had to admit.

The figure beyond that—just to my right—made my heart sink: a handsome crophaired sun-tanned suavely muscled young man in rather close-fitting sports jacket, slacks, and suede shoes, all dazzling white; his gaze was bored yet sensuous, raptorial yet veiled—oh, everybody knows Jay Astar, the newest and most successful Brando-surrogate and homegrown Mastroianni to hit stereo, cinema and TV.

My jealous and pessimistic mind instantly decided that Eduina and the blonde had to be starlets who had come to this session along with "Jastar." Such offbeat beauties could only be *his* girls. My spirits sank.

Why would the Doctor have *him* here? But then the Doctor rather liked film folks, the old fool.

A lank figure straightened briskly up from the only chair I couldn't see into, the one in front of me, and turned to face me with a supple unrigid military erectness. At times Dr. Hugo Dragonet looks remarkably like a Prussian or Czarist offficer, or diplomat perhaps. His silvery hair was crewcut, his wrinkle-netted eyes gleamed with youth, the other lines of his long face were cynical-genial.

"Arthur!" he said, smiling warmly. Then the smile thinned a trifle. "Stop smooching my niece!"

I tried brazenly to hang onto her, but Eduina unhooked herself from my arm with a full turn that swirled her velvet cape away from her black-fitted body.

Dr. Dragonet's eyes twinkled. "Eduina, Mister Arthur Gray," he said formally. "Arthur, Senorita Eduina Capasombrio."

I bowed peevishly. My pessimistic mind—which at my birth had declared a cold war against my optimistic feelings—slightly redeployed its thoughts about Eduina: she wasn't the girl Jastar had brought, but the one he had come here to fascinate and lay claim to, probably had already done so. And the blonde too, of course. Who can win against stereo stars?

Dr. Dragonet might prove my ally, of course. I could even imagine him saying "Stop necking my niece," to Jastar too. But he was an old man, lost in his experiments and inventions.

Eduina went up to him. "Dear Uncle Hugo," she said softly. He bowed to her and as she pressed a kiss on his forehead, she looked sidewise at me with a peculiarly sly smile. By some chance his lips quirked at the same moment. Was Uncle Hugo really so old? Then she swirled down into the empty chair next to his.

To fill the conversational pause, but mostly because I was really curious, I asked, "Was the other young woman actually seeing or clairvoying a scene on another planet? And is she under the influence of—" I hesitated.

"Of my new drug? Yes," he finished for me. "As to your first question, it's rather improbable she was getting anything interplanetary or interstellar. More likely something from her subconscious, or from the subconscious mind of one of us. Some forgotten fairytale, perhaps.

"However, there's this to be said for your suggestion," he went on. "Whenever I ask the young lady where her vision is coming from, she points toward the constellation Cygnus—the Swan or Northern Cross, as you know—whether it happens to be below or, as now, above the horizon, or night or day at the time. As far as I know, she has no knowledge of field astronomy. It's a suggestive circumstance, though really nothing to build on."

I nodded. Quite restrained for Dr. Dragonet, I thought, remembering the black goggles with which he had let us glimpse the glow of mentality diffusing from the galaxy and with which he had (so he claimed!) discovered the Greater Cosmic Fellowship to be a secret outpost—peaceful, he hoped, he told us—of black giant centipedal Martians—a good example of the stranger denizens of Hollywood, if you can believe the Doctor.

The memory gave me a start. I wondered if *my* black leopard could be some creature or projection of the Martians.

The priest and the professor were looking at me peculiarly. I realized I was still holding my naked swordcane. Karl silently handed me its sheath.

Eduina began chattily to tell her uncle about the eruption of police and the capture of the escaped leopard. I waited for her to finish, intending to add my theory—conviction, rather—that there had been two black leopards.

Meanwhile the fair-haired girl sat up on the couch, resting her chin in her hand. Her eyes were open now, but her classic face was still dreamy. She wasn't so long after all—it had been that white dress.

Jay Astar looked at her loosely draped form with a cool appraisal I found infuriating.

The two other men in the circle had begun to talk about the Siberian explosion that had us on the brink of war. Professor Seibold was claiming it had been a giant underground atomic test-blast which had got out of control and vented in spite of all Soviet precautions and secrecy measures. Father Minturn supported the minority guess that it had been an enemy atomic rocket, aimed at Krasnoyarsk and overshooting north. A Chinese rocket, perhaps, or—who dared say?

Palm outthrust protestingly, Dr. Dragonet called briskly, "Ladies, gentlemen, enough of these trivia! Roxane! —bring the psionic elixir!"

I looked toward the girl in white as he called "Roxane!" but she didn't react . . . and then from the next room came a third young lady bearing a tray with crystal-gleaming goblets and two bottles. She too was slim, wearing a blue suit and wraparound blue sun-glasses which somehow reminded me of the blue planet I'd heard described. Really, the girl in white should have been wearing them.

The third girl had dark red hair bobbed rather long. Beneath the masking glasses her lips were curved in an impudent, knowing smile. She wore blue net stockings.

Again my heart did that delightful business of jumping a yard away from Eduina, or this time as much as two.

The newcomer set the tray down on a high taboret beside Dr. Dragonet's chair. Smiling compassionately at me, the Doctor said, "Arthur! Let me introduce you to my nieces Mademoiselle Roxane Rougecheveu—" He indicated the redhead, who sketched a curtsy "—and to Frauline Blondine Haarlang—" The girl in white nodded vaguely "—who belong respectively to the French and German branches of the Dragonet family, through the

FAR REACH TO CYGNUS

maternal line, just as Senorita Capsasombrio does to the Spanish.

"Oh, by the way, Blondine," he called to the girl in white, "if you see any more of the blue planet, don't hesitate to break in on us, no matter what we're discussing." She gave another vague nod.

The redhead sat down in the farther of the remaining chairs and I in the remaining one—in the exact spot where my heart still vacillated midway between Eduina and Roxane, which was a good thing for my physiological integrity. Bad to have one's anatomic and amatory hearts in different places.

Working with skilled rapidity, Dr. Dragonet poured a pale yellow wine into seven of the goblets, then using a pipette, added to each exactly three drops of a colorless fluid from a glass-stoppered crystal bottle.

Gradually all eyes, even the lazy ones of Jastar, became fixed on the Doctor and his speeding hands. As he worked, he began to speak, quite casually.

"One of life's most fascinating problems, which science refuses to tackle, or shrugs off as 'metaphysics,' is the hook-up between the mind and the world."

I thought, *Oh, nuts, a lecture on philosophy—when I want to hear about blue planets and black leopards and golden elixirs.*

Flaring his nostrils at me, as if he'd caught my thoughts, the Doctor continued, "To put it simply, *where* in the brain—or elsewhere!—is the space of my—or your —consciousness? Where is that clearcut shining scene which each sighted man or woman sees outspread before him while he wakes, or shimmering strangely in dreams?" He tapped the silver-lawned side of his skull. "Is it inside here?" He swept five outstretched fingers in front of him. "Or is it . . . out there?"

I thought, *Say, maybe this applies. Was my black leopard a living thing . . . out there? Or was it a projection from my mind?—or from someone else's mind! True, my sword had bent and my arm had been shocked. Yet the black leopard had had that glimmering appearance of a projection and the super-realness one associates with fever-visions rather than reality. And something had momentarily blacked out my vision, too.*

Professor Seibold muttered to himself, intending to be overheard, I'm sure, "To try to measure pictures in the mind against the great world of matter as if they were two maps which could be fitted to each other—naive!"

Dr. Dragonet caught it. He said, smiling, "When I was a child, I decided to be naive—which incidentally means 'natural'—forever. It's paid off—in fun and money too. Now to explore the problem." He lifted one finger. "First, is the space of consciousness *in* the brain? That would analyze down only to a pattern of firing neurons or lectric fields, not the vivid theater-like scene itself."

He held up two fingers. "Or is the space of consciousness in another set of dimensions altogether? But that means there are at least two worlds, the world of things and the inner one—which offend against science's Law of Parsimony: the need to find the simplest explanation possible, to avoid assuming one more factor than necessary."

"I go for simplicity myself," Jay Astar observed, that rough sonorous voice of his ringing out for the first time, but it was hard to tell whether he was talking about scientific assumptions, or styles of acting, or clothes maybe—or at any rate I told myself that. I glanced to see if Eduina or Roxane were hanging onto the words of the white-clad male love-god. They didn't seem to be.

Dr. Dragonet continued, "Actually the second explanation involves a gigantic offense against the Law of Parsimony, for if each conscious being has an inner world approximating even to a small degree the world of things, then we are assuming trillions upon trillions of separate worlds—a vast unnecessary multiplication of structures."

FAR REACH TO CYGNUS

Professor Seibold snorted, "You're just hanging sense data on a pre-Kantian space-time framework."

"Do you dig this?" I whispered experimentally to Eduina. She nodded curtly without looking at me. From Roxane's direction I heard a very faint chuckle. I cursed myself and concentrated.

"Or—" Dr. Dragonet went on, three fingers in the air, his eyes gleaming over his pipette, to the top of which his thumb was clamped to check its drip— "does the inner world lie out there in the world of things?—like paint on a house, or make-up on a woman's face, or wrappings of finest tissue on a box. De Broglie has said that each electron extends, however tenuously, to the ends of the universe. Why not the conscious mind? What if all our inner worlds lie out there, nested on objects and on fields, clothing with color and feeling the skeleton world of things?"

"More 200-year-old British metaphysics!" the professor jeered.

"Perhaps forming together one single great diversified communal mind, Doctor?" the tall veiled black nun across the circle from me observed in a harsh mechanic whisper which made me shiver. There was a faint dry rustling as she leaned forward. Jay Astar, sitting on her left, looked at her sharply.

Dr. Dragonet nodded. "Perhaps, Sister Marcia."

"The Mind of God," Father Minturn murmured on her right.

Dr. Dragonet frowned. "God—a word," he said harshly, "yet not altogether inacceptable. The communal mind would of course have within it a multitude of foci—our individualities. Not a Trinity, but almost an Infinity."

"Bits of mind strewn about," Eduina observed. "You make it sound like ectoplasm, Uncle Hugo." From my other side Roxane chuckled. The Doctor made a face at them.

Professor Seibold was angrily waving his hand. "I can see the stars," he asserted emphatically, but only for a moment mystifyingly. "How can bits of my consciousness lie that far out—hundreds and billions of light years away?"

The Doctor replied quietly, "Aristotle had an insight which we've neglected and derided: that vision goes out from the eye to the object and then returns to the eye. Perhaps consciousness operates that way, moving instantaneously or almost so, even though physical vision doesn't. Modern investigations suggest that psi-or esp-forces move at velocities at least far greater than light."

"But what I see in the stars happened hundreds and billions of years ago!" Professor Seibold rapped back. "The stars have moved since—they and the mind bits would not be congruent!"

"Most of the stars haven't moved far," the Doctor countered. "The dis-congruence would not be great and since we've hardly begun to log psi-observations we wouldn't have detected it just as the apparent movement of the stars with the seasons was indetectable to the ancients and medievals, so that they decided all the stars were set in one vast crystal sphere at the outer limits of the cosmos."

"You talk of psi-forces and forces of consciousness," the thin professor hammered on. "If they're forces, why haven't we detected them, I ask you, sir?"

"They are too feeble for our instruments to pick up," the Doctor retorted. "Psi-forces may be basic, yet so weak under most terrestrial conditions as to be almost indiscoverable—just as the basic force of gravity itself might never be discovered in a feathery world of free fall. Besides, most of us haven't the right instruments. The gravito-electric and gravito-magnetic spectra exist in theory, but they've never been observed in practice—with the exception of Ehrenfels' experiment and one other."

"Hugo," I cut in. "Would it ever be possible for the parts of the inner world which lie in the world of things to . . . well . . . operate independently?" I was thinking of my black leopard.

"There we enter a more speculative realm," the Doctor said thoughtfully. "But yes, Arthur, some of my most recent trials of the elixir have indicated to me that under certain conditions the contents of the subconscious mind of a highly repressed, highly energized person—a person with powerful drives—might be projected into the world of things, there taking individualized form, possibly animal, like some of Jung's archetypes, and operating for a while independently, with powers to move about and help or harm."

"This is preposterous! I ask you what—" Professor Seibold burst out contentiously, but at that moment Blondine Haarlang began to speak from her central position on the low couch, her eyes again closed, her voice a pleasant yet imperious monotone:

"Great black and silver spaceships are orbiting now around the blue planet. Boats land from the spaceships and discharge beings in great helmets and protective suits—perhaps the air is poisonous to them. They are humanoid but I cannot see their faces. They begin to explore and to test the direction of the wind. The elvish folk hide from them in the deep blue grass."

Although the room was light now, I again had the illusion that the scene Blondine was describing was hovering between me and her. For a brief moment it was frighteningly realistic: I could see the heavy-suited trampers through the grass and I peered in vain to glimpse their faces. I asked myself if it were remotely conceivable that her consciousness, traveling some unknown superhighway, had gone out to a planet circling a star in the Northern Cross. On impulse I asked, "Where's the blue planet, Frauline Haarlang?"

Without opening her eyes, she pointed toward me, which was east—I know my directions in Dragonet's house—then raised her hand halfway overhead before she dropped it. That would be right for the Northern Cross at this time of summer.

"I think it's time we drank the elixir—before our speculations get too far out without its help," Dr. Dragonet said, grimacing apologetically at Professor Seibold. "Roxane, pass around the goblets!"

The professor frowned, grasping his goblet when it came as if it were a ceremonial mace. "I have further objections," he said, "but I'll reserve them."

I sniffed at mine, detecting no odor but that of Riesling. Some of the others sniffed too. I noted that Sister Marcia, the black nun, was holding her goblet close to her narrow chest in short black-gloved fingers.

When Roxane came to him, Dr. Dragonet waved her on. "The bartender should never drink," he quipped. "Besides, I have acquired a residual sensitivity from repeated doses."

He dropped his hand to the side of his chair and the lights very slowly began to dim. He said, "Cortisone is the best medical analogy I can find for my psychic or psionic elixir—which incidentally is extracted from the pineal glands of a strain of rhesus monkeys which have undergone certain stresses and been injected with various lesser drugs. Little has been discovered about the pineal's function in a century of research—but if the function is psionic, what orthodox researcher is going to discover that?—or go out on a limb about it if he does?" He shrugged.

"Cortisone makes tissues more permeable, so that healing substances can reach their targets more readily. It weakens the wall between cell and cell.

"My psionic elixir weakens the walls between the cells of the mind, between the conscious and unconscious and all the other areas, many of them unmapped, unknown, unexplored.

"To an even greater degree it weakens the wall between mind and mind, between minds that are near and minds that are far, between minds that are almost alike and minds that are unutterably divergent, indicating that we are not lonely little forts of mind, solitary 'I'-machines, but instead we are points or rather foci in a great continuum of feeling."

The room had darkened considerably from the Doctor's rheostat, but I could still see faces, most of them with gazes fixed on his sardonic-lined yet now almost sorcerous one. Between myself and the Doctor, Eduina: a humorous "cool" girl, yet ageless-seeming now, a sphinx. To my left Roxane, her smile made enigmatic by her blue wraparound glasses. To her left, Professor Seibold: suspicious, hostile, rigidly poised—yet I could see his chest move with his rapid breathing. Then Father Minturn: benign, calm, perhaps too calm. Then the inscrutable black-veiled Sister Marcia. Then Jay Astar, lazily smiling, another calm one—but perhaps his hand was shaking slightly, for now he casually steadied his goblet against his white-trousered knee. And so back around the circle to Dr. Dragonet. In the shadows behind him was a dark blocky form—Karl.

And in the center of the circle, Blondine. She faced me rather than the Doctor, but she was not looking directly at me, but somewhat over my head. And her gaze seemed to go far beyond, through the wall, out into space, perhaps to her blue planet.

My heart skipped a beat as a black shape leaped to the back of Father Seibold's chair. Impet. The black housecat silently settled down there behind the cleric's head, though I doubt he was aware of her presence. She directed her slit-eyed gaze at Sister Marcia.

I thought about what the Doctor had said about subconscious minds being projected in animal form, and I shivered at the idea while I tried to reject it. I wondered about the subconscious drives of those around me.

The Doctor said, "We will drink one by one, around the circle, clockwise. That way the effects will be more interesting, particularly to those who drink first. I will point each time to the person who is to drink and snap my fingers to tell him when."

The forefinger of his right hand aimed at me and then the mid-finger slipped off the thumb and struck the groove between bent ring-finger and palm with a solid *click*.

The gazes shifted to me. I felt flustered—and a little resentful that the Doctor had made me the first to take the plunge into the unknown. For the first time I wondered if this drug were safe, had been tested enough—or, contrariwise, if it were only three drops of water. I glanced around quickly—why the devil should the gathering shadows pick this time to remind me of the black leopard the police hadn't netted? My left hand touched my sword-cane by the side of my chair.

I was taking too long, I knew, making Eduina and Roxane think me timid.

Then I realized I had drained the goblet and was carefully setting it on the floor.

The Riesling's mild astringent sting was pleasant in my throat. There was no other taste.

Long moments passed. I leaned back. I no longer worried about black leopards or what others thought of me. I was feeling relaxed and at home, as if some age-old stricture was being loosened. I wasn't even bothered that the drug was having no particular effect on me. Why did human beings go around tense and unhappy, thinking everything mattered so much? They missed the real juice of life.

I looked at Blondine, since that was easiest. The room was almost black now, but the Doctor must have switched a soft spotlight on her, perhaps to give us a common focal point, for her complexion glowed. I lost myself in her face. I'd always thought it was jewel-juggling or tiffany-flattery when a poet spoke of a girl having lips like rubies or rose-petals, cheeks like mother-of-pearl faintly shot with pink, eyes like sapphires, hair like a cloud of the finest gold wires. Now I realized that—funny!—it could be literally true.

Roxane chuckled. I was glad she appreciated my point. "Do you notice any effects, Arthur?"

"The colors are richer," I heard myself tell Dr. Dragonet.

"Colors are richer," he repeated quietly. "In fully fifty percent of cases that is the first reaction to LSD or any of the mind-enlarging drugs, including my elixir. I suggest this is because they—and especailly my elixir—open the mind of the drug-taker to the minds of those around him, so that he sees things not only through his own eyes, but also through those of others, which since we all see things and even colors differently, has an inevitable enriching effect. Incidentally, this would explain why mind-enlarging drugs have their greatest effect when taken in company, their least when taken alone."

Midway in this statement, he had clicked his fingers and I knew that Roxane had drunk. I agreed with what he said, in an idle sort of way, but continued to watch Blondine. Now it seemed that the light on her was moonlight—the Doctor has full-spectrum illumination in his house—for her lips had gone toward grape or amethyst, the mother-of-pearl or opal of her cheeks was faintly violet, the sapphire of her eyes more intense, the gold of her hair paler but with a note of turquoise or, no, jade. It might not be moonlight, but a scene undersea, with Blondine a jewel-scaled mermaid.

"Roxane," I said, "there's more green in those wrap-around glasses than I'd have guessed."

Only then did I realize the implication of what I had said. Not that it much surprised me. Meanwhile there had come another resonant *click*: signal for Professor Seibold to drink.

"*Oui*," Roxane replied softly. "And you, *monsieur*, have an exalted vision of girls. Expensive too."

"Hugo," I observed, "you've got almost too much light on Blondine."

"Young man," Father Minturn answered for him, "the room is nearly pitch dark."

I noted that except for Blondine the room *was*, well, moderately dark. I continued to watch her face. Gradually a discordant, amost angry note came into it. Not anything obvious. She was still beautiful, but it was as if her face had been dissected by almost invisible cuts into its parts—forehead, eyes, nose, etc.—like a subtly cubistic painting. After a bit I began also to see, faintly, a red network beneath her skin and then, more faintly still, a silvery one: blood vessels and nerves.

It occurred to me that Professor Seibold was making *his* contribution to the image—and that if this was the way a materialist saw the world and pretty girls, I didn't want any more than the sample.

At the same time the image was getting a surreal appearance, suggestive of Piccaso, which puzzled me, since I hadn't thought the professor was consciously art-minded, only analytic.

I suppose there must have been another *click* a while back, though I hadn't heard it, for a palely glowing tone came into Blondine's face, soothing the discords, brushing them over with a moonlight like Roxane's but milkier, so that the face acquired an additional quality like that of a china statue. This must be coming from Father Minturn, the idealizer, the spiritualizer.

But the Picasso-look was stronger than ever. The image of Blondine was appearing to me both full-face and, at the same time, in complete profile.

Then I realized that Roxane and I were seeing her full face, while Seibold and Minturn, sitting a quarter way around the circle from us, were viewing her profile. It was as simple as that.

All the varied images still added up to a girl's face. The totality, though strange, was still beautiful.

There was still another *click*. This time I heard it and I watched Sister Marcia's goblet creep up under her heavy black veil—which I still couldn't see through, although the light came up on her as I watched her, as it did on everything I watched.

There was an odd prolonged sipping or sucking sound, barely audible, and the goblet came out empty.

Just then Blondine began to speak again, a note of agitation rippling the sweet monotony.

"The helmeted invaders are firing the blue grass with flame-throwers! Towering red-yellow walls, smoke-topped, rush with the wind across the great savannas or creep against it. The elvish fold crouch unresisting in their grassy hollows, eyes shut, emaciated from privation or from intense thought."

I began to get a vision of that too—there were ghostly flames between us—but just then all my attention was engulfed by another change taking place in Blondine's hair and form. It was an image of her back—Sister Marcia sat across the circle from me—but it was an image which broke up the gold of her hair and the white of her dress into a checkerboard of large dots, like a very coarse-grained newspaper reproduction.

It was Blondine as seen through an insect's eyes, or possibly an arachnid's or chilopod's.

At the same time I found myself salivating and thinking, to my horror, that Blondine would be *good to eat*. The only reassuring thing about the impulse this thought gave me was that it seemed to be strictly inhibited.

I asked myself if Dr. Dragonet might conceivably have smuggled into our group one of the giant centipedal Martians from the Greater Cosmic Fellowship. I found this difficult to accept, as I had actually never seen one of the beasts myself and, to tell truth, half doubted all his stories about them. But if it were so, he was on closer terms with them than he'd ever told me—and of course the black-nun disguise was a brilliant one. Mars—Sister Marcia—oh Good Lord!

Eduina's hand tugged gently at my elbow. I leaned toward her. She whispered in my ear, "Arthur I think you know that Uncle is an ardent desegregationist. Just keep that in mind."

In my excitement I must have missed another *click*, for now I heard Jay Astar say lazily, "This'll be only my second drink today. Just another touch of wind and Doc's good old Elixir," and I saw him drain his goblet.

"Jastar and I had a session this morning," the Doctor explained casually, though with a hint of annoyance.

I felt a stab of jealousy that the stereo star should be deeper in the Doctor's secrets than I. Eduina and I were still leaning together. Impulsively I whispered, "Has that big white ape from the underside of the Panhandle ever made a pass at you?"

"Dozens," she assured me impatiently, as though I should have known the answer to that one. "I brush him off as gently as I can, he's such a child. My heart's still mostly with the family—you know, Uncle Hugo."

"Child gorilla?" I asked, still whispering, of course. "Another of those poor panting leopards?"

She shrugged, then quirked me a quick smile.

At that happy (to me) moment, Blondine burst out more agitatedly with: "I've looked into the helmet of one of the destroyers! They're a cat-people, black-furred!"

There was a flurry of small movements around the circle, touched off by the intensity of her voice, I suppose —or perhaps others here knew about the second black leopard. I know *I* started to think about it again—first the wild notion that Blondine had materialized on earth one of the cat-people invading the blue planet, then Dr. Dragonet's suggestion about a subconscious mind on the loose in animal form. *Whose* would it be, I wondered? Professor Seibold had shown constant irritation and a half repressed anger—*that* might be indicative. Yet the milky calm of Father Minturn's mind might be an even stronger sign of murky unconscious depths. Eduina *dressed* like a black leopard—that could be a clue; while Sister Marcia . . . there were simply too many hints! Why, even I . . . So far the elixir had given me no sight of my own unconscious mind, as the Doctor had said it would. Did that mean my subconscious had gone out of me? True, I had struck at the leopard, but would I know my own subconscious mind if I met it? Would anybody?

The room seemed to have grown darker now, although Blondine's strange image still was bright, and I began to catch movements in the shadows behind the chairs—movements which stopped as soon as I looked straight at them. I wanted to call for real lights.

There was a *click*—signal for Eduina to drink. We'd be finished soon, I thought hopefully.

I returned to Blondine's image. Jastar's drinking seemed to have added nothing to it at all. Nothing rich in *that* mind, I told myself with a certain satisfaction.

Or perhaps the effects of the elixir were wearing off for me. Even the quintuple-exposure of Blondine was beginning to darken.

Yet at the same time I began to feel a growing tension and I sensed again the illusion—or reality—of movement in the shadows by the walls, as if some sinuous black beast were pacing there. Half rising, I openly peered around the room—even behind my chair, I have to admit. I didn't see any slinking animal either, but it could have been hiding behind one of the chairs.

The tension continued to grow. Sister Marcia was leaning forward now, looking taller and thinner than ever. Father Minturn's hands made fat white blobs where they gripped the arms of his chair. Professor Seibold was writhing his narrow shoulders and jogging his right knee very fast, like a chess player with a minute in which to make twenty moves. Roxane no longer smiled below her wraparound glasses. Eduina had slipped off her cloak and was holding it over her left arm. Dr. Dragonet was sitting very erect, his gaze switching quickly from side to side. Only Jay Astar leaned back, serene—or just stupid.

I was leaning forward myself now, my left hand gripping my sword cane, my right hand on its hilt.

Her soft fur bristling, Impet came erect behind Father Minturn's shoulders with a spitting *hiss*. The plump priest threw himself forward on the floor. I didn't blame him one bit.

At first I was sure Impet was hissing at Sister Marcia. Then I saw that the target of the cat's alarm and anger lay beyond. Out of the shadow behind Jay Astar's chair there rose a narrow, high-domed, shimmering black muzzle with ears like silky spear points, eyes that were pulsing blue sparks, fangs that gleamed like steel.

Eduina sprang to the seat of her chair. Stamping on its arm and waving her black cloak forward, she shouted at the top of her voice at the black apparition, *"Gato! Hey, gato!"*

She was citing the black leopard as if it were a bull; she was calling, "Hey, cat!"

The leopard vaulted over Jastar and his chair in one enormous bound—a great curving brushstroke of glimmering black against the lesser darkness. But I had snatched my sword from its sheath and now I lunged high.

A dazzling blue flicker ran along the blade. Lightning flashed in the room, showing the pictures on the walls.

The blade bent double and broke. I felt twice the shock I had on the terrace, but my vision didn't go. I drew back to thrust again with my numb hand, not knowing even if it still held the broken sword.

The black leopard came weaving forward again, then turned abruptly and sprang sideways, out of range of my defense, at Roxane.

An instant earlier Sister Marcia had launched herself forward, seeming to lengthen almost impossibly, in a long arc of her own, her black habit streaming. She dove over Father Minturn and Blondine, whose image had dimmed almost to darkness now, and met the leopard in midair. They dropped to the floor together and for a moment there was a scuffling and a horrid dry rustling, then sudden silence, broken almost immediately by our frantic voices.

The darkness was now complete.

"Keep quiet and keep your places!" Dr. Dragonet commanded.

A few moments later enough lights for an operating theater came on. They showed us all on our feet, with one exception.

Sister Marcia was standing like a lightly disheveled black pillar beside the door, half open now, to the terrace.

There was no sight of the black leopard anywhere.

In that mechanical voice, so chillingly suggestive of a voder rather than speech from a living throat, the black nun said, "I must return to my devotions. Thank you, Doctor, for an interesting session. Good night, friends."

Taking mincing steps and ducking her head to miss the lintel, which would have cleared my own head by two feet, she rustled from the room.

I wanted to ask her, "Do subconscious minds taste good, Sister?"

Professor Seibold wiped his forehead and gave off with an inelegant, unscientific "Whew!"

The one of us remaining in his chair, so quiet he might be a stereo still of himself, or dead, was Jay Astar. But when the Doctor lightly shook his shoulder, he came to with a headshake and a "Huh?" and then said in a voice from which most of the glamorous resonance was gone, "How'd the session go, Doc? I must of fell asleep though I never thought I'd even relax, let alone nap. That Black Sister's starched underthings kept rustling like one of the big centipedes we had down in my granddaddy's house in Old Mississip."

"I heard nothing," Father Minturn said, a shade loftily. "But then I don't listen for such things."

Jay stood up shakily. "Gee, I feel awful weak on my pins. Like I was empty inside."

The Doctor steadied him, saying, "Karl will drive you home." Then, "I think we'd all be better for a breath of fresh air." He indicated the terrace.

I wanted to go beside Eduina, to compliment her on her technique as a *torero*—or *gatero!*—and maybe fish for a compliment back on my own showing as a *matador*—or *gatador!*—but she was chattering excitedly with Roxane. Father Minturn followed, half supporting Jastar, and behind them went Professor Seibold and Blondine. Dr. Dragonet gently held me back and as we drifted after them, he leaned his head and told me confidentially, "I suspected it was Jastar's unconscious mind all along. I like the film colony—I make my living off them!—but some of the newcomers are so single-mindedly ambitious and pushing that they're a public danger. They need their teeth—I mean their drives—drawn and I look upon it as a sort of civic duty to do so. Now he'll be a hollow man for months."

"Won't it ruin his career?" I asked, not too concerned.

"No. Most actors are only lay figures—puppets. His directors will position him properly and use a needle spot to make his eyes gleam and re-resonate his voice with an echo chamber and maybe use collodion to twist his mouth into the smirk his fans love, until something of his old energy returns."

I asked, "Would being rejected by just one girl fill a man like Jastar with such seething resentments?"

He looked at me sharply. "So Eduina's been telling you things? Yes, of course, the littler the big man, the more sensitive he is to slights."

"What do you think would have happened, Doctor, if the leopard had reached Eduina or Roxane?"

He shrugged. "Perhaps nothing. Perhaps a mild electric shock. *I* think she'd have had her face scratched off: Jay has—or had—a very strong feminine component, completely repressed."

"One more thing, Doctor. Is Sister Marcia really—"

FAR REACH TO CYGNUS

I began, but we were on the terrace now, near the others, and he lightly squeezed my arm for silence.

"Some creatures, even highly intelligent ones, feed on the body electricity of emotion as well as on flesh," he whispered briskly. "That's all I can tell you."

Now we were all under the stars, bright in the windswept sky. Automatically my gaze went up to Cygnus, that great five-starred swan winging high through the dark. Blondine looked up and then the others too, as she said tranquilly, "A terrible cold radiates from the pale blue dreaming elvish folk. The great fires in the blue grass shrink and flicker and die. The helmeted invaders rush back to their boats, but some of them are frozen in their tracks and shattered by their hurtling comrades —their heat vanished like neutrinos or spectrons. The boats take off and then the spaceships that brought them. But—" there was a catch in her voice "—the elvish folk crouch frozen too. Forever frozen, unless . . ."

At that instant, from a point in the heavens between Cygnus and Lyra, there came a tiny flash of blue light which lasted perhaps a second. The blue was the same shade as the grass of Blondine's planet. Real light, I asked myself, or the reflected gleam of consciousness? I had no way of knowing, but murmurs told me the others had seen it too.

"It didn't even come from Cygnus," Professor Seibold protested, possibly in some last-ditch inner defense of his materialism.

"No," the Doctor agreed. "Perhaps the star towing Blondine's planet has moved that far during the millennia it takes its physical light to reach us. Your own point, Professor."

"Doctor," I asked, "do you think there's any possible connection between the black felinoids invading the blue planet and our own black leopard?"

He shrugged thoughtfully. "It is one of those grand coincidences, or congruences, which we'll only begin to understand when we've seriously studied the innumerable fields of psionics for fifty years or so."

We asked Blondine questions but, "I don't see anything any more. It's over," was all she would answer.

I joined Eduina and Roxane. The latter, with a grin, drifted away toward the Doctor, who was calling, "Karl! Better get the car out."

Just then a siren sounded far off and came weaving up through the hills. We all stopped to listen to it—a little apprehensively, I imagine. Even the Doctor's elixir leaves one a shade jittery.

I scanned around. Below us, the lawns and flowerbeds and and gilt domed buildings of Greater Cosmic Fellowship were dark, except for the tiny golden flame of one peace candle burning steadily.

Presently there was no doubt of the siren's destination, for it grew very loud and high white headlights came hurtling with it up the road. A squeal of brakes, a clatter of footsteps, and then three uniformed policemen and two detectives had run up the stairway onto the black-flagged terrace.

"Any of you here found a little black suitcase, sealed?" the first detective breathlessly demanded of us.

Karl stepped out of the shadows and handed him the suitcase I'd seen earlier lying in the bushes.

The first detective grabbed it, examined the seals closely, breathed a "Thank God," and then—although the other detective was signing him to be quiet—burst out with, "You people have saved our bacon! This suitcase has got in it the biggest haul of heroin we ever made in a single raid! When they went to get the leopard, some boob grabbed it up, thinking it was a case of teargas bombs, and then lost it here. We owe you a vote of thanks!"

The second detective pulled him toward the stairs.

Heroin, I thought contemptuously—and breathed a prayer for all poor thrill-seekers hooked on mind-darkening drugs instead of mind-enlarging ones—and administered without the benefit of Dr. Dragonet.

Karl helped Jastar down the stairs after the police. Professor Seibold followed with Father Minturn. Roxane, Blondine, and the Doctor went inside. I was alone with Eduina.

"Darling," I began, turning to her, "as a *gatero* you were magnificent—"

She interrupted me with, "Verbal compliments are uncool, Arthur."

I put my arms on her shoulders and drew her to me.

"Arthur!" Dr. Dragonet's voice came sharply from the doorway. "I told you not to smooch my niece. Come inside, Eduina."

I tightened my hands on her shoulders, but she shook her head slightly, brushed her lips against mine, and drew away from me with a smile.

I thought, as she crossed the terrace, *Damn the man! Aren't two nieces enough for him?*

NIGHT PASSAGE

THE LARGE GOLD COIN rang and settled on the green felt where the newly arriving young lady crying out "Eight!" had pitched it and the ivory marble clicked against the diamond-shaped silvery point in the darkly gleaming mahogany bowl while a voice called, "No more bets. Game closed." The golden coin's worn face faintly revealed to my glance a circle that was horned and had a pendant cross. Then the ivory ball clattered into a slowly revolving metal square.

"Eight. Black," the croupier called and the banker's large, meaty, well-manicured white hand with wiry black hairs sprouting from its back closed on the coin and lifted it off the eight square.

"That bet came too late. Sorry," he said and tossed it back.

The young lady did not pick it up, but stared across the table at the house.

The banker and the croupier stared back—and the pit boss too, come up opportunely behind them.

For a moment they made an arresting tableau of challenge. The young lady very slender and standing tall, dark hair piled high, profile neat as one on a coin, wearing a thin, thigh-length cotton dress (snug but not tight around the narrow waist) of black and carnation red, both colors harmoniously faded. The three men oldish young, gone beefy around the necks like tomcats, leaning a little toward her aggressively. All three in evening dress with the blank, stupid faces of athletes and ward politicians, but with a diamond glint deep in their eyes.

Beside me, the thin old man who looked like a bad-tempered high school physics teacher volunteered, "I heard the ball click out before the bet landed. It was too late."

The banker started a smile, then changed it tentatively to a frown as I said, "I heard it the other way. First the bet landed. Then the ball clicked out."

Immediately two ladies across the table, who looked the sort who are always eager to back up authority, said together, "No, the bet was too late. We were watching," and three other players nodded.

The banker's smile blossomed after all. "Sorry," he repeated.

The young lady snatched up her coin, turned her back, and walked away swiftly.

I had won a small wager split between eight and eleven. I cashed in my violet roulette chips and shoved the general house chips I got in return into the right-hand side pocket of my jacket, which I needed—the air conditioning made the Zodiac's casino almost frigid despite the moderate crowd and furious Mojave heat outside; early that morning I'd opened my bedroom door, which faced the east and let onto an outside balcony, and the radiance of the new risen sun had been like a physical blow—as if it had been trying to knock me over with one sneaky shot.

I asked the old man beside me (he seemed sharp-eyed at least), "Did you notice what kind of coin that was she bet?"

"That was no coin," he told me as if I were one of his poorer students. "That was a yellow ten-dollar chip."

I wandered up and down the luxurious aisles, wondering whether to have a go at blackjack, or rest a bit while making a few keeno bets, or even more sensibly take a long nap before my night-long drive. I glanced at my wrist, but I'd left my watch in my room. I started to look around before I remembered that there are no clocks in Vegas, at least anywhere in the casinos.

They keep it a timeless place so one won't be reminded of appointments that should be kept, whether for business or food or sleep or work or love, and so be tempted to cut short a winning streak before it turns into a losing one, or the latter ever, but I like to fancy it makes time travel possible—enter the timeless world from anywhere and later exit at any time future or past one chooses.

Off in a shadowy corner I saw a slender patch of harmoniously faded black and carnation red. They'd put a small bar there. I eased myself onto the stool beside her and ordered a scotch and water.

She turned dark eyes on me. "Thank you for your support," she said and smiled.

"It didn't help," I reminded her with a shrug. "Tell me, isn't a horned circle with a cross below—a horned ankh, one could almost say—a sign of Mercury?"

"I think so," she replied, wrinkling her neat, straight, rather short nose a little as the dark eyes studied me. "But that's not so strange. We're on the edge of Astrological Territory." She said it with capitals just like that, as one would say Western Reserve or Hopi Reservation . . . or Eldorado.

"Right in the middle of the Zodiac," I agreed. "I thought of the planet Mercury this morning when the sun looked in my bedroom door as I opened it and almost floored me—how the people on Mercury must live in capsules of chilliness to make the heat endurable."

"Yes, the sun's glance can be deadly, his diamond eye," she said oddly. "So you're not surprised at the idea of planet people?"

"I can't afford to be," I told her. "I write science fiction stories for a living."

"And you think the Zodiac Hotel is like a Mercurian capsule, only bigger?"

"Exactly. Aren't you chilly?" I asked, looking down at her thin dress. Although it was completely opaque, she seemed to be wearing little under it.

She picked up the pony of brandy in front of her and drained it, the tip of her tongue slipping out to capture the last drop.

"Not after that," she said.

There was nothing else in front of her on the bar and she wasn't carrying a purse. In fact, she was clean from her small flat ears fully revealed by her upswept, high-piled hair to her toes looking out of the ends of her flimsy shoes through finely textured dark stockings. I wondered where she kept the gold piece.

"Would you have dinner with me?" I asked.

"I'm sorry," she said pleasantly, "but I'm driving south tonight soon as I take a nap."

"That's a coincidence," I said. "So am I too, as far as Lordsburg. Perhaps we could combine—"

Her dark eyes (they were blue) which had been smiling at mine looked past me and grew serious. I looked around.

The pit boss from the roulette table was looking serious too in his beefy way. I thought he was going to speak to her, but instead he took a small green notebook out of his pocket and handed it to me.

"You left it at the table," he told me.

It was mine, all right, though I'd have sworn I hadn't taken it out of my left-hand jacket pocket. "Thanks," I said.

"No trouble," he assured me and walked on. It occurred to me it might have been lifted off me—Gods knows why, maybe to check on my antecedents. In that case they'd found nothing suspicious except the behavior of two Martians when confronted by an emissary from Galaxy Center. The notebook was for story notes as they occurred to me.

I looked back. The young lady was gone, nowhere in sight, but by the pony glass was a curled-up green bill.

"That was funny," the bartender observed to me as he spread it open. It was a Two. "She had it in her hair."

Oh well, not everyone wants to know you better, I philosophized grumpily, but why does it always have to be svelte, long-limbed young ladies with gold pieces tucked away in their high-piled dark hair?

I went and put my wristwatch on and had my nap. When I woke it was fully dark outside, but still oven-hot and my car had no refrigeration—one of the reasons that I drove at night. I dressed in brown cotton pyjamas that almost looked like slacks and shirt, but were a lot cooler, then checked out. Dunkirk (my little Datsun station wagon) was like a furnace. I opened her up and gave her a chance to get less hot before I got in.

Over the parking lot, despite the upward glare of the casinos along the Strip, the desert night showed some bright stars: the triangle of Vega, Deneb, and Altair, and to the south red Mars in Sagittarius. Vega from Vegas? The asphalt under my feet was baking hot.

On a slightly higher section of the parking lot near its exit, beyond an intervening row of cars, light spilling sideways from the Zodiac showed two white roadsters with tops down parked next to each other. Beside one was a slender figure with head held as if in thought or meditation. Even at the distance there was no mistaking that profile and she was still wearing the harmoniously faded red and black cotton dress.

As I considered strolling over, she quickly scurried around to the other white roadster and got behind the wheel. And then just before driving out she seemed to look straight at me and she lifted her hand and waved twice, rather solemnly.

Perhaps, I thought, my spirits rising, we'd meet somewhere along the lonely way. I got in Dunkirk (the seat was still hot) and started her and let her run quietly while I checked that my maps and flash and tissue were on the dashboard, my pocketbook, notebook, and pens in my pyjama pockets, Dunkirk's tank full, her hot oil coursing, and her lights all working.

We took off softly. Just before the exit I glanced at the open white roadster with the empty space beside it. From a point near the center of the white hood—from the car's heart, you might say—a single intense highlight reflected by God knows what or from what source, dazzled my eyes so that I flinched them away. It made me wonder, but I didn't try to look back—and wouldn't have even if I'd wanted to, because there was an empty spot coming in the traffic ahead that I wanted to catch, and did.

A quarter mile farther on I heard fire sirens behind me. Looking quickly back, I saw a shaft of intense white flame shooting up from somewhere close to the Zodiac. I wondered if there could have been a connection and if it were the white roadster burning. No, I told myself, the highlight and the shaft of flame could have had no relation.

Just the same, a black spot was still dancing in front of my eyes. That highlight had been *bright*.

I soon turned out of the traffic streaming toward California and Los Angeles onto the narrower, emptier route leading to Boulder Dam and Arizona. The night stayed hot. At Boulder City I checked Dunkirk's tires, letting out some air. I also checked the oil and water, filled my plastic two-gallon bottle of the latter, and topped off the gas tank.

I kept a sort of watch (not a very serious one, I told myself) for a white roadster and, on a straight stretch just beyond Boulder City, I thought I glimpsed one disappearing around the far bend, its red tail lights winking. I speeded up, but when I came to the next straight stretch, a much longer one, there wasn't any car ahead at all, though I thought I saw a car, maybe a white one, sneaking away from the highway down a wooded side road.

Well, if that were she, I told myself, she hadn't been driving very far south.

Boulder Dam, when I got to it, was magnificent in a monstrous way. The highway went across the top of it, from Nevada into Arizona, but it was so wide and very brightly lit that one could see little of its surrounds and nothing of the Colorado River. There was also much heavy mesh wire fencing. The smell of security was very strong, so that one got the feeling it had beeen built not for Herbert but for Edgar Hoover. There were several great squat chunky towers, like banks or forts—in fact, to me with my peculiar imagination, it had the feeling of a fortress on Jupiter, built for a heavier gravity than ours. It had a Jovian look, or a Vulcanian.

The shouldering crags at either end were correspondingly hulking, and on them were short, burly, immensely strong-looking openwork towers of steel beams bearing on their huge insulators the thick heavy copper wires that carried off the power the dam generated.

This is electricity's heartland, I told myself, a castle of the lightning. From here the stuff goes out to the great military and space establishments and to the myriad industrial complexes and to the multi-million lights of the Vegas Strip challenging the stars. It somehow made my liberal heart feel lonely and oppressed. Dunkirk the Datsun seemed to feel it too—a little Japanese bowing nervously to giants as she scurried past them.

On the other side it got rapidly darker and the empty road led steadily down and the night got hotter still. I reminded myself that the county containing this corner of Arizona is called Mohave—I checked it by my map. On my right were Black Canyon and the Eldorado Mountains, on my left the Cerbats with Mount Wilson and Squaw Peak—but you can't see such things in the dark from a car with a top.

The shoulders of the road widened for a little settlement. I slowed down and then pulled up across from a small old cafe that was still open. Better get a little to eat, I told myself, it was a long empty stretch ahead. And some coffee too, despite the heat.

I got out. The stars crusted the desert night so luxuriously that one almost forgot they marched in unalterable order. Deneb, Altair, and Mars were merely brighter points in the great, eddying river of the Milky Way. Only Vega was still somewhat lonely.

There was a counter with two Indian women behind it. The older, who looked toothless, cooked. The younger (but not that young) was very stolid and taciturn in dark shapeless clothes. I told her coffee and a beef enchilada. She went back and leaned near the older woman. Whatever culture they belonged to, it was apart.

The screen door creaked and a modern cowboy (I took him to be) walked in stiffly. His blue levis were caked with whitish dust. So was his wide-brimmed black hat, which he didn't remove. So were his sunken cheeks. And he was very bowlegged. He wearily settled down and ordered tacos. He looked every bit as authentic as the Indian women.

Our food came. The coffee was strong and bitter. My enchilada tasted all right but was too heavy, while orange grease dripped from the end of the cowboy's huge taco, which he munched steadily. I made some notes in my little green book.

I heard another car draw up across the road, but no one came in.

I finished my coffee and some of my enchilada, paid (including a tip), and went out. As I passed the cowboy, he said to the Indian woman and the cafe in general with the solemnity of William S. Hart, "That was the best taco I ever ate, and I've eaten many a taco."

The white roadster was parked off the road on the wide shoulder, but *she* was standing close beside Dunkirk, looking toward me quite gravely. But as I crossed the highway she started to smile, and when I got to her, she said, "You were saying, 'Perhaps we could combine—' and I'm accepting your offer."

NIGHT PASSAGE

I *had* to chuckle. I had been saying exactly that . . . some six hours ago.

"My car konked out," she explained quickly. "A vapor block. I'm leaving it here—I can send back for it tomorrow. But I must get south tonight."

"Where are you going?" I asked.

"To Gila Peak beyond the Superstition Mountains. That's just beyond Globe and the San Carlos Indian Reservation south of the Apache. I'll bet out at Geronimo." She added anxiously, "You are going to Lordsburg by that route?"

"I can," I temporized. (National Interstate 10 through Tucson might be quicker.) It had just occurred to me that this all fitted a classic hitch-hike situation—the girl the bait. You agreed to give her a lift, then the boys appeared, bent on . . . who knows what?

But I had met her in Vegas at the Zodiac. Besides . . . I was very aware of her dark, very slender height so near to me, of her slim fingers . . .

"Of course I can," I said with a smile. "Get in."

She gave me a smile in return and obeyed me quickly, walking around Dunkirk.

"Hey, wait a minute, what about your car?" I asked, ducking my head and looking at her through the driver's window.

"It's locked, it'll be all right," she assured me with another smile from where she was already sitting neatly and decorously in the shadowy interior. "Come on, let's drive."

I opened the door and started to get in. "But where's your luggage?" I asked.

"Locked in the trunk. I've got everything I need. Get in." Her eyes were dark pools, her smile was sure, but her voice was anxious.

I had a last try as I complied. "You're sure you wouldn't like some coffee? We could—"

"No, that's why I waited outside. Let's drive."

I toed the starter and nosed Dunkirk out. At least no

guys had appeared. As I shifted to second, my hand on the short stick between our feet, I glanced toward her white roadster sliding past and saw in the heart of the hood that same damn dazzling diamond headlight I had seen in Vegas.

Her fingers touched my forearm briefly but peremptorily. She said, *"Keep driving."*

For a moment I had no intention of doing anything else. The black spot was dancing in front of my eyes again, worse than the first time, and I was busy shifting up. Then I started to look back but—

"That gold coin I bet was a genuine Mercurian double eagle," she said rapidly. "I was surprised you spotted it."

She almost took my mind completely off whatever it was that was happening behind. Besides, there was a curve coming up ahead and from beyond it there were the lights of an approaching car. But then I caught a white flash in the rearview mirror.

"I'm a Mercurian, you see, a Mercury person," she went on desperately, "and I play a special game with some Jovian dealers there—Jupiter people. But today—"

But despite that and her slender, wiry fingers touching me again, I did manage to look back very briefly as we went around the curve and see. . . .

It was almost my last look too, for the curve was sharper than I'd anticipated and I'd let Dunkirk drift toward the center of the two-lane highway and the approaching car came around the curve very fast and in *my* lane, so it was only by dodging very sharply over into *his* lane and passing him on the wrong side that I missed him—and even at that there was a greet *whoosh* of squeezed air and Dunkirk shook at the nearness of his passage. If I'd done the automatic thing and tried to dodge him by getting back into my lane and out onto my shoulder—ugh!

I was "real shook" myself, needless to say, and for a bit I was very busy getting Dunkirk straightened out and back where she belonged and making sure there weren't any more bats coming out of hell. Then I started to slow down, but—

"Zowie! that was close," my passenger said with girlish excitement, not to say enthusiasm. "Wow! But he'll sure be mad. Better not stop."

She touched two of my weak spots there: my tendency always to blame myself first for anything and my dread of getting into any sort of strident and wearisome confrontation (perhaps the two are related). Besides, by now what I'd seen (or thought I'd seen) in that one glimpse back was all mixed up with those blinding headlights hurtling at me from ambush and the way Dunkirk had rocked. It took me time to get them sorted out. And while I did that I continued to drive on.

What I believed I'd seen (and it was very clear-etched when I got it) was a pillar of bright white flame going straight up from the roadside across from the Indian cafe and standing in the middle of the road staring at it and silhouetted by its glare my taco-stuffed cowboy. He was quite tiny with distance, but the hat, bent back, and bowlegs were unmistakable—almost too good.

I drove on for a while, thinking about it and wondering how much if not all of her wild story had been impromptu diversion and how much of it one of those strange bags someone is always opening up for you in these changing days of flamboyant individuality—and giving her a chance to continue her wild story, only she didn't, but stayed strangely (in view of its hysterically swift opening) or perhaps strategically silent. But all the while I was feeling this deep-down thankfulness that I was getting farther away every second from possible trouble and that there were no cars chasing me and that things were smoothing out quietly, just as I always like it.

Meanwhile the heat became really quite astonishing. I found I had to keep Dunkirk down to forty miles an hour, or else the temperature pointer on the dash would lean dangerously toward the red. Soon I was driving by the feel on my face of the air pouring in the side window. If it cooled a bit, Dunkirk would spring ahead. If there were a warm wash, Dunkirk would lag.

Finally on one of the latter occasions I let her keep lagging until she stopped and I looked around at my young mystery lady, sitting beside me like a bundle of gleaming slim shadows and I demanded, "Now just what is all this nonsense about planet people and gold coins brought here from the planet Mercury?"

"Oh, they're not imported from Mercury," she protested. "That *would* be ridiculous. No, they're struck here from gold mined here or made here, by the old prenuclear alchemy, for local use by Mercury people temporarily in residence here, mostly for gambling with other planet people, but for ritual and diplomatic purposes too."

"Oh, really!" I said, unable to keep back a little laugh. "You don't expect me to believe that all you planet people shift about around here among us earth folk, even gambling against each other, and conducting all sorts of interplanetary intrigues—"

"Yes, that is exactly what I expect you to believe," she countered. "The different worlds aren't nearly so separated, at least in Arizona, as you seem to imagine. As I told you, this is Astrological Territory. They all drift here, star folk and planet people."

". . . and even waging interplanetary wars," I continued, "or at least serious skirmishes *in which you burn each other's cars?*"

"We *never* burn cars, we Mercury people!" she denied vehemently. "It's only the barbarous Solarians who do that—" She broke off and looked at me reproachfully. "You tricked me into saying that," she said, "but perhaps that is because I never thanked you properly for standing up for me at the roulette table," and she advanced her hands along the curve of my jaw on either side until her fingers touched my ears and she drew my face to hers and kissed me rather briefly but emphatically and then she sat back and said, "There. Drive on."

I obeyed thoughtfully. That kiss had tingled like electricity and as for her fingers—well, fingers are really the most amazing erotic tools, except that they have so many other uses that their sexual one is somewhat overshadowed.

When I did speak again, it was to tell her my impressions of Hoover, or Boulder Dam.

"You really are quite intuitive," she said with interest, almost with respect. "Hoover Dam actually was designed and built under the influence of Jovians. Jupiter men had most of the Vegas casinos in those days and for a long while afterwards. That was when I got hooked on roulette. The Jupiter men were sort of rough, of course, but in a nice and genial—I might say jovial—way, like good bears. But the last year or so the Solarians started moving in and taking over—"

"Solarians—that would be Sun people, wouldn't it?" I interrupted. "Now, really, how can you have people at a temperature of millions of degrees?"

"Some people can be awfully tough," she assured me, "as if they were made of nothing but asbestos. That's the Sun men for you—very macho and rough (You saw them!) but in a mean and nasty way, like bad bears. Each of them carries in his asbestos heart a tiny spark of killing nuclear fire, which puts the diamond glint into his eyes and with which his eyes, like two burning glasses, can focus on things and make them white hot—if they concentrate."

"In New York City they call it a double whammy, I believe," I commented.

"Well, if you're going to joke . . ." she murmured huffily and leaned back and looked straight ahead.

Really it was a strange mood I was getting into, though not unpleasant, listening to her wacky fairy tales and letting my own mind drift between the real and the unreal. On the black road ahead there appeared a wavy white line that wriggled like a snake as it went under Dunkirk's hood. It ended in a white arrowhead that pointed at a rectangle of road that had been filled in with gravel but not yet resurfaced, which, now forewarned, I dodged around. It occurred to me that a timeless mind had invented that warning.

After a while there was another white snake and then more kept coming and suddenly there was a detour sign which in this case did not mean a change of road but only that for a stretch it became one of unsurfaced, wicked-looking gravel that forced cars to go very slowly. I got the impression that a whole people (men, women, and children) had toiled for centuries to find all the pointiest (though well worn) little rocks, all the tetrahedrons, and pack them carefully, point up, like caltrops of stone, to hurt the hoofs of unshod horses and barefoot poets and pop the tires of speeding cars.

I had to go so slowly that I could try to make out the inky horizon in the torrid night, the Black Mountains on her side, the Cerbats still on mine, guessing at hills and gaps, drawing reflexively back from breaths of hotter wind. But it was hard to tell whether the lowest stars were stars at all or the lights of low castles topping invisible crags. Everywhere I could sense the workings of that timeless mind, that ancient culture. I began to feel that the Indians still secretly ruled Arizona, patiently tolerating the ephemeral White Man, catering to his crazy cars and other childish whims, and succoring dusty cowboys.

I even entertained the fancy that my young mystery lady with her high-piled dark hair, sitting in her gloomy corner of the front seat, was one of them. It was decades of blinding sun and dry winds that had made her so slim and shadowy, such a wraith.

I told her all that I'd been fancying.

"You're being quite intuitive again," she said still somewhat grumpily (at first) but with a certain respect. "Ancienter peoples *are* in charge down here, most secretly, only they came here (from up there) a long time before the Indians. They were drawn to Arizona because it's always had a lot of magic in it, especially at night under the moon, as you could see for yourself if the moon weren't new. They all revered (*pace* the Solarians!) the moon goddess. They had their little differences, of course, their little feuds, but settled them all by high diplomacy, codes of civilized behavior as old as the stars. And when the Indians came wandering down at last from the far north, the planet people got along fine with them and they had hardly any more difficulty adapting themselves to the White Man, gold-crazy Latinos from the south full of pot and loco weed and drunken Anglos from the east and west.

"But then those brutal, vicious Sun men began to turn up, with their diamond eyes, who burn cars and ignore the age-old usages of diplomacy and *hate* the Moon Goddess and us Mercury people especially because our planet is closest to their huge hairy home and we sneer at all their macho heat, safe in our cool, cool capsules."

"Is that how they spotted you at the Zodiac," I interjected, "when you flashed that Mercurian gold piece?"

"Of course," she said. "I thought they were three Jupiter men and we could play the old game we always do right under the eyes of you terrestrials. The Zodiac was supposed to be Jovian still, although most of the other casinos are Solarian now. In fact, there's a big interplanetary conference scheduled for the Zodiac day after tomorrow. I'm on the Mercurian delegation, but I'd gone up early to play roulette.

"But as soon as those three hulking bastards (whom I'd taken for Jovians) refused to honor my bet (you *know* it wasn't late!) and I saw the diamond glint in their eyes, I *knew* they were Solarians and that I'd have to get back south and warn my people before the whole conference was ambushed and wiped out (their obvious intention). But I also knew that they knew that I knew and would do their damnedest to stop me!"

"But if the Sun men have as little regard for rules as you say," I objected, "why didn't they kidnap you or (excuse me) rub you out while you were still at the Zodiac where they're top dogs?"

"Even the Sun can't afford to do anything that openly inside the Zodiac with all you squares around. Besides, they did try to burn me in my car (they're *great* at burning cars) right in the parking lot, only I fooled them into thinking my car was another that looked just like mine. And it worked. When I got outside the Vegas city limits I looked back and could see it burning."

"But why couldn't you have warned your people simply by telephone or special short-wave radio or something?" I asked.

"My God, you must think we are really stupid if you think we'd ever go around breaking cover like that," she fumed at me, subsiding. "Short-wave radio!"

"Or couldn't you just use telepathy?" I persisted, "—you being so astrological and occult and all?"

"For your information, the planet people do not happen to be telepathic," she informed me and lapsed into an offended silence, only shifting position from time to time to look behind us.

We went through Kingman, which seemed all asleep, and then east on National Interstate 40 for a bit, where we met some cars and were passed by a couple, and then south on U.S. 93 again for another lonely, long, quite straight flat stretch along the Sandy River between the Hualapai Mountains on her side and the Aquarius Mountains on mine. I mentioned the last to her.

"I told you we were in the heart of Astrological Territory," she said shortly.

The long, rather slight curves in the road were all marked with little round reflectors that were born like little yellow stars at the first touch of Dunkirk's headlights beam, or like tiny rockets born on their blasting pads that did not move at first, then slowly toward us, and then took of swiftly as we passed them by. I got on my timeless-intelligence kick again and thought of worn fellahin fingers patiently teasing apart with cracked dry fingernails the sheets of yellowish mica to make the reflectors.

I saw a new star, as bright as Sirius, on the horizon ahead. Then it winked out. After quite a bit it flashed on again, somewhat brighter, then off again, then on again, brighter still, and came on steadily. I'd just decided (with some amazement) it was the headlight of an approaching motorcycle, when it divided into two and I realized it was the headlights of a car, but first seen so far away through the incredibly clear desert air that they merged into one. The first bright flash must have come when we were aimed exactly at each other from the tops of almost imperceptible hills many miles apart. That really seemed quite amazing to me, worth commenting on.

My sulking (or merely sleepy?) companion appeared to digest the information I gave her and then remarked in rather lofty tones (and somewhat repetitiously), "For your information, I have been observing the same phenomenon behind us. There appears to be a car hanging on there a few miles back." She subsided.

"And?" I said.

"Its merged headlights have a peculiar diamond glint, to my eye."

"And?" I persisted.

"The Solarians do not give up easily," she observed. dispassionately.

"You think some people from the Zodiac are chasing us?" I asked.

She shrugged, somewhat elaborately.

A diamond glint?—I thought with a little shiver that surprised me. But the merged headlights of that approaching car I'd watched had been startlingly bright, too, and the same thing could work in the opposite direction, surely.

Nevertheless after a half minute or so, I speeded up. It was getting a bit less hot anyway and I no longer needed to hold Dunkirk down so much.

Twice more I saw horizon stars ahead that changed to cars.

My companion looked back from time to time, but didn't offer any information as to whether we'd shaken the car behind and I didn't ask her.

My science-fiction mind dredged up something that seemed worth repeating.

"If you were out on Pluto, the sun would be just a point of light like any other star, and yet it would be many, many times brighter than the whole full moon. A single point of light, but painfully intense. That sounds to me quite like your diamond glint."

"Um," she said in recognition of my speaking. If I'd scared anyone, it was myself. I lit a cigarette and offered her one and she took it. Lighting it off a match from a book of them she had tucked in her hair, she bent close to the dashboard and saw "Dunkirk" taped there. I told her it was the car's name and she asked me why.

I said, "Because I figure I can always depend on her to get me out of really desperate situations."

"You know, I'm relieved to hear that," she said shortly.

I saw her point. We both smoked quite a bit off and on after that, and didn't talk much. We both had, I think, that sense of shared monotony and watchfulness that comes with any long drive, but intensified here by the heat and the loneliness and the dark and whatever it was that hung behind us and we weren't talking about so much any more. Darting fantasy had given way to a sort of wakeful trance.

We passed through Wikieup, a sort of ghost place in the small hours, and then through Wickenburg, somewhat bigger, the Date Creek Mountains on my side now and the Vulture Mountains on hers. The last of Wickenburg's lights, industrial, showed me a forest of Joshua trees. The tall, twisted cactuses reminded me of something on a moon of Saturn and I told her so.

She said "Um" again and, after a bit, "The Saturnians are the oldest planet people. Very conservative. They're on our side."

Sometimes I was very conscious of her long slim youthfulness, but sometimes as she leaned back in the shadows I got the impression that she was ages old, desiccated by the centuries, the slender mummy of an ancient princess.

The desert gave way to scattered dark settlements and then I saw great openwork towers covered with colored lights.

"My God," I said, startled for a moment, "It almost looks as if we were back on the Vegas Strip again."

"No," she said, "they're cracking plants for petroleum, not casinos." (I'd realized that by then.) She added, "The planet people—Martians especially—had a lot to do with determining the form of both sets of structures."

"There's no accounting for tastes," I said, shaking my head. "Perhaps they're supposed to resemble space-to-space vehicles."

Soon we were into Phoenix, quiet a couple of hours or so before the dawn. I stopped at a sleepy station to top off Dunkirk's tank again, add water and a pint of oil, and get us two cups of coffee apiece out of a machine (She vetoed breakfast and I didn't argue.) She drank her coffee thirstily, but seemed preoccupied until we were rolling again. I studied my map.

When we were out in the desert countryside again, more rolling now, heading east, I said cheerily, "The Superstition Mountains and the Tonto National Forest should be coming up soon on my side. Then Globe and the Indian Reservation and Geronimo under your Gila Peak—all in an hour or so!"

"Yes," she agreed, somewhat dubiously, "in an hour or so."

I thought gayly, intoxicated by coffee, yes, she's a somber Indian princess, all right, no pleasing her, and when she's mummified, they'll lay her pet Gila monster, reddish and black to match her little tunic, at her feet, mummified too.

But it was distinctly cooler now. She'd closed the window on her side, and I cranked mine halfway up. Dunkirk became sprightly and began to thumb her nose at Arizona's sixty-mile speed limit. All night she'd been frightened and rather miserable, her tires tender and her heart careful for itself in the heat, a lonely Japanese in an arid, gritty land most unlike her moist and mountainous Honshu, ducking away from rocky phantoms, watching for poisonous snakes and dry furry big spiders (and Gila monsters). But here with wooded hills to the north at least and now that it was cooler she could imagine she was home in Japan and foot it lightly.

I found myself feeling livelier too (although underneath there was a great weariness) and taking a livelier and more detailed interest in my companion. She had high cheekbones and, under her short straight nose, a rather wide, very mobile mouth. The upper lip was a bit fuller than the lower. I remembered the electricity of that single emphatic kiss. Her hands were narrow with long restless fingers and thumb that narrowed at their tips. She had a way of playing with her cigarette close by her face, as if it were a tiny baton orchestrating her thoughts, and sometimes she held it almost alarmingly close to her high-piled dark hair.

She was becoming livelier (or uneasier?) herself. She'd look ahead, then back, then off to the side, then light another cigarette (I had two packs on the dash), never at rest. But she didn't seem to want to talk.

Dunkirk was climbing now. Globe was faintly astir as we ghosted through, although even astronomical twilight seemed hardly to have begun. And now the way was down and Dunkirk fairly leaped and then the way got straighter and more desert like again as we traversed the Indian Reservation.

I was running out of time with her, I knew, and now I felt impelled to make a move.

NIGHT PASSAGE

"Do you realize," I said, really struck by it, "that we haven't told each other our names?"

She'd been looking back. "I'm sorry," she said, twisting around, her eyes wide with excitement or fear, or both, "but now I'm sure of it—it must be they. They've been behind us again ever since Globe and now they're closing in."

"Who are?" I asked. Then after a moment, "Those Sun men?"

In my more immediate interest in her I'd actually almost forgotten that game we'd played. I suddenly felt very furious with her and had a shockingly strong impulse to grab that flimsy dress at the neck and—

"Yes, the Solarians, who else?" she said sharply. "What's more, I'm certain they've put a mental tail on us, so that we've got to blank our minds or think of something different to mislead them—anything except about them!"

"A *mental* tail?" I exploded. "Those dumb macho Sun men with asbestos brains? Besides, you told me none of the planet people are telepathic."

"The Solarians are star folk, not planet people," she countered angrily. "And all star folk are highly telepathic. Or didn't they teach you in third grade the sun's a star? Now listen to me closely, dumbbell, I know this territory like I know my crotch, and we've only one chance now to stay alive, or at most two. Behind each of the next two rises a side road goes off sharply to the left. You whip around the first one and douse your lights and stop quick as you can and start thinking for all you're worth of something very different—I'll tell you what."

During the last part of that she had been lighting a cigarette with very nervous fingers. She took a deep, furious drag now and started to cough. Then I was yelling, "Like hell I will!" and we were going over the rise and she was yelling "Turn here!" between coughs and I wasn't turning and then suddenly there was a bright white flash, a needle of very intense white light lancing through Dunkirk's rear window and I smelled the stink of something burning and then I was steering with my left hand while I clamped the palm of my right to the side of her head to put out the fire in her hair there—a ghostly blue flame traveling swiftly upward.

Somehow that put a different complexion on the whole business and incidentally scared me half to death. I managed to get the fire out (my palm stung, but I hardly noticed) and keep the car on the road and even to speed up. And when we topped the next rise I braked sharply and followed her first orders exactly, and no mistakes. She needn't have shouted, "Then turn *here*, dumbbell!" The side road was there, all right, just as she'd said, and I was down it and Dunkirk's lights were out and she was stopped—and *she* was in my arms and pressed against me and her lips were giving those electric kisses (the shock is greater when there's moisture, as you'd expect) and her fingers were busy with me and mine with her—one of my hands was near the neck of her dress, but it wasn't tearing it—and I had realized what the "something different" thing was we were to think about exclusively.

There is really something very special about fingers, they're so deft and clever, they *know* so much more than any other parts of the body, even the lips and tongue. And there is also something very special about skin felt through thin clothing, even two layers of it, say cotton and fine silk. The three textures move against each other most interestingly. Together they provide a very special sort of enjoyment that can go on and on. It is an argument for bundling, when you think about it.

After quite a long while (the sky was pale, the stars were gone except for Sirius) she murmured softly, "You know, my dear, we *know* we can't have been thinking about anything else, either of us, or they'd have come back and got us."

It occurred to me that I hadn't once even seen the Solarian car. I started to tell her so, but she put her lips down on mine and turned on the electricity again, gently at first.

When I woke again, it was because a bright red ray of sun was poking me in the eye just as it had yesterday morning, and just as then, only worse, I felt I was being shot at. Were Sun men out by day, as their star was? I turned to ask her that, but she was gone.

Well, there's not much to tell after that. I didn't find her then and I haven't found her since, my slim Mercurian. She's gone completely back into Astrological Territory, I guess. Did the Solarians actually set her hair afire, or was it her cigarette? I really have no way of knowing, while cars burn up on our highways every day.

Anyhow, I was still about seventy-five miles from Lordsburg and very tired and all hot again and somehow very uneasy about that sun up there, getting higher and hotter every minute.

So after a bit I headed towards Lordsburg, fast as I dared. Dunkirk met a surprising number of light Datsun trucks used by the farmers thereabouts and wanted to linger and gossip with them about Japan, but I wouldn't let her. That sun was really bothering me and making me nervous. I wanted to get entirely away from it and the heat, and sleep.

I stopped at the first refrigerated motel I spotted at Lordsburg—they call them that instead of air conditioned to distinguish them from the old breeze-and-hanging-wet-blanket type. The manager gave my pyjamas an odd look, but let me register since I was paying in advance —maybe he figured they proved I just wanted to sleep.

The shades were drawn in my cabin, the lights off, and the refrigeration on. I didn't change any of those— it was so great to get out of the sun and heat. I made my way through the gloom to the bathroom and there I did need light—it was just too dark. So I flicked the switch.

No light came on, but *heat* struck the top of my head and the back of my neck. I got the damnedest, eeriest, most frightening feeling that the sun had come inside after me and I'd never be able to get away from him. She'd said the Sun men were very persistent. And now there began to come a dark, reddish glow.

I glanced from where I'd flinched down and saw three of those flat-faced infrared bulbs set in the ceiling to warm a person while he washed or shaved on chilly mornings. I'd just flicked the wrong switch.

NICE GIRL WITH FIVE HUSBANDS

To BE GIVEN paid-up leisure and find yourself unable to create is unpleasant for any artist. To be stranded in a cluster of desert cabins with a dozen lonely people in the same predicament only makes it worse. So Tom Dorset was understandably irked with himself and the Tosker-Brown Vacation Fellowships as he climbed with the sun into the valley of red stones. He accepted the chafing of his camera strap against his shoulder as the nagging of conscience. He agreed with the disparaging hisses of the grains of sand crushed by his sneakers, and he wished that the occasional breezes, which faintly echoed the same criticisms, could blow him into a friendlier, less jealous age.

He had no way of knowing that just as there are winds that blow through space, so there are winds that blow through time. Such winds may be strong or weak. The strong ones are rare and seldom blow for short distances, or more of us would know about them. What they pick up is almost always whirled far into the future or past.

This has happened to people. There was Ambrose Bierce, who walked out of America and existence, and there are thousands of others who have disappeared without a trace, though many of these may not have been caught up by time tornadoes and I do not know if a time gale blew across the deck of the *Marie Celeste*.

Sometimes a time wind is playful, snatching up an object, sporting with it for a season and then returning it unharmed to its original place. Sometimes we may be blown about by whimsical time winds without realizing it. Memory, for example, is a tiny time breeze, so weak that it can ripple only the mind.

A very few time winds are like the monsoon, blowing at fixed intervals first in one direction, then the other. Such a time wind blows near a balancing rock in a valley of red stones in the American Southwest. Every morning at ten o'clock, it blows a hundred years into the future; every afternoon at two, it blows a hundred years into the past.

Quite a number of people have unwittingly seen time winds in operation. There are misty spots on the sea's horizon and wavy patches over desert sands. There are mirages and will o' the wisps and ice blinds. And there are dust devils, such as Tom Dorset walked into near the balancing rock.

It seemed to him no more than a spiteful upgust of sand, against which he closed his eyes until the warm granules stopped peppering the lids. He opened them to see the balancing rock had silently fallen and lay a quarter buried—no, that couldn't be, he told himself instantly. He had been preoccupied; he must have passed the balancing rock and held its image in his mind.

Despite this rationalization he was quite shaken. The strap of his camera slipped slowly down his arm without his feeling it. And just then there stepped around the giant bobbin of the rock an extraordinarily pretty girl with hair the same pinkish copper color.

She was barefoot and wearing a pale blue playsuit rather like a Grecian tunic. But most important, as she stood there toeing his rough shadow in the sand, there was a complete naturalness about her, an absence of sharp edges, as if her personality had weathered without aging, just as the valley seemed to have taken another step toward eternity in the space of an instant.

She must have assumed something of the same gentleness in him, for her faint surprise faded and she asked him, as easily as if he were a friend of five years' standing. "Tell now, do you think a woman can love just one man? All her life? And a man just one woman?"

Tom Dorset made a dazed sound.

His mind searched wildly.

"I do," she said, looking at him as calmly as at a mountain. "I think a man and woman can be each other's world, like Tristan and Isolde or Frederic and Catherine. Those old authors were wise. I don't see why on earth a girl has to spread her love around, no matter how enriching the experiences may be."

"You know, I agree with you," Tom said, thinking he'd caught her idea—it was impossible not to catch her casualness. "I think there's something cheap about the way everybody's supposed to run after sex these days."

"I don't mean that exactly. Tenderness is beautiful, but—" She pouted. "A big family can be vastly crushing. I wanted to declare today a holiday, but they outvoted me. Jock said it didn't chime with our mood cycles. But I was angry with them, so I put on my clothes—"

"Put on—?"

"To make it a holiday," she explained baffingly. "And I walked here for a tantrum." She stepped out of Tom's shadow and hopped back. "Ow, the sand's getting hot," she said, rubbing the grains from the pale and uncramped toes.

"You go barefoot a lot?" Tom guessed.

"No, mostly digitals," she replied and took something shimmering from a pocket at her hip and drew it on her foot. It was a high-ankled, transparent mocassin with five separate toes. She zipped it shut with the speed of a card trick, then similarly gloved the other foot. Again the metal-edged slit down the front seemed to close itself.

"I'm behind on the fashions," Tom said, curious. They were walking side by side now, the way she'd come and he'd been going. "How does that zipper work?"

"Magnetic. They're on all my clothes. Very simple." She parted her tunic to the waist, then let it zip together.

"Clever," Tom remarked with a gulp. There seemed no limits to this girl's naturalness.

"I see you're a button man," she said. "You actually believe it's possible for a man and woman to love just each other?"

His chuckle was bitter. He was thinking of Elinore Murphy at Tosker-Brown and a bit about cold-faced Miss Tosker herself. "I sometimes wonder if it's possible for anyone to love anyone."

"You haven't met the right girls," she said.

"Girl," he corrected.

She grinned at him. "You'll make me think you really are a monogamist. What group do you come from?"

"Let's not talk about that," he requested. He was willing to forego knowing how she'd guessed he was from an art group, if he could be spared talking about the Vacation Fellowships and those nervous little cabins.

"My group's very nice on the whole," the girl said, "but at times they can be nefandously exasperating. Jock's the worst, quietly guiding the rest of us like an analyst. How I loathe that man! But Larry's almost as bad, with his shame-faced bumptiousness, as if we'd all sneaked off on a joyride to Venus. And there's Jokichi at the opposite extreme, forever scared he won't distribute his affection equally, dividing it up into mean little packets like candy for jealous children who would scream if they got one chewy less. And then there's Sasha and Ernest—"

"Who are you talking about?" Tom asked.

"My husbands." She shook her head dolefully. "To find five more difficult men would be positively Martian."

Tom's mind backtracked frantically, searching all conversations at Tosker-Brown for gossip about cultists in the neighborhood. It found nothing and embarked on a wider search. There were the Mormons (Was that the word that had sounded like Martian?) but it wasn't the

NICE GIRL WITH FIVE HUSBANDS

Mormon husbands who were plural. And then there were Oneidas. (Weren't husbands and wives both plural there?) but that was 19th century New England.

"Five husbands?" he repeated. She nodded. He went on, "Do you mean to say five men have got you alone somewhere up here?"

"To be sure not," she replied. "There are my kwives."

"Kwives?"

"Co-wives," she said more slowly. "They can be fascinerously exasperating, too."

Tom's mind did some more searching. "And yet you believe in monogamy?"

She smiled. "Only when I'm having tantrums. It was civilized of you to agree with me."

"But I actually do believe in monogamy," he protested.

She gave his hand a little squeeze. "You are nice, but let's rush now. I've finished my tantrum and I want you to meet my group. You can fresh yourself with us."

As they hurried across the heated sands, Tom Dorset felt for the first time a twinge of uneasiness. There was something about this girl, more than her strange clothes and the odd words she used now and then, something almost—though ghosts don't wear digitals—spectral.

They scrambled up a little rise, digging their footgear into the sand, until they stood on a long flat. And there, serpentining around two great clumps of rock, was a many-windowed adobe ranch house with a roof like fresh soot.

"Oh, they've put on their clothes," his companion exclaimed with pleasure. "They've decided to make it a holiday after all."

Tom spotted a beard in the group swarming out to meet them. Its cultish look gave him a momentary feeling of superiority, followed by an equally momentary apprehension—the five husbands were certainly husky. Then both feelings were swallowed up in the swirl of introduction.

He told his own name, found that his companion's was Lois Wolver, then smiling faces began to bob toward his,

his hands were shaken, his cheeks were kissed, he was even spun around like blind man's bluff, so that he lost track of the husbands and failed to attach Mary, Rachel, Simone and Joyce to the right owners.

He did notice that Jokichi was an Oriental with a skin as tight as enameled china, and that Rachel was a tall slim Negro girl. Also someone said, "Joyce isn't a Wolver, she's just visiting."

He got a much clearer impression of the clothes than the names. They were colorful, costly-looking, and mostly Egyptian and Cretan in inspiration. Some of them would have been quite immodest, even compared to Miss Tosker's famous playsuits, except that the wearers didn't seem to feel so.

"There goes the middle-morning rocket!" one of them eagerly cried.

Tom looked up with the rest, but his eyes caught the dazzling sun. However, he heard a faint roaring that quickly sank in volume and pitch, and it reminded him that the Army had a rocket testing range in this area. He had little interest in science, but he hadn't known they were on a daily schedule.

"Do you suppose it's off the track?" he asked anxiously.

"Not a chance," someone told him—the beard, he thought. The assurance of the tones gave him a possible solution. Scientists came from all over the world these days and might have all sorts of advanced ideas. This could be a group working at a nearby atomic project and leading its peculiar private life on the side.

As they eddied toward the house he heard Lois remind someone, "But you finally did declare it a holiday," and a husband who looked like a gay pharaoh responded, "I had another see at the mood charts and I found a subtle surge I'd missed."

Meanwhile the beard (a black one) had taken Tom in charge. Tom wasn't sure of his name, but he had a tan skin, a green sarong, and a fiercely jovial expression.

"The swimming pool's around there, the landing spot's on the other side," he began, then noticed Tom gazing at the sooty roof. "Sun power cells," he explained proudly. "They store all the current we need."

Tom felt his idea confirmed. "Wonder you don't use atomic power," he observed lightly.

The beard nodded. "We've been asked that. Matter of esthetics. Why waste sunlight or use hard radiations needlessly? Of course, you might feel differently. What's your group, did you say?"

"Tosker-Brown," Tom told him, adding when the beard frowned, "the Fellowship people, you know."

"I don't," the beard confessed. "Where are you located?"

Tom briefly described the ranch house and cabins at the other end of the valley.

"Comic, I can't place it." The beard shrugged. "Here come the children."

A dozen naked youngsters raced around the ranch followed by a woman in a vaguely African dress open down the sides.

"Yours?" Tom asked.

"Ours," the beard answered.

"C'est un homme!"

"Regardez des vêtements!"

"No need to practice, kids; this is a holiday," the beard told them. "Tom, Helen," he said, introducing the woman with the air-conditioned garment. "Her turn today to companion die Kinder."

One of the latter rapped on the beard's knee. "May we show the stranger our things?" Instantly the others joined in pleading. The beard shot an inquiring glance at Tom, who nodded. A moment later the small troupe was hurrying him toward a spacious lean-to at the end of the ranch house. It was chuckful of strange toys, rocks and plants, small animals in cages and out, and the oddest model airplanes, or submarines. But Tom was given no time to look at any one thing for long.

"See my crystals? I grew them."

"Smell my mutated gardenias. Tell now, isn't there a difference?" There didn't seem to be, but he nodded.

"Look at my squabbits." This referred to some long-eared white squirrels nibbling carrots and nuts.

"Here's my newest model spaceship, a DS-57-B. Notice the detail." The oldest boy shoved one of the submarine affairs in his face.

Tom felt like a figure that is being tugged about in a rococo painting by wide pink ribbons in the chubby hands of naked cherubs, except that these cherubs were slim and tanned, fantastically energetic, and apparently of depressingly high IQ. (what these scientists did to children!) He missed Lois and was grateful for the single little girl solemnly skipping rope in a corner and paying no attention to him.

The odd lingo she repeated stuck in his mind: "Gik-lo, I-o, Rik-o, Gis-so, Gik-lo, I-o..."

Suddenly the air was filled with soft chimes. "Lunch," the children shouted and ran away.

Tom followed at a soberer pace along the wall of the ranch house. He glanced in the huge windows, curious about the living and sleeping arrangements of the Wolvers, but the panes were strangely darkened. Then he entered the wide doorway through which the children had scampered and his curiosity turned to wonder:

A resilient green floor that wasn't flat, but sloped up toward the white of the far wall like a breaking wave. Chairs like giants' hands tenderly cupped. Little tables growing like mushrooms and broadleafed plants out of the green floor. A vast picture window showing the red rocks.

Yet it was the wood-paneled walls that electrified his artistic interest. They blossomed with fruits and flowers, deep and poignantly carved in several styles. He had never seen such work.

He became aware of a silence and realized that his

hosts and hostesses were smiling at him from around a long table. Moved by a sudden humility, he knelt and unlaced his sneakers and added them to the pile of sandles and digitals by the door. As he rose, a soft and comic piping started and he realized that beyond the table the children were lined up, solemnly puffing at little wooden flutes and recorders. He saw the empty chair at the table and went toward it, conscious for the moment of nothing but his dusty feet.

He was disappointed that Lois wasn't sitting next to him, but the food reminded him that he was hungry. There was a charming little steak, striped black and brown with perfection, and all sorts of vegetables and fruits, one or two of which he didn't recognize.

"Flown from Africa," someone explained to him.

These sly scientists, he thought, living behind their security curtain in the most improbable world!

When they were sitting with coffee and wine, and the children had finished their concert and were busy at another table, he asked, "How do you manage all this?"

Jock, the gay pharaoh, shrugged. "It's not difficult."

Rachel, the slim Negro, chuckled in her throat. "We're just people, Tom."

He tried to phrase his question without mentioning money. "What do you all do?"

"Jock's a uranium miner," Larry (the beard) answered, briskly taking over. "Rachel's an algae farmer. I'm a rocket pilot. Lois—"

Although pleased at this final confirmation of his guess, Tom couldn't help feeling a surge of uneasiness. "Sure you should be telling me these things?"

Larry laughed. "Why not? Lois and Jokichi have been exchange-workers in China the last six months."

"Mostly digging ditches," Jokichi put in with a smile.

"—and Sasha's in an assembly plant. Helen's a psychiatrist. Oh, we just do ordinary things. Now we're on grand vacation."

"When all of us have a vacation together," Larry explained. "What do you do?"

"I'm an artist," Tom said, taking out a cigarette.

"But what else?" Larry asked.

Tom felt an angry embarrassment. "Just an artist," he mumbled, cigarette in mouth, digging in his pockets for a match.

"Hold on," said Joyce beside him and pointed a silver pencil at the tip of the cigarette. He felt a faint thrill in his lips and then started back, coughing. The cigarette was lighted.

"Please mutate my poppy seeds, Mommy." A little girl had darted to Joyce from the children's table.

"You're a very dirty little girl," Joyce told her without reproof. "Hold them out." She briefly directed the silver pencil at the clay pellets on the grimy little palm. The little girl shivered delightedly. "I love ultrasonics, they feel so funny." She scampered off.

Tom cleared his throat. "I must say I'm tremendously impressed with the wood carvings. I'd like to photograph them. Oh, Lord!"

"What's the matter?" Rachel asked.

"I lost my camera somewhere."

"Camera?" Jokichi showed interest. "You mean one for stills?"

"Yes."

"What kind?"

"A Leica," Tom told him.

Jokichi seemed impressed. "That is interesting. I've never seen one of those old ones."

"Tom's a button man," Lois remarked by way of explanation, apparently. "Was the camera in a brown case? You dropped it where we met. We can get it later."

"Good, I'd really like to take those pictures," Tom said. "Incidentally, who did the carvings?"

"We did," Jock said. "Together."

Tom was grateful that the scamper of the children out of the room saved him from having to reply. He couldn't think of anything but a grunt of astonishment.

The conversation split into a group of chats about something called a psych machine, trips to Russia, the planet Mars, and several artists Tom had never heard of. He wanted to talk to Lois, but she was one of the group gabbling about Mars like children. He felt suddenly uneasy and out of things, and neither Rachel's deprecating remarks about her section of the wood carvings nor Joyce's interesting smiles helped much. He wandered outside and made his way to the children's lean-to, feeling very depressed.

Once again he was the center of a friendly naked cluster, except for the same solemn-faced little girl skipping rope. A rather malicious but not very hopeful whim prompted him to ask the youngest, "What's one and one?"

"Ten," the shaver answered glibly. Tom felt pleased.

"It could also be two," the oldest boy remarked.

"I'll say," Tom agreed. "What's the population of the world?"

"About seven hundred million."

Tom nodded noncommittally and, grabbing at the first long word that he thought of, turned to the eldest girl. "What's poliomyelitis?"

"Never heard of it," she said.

The solemn little girl kept droning the same ridiculous chant: "Gik-lo, I-o, Rik-o, Gis-so."

His ego eased, Tom went outside and there was Lois.

"What's the matter?" she asked.

"Nothing," he said.

She took his hand. "Have we pushed ourselves at you too much? Has our jabbering bothered you? We're a loudmouthed family and I didn't think to ask if you were loning."

"Loning?"

"Solituding."

"In a way," he said. They didn't speak for a moment.

Then, "Are you happy, Lois, in your life here?" he asked.

Her smile was instant. "Of course. Don't you like my group?"

He hesitated. "They make me feel rather no good," he said, and then admitted, "but in a way I'm more attracted to them than any people I've ever met."

"You are?" Her grip on his hand tightened. "Then why don't you stay with us for awhile? I like you. It's too early to propose anything, but I think you have a quality our group lacks. You could see how you fit in. And there's Joyce. She's just visiting, too. You wouldn't have to lone unless you wanted."

Before he could think, there was a rhythmic rush of feet and the Wolvers were around them.

"We're swimming," Simone announced.

Lois looked at Tom inquiringly. He smiled his willingness, started to mention he didn't have trunks, then realized that wouldn't be news here. He wondered whether he would blush.

Jock fell in beside him as they rounded the ranch house. "Larry's been telling me about your group at the other end of the valley. It's comic, but I've whirled down the valley a dozen times and never spotted any sort of place there. What's it like?"

"A ranch house and several cabins."

Jock frowned. "Comic I never saw it." His face cleared. "How about whirling over there? You could point it out to me."

"It's really there," Tom said uneasily. "I'm not making it up."

"Of course," Jock assured him. "It was just an idea."

"We could pick up your camera on the way," Lois put in.

The rest of the group had turned back from the huge oval pool and the dark blue and flashing thing beyond it, and stood gay-colored against the pool's pale blue shimmer.

"How about it?" Jock asked them. "A whirl before we bathe?"

Two or three said yes besides Lois, and Jock led the way toward the helicopter that Tom now saw standing beyond the pool, its beetle body as blue as a scarab, its vanes flashing silver.

The others piled in. Tom followed as casually as he could, trying to suppress the pounding of his heart. "Wonder you don't go by rocket," he remarked lightly.

Jock laughed. "For such a short trip?"

The vanes began to thrum. Tom sat stiffly, gripping the sides of the seat, then realized that the others had sunk back lazily in the cushions. There was a moment of strain and they were falling ahead and up. Looking out the side, Tom saw for a moment the sooty roof of the ranch house and the blue of the pool and the pinkish umber of tanned bodies. Then the helicopter lurched gently around. Without warning a miserable uneasiness gripped him, a desire to cling mixed with an urge to escape. He tried to convince himself it was fear of the height.

He heard Lois tell Jock, "That's the place, down by that rock that looks like a wrecked spaceship."

The helicopter began to fall forward. Tom felt Lois' hand on his.

"You haven't answered my question," she said.

"What?" he asked dully.

"Whether you'll stay with us. At least for awhile."

He looked at her. Her smile was a comfort. He said, "If I possibly can."

"What could possibly stop you?"

"I don't know," he answered abstractedly.

"You're strange," Lois told him. "There's a weight of sadness in you. As if you lived in a less happy age. As if it weren't 2050."

"Twenty?" he repeated, awakening from his thoughts with a jerk. "What's the time?" he asked anxiously.

Two," Jock said. The word sounded like a knell.

"You need cheering," Lois announced firmly.

Amid a whoosh of air rebounding from earth, they jounced gently down. Lois vaulted out. "Come on," she said.

Tom followed her. "Where?" he asked stupidly, looking around at the red rocks through the settling sand cloud stirred by the vanes.

"Your camera," she told him, laughing. "Over there. Come on, I'll race you."

He started to run with her and then his uneasiness got beyond his control. He ran faster and faster. He saw Lois catch her foot on a rock and go down sprawling, but he couldn't stop. He ran desperately around the rock and into a gust of up-whirling sand that terrified him with its suddenness. He tried to escape from the stinging, blinding gust, but there was the nightmarish fright that his wild strides were carrying him nowhere.

Then the sand settled. He stopped running and looked around him. He was standing by the balancing rock. He was gasping. At his feet the rusty brown leather of the camera case peeped from the sand. Lois was nowhere in sight. Neither was the helicopter. The valley seemed different, rawer—one might almost have said younger.

Hours after dark he trailed into Tosker-Brown. Curtained lights still glowed from a few cabins. He was footsore, bewildered, frightened. All afternoon and through the twilight and into the moonlit evening that turned the red rocks black, he had searched the valley. Nowhere had he been able to find the soot roofed ranch house of the Wolvers. He hadn't even been able to locate the rock like a giant bobbin where he'd met Lois.

During the next days he often returned to the valley. But he never found anything. And he never happened to be near the balancing rock when the time winds blew at ten and two, though once or twice he did see dust devils. Then he went away and eventually forgot.

In his casual reading he ran across popular science articles describing the binary system of numbers used in electronic calculating machines, where one and one make ten. He always skipped them. And more than once he saw the four equations expressing Einstein's generalized theory of gravitation:

$$"g^{i}_{+-}K_{;}l=0; \Gamma i=0; Rik=0, \mathcal{G}^{is}_{\underset{s}{v}}=0"!$$

He never connected them with the little girl's chant: "Gik-lo, I-o, Rik-o, Gis-so."

WHEN THE CHANGE-WINDS BLOW

I WAS HALFWAY between Arcadia and Utopia, flying a long archeologic scout, looking for coleopt hives, lepidopteroid stiltcities, and ruined villas of the Old Ones.

On Mars they've stuck to the fanciful names the old astronomers dreamed onto their charts. They've got an Elysium and an Ophir too.

I judged I was somewhere near the Acid Sea, which by a rare coincidence does become a poisonous shallow marsh, rich in hydrogen ions, when the northern icecap melts.

But I saw no sign of it below me, nor any archeologic features either—only the endless dull rosy plain of felsite dust and iron-oxide powder slipping steadily west under my flier, with here and there a shallow canyon or low hill, looking for all the world (Earth? Mars?) like parts of the Mojave.

The sun was behind me, its low light flooding the cabin. A few stars glittered in the dark blue sky. I recognized the constellations of Sagittarius and Scorpio, the red pinpoint of Antares.

I was wearing my pilot's red spacesuit. They've enough air on Mars for flying now, but not for breathing if you fly even a few hundred yards above the surface.

Beside me sat my copilot's green spacesuit, which would have had someone in it if I were more sociable or merely mindful of flying regulations. From time to time it swayed and jogged just a little.

And things were feeling eerie, which isn't how they ought to feel to someone who loves solitude as much as I do, or pretend to myself I do. But the Martian landscape is even more spectral than that of Arabia or the American Southwest—lonely and beautiful and obsessed with death and immensity and sometimes it strikes through.

From some old poem the words came, " . . . and strange thoughts grow, with a certain humming in my ears, about the life before I lived this life."

I had to stop myself from leaning forward and looking around into the faceplate of the green spacesuit to see if there weren't someone there now. A thin man. Or a tall slim woman. Or a black crabjointed Martian coleopteroid, who needs a spacesuit about as much as a spacesuit does. Or . . . who knows?

It was very still in the cabin. The silence did almost hum. I had been listening to Deimos Station, but now the outer moonlet had dropped below the southern horizon. They'd been broadcasting a suggestions program about dragging Mercury away from the sun to make it the moon of Venus—and giving both planets rotation too—so as to stir up the thick smoggy furnace-hot atmosphere of Venus and make it habitable.

Better finish fixing up Mars first, I'd thought.

But then almost immediately the rider to that thought had come: No, I *want Mars to stay lonely. That's why I came here. Earth got crowded and look what happened.*

Yet there are times on Mars when it would be pleasant, even to an old solitary like me, to have a companion. That is if you could be sure of picking your companion.

Once again I felt the compulsion to peer inside the green spacesuit.

Instead I scanned around. Still only the dust-desert drawing toward sunset: almost featureless, yet darkly rosy as an old peach. "True peach, rosy and flawless . . . Peachblossom marble all, the rare, the ripe as fresh-poured wine of nighty pulse...." *What* was *that* poem? —my mind nagged.

On the seat beside me, almost under the thigh of the green spacesuit, vibrating with it a little, was a tape: *Vanished Churches and Cathedrals of Terra.* Old buildings are an abiding interest with me, of course, and then some of the hills or hives of the black coleopts are remarkably suggestive of Earth towers and spires, even to details like lancet windows and flying buttresses, so much that it's been suggested there is an imitative element, perhaps telepathic, in architecture of those strange beings who despite their humanoid intelligence are very like social insects. I'd been scanning the book at my last stop, hunting out coleopt-hill resemblances, but then a cathedral interior had reminded me of the Rockefeller Chapel at the University of Chicago and I'd slipped the tape out of the projector. That chapel was where Monica had been, getting her Ph.D. in physics on a bright June morning, when the fusion blast licked the southern end of Lake Michigan, and I didn't want to think about Monica. Or rather I wanted too much to think about her.

"What's done is done, and she is dead beside, dead long ago...." Now I recognized the poem!—Browning's *The Bishop Orders His Tomb at St. Praxed's Church.* That was a distant cry!—Had there been a view of St. Praxed's on the tape?—The 16th Century . . . and the dying bishop pleading with his sons for a grotesquely grand tomb—a frieze of satyrs, nymphs, the Savior, Moses, lynxes—while he thinks of their mother, his mistress....

"Your tall pale mother with her talking eyes.... Old Grandolf envied me, so fair she was!"

Robert Browning and Elizabeth Barrett and their great love....

Monica and myself and our love that never got started....

Monica's eyes talked. She was tall and slim and proud....

Maybe if I had more character, or only energy, I'd find myself someone else to love—a new planet, a new girl!—I wouldn't stay uselessly faithful to that old romance, I wouldn't go courting loneliness, locked in a dreaming life-in-death on Mars. . . .

"Hours and long hours in the dead night, I ask, 'Do I live, am I dead?'"

But for me the loss of Monica is tied up, in a way I can't untangle, with the failure of Earth, with my loathing of what Terra did to herself in her pride of money and power and success (communist and capitalist alike), with that unneccessary atomic war that came just when they thought they had everything safe and solved, as they felt before the one in 1914. It didn't wipe out all Earth by any means, only about a third, but it wiped out my trust in human nature—and the divine too, I'm afraid —and it wiped out Monica. . . .

"And as she died so must we die ourselves, and thence ye may perceive the world's a dream."

A dream? Maybe we lack a Browning to make real those moments of modern history gone over the Niagara of the past, to find them again needle-in-haystack, atom-in-whirlpool, and etch them perfectly, the moments of starflight and planet-landing etched as he had etched the moments of the Renaissance.

Yet—the world (Mars? Terra?) only a dream? Well, maybe. A bad dream sometimes, that's for sure! I told myself as I jerked my wandering thoughts back to the flier and the unchanging rosy desert under the small sun.

Apparently I hadn't missed anything—my second mind had been faithfully watching and instrument-tending while my first mind rambled in imaginings and memories.

But things were feeling eerier than ever. The silence did hum now, brassily, as if a great peal of bells had just clanged, or were about to. There was menace now in the small sun about to set behind me, bringing the Martian night and what Martian were-things there may be that they don't know of yet. The rosy plain had turned sinister. And for a moment I was sure that if I looked into the green spacesuit, I would see a dark wraith thinner than any coleopt, or else a bone-brown visage fleshlessly grinning—the King of Terrors.

"Swift as a weaver's shuttle fleet our years: Man goeth to the grave, and where is he?"

You know, the weird and the supernatural didn't just evaporate when the world got crowded and smart and technical. They moved outward—to Luna, to Mars, to the Jovian satellites, to the black tangled forest of space and the astronomic marches and the unimaginably distant bulls-eye windows of the stars. Out to the realms of the unknown, where the unexpected still happens every other hour and the impossible every other day—

And right at that moment I saw the impossible standing 400 feet tall and cloaked in lacy gray in the desert ahead of me.

And while my first mind froze for seconds that stretched toward minutes and my central vision stayed blankly fixed on that upwardly bifurcated incredibility with its dark hint of rainbow caught in the gray lace, my second mind and my periferal vision brought my flier down to a swift, dream-smooth, skimmering landing on its long skis in the rosy dust. I brushed a control and the cabin walls swung silently downward to either side of the pilot's seat, and I stepped down through the dream-easy Martian gravity to the peach-dark pillowy floor, and I stood looking at the wonder, and my first mind began to move at last.

There could be no doubt about the name of this, for I'd been looking at a taped view of it not five hours before—this was the West Front of Chartres Cathedral, that Gothic masterpiece, with its plain 12th Century spire, the *Clocher Vieux*, to the north and between them the great rose window fifty feet across and below that the icon-crowded triple-arched West Porch.

Swiftly now my first mind moved to one theory after

another of this grotesque miracle and rebounded from them almost as swiftly as if they were like magnetic poles.

I was hallucinating from the taped pictures. Yes, maybe the world's a dream. That's always a theory and never a useful one.

A transparency of Chartres had got pasted against my faceplate. Shake my helmet. No.

I was seeing a mirage that had traveled across fifty million miles of space ... and some years of time too, for Chartres had vanished with the Paris Bomb that near-missed toward Le Mans, just as Rockefeller Chapel had gone with the Michigan Bomb and St. Praxed's with the Rome.

The thing was a mimic-structure built by the coleopteroids to a plan telepathized from a memory picture of Chartres in some man's mind. But most memory pictures don't have anywhere near such precision and I never heard of the coleopts mimicking stained glass though they do build spired nests a half thousand feet high.

It was all one of those great hypnotism-traps the Arean jingoists are forever claiming the coleopts are setting us. Yes, and the whole universe was built by demons to deceive only me—and possibly Adolf Hitler—as Descartes once hypothesized. *Stop it.*

They'd moved Hollywood to Mars as they'd earlier moved it to Mexico and Spain and Egypt and the Congo to cut expenses, and they'd just finished an epic of the Middle Ages—The *Hunchback of Notre Dame,* no doubt, with some witless producer substituting Notre Dame of Chartres for Notre Dame of Paris because his leading mistress liked its looks better and the public wouldn't know the difference. Yes, and probably hired hordes of black coleopts at next to nothing to play monks, wearing robes and humanoid masks. And why not a coleopt to play Quasimodo?—improve race relations. *Don't hunt for comedy in the incredible.*

Or they'd been giving the Martian tour to the last mad

president of La Belle France to quiet his nerves and they'd propped up a fake cathedral of Chartres, all west facade, to humor him, just like the Russians had put up papier-mache villages to impress Peter III's German wife. The Fourth Republic on the fourth planet! *No, don't get hysterical. This thing is here.*

Or maybe—and here my first mind lingered—past and future forever exist somehow, somewhere (the Mind of God? the fourth dimension?) in a sort of suspended animation, with little trails of somnambulant change running through the future as our willed present actions change it and perhaps, who knows, other little trails running through the past too?—for there may be professional timetravelers. And maybe, once in a million millennia, an amateur accidentally finds a Door.

A Door to Chartres. But when?

As I lingered on those thoughts, staring at the gray prodigy— "Do I live, am I dead?" —there came a moaning and a rustling behind me and I turned to see the green spacesuit diving out of the flier toward me, but with its head ducked so I still couldn't see inside the faceplate. I could no more move than in a nightmare. But before the suit reached me, I saw that there was with it, perhaps carrying it, a wind that shook the flier and swept up the feather-soft rose dust in great plumes and waves. And then the wind bowled me over—one hasn't much anchorage in Mars gravity—and I was rolling away from the flier with the billowing dust and the green spacesuit that went somersaulting faster and higher than I, as if it were empty, but then wraiths are light.

The wind was stronger than any wind on Mars should be, certainly than any unheralded gust, and as I went tumbling deliriously on, cushioned by my suit and the low gravity, clutching futilely toward the small low rocky outcrops through whose long shadows I was rolling, I found myself thinking with the serenity of fever that this wind wasn't blowing across Mars-space only but through time too.

A mixutre of space-wind and time-wind—what a puzzle for the physicist and drawer of vectors! It seemed unfair—I thought as I tumbled—like giving a psychiatrist a patient with psychosis overlaid by alcoholism. But reality's always mixed and I knew from experience that only a few minutes in an anechoic, lightness, null-G chamber will set the most normal mind veering uncontrollably into fantasy—or is it always fantasy?

One of the smaller rocky outcrops took for an instant the twisted shape of Monica's dog Brush as he died— not in the blast with her, but of fallout, three weeks later, hairless and swollen and oozing. I winced.

Then the wind died and the West Front of Chartres was shooting vertically up above me and I found myself crouched on the dust-drifted steps of the south bay with the great sculpture of the Virgin looking severely out from above the high doorway at the Martian desert, and the figures of the four liberal arts ranged below her—Grammar, Rhetoric, Music, and Dialectic—and Aristotle with frowning forehead dipping a stone pen into stone ink.

The figure of Music hammering her little stone bells made me think of Monica and how she'd studied piano and Brush had barked when she practiced. Next I remembered from the tape that Chartres is the legendary resting place of St. Modesta, a beautiful girl tortured to death for her faith by her father Quirinus in the Emperor Diocletian's day. Modesta—Music—Monica.

The double door was open a little and the green spacesuit was sprawled on its belly there, helmet lifted, as if peering inside at floor level.

I pushed to my feet and walked up the rose-mounded steps. *Dust blowing through time? Grotesque. Yet was I more than dust? "Do I live, am I dead?"*

I hurried faster and faster, kicking up the fine powder in peach-red swirls, and almost hurled myself down on the green spacesuit to turn it over and peer into the faceplate. But before I could quite do that I had looked into the doorway and what I saw stopped me. Slowly I got to my feet again and took a step beyond the prone green spacesuit and then another step.

Instead of the great Gothic nave of Chartres, long as a football field, high as a sequois, alive with stained light, there was a smaller, darker interior—churchly, too, but Romanesque, even Latin, with burly granite columns and rich red marble steps leading up toward an altar where mosaics glittered in the gloom. One thin stream of flat light, coming through another open door like a theatrical spot in the wings, struck on the wall opposite me and revealed a gloriously ornate tomb where a sculptured mortuary figure—a bishop by his miter and crook—lay above a crowded bronze frieze on a bright green jasper slab with a blue lapis-lazuli globe of Earth between his stone knees and nine thin columns of peach-blossom marble rising around him to the canopy....

But of course: this was the bishop's tomb of Browning's poem. This was St. Praxed's church, powdered by the Rome Bomb, the church sacred to the martyred Praxed, daughter of Pudens, pupil of St. Peter tucked even further into the past than Chartres' martyed Modesta. Napoleon had planned to liberate those red marble steps and take them to Paris. But with this realization came almost instantly the companion memory: that although St. Praxed's church had been real, the tomb of Browning's bishop had existed only in Browning's imagination and the minds of his readers.

Can it be, I thought, that not only do the past and future exist forever, but also all the possibilities that were never and will never be realized . . . somehow, somewhere (the fifth dimension? the Imagination of God?) as if in a dream within a dream.... Crawling with change too, as artists or anyone thinks of them.... Change-winds mixed with time-winds with space-winds....

In that moment I became aware of two dark-clad

figures in the aisle beside the tomb and studying it—a pale man with dark beard covering his cheeks and a pale woman with dark straight hair covering hers under a filmy veil. There was movement near their feet and a fat dark sluglike beast, almost hairless, crawled away from them into the shadows.

I didn't like it. I didn't like that beast. I didn't like it disappearing. For the first time I felt actively frightened.

And then the woman moved too, so that her dark wide floor-brushing skirt jogged, and in a very British voice she called, "Flush! Come here, Flush!" and I remembered that was the name of the dog Elizabeth Barrett had taken with her from Wimpole Street when she ran off with Browning.

Then the voice called again, anxiously, but the British had gone out of it now; in fact it was a voice I knew, a voice that froze me inside, and the dog's name had changed to Brush, and I looked up, and the gaudy tomb was gone and the walls had grayed and receded, but not so far as those of Chartres, only so far as those of the Rockefeller Chapel, and there coming toward me down the center aisle, tall and slim in a black academic robe with the three velvet doctor's bars on the sleeves, with the brown of science edging the hood, was Monica.

I think she saw me, I think she recognized me through my faceplate, I think she smiled at me fearfully, wonderingly.

Then there was a rosy glow behind her, making a hazily-gleaming nimbus of her hair, like the glory of a saint. But then the glow became too bright, intolerably so, and something struck at me, driving me back through the doorway, whirling me over and over, so that all I saw were swirls of rose dust and star-pricked sky.

I think what struck at me was the ghost of the front of an atomic blast.

In my mind was the thought: St. Praxed, St. Modesta, and Monica the atheist saint martyred by the bomb.

Then all winds were gone and I was picking myself up from the dust near the flier.

I scanned around through ebbing dust-swirls. The cathedral was gone. No hill or structure anywhere relieved the flatness of the Martian horizon.

Leaning against the flier, as if lodged there by the wind yet on its feet, was the green spacesuit, its back toward me, its head and shoulders sunk in an attitude mimicking profound dejection.

I moved toward it quickly. I had the thought that it might have gone with me to bring someone back.

It seemed to shrink from me a little as I turned it around. The faceplate was empty. There on the inside, below the transparency, distorted by my angle of view was the little complex console of dials and levers, but no face above them.

I took the suit up very gently in my arms, carrying it as if it were a person, and I started toward the door of the cabin.

It's in the things we've lost that we exist most fully.

There was a faint green flash from the sun as its last silver vanished on the horizon.

All the stars came out.

Gleaming green among them and brightest of all, low in the sky where the sun had gone, was the Evening Star—Earth.

237 TALKING STATUES, ETC.

DURING THE LAST FIVE YEARS of his life, when his theatrical career was largely over, the famous actor Francis Legrande spent considerable time making portraits of himself: plaster heads and busts, some larger statues, oil paintings, sketches in various media, and photographic self-studies. Most of them showed him in roles in which he had starred on the stage and screen. Legrande had always been a versatile craftsman and the results were artistically adequate.

After his death, his wife devoted herself to caring for the self-portraits along with other tangible and intangible memories of the great man. Keeping them alive, as it were, or at least dusted and cleaned and even pampered with an occasional change of air and prospect. There were 237 of them on view, distributed throughout Legrande's studio, the living room and halls and bedrooms of the house, and in the garden.

Legrande had a son, Francis Legrande II, who had no more self content or success in life than most sons of prominent and widely admired men. After the collapse of his third marriage and his eleventh job, young Francis —who was well over forty—retreated for a time to his father's house.

His relations with his mother were amicable but limited: they said loud cheery things to each other when they met, but after a bit they began to keep their daily orbits separate—by accident, as it were.

Young Francis was drinking rather too heavily and trying hard to control it, yet without any definite program for the future—a poor formula for quiet nerves.

After six weeks his father's selfportraits began to talk to him. It came as no great surprise, since they had been following him with their eyes for at least a week, and for the past two days they had been frowning and smiling at him—critically, he was certain—glaring and smirking—and this morning the air was full of ominous hangoverish noises on the verge of intelligibility.

He was alone in the studio. In fact he was alone in the whole house, since his mother was calling on a neighbor. There came a tiny but nerve-rasping dry grating sound, exactly as if chalk were coughing or plaster had cleared its throat. He quickly glanced at a white bust of his father as Julius Caesar and he distinctly saw the plaster lips part a little and the tip of a plaster tongue come out and quickly run around them. Then—

FATHER: I irritate you, don't I? Or perhaps I should say *we* irritate you?

SON (*startled but quickly accepting the situation and deciding to speak frankly*): Well, yes, you do. Most sons are bugged by their fathers—any psychologist who knows his stuff will tell you that. By the actual father or by his memory. If the father happens to be a famous man, the son is that much more intimidated and inhibited and overawed. And if, in addition, the father leaves behind dozens of faces of himself, created by himself, if he insists on going on living after death . . .
(*He shrugs.*)

FATHER (*smiling compassionately from a painting of himself as Jesus of Nazareth*): In short, you hate me.

SON: Oh, I wouldn't go as far as that. It's more that you weary me. Seeing you around everywhere, all the time, I get bored.

FATHER (*in dark colors, as Strindberg's Captain*): You get bored? You've only been here six weeks. Think of me having nothing to look at for ten whole years but your mother.

SON (*with a certain satisfaction*): I always thought your affection and devotion to mother were overdone.

FATHER (*as Romeo, a pastel sketch*): No, son, they weren't, but . . .

FATHER (*a head of Don Juan, interrupting*): But it *has* been a dull time. There have been exactly three beautiful girls inside this house during the last decade, and one of those was collecting for Community Chest and only stayed five minutes. And none of them got undressed.

FATHER (*as Socrates*): And then there are so many of me to be bored and just one of you. I've sometimes wished I hadn't been quite so enthusiastic about multiplying myself.

SON (*wincing from a crick in the neck got from swiveling his head rapidly from portrait to portrait*): Serves you right! Two hundred and thirty-seven self-portraits!

FATHER: Actually there are about 450, but the others are put away.

SON: Good Lord! Are they alive too?

FATHER: Well, yes, in an imprisoned drugged sort of way . . . (*From various cabinets and drawers comes a low but tumultuous groaning and muttering.*)

SON (*rushing out of the studio into the living room in a sudden spasm of terror which he tries to conceal by speaking loudly and contemptuously*): What collosal vanity! Four hundred and fifty self-portraits! What narcissism!

FATHER (*from a full-length painting of King Lear over the fireplace*): I don't think it was vanity, son, not chiefly. All my life I was used to making up my face and getting into costume. Spending half an hour at it, or if there were something special like a beard (*the portrait touches its long white one with wrinkle-painted fingers*) an hour or more. When I retired from the stage, I still had the make-up habit, the itch to work my face over. I took it out in doing self-portraits. It was as simple as that.

SON: I might have known you'd have an innocent fine-sounding explanation. You always did.

FATHER: In an average acting year I made myself up at least two hundred and fifty times. So even 237 self-portraits are less than a year at the dressing-room table, and 450 less than two years.

SON: You'd never have been able to do so many portraits except you cheated. You worked from photographs and life-masks of yourself.

FATHER (*self-painted as Leonardo da Vinci*): Son, great artists have been cheating that way for five thousand years.

SON: All right, all right!

FATHER (*being very fair about it*): I'll admit that in addition the self-portraits let me relive my triumphs and keep up the illusion I was still acting.

SON (*cruelly*): You never stopped! On the stage or off you were always acting.

FATHER (*as Moses*): That's hardly just. I never talked a great deal. I was never domineering and (*pointedly*) I never ranted.

SON (*stung*): That's right!—offstage you preferred the quiet starring roles to the windy ones. Your favorite was a sickeningly noble, serene, infallible, pipesmoking older hero—a modern Brutus, a worldly Christ, a less folksy Will Rogers. But no matter how restrained your offstage characterizations, you managed to stay stage center.

FATHER (*shrugging pen-and-ink shoulders*): Laymen always accuse actors of acting. Because we can portray genuine emotion, we're supposed to be unable to feel it. It's the oldest charge made against us.

SON: And it's true!

FATHER (*very kindly, from a jaunty portrait of Cyrano de Bergerac*): My child, I do believe you're jealous of me.

SON (*pacing wildly and waving his arms*): Certainly

237 TALKING STATUES, ETC.

I am! What son wouldn't be?—surrounded, stifled, suffocated by a father disguised as all the great men who ever were or are or will be! All the great sages! All the great adventurers! All the great lovers!

FATHER (*gently, from the gape-mouth of a gaunt plaster head of Lazarus lifting from a plaster gravehole*): But there's no reason to be jealous of me any longer, son. I'm dead.

SON: You don't act as if you were! You're alive 237 times—450, if we count your reserve battalions. You're all over the place!

FATHER (*as Peer Gynt*): Oh son, these are only poor phantoms, roused for a moment from the nightmarish waking-sleep of Hell. Only powerless ghosts. . . . (*All the portraits cry out softly and confusedly and there comes again the muttering and groaning of the ones shut away in darkness.*)

SON (*overcome by another gust of terror and banging the door as he rushes out into the garden*): They are not! They're all facets of your perfection, damn you! Your miserable perfection, which you spent a lifetime polishing.

FATHER (*from a gauntcheeked bas relief of Don Quixote on the patio wall*): Every human being believes he is perfect in his way, even the most miserable scoundrel or dreamer.

SON: Not to the degree you believed you were perfect. You practiced perfection in front of the mirror. You rehearsed it. You watched your least word and gesture and you never made a slip.

FATHER (*incredulous*): Did I actually seem like that to you?

SON: Seem? My God, if you knew how I prayed for you to make a mistake. Just one, just once. Make it and own up to it. But you never did.

FATHER (*shaking a green-tarnished bronze head across a screen of leaves*): I never suspected you felt that way. Naturally a parent pretends to his child to be a little more perfect than he actually is. To admit any of his real weaknesses would be too much like encouraging vice. He wants to be sure his child is law-abiding during the formative years—later he may be able to stand the truth. Children can't distinguish between black and the palest shade of gray. It's the parent's duty to set as good an example as he can, even if he has to cover up some things and cheat a bit, until the child has mature judgment.

SON: And as a result the child is utterly crushed by this great white marble image of perfection!

FATHER: I suppose that conceivably could happen. Do you mean to tell me, son, that you didn't know your father was as other men?—that he had every last one of their weaknesses?

SON (*a hope dawning*): You really mean that? You're honestly saying . . . (*Then, recovering himself*) Oh, oh, I smell another of your lily-white, high-sounding explanations coming.

FATHER (*still from bronze head, which is that of Hamlet*): No, son! I could accuse me of such things that it were better my mother had not borne me. I was very proud, revengeful, ambitious, with more offenses at my beck than I had thoughts to put them in, imagination to give them shape, or time to act them in. I itched to excell at everything. Because my life depended on being the best actor, I was bitterly jealous of everyone's least accomplishments, even your own. I hid my scorn of all mankind under a mask of tolerant serenity—which I had trouble keeping in place, believe me. I lived for applause. During my last years I was bitterly resentful that ill-advised friends and greedy managers did not force me to come out of retirement and make farewell tours. I wronged your mother by lusting after other women, and myself by never having the nerve to yield to temptation—

SON: What, never?

FATHER: Well, hardly ever.

SON: Dad, that's terrific!

FATHER (*modestly*): Well, inspired by the great characters I portray, I sometimes get carried away. A little of them rubs off on me.

SON (*rather breathless*): This puts a different complexion on everything. What a relief! Dad, I feel wonderful. (*He laughs, a touch hysterically.*)

FATHER: Wait, son, I did worse than that. I watched your mother's personality fade, I watched her change into a mere adjunct of myself, and I let it happen, merely because life was a trifle easier for me that way. I watched you blunder along under a load of anxiety and guilt and I never tried to get close to you or tell you the truth about myself, which might have helped you, simply because it would have been difficult and uncomfortable for me to have done so and because I—

SON (*concerned*): Now you are going too far, Dad. You mustn't blame yourself for—

FATHER (*ignoring the sympathy*): —and because I actually enjoyed your awed embittered admiration. You were such a gullible audience! And then during the last years, instead of turning outward, I lost interest in almost everything except the self-portraits. I poured all of myself into them, finally the life-force itself, so that now I live on in them—a solitary self-created Hell. A human being's punishment for his misdeeds is having to watch and sometimes suffer their consequences . . . but to have to watch them minute after minute from 237 vantage points, unable to take the slightest action, unable even to comment, without the boon of a moment's forgetfulness, a moment's nirvana . . . (*His voice grows ghostly.*) Ten years! Thirty-six hundred interminable twilights. Thirty-six hundred empty dawns. To have to watch this house and garden die. To watch your mother mooning about day after day, wasting herself on memories and sentimental bric-a-brac. To watch you narrow your life down as I did mine, but before you've even lived it, and all your sodden drinking. To have to observe in all its loathsome detail the soul-rotting, snail-slow creep of inanition . . .

SON (*angry again, in spite of himself, and once more quiet frightened*): Well don't bellyache to me about it. It's your own fault that there are 237 of you, all corroding with life-force—another man would have been satisfied with being damned just once. There's nothing I can do for you.

FATHER (*grinning evilly from the head of Mephistopheles peering from between bushes opposite Hamlet*): But there is. Break us, burn us, melt us down. Give us oblivion. *Smash us!*

SON (*rushing back into house, partly to grab up poker from fireplace and partly because, all in all, the talking portraits in the house are less eerie than those hidden about the garden*): By God, I'd like to! I don't know how often I've thought of this house as a musty old museum, the lumber room of one man's vanity.

FATHER (*a chorus*): *Strike!*

SON (*hesitating with poker lifted above his head*): But they'd think I was crazy. They'd believe that envy of you pushed me over the line into psychosis. They'd probably put me away.

FATHER (*as Leonardo again*): Nonsense! They'd merely say that you were ridding the world of some amateurish daubs and thumb-scoopings. *Smash us!*

SON (*veering into argument*): Amateurish is too strong a word. They're not that bad, certainly.

FATHER (*pleased*): You think my work has enduring professional quality?

SON (*frowns*): No, that would be going too far in the opposite drection.

FATHER: *Smash us!*

SON (*raises the poker, but again hesitates*): There's another thing: mother would never forgive me.

FATHER: *Don't bring your mother into this!*

SON: Why not? For that matter, if you've really been wanting oblivion for ten years, why didn't you ask mother to smash you? Or at least to put you all away, where you'd have something nearer oblivion, I gather. Or *give* you all away to people who would either destroy you or provide you with more diverse environments and a more interesting shadowlife.

FATHER: Son, I've never been able to make things like that clear to your mother. Somehow the more she fitted herself to me, the less she was really in touch with me. She was as close to me and yet as far beyond my ken as . . . my gall bladder. I've tried to talk to her, but she doesn't hear. I don't think she even sees my self-portraits any more, but only the image of me—her own creation—which she carries in her mind. But *you*, at long last, hear me. And I tell you: *smash us!*

FATHER (*as plaster head of Don Juan, calling from studio*): Think of the fiery impetuous philanderer imprisoned in the icy rigid statue he invites for dinner. Three girls glimpsed in ten years! *Smash us!*

FATHER (*as the painted Leonardo*): You were always scared to take action. I wasn't!—I expressed myself, even in these miserable self-portraits. Now it's your turn—and your opportunity. *Smash us!*

FATHER (*as Peer Gynt*): Plunge me back in the crucible. Melt me down.

FATHER (*as Beethoven*): Strike a great healing discord!

FATHER (*as Jean Valjean*): Explode the prison!

FATHER (*as St. John the Divine*): Unleash the apocalypse!

FATHER (*A muffled chorus of photographs*): Break our glass, shred us, touch a match to us. Destroy us!

FATHER (*all 237 with the dark undertones of the imprisoned ones*): SMASH US!

SON (*swings up the poker a third time, then lowers its tip to the floor with a smile, his manner suddenly easy*): No. Why should I let myself be agitated by a bunch of old pictures and sculptures, even if they do talk? How would destroying them change me? And why should I be intimidated by a dead father, even if he lives on in various obscure ways? It's ridiculous.

FATHER (*once more King Lear*): Have you lost your respect for us? Are you not at least filled with supernatural terror at this morning's events?

SON (*shaking his head*): No. I think it's just my hangover talking with a strong psychotic accent—or 237 accents. And if it really *is* you, Dad, somehow talking from somewhere, I think you mean me well and so I'm not frightened. And finally, to be very honest with you, I don't think you *really* want to be destroyed, Dad, even in effigy—or effigies. I think you've just been getting your feelings off your chest, especailly your boredom.

FATHER (*as Peer Gynt, smiling an inscrutable smile, perhaps of relief, perhaps of triumph, perhaps of resignation*): Well, if you can't bring yourself to destroy us, at least stir up this old house, stir up your own life.

SON (*nodding*): There's something to that, all right, Dad.

FATHER: If you don't take the initiative—and moderate your drinking, too—we'll probably start talking again some morning or night, and not nearly as pleasantly, or even sanely. So stir things up.

SON (*seriously*): I'll remember that, Dad.

FATHER (*calling as Don Juan, from studio*): Invite some—(*The voice breaks off abruptly.*)

SON *looks around at the portraits. They have suddenly all gone mum. He can detect no movement in any of them, or changes in their features. The front door opens and his mother comes in excitedly with an opened letter in her hand.*

MOTHER: Francis, I've just received the most interesting request. The Merrivale Young Ladies' Academy wants a bust of your father for their library or lounge room. I think we should grant their request—that is, if you agree.

SON (*poking elaborately at the ashes in the fireplace, to account for the poker*): Why not? (*Then getting an inspiration and growing wily*) How about the Hamlet head?

MOTHER: Out of the question—that's his masterpiece. Besides, it's rivetted to its pillar in the garden.

SON: Well, then the Lear.

MOTHER: Certainly not, it's my favorite. Besides, it's a painting, not a bust.

SON (*baiting his trap*): Well, I suppose you could give them . . . No, it's not good enough.

MOTHER (*instantly contentious*): What's not good enough?

SON (*as if reluctantly*): I was going to say the bust of Don Juan, but—

MOTHER: I think that's a very fine piece of work—and an excellent choice in this instance.

SON: Perhaps you're right about that, mother. In any case, I bow to your judgment.

MOTHER: Thank you, Francis. I've never given any of the statues away before, but I think I should begin to. I'll write Merrivale Young Ladies' Academy they may have the bust of Don Juan. (*Starts out.*)

SON: I think you'll feel happier when you've done this, mother. And I think father will feel happier too.

MOTHER (*pausing in doorway*): What's happened to you, Francis? You're usually so cynical about these matters.

SON (*shrugs*): I don't know. Maybe I'm growing. (*As his mother leaves, he begins to smile. Suddenly he whirls toward the portrait of Peer Gynt. It had seemed to wink, but now it presents only its fixed painted expression. Francis Legrande II continues to smile as he hears someone in the studio begin faintly to hum an air from Don Giovanni.*")

THE IMPROPER AUTHORITIES

As SOON AS Ronald Flecker fully convinced himself that he had discovered in his eccentric aunt's cluttered basement a small battery that stored the force of gravity instead of electricity—a battery that held in complete essence the power of fuelless spaceflight, levitation, and any number of lesser marvels—he sat down to do some very serious thinking.

The discovery had come about while he was repairing his aunt's doorbell—one of the innumerable small tasks she hesitantly but in the end always rather firmly set him, although she had more than enough money to hire professional household mechanics, and that Ronald in any case always felt obliged to discharge in return for the privilege of sleeping over her garage. He had found the thin wires in a monstrous tangle close under the dusty rafters. It turned out the system wasn't even worked by a step-down transformer but by dry cells and some idiot had hooked up the cells in parallels rather than series, accounting in large part for the doorbell's feeble performance. His aunt recalled that the last person before Ronald to revive the doorbell had been the kindly but abstracted and rather smelly Dr. Yorn, the second-to-last in her unending series of spiritual counselors—a yogi, medium, hypnotist, dynamic psychologist, something like that. Mrs. Wycherly liked variety and versatile men. Dr. Yorn's successor, the gleaming-eyed and dapper Mr.

Espy, seemed equally obliging and would almost certainly have been willing to tackle the doorbell, but now Mrs. Wycherly had Ronald for those things.

Ronald had picked out the three freshest looking dry cells, setting the other two, which still had short bent lengths of wire untidily attached to their terminals, down on the scarred top of an upended trunk beside the stepladder on which he was working. It was still day outside, barely, although of course he had a flashlight to see up into the cobwebby rafters, and just as he'd about connected up the three newer looking cells properly, working a little gingerly because of his apprehension of spiders, a beam of yellow light from the setting sun struck brightly through one of the low oblong windows and across the top of the trunk. It showed a lot more dust motes trembling in the air than Ronald's flashlight revealed, and immediately Ronald felt a sneeze coming on. But then it showed something so much more strange and arresting that the sneeze never came and Ronald quite forgot that his nasal passages had been tickling.

One of the rejected batteries carried attached to one terminal a length of gray-insulated wire so sharply curved that its other end now chanced to touch the other terminal, shorting the battery out—except that the battery had looked to Ronald too dingy and old to have any juice left to short.

The dust motes were whirling in orderly circles around the wire, forming a dim tube that curved from terminal to terminal with the wire running down the center or axis of the shadowy tube. The circular orbiting of the dust motes was clearest within an inch of the wire, but even as he watched he saw some of the more distant motes begin to take up the movement, swinging in larger, slower circles.

Ronald's face grew blank with attention. He leaned down very slowly until his eyes were only inches from the phenomenon. Fearfully, almost reverently, he blew softly at the wire. The motes eddied away wildly and then almost immediately began to resume their circling, those nearest the wire taking it up most quickly, then those further off starting once more to join in.

Ronald thought: *There's a force moving those particles. They're in a force-field. If they were powdered iron or black iron oxide (but they aren't) it would be a magnetic field moving them, a magnetic field created by an electric current moving through the wire, though I think it would have to be a lot stronger current than a dry cell could furnish.*

But the particles aren't iron or iron oxide (too heavy to float in air, besides this has to be just Wycherly basement dust—ashes, lint, earth, powdered wood and paper) so it can't be a magnetic field that's moving them, though they're moving exactly as if they were in a force-field of some sort. So it has to be gravity . . . a gravitic forcefield they're moving in, at least that's the only other force I know of it could be.

An electric current moving through a conductor creates a magnetic field.

A what?-current . . . call it a gravitic current anyway . . . though it could be a magnetic current . . . a gravitic current moving through a conductor creates a gravitic field.

The sunlight faded swiftly. As the yellow beam moved upward, dimming, its last rays showed more and more dust motes pouring into the vortex, joining in the frenzied yet orderly circling.

As the dark basement twilight closed in, Ronald reached out and grasped the battery protectively, possessively. With his other hand he bent the wire away from the terminal. Already he had begun to worry about the battery running down.

A minute or so later it occurred to him to use his flashlight to examine the battery more closely. It was a distinctly smaller cylinder than the other dry cells, he saw now—only about five inches high and an inch-and-a-half in diameter—and it had no cardboard sheath around it, which had been the chief reason he'd thought of it as older and more likely to be completely exhausted than the others. And the terminals, although of the screw-on, knurled-nut type, didn't seem to be brass, but something grayer, like the zinc, or whatever it was, of the battery's body.

He tried to force himself to think in a systematic way about the possible *source* of the thing, granting that it really *was* a gravity battery—something that another part of his mind was already working out delightful ways to check. *Let's see,* he thought, *it could be a genuine gravity battery manufactured as such by human beings engaged in secret government-sponsored anti-gravity research either in this country or elsewhere—there are such projects—though then how it should get into Aunt Wycherly's basement seems to require very weird assumptions. Or else—my God, this gets fantastic—it could come from off this earth and have been manufactured by extra-terrestrials—got to consider every possibility—though that involves us in even more weird assumptions.*

Or it could just have happened. I mean the battery could have started out as an ordinary battery, but sitting here in Aunt Wycherly's basement and undergoing all sorts of rhythmical temperature changes and God knows what else, the chemicals in it could have been transformed into substances generating a current—gravitic, magnetic, how should I know what jargon to use?—that in turn creates a gravitic field. Like spontaneous combustion, or something. Old rags. That's not unusual.

Or it could all be illusion or freak air currents.

Or I could just be going nuts—that's something to keep in mind too.

But while Ronald was making his brain hammer out these possibilities, another section of his thoughts was darting around like kittens to investigate all sorts of wonderful ideas, making use of the thirty years' rag-tag accumulation of information in Ronald's mind—a quite remarkable and varied assortment. For one thing he was thinking that since this basement phenomenon behaved so much like magnetism, it must be a dipolar gravity field he had here, promising both positive and negative gravity if properly harnessed; that is, not only gravitic attraction but gravitic repulsion—in other words, antigravity, the secret of rocketless spaceflight! There were ways to check that, of course. And what *was* the wonderful stuff that flowed through the wire and made the field grab and the motes spin? Gravitic fluid, could you call it? Liquid gravity? Was it particles, like electrons? Gravitrons, would you call them? Hell, nobody really understood electricity yet! Still—

"Ronald, why are you taking so long? Mr. Espy will be coming soon and I don't want to have to watch for him at the window."

Ronald looked down at his aunt's pudgy, thin-lipped face, realizing that she had come creaking and clumping all the way down to the basement without his being aware of it. He nodded slowly at her without a word, put away the battery he was holding, and like a man in a dream began to make the last connections in the bell system.

The bell rang strongly at the first test. Mrs. Wycherly thanked Ronald profusely in the kitchen and seemed on the point of bringing up some additional matter, but just then Ronald rather abruptly wandered off toward the garage, still acting like a man in a dream.

Mrs. Wycherly made a little humorous face. She'd been debating giving Ronald two dollars for his labors and had almost decided to, but if he chose to go mooning off that way . . .

She was still wondering, too, why he had so carefully put one of her batteries into the inside breast pocket of his coat, buttoning the coat afterwards. It was almost like a psychiatric symptom, with some deep symbolic meaning—perhaps she should ask Mr. Espy about it. But no, Ronald probably just wanted it for something in the garage. Well, she wouldn't grudge it to him, though of course he ought to have asked her first.

Convincing himself that his find really was a gravity battery occupied Ronald most of the night and next day. He made his tests with great care, only after thinking each through in detail first. He kept them as few and brief as his delight and wonder would let him. The possibility of the battery running down had begun to prey on his mind more and more seriously, especially after a search of the basement next morning revealed no more dry cells of similar appearance.

The chief test, or rather set of tests, involved making a coil of the wire joining the terminals, so as to give direction and greater power to the gravitic field, exactly as one would do in making an electromagnet. The most obvious and interesting cylinder around which to wind the coil was the battery itself. Ronald started out with just a dozen loops, winding the wire down the body of the battery from one terminal and returning it through the air to the other.

The result was more than gratifying. *Held terminals-end-up the battery almost doubled in weight as soon as he connected the coil.* Of course he was just judging the weight by feel, but he was sure he couldn't be fooling himself to that degree. Moreover, the coils strained toward the floor in that position, tending to creep along the cylinder and bunch together. (In later tests he made a point of anchoring them individually with adhesive tape.)

Held terminals-end-down the battery weighed almost nothing at all. It seemed as light as if it were a painted balsa-wood model of itself. The transition from twice-weight to no-weight, as felt by his hand, was as mysteriously alarming and delightful as a mild electric shock.

Clearly the gravitic field was dipolar as he'd surmised. The terminal-end was the negative or repulsive pole, seeking to push away the earth—or push the earth away! The other end was the positive or attractive one. (A bit later he discovered what he told himself he should have guessed at once: that if he wound the coil the opposite way, say clockwise instead of counter-clockwise, it reversed the poles—they really had nothing to do with the location of the terminals on the battery.)

For light objects nearby, the battery's tiny gravitic field was more powerful than that of the earth—a circumstance that shouldn't surprise him, Ronald reminded himself, as earth's center of gravity was 4,000 miles away while the battery's was right in his hand. The attractive pole would snatch a cork off the floor from two feet—he could actually see the cork falling upward faster and faster—while the repulsive pole would bat away the same cork dropped on it from above. And the attractive pole always became covered with dust when used, while the other pole stayed clean.

Brought close to his forearm, the repulsive pole made a shallow, saucer-shaped dimple in the flesh, while the attractive one tugged at the tissue in a way that somehow felt deeper than suction.

It was vastly exciting to say the very least, and Ronald could hardly wait to step up the power of the field by increasing the number of turns in the coil—this being one of the times when his delight and wonder got the better of him.

However, he retained at least minimal prudence and added only six turns. He told himself that if the effect wasn't enough, he could always add more.

He was glad that he had been conservative. The repuslive pole was downward when he touched the return wire to the second terminal, and the battery tugged his hand sharply upward, as if it were, not a small, but say a *medium-size* bird trying to escape. Or maybe a weather balloon. The sensation was peculiarly delightful—his hand was not only tugged but indescribably tickled (presumably by the curving components of the dipolar gravitic field) —and despite his concern about the battery running down, it was all Ronald could do not to stand there all night holding the up-surging battery with a happy, dazed smile on his face.

And in fact Ronald did not disconnect it right away. He'd got the impression that the wire of the coil had changed color in some way and on an impulse he switched off the light he'd been working by, a hanging and unshaded 150-watt globe (which he kept secret from his aunt, for she had a thing about wasting electricity and kept nothing stronger than 40 watts in her whole mansion).

The consequences were sudden, spectacular, and almost disastrous.

In the darkness the coil was outlined in bright white light.

Ronald was so startled that he opened his hand.

The white-spiraled battery sprang upward and for an instant Ronald had the dreadful fear that the thing had got away from him forever, and from the earth too, although he knew very well that the ceiling of his garage apartment must stop it.

But then almost immediately, without touching the ceiling, the thing flipped over, dove down, and hit the floor with a sharp crack.

Its light went out.

Ronald's feelings were intense and mixed. He was relieved that the battery hadn't escaped, doubly relieved to discover that apparently it couldn't escape from earth —that released repulsive pole down it would simply flip over and dive. (There was the possibility that he had started the battery flipping over with a twist of his hand when he released it, but that possibility didn't bulk large in his mind.)

And of course, beyond all else, he was fearful that the fall had somehow ruined the battery forever. For instance, if its ability to generate gravitic energy depended on some rare and delicate spontaneous chemical transformation that had taken place inside it, then even something as slight as a sudden jar might well reverse the transformation.

He switched on the light and picked up the battery as if it were a wounded bird. He was considerably relieved to find that the wire had jarred loose from one of the terminals. He reconnected it, the battery surged in his hand, and his relief was complete.

But thereafter his carefulness was doubled and also tainted with suspicion.

He made a number of other interesting discoveries about the battery besides the epi-phenomenon of the white glow. For instance, it turned out to be the *insulation* on the wire that carried the gravitic current. A bare copper wire didn't work at all. A nylon cord worked beautifully, provided he wrapped it in tinfoil so that it didn't short itself out. In fact, there seemed to be a half dozen new sciences implicit in the battery and Ronald would have liked nothing better than to spend the next six months in investigating them all, provided he had a dozen batteries to work with, or even just one to hold in reserve.

That was the fly in the ointment, of course. His battery was goose and golden egg rolled into one, a bird in the hand but none at all in the bushes. So about the middle of the next afternoon he sat down to do some serious, really serious thinking—meaning of course thinking about discovery to profit himself.

First he carefully locked away the battery and went out into the garden to meditate it through, but he found he couldn't bear to be that far away from his find. So he went back to his garage apartment and sat beside the window that looked into the garden, feeling a little giddy from lack of sleep.

His aunt had noted his abstracted and somewhat agitated behavior, however, from one of her lace-curtained watch-windows, just as she'd early that morning been aware of him poking around in the basement without her permission. She frowned, remembering his distinctly odd behavior with her battery. She hadn't discussed the matter with Mr. Espy yesterday but she decided she certainly would tonight.

Serious thinking is always apt to be a somewhat chilling business. The more Ronald applied his mind to the problem of how to make *money* out of one small and presumably irreplaceable gravitic and antigravitic battery, the chillier the prospects came to look to him.

One thing he was fatalistically certain of from the start: that if he reported his find to any "proper authorities" (military, scientific, industrial, academic, governmental—authorities are always governmental to the end) he would get nothing whatever for himself except trouble. To begin with—the governmental authorities would know very well whether one of their secret projects had or had not started to manufacture gravitic batteries. In either case they would grab the battery—either for safekeeping or for feverish secret research into its mysteries —and at the same time loudly proclaim that it did not exist. Ronald's protests would be laughed at. He would be left out in the cold or, more likely, grabbed himself and awarded a lifetime of protective custody and unending interrogation. Where a discovery of such fabulous military importance as antigravity was concerned, an individual's rights just wouldn't count.

Perhaps he could investigate the battery himself, carefully open it and find out what made it work? Ronald's reaction to this idea was simply to shudder. True, he fancied a bit his talent for scientific thinking, but he wasn't *that* egotistical. Cutting or prying the battery open in hope of discovering its secrets struck Ronald as some seven degrees more unpromising than an infant taking apart a gold wristwatch to find out what made it work. This seemed particularly to the point as Ronald now inclined more and more to the theory that the battery was something that had been spontaneously generated in his aunt's basement by complex cycles of temperature change or the like—which also brought him back once more to the fact that he only had *one* battery, that as far as he knew there was only one on Earth. And if *that* were the case, why the chances were that the properest scientific authorities in the world wouldn't be any too successful in probing the battery's secrets. They'd play with it—at a little more sophisticated level than he, to be sure—until its power gave out, and then dissect it into microscopic slides and peer and poke at it, and like as not end up knowing little or nothing more than at the first testing.

These general considerations also made Ronald shy away from the plan of finding and privately enlisting the services of some brilliant young technician or engineering student, or offering such a person a partnership in the battery.

Perhaps he could *sell* the battery? No, any substantial businessman would be fearfully suspicious of such an offer. He'd think it was the Keeley motor over again or some perpetual motion crank or the powder that added to water makes gasoline. Ronald could arrange brilliant demonstrations, of course, but the more brilliant they were the more his prospect would suspect trickery. Experts would have to be called in and he would be back once more with the proper authorities, who would be snatching at his battery with rapacious fingers.

Suppose he were to find a millionaire gambler and bet him that—Ronald irritably shook his head. In the first place he didn't know any such gamblers or how to approach them and in the second place the last thing a Bet-a-million Gates would bet on was something that looked like a cast-iron certainty to win. The maker of such a tempting offer would be bound to have something up his sleeve.

Maybe he could use the battery to put on a magic or

spiritualist act? Causing something to float without wires, or levitating small objects in a slightly darkened room for the edification of wealthy crackpots like his aunt—do the Poltergeist bit. Now that, Ronald told himself, was cutting his problem down close to size. The trouble was, of course, as with so many other plans, that the battery would eventually run down and probably sooner than later. But more than that, the magic-act plan ran up against the objection that Ronald simply wasn't even a passable third-rate showman or conman and knew it very well.

Sitting in his chilly hole-over-a-garage and gazing out at the darkening garden—for a full twenty-four hours had passed since his great discovery—Ronald gave an irritated little sigh. His utter incapacity as a showman and conman was an old sore point with him. Why, as long as ten years ago he'd been the one to get his aunt interested in occultism, but had he reaped any of the benefits of her craze? No! That had been reserved for the slick operators like Mr. Espy, Dr. Yorn, and their dozen or so predecessors. They'd taken hundreds, thousands of dollars from her over the years. She'd even sent money by mail to Tibet, Ceylon and Southern California "to further occult research," while he, who'd started the whole thing, was lucky if from time to time he got a few cans of corned beef hash or spaghetti from her pantry hoard!

Not that Ronald lay awake nights scheming how to murder his aunt without being suspected or how to defraud her on a large scale. He wasn't that sort of person at all. He just grieved occasionally that a man with a commanding gaze and a confident pseudo-professional manner should be able to charm a twenty-dollar bill out of someone else's pocket and into his own, while he, with ten times the education, ingenuity, and honest idealism, couldn't!

Now if I just had the kind of cheap ability that a Yorn or an Espy has, Ronald told himself, *I'd figure out a dozen childishly simple ways to profit from this battery and, what's more important, I'd have the nerve and know-how to put them into action.*

He shook his head and shivered. He'd just had a vision of himself, days or months hence, the battery completely dead, finally going to the "proper authorities" with a crazed gleam in his eyes and assuring them that, yes, once this battery had held gravitic energy . . .

What I obviously need, he told himself, *is an improper authority.*

His gaze lit on Mr. Espy and his aunt talking at the far end of the garden. Almost at once his aunt went inside and Mr. Espy lit a cigarette and began to stroll.

Normally Ronald was anything but a man of action, but sleeplessness and desperation had transformed him. He grabbed the battery and completed the connection. It glowed brilliantly and surged powerfully upward in his hand, the coil consisting now of some twenty turns of tinfoil-wrapped nylon. Ronald headed for the garden.

Strike while the iron is hot, he told himself exultantly. *Espy's my man. With this to show him and let him feel it won't take me twenty seconds to make my pitch. And with his conning ability and my battery . . .*

Ronald certainly did make an arresting sight as he hurried through the darkening garden, holding high his glowing hand. Mr. Espy stopped dead and stared at Ronald.

There was something peculiar about the stare, though. It seemed to Ronald to go through him like a knife. Intending to startle, Ronald found himself startled in return . . . momentarily almost paralyzed.

He realized with horror that the battery had sprung from his limp fingers.

He waited for it to flip over and crash, thanking God that the ground was soft.

It didn't flip over. Buzzing faintly now and seeming to spin, it bulleted straight upward at ever-increasing velocity, one more bright point of light headed toward the first stars of evening.

It faded and was gone forever.

Ronald realized that Mr. Espy had hold of his shoulder and was shaking him.

"Young man!" Mr. Espy was saying, "Do you realize that you possess astounding occult powers? That was the most impressive demonstration of telekinesis I have ever witnessed in a long and rather far-flung life!"

Lieutenant J. C. Arnold and S. Abramson, USAF, were on a routine jet mission at 30,000 feet when the phenomenon shot by them at a distance of only a few yards, its velocity now considerable.

"Jack, a meteor!" the second gasped.

"Be your age, Sammy," the first admonished him. "Would a shooting star shoot up?" He paused before adding, "But what could it have been?"

Rather later that evening Mr. Espy was preparing a sort of telegram for transmission, though not by Western Union. It read in part:

> You will also be pleased to hear that the last of the batteries the saintly Yorn absent-mindedly distributed around in his chuckle-headed way before he was reassigned to a less critical post, has been located and safely disposed of. It is no longer on Earth. One worry less for all of us! To get it away painlessly from the young human who had discovered it and was beginning to probe its more superficial powers, I was forced to employ what on this planet they quaintly call "the whammy." He was most startled and considerably grieved to see the battery star-trend, having apparently not anticipated all the consequences of the gyral effect or the cube law on the coils. I calmed him and reconciled him in part to his loss without having to wipe his memory.

So . . . our observation station on Sol Three is once more reasonably secure from discovery. It will not be necessary now to find new patrons—we can continue to depend for local financing on Mrs. Wycherly and the other ladies who knowingly but so very kindly support out little enterprise.

OUR SAUCER VACATION

"DAD," I SAID, "how does a planet come to blow up?"

Dad briefly closed two of his eyes—the "thinking" ones. Then, "I don't rightly know, Son," he told me. "Let's go see."

That is like Dad—thoughtful but to the point, no pretenses, and no wasted motions! Dad is the sort who could strangle two and a half Antarean multibrachs while using his sixth and seventh tentacles to read the latest supplement to the *Acta Cosmica*.

At first Sis and Shorty thought he was kidding, but I have come to know Dad well enough to know that he never kids about anything involving a lawful desire to enlarge consciousness. (Or unlawful, for that matter, if he knows you well enough. But don't tell Mom.)

"Let's see . . ." Dad continued. "I have a sabbatical due, it happens. Galaxy Center is a hard master, but every googolth day the mills of the gods grind a little gold dust. I'll pulse Vrup and find out what planets are budding. Happens the old sock is pretty full of dinero—we could even squeeze out a trip to one of the Megellanic Clouds or Andromeda if that's where we have to go to find a lusty pod getting ready to pop . . ."

Mom knew he wasn't kidding either. She turned a faint purple and began to introspect like fury. Dad took no notice. Dad told me once, in private, that that is the best way to handle Mom. Women have to suffer their way through things, he said, and turning purple once in a while actually does Mom good.

Two orbits later Dad wafted in from the office waving the tickets. "Vrup pulsed over," he said, "and let me help him scan for buds. We found a beauty right in our own galaxy, out toward the rim. Mother won't have to pack our intergalactic underwear after all." He grinned at us kids. "I dropped in on your mentors," he told us. "Updating your three long vacations is okay with them, but Sis will have to coach Shorty on Intermediate Galactic History II and III and finish weaving her Stellar Tribes tapestry, while you, my young heptapus—" (he looked at me with all five eyes) "—will have to keep up with your tensor calculus class all on your lonesome."

That's like Dad too—the heavy tentacle and the light touch. Modest as well—to all outward appearances Dad isn't a very important guy, he likes it that way, but what he says has a way of counting with the really important people, such as Vrup.

I wasn't poisoned too purple by the news about vacation homework, though I didn't pretend to like it. Multidimensional geometry comes easy if you have seven tentacles to feel it out with. Shorty and Sis raised a stink of course, but Mom made them blow it out of the home.

I sometimes think that, for Dad, Education and the Cosmic All-Father are one and the same.

The tickets were for the instantaneous jump to the neighborhood of the star warming the bud world. There we would contact the Tour Boss.

Would the Tour Boss run our lives and be a tyrant like the old Heptarchs?—Sis wanted to know.

"I suppose he can try," Dad said, thickening his tentacles aggressively.

What was the name of the planet we were going to? Shorty demanded.

"It's still just a number in the galactic charts," Dad

revealed. "In the hundred-odd argots the natives use it is variously referred to as—" (Dad suddenly began to grunt—turns out the natives use sound for communication) "—das Welt, el mundo, Terra . . . oh yes, and Earth."

What were we going to do when we got there and were we coming back in time for the swimfests?

"If you don't mind, we'll live the future as it's served out to us, one day at a time," Dad informed him drily, "and just hope we don't meet any green weavers, especially the lambent kind."

Dad wouldn't say another word about green weavers and I couldn't find any references to them in the thought capsules from his library I now began to soak up—*Planets of the Swarm, Dawn Cultures, Rim worlds,* Vrup's own *The March of Consciousness, Good Manners for Galactic Sight-seers,* and so on.

I found out a good deal about how bud planets come to suicide, though. It seems that when most infant races discover fission and fusion, they are still in a war phase. They get to experimenting with underground atomic explosions, or they stockpile their fusionables too deep, or their nations even try to mine and counter-mine each other— and pretty soon if they don't watch their step they trigger the Core Effect and flame out as a micronova.

If they get over the psycho-social hump of the primitive war phase, well and good. They discover the Galactic Union for themselves and are admitted as junior members, with much whoop-tee-rah.

If not—well, they wouldn't have been good neighbors anyway, and astronomers always squeeze a lot of technical information and plain saddistic enjoyment out of a micronova.

In the meantime, however, while it's deciding whether or not to pop, the bud planet is just about the most interesting object in the whole cosmos. Alerted by the Mind Watchers who from their extragalactic eyrie keep an extrasensory eye on all burgeoning orbs, students and specialists and just plain sensation-seekers come swarming in from all over the galaxy (and a good many from outside it) to feed their minds and watch out not to give the budlings the slightest hint that they have become the leading actors in the universe's most exciting melodrama, that for the moment they are putting on the Big Show—it would botch their free psycho-social choice if they caught on—so the whole business is pretty carefully policed, even though all us cosmicians are considered thrillingly mature. (Dad says no.)

Of course it is all supposed to be in the interests of Science and Education, but I know for a fact that a lot of folks visit bud planets just for kicks—because they happen to have the necessary dough and pull, and even Mind Watchers have been known to blink at the rule book. A sorry state, maybe, but that's the way the universe is—corrupt.

Anyway, Dad says that even deep dyed villains and custard heads have a right to all the Education they can wangle.

As we waited our turn at the translation point—Shorty restless and squirming, Mom introspecting at core depths—I told Dad a little about my reading.

"Seems now that we're due to go," I said modestly, "I've already got most of the answers to my original question."

"That's the way Education works, Son—by anticlimax," Dad said with the flip of a tentacle. What he told me next he tight-beamed, so Mom wouldn't catch it. "And I wouldn't be too sure that you're just going to see a textbook in action. The real yorfis always has greener fangs than the nightmare."

The trip was a great disappointment to Shorty—no suns flashing past meteor-scarred portholes. Just "Prepare for translation!" and—*blip!*—there we were floating along with a lot of other heptapussies and various galactic beings inside the great transparent sphere of a spatial reception center, looking from a distance of about three diameters at the planet of our choice.

The Shell of the Reception Center was almost invisible. Air pressure and not inherent rigidity kept it spherical. We were just a gaggle of greenish translucent heptapussies free-falling against a background of star-spangled night, except for the raggledly-tentacled star that warmed this volume of space and the blue-brown planet that had lured us here.

Earth (to use Dad's grunt) seemed to have more water than land. The two continents I could see looked like two gorged grinnies, one clutching an ice cap, the other hanging onto his tail. The continents on the other side, I discovered later, made a more confused picture—maybe a yorfis killing a grunch, while a fat sway-backed flutch quaked in terror nearby. A real crazy orb.

For ten pulsations it was awe-inspiring. Then Shorty started to squirm and ask about the bathroom, Sis spotted a female or our acquaintance we'd never dreamed of running into here, Mom whampsed up out of her introspection and started to gossip like mad with said female (which must have been a great relief to Dad) and Dad himself said to me, "Come on, Son, let's waft around and find the Tour Boss."

Less than an orbit later we were happily settled in our own living quarters. What was far more exciting—to me, at least—yes, and just plain astounding—we had a flying saucer for our own exclusive use!

Dad had flashed a letter from Vrup and the Tour Boss had tied himself into knots being obliging.

It bothered me sort of—that suggestion of bribery or at least special privilege. I told Dad how I felt.

"Son," he said, "always remember that we've got heptapi to work with, not angels. Happens I'd been doing some extra kortling for Vrup and he wanted to show his appreciation." He closed his thinking eyes and gave out with a proverb: "Thou shalt not plug the throat of the grunch that hunteth grinnies for thy soup tureen."

That satisfied me, pretty well. I don't suppose I'd have been too bothered even if I'd gone on feeling we were cheating—our saucer was just too much of a sweetheart. Transparent to the point of invisibility and with tentacle-tip controls, it held the five of us neatly—with room for a couple of extra passengers if we felt so inclined.

In it we could go anywhere we wanted on Earth, hover indefinitely over points of special interest, even land briefly at lonely spots—if we took the proper precautions.

You can bet we always took them! —Dad had every one of us kids, Shorty in particular, memorize *the entire tourists' rule book*.

And once each orbit, without fail, we docked the saucer at Center, cleaned and polished it and rubbed it down with air-wax to maintain its invisibility. Dad was a perfect stickler.

Sometimes I think Dad is almost too saintly a custodian. (But then his worldly side will emerge to confute me.)

Earth was as exciting as a basketful of baby grunch, of course. We first surveyed it all from about one-half tentacle of radius, then began to make closer approaches. We would observe Earthan tests of nuclear weapons— the bulletin board back at Center kept us pretty well posted on the when and where of things like that. The police, you see, kept up systematic study of Earth, though by now the Mind Watchers had turned their extrasensory eyes on newer and (to them) more interesting orbs.

Once Dad dipped down into the soupier atmosphere and steered real close to a big clumsy Earthan airship. It was quite a sight with its rigid fins and hot squirters. They hadn't the faintest suspicion of our presence of course, though Dad followed it closely for some time.

And once another saucer came within an ace of getting itself speared by an experimental Earthan rocket. There were a bunch of saucers hovering around to see the shoot and this one went way inside the bounds our police had set up. There was quite a fuss and even talk of restricting all saucers, but in the end nothing was done—even the rule-breakers weren't disciplined.

I felt pretty embarrassed. The offending saucer had been manned by heptapussies and that seemed to reflect on us. I got to be as big a stickler as Dad. Once I spanked Shorty for using a flashlight two diameters away from Earth. It couldn't possibly have been seen by Earthans, but it was the principle of the thing.

There were a lot of heptapussies among the tourists, the Tour Boss himself was one and so were most of the police—in fact, we formed a plurality. That's the way galactic touring is apt to go, Dad says—one person decides to make a certain trip and pretty soon fifty of his neighbors get the same idea. One reason Vrup and he had picked Earth was that there were a lot of heptapussies already visiting it. All of them had their personal flying saucers, incidently, even the solo travelers. The saucers were military surplus, I discovered, and the Tour Boss passed them out like free seaweed. I remembered my worries about special privilege and felt pretty sour.

But there wasn't a single Antarean multibrach among the tourists or officials, which was a relief though we made a point of not commenting.

The Earthan natives themselves gave me the creeps, I have to admit, when we got through our student period and were privileged to hover real low and make landings. There is something just plain sickening about appendages that look like tentacles but turn out to be rigid except for a couple of joints—it makes one think of paralysis and calcification, a sort of living death. These Earthans looked like arthritic heptapussies with only four tentacles, the other three either cropped off (ugh!) or twined in a permanent tight knot at the tops of their bodies (double ugh!).

When Sis first discovered that the Earthans had bones inside their tentacles she actually took sick!

But Education dispells all hostilities (except toward Antareans—I'll have to spring that point on Dad some day). The more I observed and studied Earthans, the more I got to sympathize with them and the less their unfortunate forms disturbed my appetite. There were a lot of background capsules on Earthan culture available at Center, with new bulletins being added every day. What's more, Dad made each of us learn a different Earthan language. For one and a half tentacles of the time (that's three fourteenths—figure it out for yourself) each of us kids had to do textbook drill or monitor Earthan broadcasts in the appropriate language on our personal radios.

Together with our vacation classwork (Dad had meant it about my tensor calculus!) and the saucer-waxing and all, we weren't left with exactly a plethora of spare time, yet somehow we all throve and managed to be happier than I ever remember. Even Mom enjoyed herself thoroughly. She got green as a girl and joined in so many of our activities that Dad had to remind her not to neglect her introspection. (Where would any family be if its deep mind quit working?)

All the other tourists seemed to be enjoying themselves equally. There is something terrifically stimulating and enriching, you see, about watching and listening in on the first gropings of an infant racial intelligence and seeing whether it will decide to love, mostly, and live— or hate, mostly, and die. It reunites you with the mainsprings of life and you have the privilege of reaffirming your own race's decision—or so the thought capsules think.

These Earthans were in a pretty perilous fix, all right. They were divided into two large federations of semi-industrialized nations, one of them believing that people should be controlled by appealing to their appetites and the other to their fears. (Dad says I am oversimplifying.) Each federation had fission and fusion weapons and was putting up unmanned and a few manned satelites. And they were both experimenting with underground nuclear explosions—shallow ones so far, fortunately.

OUR SAUCER VACATION

The Earthans were fiercely competitive, you soon saw that, and pretty strong haters, but they were warm-hearted and loving critters, too. It made me sort of shiver to think that in a few more orbits, if they took the wrong turning, they and their lovely little planet would be just a smoky red cinder. Each time Dad dove our saucer down through the silky white clouds I filled up with determination to drink in every last infinitely precious detail (I never ran across any green weavers, however, though I always kept expecting them.)

I got to feeling pretty gooey about the Earthans in spite of the bones in their tentacles and several times I caught myself wishing, especially after I'd mastered a language or two, that I could reveal myself to them and explain that there was no need to perish, that all around them was a strong brotherhood aching to receive them. I rather fancied myself in the role of boy savior, though the Earthans might have found my seven green tentacles rather wild. (I'd thought of a way around that, though.)

For a couple of orbits my gloomy feelings nearly got me down, and, just as if I were a little kid again, I found myself spending a lot of time twisting and shaping my tentacles into fantastic forms. (We are all pretty good at that sort of thing—Dad can do wonderful animal faces.) Then I took stock and whipped myself back into good humor.

About this time I started to pal around quite a bit with a young heptapus named Tab. He was quite a deep-minded logician, even more sympathetic than I towards the Earthans, and inclined to be quietly contemptuous of Mind Watchers and police, though he knew the rule book as well as I did (I tested him). Tab's parents were very intellectual too; they pulled a lot of weight at the group-fests at Center and at times (I blush to admit it) they seemed to me a shade more stylish than Dad and Mom.

When I first met Tab I thought here was my chance to start a Young Rangers patrol, but then I decided he was too intellectual for that sort of thing.

Tab had a lot of sharp ideas that were very suitable for chewing over and a lot of interesting if doubtful information—such as that the more progressive Mind Watchers had worked out nondestructive methods for maturing infant races, but that the conservative majority had blocked their employment.

A couple of times I went for a ride in Tab's family's saucer. It was pretty aesthetic the way they appreciated Earth—there was none of the wisecracking that Dad and us kids (and even Mom) would have been doing. Tab's father had a way of steering towards things that made them more beautiful. They took me to several of their favorite spots on Earth, especially a wooded mountain with a big dome on it housing some sort of telescope, I believe. We landed there and got out to stretch our tentacles—not by the dome, though, but in a little glade down the mountain side. It was one of their "secret places," Tab's mother explained—none of the other tourists had discovered it yet, she said, and she asked me not to tell. I didn't see anything very wonderful about it, I must admit, though it was nice enough. We rested there for some time, idly spying on an Earthan who came out of a little house and sniffed around for a while as if he sensed something out of the ordinary. In fact he muttered something about "hearing things" in the argot of the area, which happened to be the one I knew (American, it's called) and even spread his arms wide (he was a solemn chap) and intoned: "Oh spirits, if you have come, speak!" At that moment I caught Tab's father giving Tab a sharp negate, though I hadn't caught what Tab's question or suggestion had been. (This only stuck in my memory because both Tab's father and Tab froze when they realized I might be listening.) Very soon after we took off again.

And once Tab went for a ride in our saucer. He was polite but he hardly said a word, although Dad tried to draw him out, and I got the impression that he disapproved, in a kindly fashion, of the way my family did things. After that our friendship chilled considerably.

Eventually I told Dad something of my private sympathies for the maybe-doomed Earthans and even about my guilty dreams of helping them.

Dad just looked at me very seriously and said, "Now you understand, Son, why the rule book is so danged persnickety. Always remember, Son, that for all his mighty civilization the heptapus is the most lawless animal in the whole universe—fierce, reckless and bloody. Compared to him, the yorfis is a grinni. Civilized—my sixth eye! He needs rules, plenty of them!"

Privately I thought Dad was being romantic, describing us heptapussies that way. Still, I'll admit it made me suck in my tentacles a bit with a sort of embarrassed pride.

Me—seven-branch killer! Hah!

Not three orbits later I'd changed my mind about Dad—he was a complete realist on heptapussies, I decided, at least when it came to the lawless part.

It wasn't any one big thing that made me change my mind, it was that a lot of little incidents had multiplied to the point where they couldn't be ignored or euphemized any more, by me or anyone else.

It amounted to this: *most of the tourists, but the heptapussies in particular, were getting so careless about the way they handled their personal vehicles that Earthans were becoming aware that there were alien spacecraft in their skies.*

We'd noticed instances before—I've mentioned one or two of them—but thought them exceptions. Now it was clear that the exception was becoming the rule and the rule book a dead letter.

Tourists were letting their saucers become positively opaque—I honestly believe some of them hadn't been airwaxed since the Tour Boss assigned them.

Other saucers were airwaxed so sloppily—the goo just thrown on—that there were conspicuous highlights.

Routine precautions against creating vapor trails were just plain neglected.

Pilots of such slop-saucers (as Dad called them) seemed to make a special point of hovering over Earthan towns, stunting over cities, buzzing known atomic installations, playing "chicken" with Earthan aircraft and tag with each other, and the like.

Some dumped garbage, if you can believe it. Dad said the behavior of some tourists is beyond belief. It takes great faith.

Saucers skimming low through Earth's cone of night followed Earthan roads, deliberately flashed lights at Earthan landcraft, let themselves be silhouetted against the Moon, and I don't know what else. Slop-saucers joined together to cut these didoes in formation, in groups of five and seven!

As for the things we heard about the high jinks engaged in by tourists landed from saucers, sometimes in populous areas—well, they were just plain incredible.

But I remembered what Dad had said about "great faith." I knotted my thinking tentacles and managed to credit.

What was happening added up to an outbreak of mass mischief, kindergarten level, among the majority of the tourists—a disgusting enough outbreak to turn even a juvenile delinquent (as Dad often describes me) into a confirmed lawman.

Even back at Reception Center the atmosphere of giggly hysteria was so thick you could have used it to curdle interstellar space into an edible sickly sweet jelly. Supposedly hyper-mature tourists, including a majority of the heptapussies, acted just plain silly drunk.

Here and there were a few families who abstained from dementia, notably Tab's. Our friendship warmed up again.

Even Sis caught the bug, went for a ride in a girl-friend's saucer, and came back hee-hee-heeing about how they'd got some Earthan aircraft following them in circles and flashing lights back at them.

OUR SAUCER VACATION

I don't think it does to describe spankings. They ought to be kept a family secret, especially when a girl is involved. I'll only say I didn't know Mom had it in her.

Really, all this nonsense had been warming up for a long time, probably antedating our own arrival at Center, but we'd tried not to believe it. Now we could no longer keep our thinking eyes closed.

What's more: *the Tour Boss and the police weren't doing anything about it*. Not anything with teeth in it, that is, not anything really calculated to *stop the idiots*.

Oh, they engaged in considerable wrist slapping, but so gentle it wouldn't have stung a baby's tentacle tip. They issued a lot of "reminders" and "warnings"—they even Centerized a couple of saucers. (This last looked like business, but it turned out that the main drives of the two offending saucers had broken down and they'd been *barely snatched out of the hands of the Earthan police* before being towed back to Center for repairs.)

I'd typed the Tour Boss as a butterer-up and backslapper from the start. Now he seemed so moon-facedly in love with his reputation for good nature and helpfulness that he didn't dare chance offending one delirious custard head.

As for the police, they acted like tourists wearing badges. End of character estimate.

Don't get me wrong—it was all quite funny of course. I especially derived a sickly sort of amusement from the "reminders" and "warnings" that were forever going up on the bulletin board. For one thing, they threw considerable light on the Earthan hysteria.

Seems that Earthan beings were madly squabbling among themselves as to whether or not the saucers were real or just a silly-season phenomenon. (Small wonder that no Earthans seemed able to deduce that the saucers were both real *and* silly.) Factions and cults were formed, for and against saucers. Some even worshipped us, it was reported. Earthan enthusiasts climbed mountains and stayed up nights to watch for saucers, then spread the word like maniacs. Saucer hysteria would break out now here, now there, as our lovable little slop-saucer irresponsibles shifted their antics from one area to another. I panicked myself imagining how Earth ought soon to start rocking like a boat from Earthan saucer-bugs rushing back and forth from one side of the planet to the other.

But the next tentacle to self-panicking is self-disgust. One orbit even a joker like me wakes up to the realization that there isn't anything one bit funny about super-beings behaving like tots kootchy-kootchy tickled into prankish delirium—*or* about dawn creatures (I mean the Earthans) being goosed into hysteria in the midst of a somber and crucial struggle between their own strong loves and hates and while trying to make a for-all-times decision between life and death.

Not one bit funny at all.

We tourists were tampering with a bud planet. A few more orbits of such prankishness and Earth's potential for growth and free choice would be irremediably warped.

Once that thought was expressed in our family (I think it was Mom who put it into symbols) we went into action. At least Dad did. (Dad always says, "Son, if your thinking tentacles stop manipulating real objects it doesn't matter what beautiful thoughts they curl around.")

Dad set us kids to double-waxing our saucer, which we first wafted into an area of Center reserved for groupfests, and then he went out to organize a protest committee.

He reported back a weary time later and said he'd got a fair response. Tab's family had been the first to join with him and they'd been very eager about it, which bucked him up considerably and made him think, he said, that we actually might be able to do something by sweet reason alone.

Just the same I noticed him slip a package in nothingness fabric aboard our fanatically airwaxed saucer (which takes sharp eyes if I do say myself?). I quizzed him and he drew me in close and unwrapped it enough to show me two paralysis pistols. How he'd laid his squeezers on those I can't imagine. (Later I found he'd got the Armorer's girlfriend and then the Armorer drunk. To get the liquor in the first place, he'd had to square the Cellarer, how I never did discover. You know, I think Dad would do very well on a pirate planet.)

"Son," he said, "I'm showing you these because if we have to use them I want your squeezer around one. Strictly felonious, of course, and could get you five hundred orbits in a frost cell of Blackgarth."

I had to squeeze my eyes hard, all five of them.

I went to the groupfab Dad and Tad's father had called feeling as if I were muscled like a sea-yorfis and with a spiked iron club in each tentacle. Our family—our *two*-man family—would show these slop-saucerites something!

I came out of it feeling like a sick grinni.

Tab's father had sabotaged our whole effort!—and for the moment neither Dad nor I could figure out why; we were just stunned.

Dad had made a blistering introductory statement and then called on his supposed chief supporter. That caused a big flurry of excitement because Tab's father had come to be the chief speaker at most groupfabs, a heptapus everyone looked up to. He wafted himself to the rostrum, wrapped a couple of tentacles around the frame, and began a long rigmarole about how he supported Dad because of the principle of the thing although there was no practical need to worry about Earthans catching on to the presence of the tourists. Somehow he'd got hold of a Mind Watcher file on Earth and now he quoted it to show that Earthans were forever believing they were seeing strange objects in their skies. Thousands of earth orbits ago Earthans had been seeing fiery chariots streaking around overhead; that they should think they were seeing similar things now was just normal Earthan behavior and had nothing or almost nothing to do with our saucers! Earthan history proved that such epidemics of mass hysteria recurred at regular intervals. Still, he affirmed, he supported Dad for *aesthetic reasons!* Tourists ought always to behave beautifully for beauty's own sake, and now that everyone had been reminded of it he was sure that they would! The most important thing, he said, was for us not to fight among ourselves: tourist dissensions could harm dawn folk—and he quoted instances.

Boy, that was just the opening the Tour Boss was waiting for! With sickening joviality he promised to send everyone daily reminders to behave beautifully and then he went on to thank Tab's father for presenting the matter so smoothly and intelligently—and by implication to castigate Dad for being an uncivilized alarmist. When he finished you'd have thought Dad had tried to start a riot and Tab's father had saved the day for decorum.

I expected Dad to make a fight of it, but for once he failed me. He just looked around, a bit grimly perhaps, and wafted out of the fab without comment.

Tab's father called gayly to Tab and the rest of his family to join him right away at their saucer, that he had a little expedition in mind—a beautiful piece of good-example-setting, I thought bitterly.

I slunk out after Dad, feeling like a sick grinni to be sure, but eager to talk about the why of Tab's father's double cross.

It turned out Dad had something else on his mind, something trivial. I got real irked at him.

"Later on, son," he said. "I just remembered it's Vrup's birthday."

Dad always remembers birthdays.

The Interstellar Sender was pretty suspicious of Dad's request—probably he'd had a warning that Dad might try to go over the Tour Boss's head—but when he found Dad merely wanted to send Interstellar Greeting 3 he simmered down and got condescendingly friendly.

OUR SAUCER VACATION

All he'd have to do would be to send Vrup's planet address and a 3 and Vrup would get a message gold-embossed and a yard long with magenta fringe beginning with "May the stars show forth the secrets of the All-Father and the whole planet know on this your natal day," or some folderol like that.

It wasn't at all like Dad to use standardized messages. He must be slipping, it flashed through my mind, after the big slap he got at the fab—and instantly gave myself a big mental slap for having the thought.

Still his business with the Sender gave me time to straighten out my ideas.

"Dad," I said, tight-beaming it, as soon as he was free, "Tab's father is just too all-fired smart to believe what he said about slop-saucers *not* being responsible for Earthen saucer hysteria. He's a custard head, all right, but it's thinking custard."

"I agree, Son." Very quiet, very tight.

"So he must have another reason for not wanting sightseeing curtailed in any way. Dad, I think he *wants* the Earthans to know about us. In fact, he *must* want just that. He *must* want Earthans to know about the Galactic Union before they're adjudged to have made their free choice for life or death."

"Go on, Son."

"Well, if he *wants* something so contrary to tradition the chances are that he's *actively working* for it as well—that he's already set up or setting up contact with the Earthans."

"I triple check you, Son. Those thoughts are mine. He must be in or entering contact. But can you pin it down any further?"

"Dad, I think I can," I beamed eagerly and went on to tell about my last ride in Tab's family saucer.

"Round up Sis and Shorty, Son," Dad said as soon as I'd finished, and he was light-heartedly loose-beaming now. "I'll get Mom. I think it would be nice if we all went on a picnic—" (he tightened his beam again) "—at a certain secret glade."

I don't ever remember Earth's cloud flocks looking as soft and dazzlingly white. Maybe we didn't make our approach "beautifully" but we threaded through them without disturbing a wisp of vapor or adding or subtracting one iota of shimmer—as any well-piloted saucer should.

We spotted the wooded mountain with the big dome on it. Dad withdrew his tentacles from the controls.

"Take over, Son," he said.

This time I didn't feel any extra muscles or spiked clubs, I just felt like a grown-up heptapus with a job to do. I took us on a smooth curve to the secret glade—there was something going on there, all right!—and I brought us down, not in the glade, but in a narrow gap between two nearby trees, without jogging one lightly poised dried leaf. Grass leaned lazily away from the saucer as I landed—that was all.

Next thing Dad and I were out and advancing and there was something reassuringly solid (and responsible-making) in one of my free squeezers. We didn't send one crumb of sound or thought ahead of us, not even when we peered into the glade.

The Earthan I'd seen there before was kneeling on the far side of the glade, looking exalted. I might have guessed from that that he was a primitive esper and receiving, but I didn't need to—all around us, loose beamed, were spraying the Great Thoughts, the Secrets of the Galactic Union.

They were coming from Tab's father, who was on the near side of the glade with his family artistically grouped around him. Translucent green against the green forest, he was standing lightly on two tentacles and waving the other five in rythmic hypnotic passes—very beautifully. The stinking custard head was giving way to his sloppy desires to share and save!—and a little mystery that had nagged my mind many orbits was solved.

"Green weaver," I tight-beamed Dad, "and lambent as Old Scratch."

"Right, Son," Dad responded. "Take him, son, at median power. I'll take his brood."

Our paralysis pistols sighed as one. Tab's father, I am pleased to say, froze in a particularly graceful attitude. The Great Thoughts seemed to hang motionless in the air a moment, then fall like autumn leaves.

On the other side of the glade the Earthan slowly got to his feet. I could see and sense that he was still exalted, though beginning to be a little puzzled now.

There flashed into my mind the terrific problem still facing us. The Great Thoughts had been loosed in this bud planet, Tab's father had seen to that. By all the laws of psyco-dynamics they would spread and fill this planet, driving out all lesser thoughts, conquering all errors, until all Earthans would know about the Galactic Union and their race's situation *before making their free choice*.

Of course we could kill or kidnap this particular Earthan, or wipe his mind. Such an act would in itself be a tremendous violation of tradition. Still, we could do it—Dad had proven himself a lawless pistol-packer and I was his son.

But how could we be sure that would take care of things? The Great Thoughts had been loosed. Tab's father could have made revelations to this Earthan which he might already have passed to other Earthans.

What could we do to nullify those possibilities? How do you rope a runaway thought? I'd always been taught that it is in the nature of the Great Thoughts that they drive out lesser thoughts. What psyco-dynamic pattern (if any!) could we send out after the runaway Great Thoughts that would render them ineffectual?

As I say, all this shot into my mind in an instant. I turned toward Dad, meaning to beam a question. He was stepping confidently into the glade.

I have mentioned that Dad was very good at doing pseudo shapes with his tentacles, at imitating other forms with them simply by superb muscular control. Now two of his walking tentacles had become green legs—just like those of an Earthan though shorter and stockier than most. The tentacle tips turned up like the toes of fabulous green slippers.

His other walking tentacle and one of his handling tentacles had become stubby green arms, which looked as if they ended in little mittened hands.

His body was deep purple—I realized he must be using self-suggestion to induce our typical resentment reaction.

But the three top tentacles (one handling, two "thinking"—really, fine-handling) were his masterpiece. They were intricately yet smoothly knotted together into a large grotesque Earthan head that was mostly face. Two bold tentacle curves made a great ridged brow over cavernous eye sockets, others formed cheeks and chin. A partly contracted tentacle end made a large beaky nose. His eyes figured as buttons down his waist.

Dad had become a brawny little green man in a purple jacket.

The eyes of the Earthan on the other side of the glade grew wide. He took a staggering backward step. "Good God, no!" he cried.

The Green Dwarf—I mean Dad—raised an arm. A slit opened in his lower face.

"Afraid be not," Dad croaked—in American too, of course. "I waft in peace and love to untangle all hard-knotted confusions." He stood stock still and pointed at Tab's father, whose paralyzed form at this moment overbalanced and fell with a gentle *swush* in a pile of dried leaves.

"Him Martian. *Bad*." Dad croaked. He turned a green mitt toward his own purple middle. "Me Venusian. *Good*. I tell all. We go for a ride in my saucer—no?" He turned slowly toward me, giving me plenty of time to get ready, and extended a commanding mitt.

"Fetch same," he ordered me.

My Green Dwarf wasn't nearly as good as Dad's (for

one thing my purple jacket kept fading out) but it didn't have to be—Dad had made the crucial impression and the Earthan couldn't keep his eyes off him. I was a green-blobby reasonable facsimile.

Bowing low, I rapidly backed out of the glade. I wasn't absolutely sure yet what Dad's game was, but I had a good idea. As soon as I got back to our saucer I told everybody to ask no questions but make like Green Dwarfs, though I didn't use that exact expression because I didn't trust their knowledge of Earthan mythology. I told Shorty I'd ram his tentacles down his gullet if he cut up.

Then I wafted us back to the glade. I had to tip the saucer at an eighty degree angle to squeeze between some of the trees, but I managed.

Dad had obviously been making the most of his time. He was calling the Earthan Mister Adamovich now and the Earthan was calling him Dear Guru. They seemed like real buddies. Dad was saying, "Ah yes, that was when we built the caves under your cities which the evil ones still occupy, warping your minds with cunning rays. You need much Venus-thought to fight that. Much!"

Mister Adamovich got another shock when he saw the four of us gliding into the glade on a heat shimmer, but he got over it fast. In fact he showed himself a pretty brave man, because not long afterwards we were hoisting him aboard and strapping him down for the little spin Dad had promised. I think he almost lost his nerve as the invisible band tightened around his middle. Dad said something soothing.

It was of course just about the dullest ride imaginable, as this Earthan didn't seem able to take anything but the mildest accelerations and I surely didn't want him to pop anything inside his half-calcified carcass. It was a proud moment for me that Dad let me do the piloting. I took her up between the trees as gently as if I were transporting seven maiden aunts with lace-coral tiaras and then I put her through her paces at funeral tempo—I swear I didn't use more than 4 G's at any time.

But to see the way this Mister Adamovich kept changing color and closing his eyes and gulping and leaning this way and that and clutching first at the side-bar and then at Dad, you'd have thought we were the Special Number in some all-galactic space-o-batics show.

Between turns and jumps and drops Dad kept filling Mister Adamovich full of more stuff on us Venusians: how we'd come from Atlantis and Mu originally (here Dad's Earthen mythology began to get ahead of me, but I made him repeat it to me later) and about the Wars of the Evil Tyrants and the Great Interplanetary Migrations, and the Martian Conflict and the Giant Love-Girls, whoever they were.

Among other things Dad told Mister Adamovich that any number of Earthan beings were or had really been Venusians in disguise (or Martians sometimes): Plato, Aristotle, Cleopatra, The Black Prince, Roger Bacon Cagliostro, Madame Blavatsky, Einstein, Edgar Rice Burroughs, Greta Garbo, Peter Lorre, Bela Lugosi, Edward Teller, Gerald Heard, Richard Shaver, Hugo Gernsback, Marilyn Monroe, and I doubt if even Dad can remember all the names he gave out with.

I suppose it must have been quite an experience to Mister Adamovich dodging around through the clouds (at a snail's pace, really) with us five maniacs in a ship he could only feel and being pumped full of all this information at the same time.

Of course by now I realized exactly what Dad was doing and I was filled with the intensest admiration. No matter what or how much Tab's father had esped to this Earthan, it couldn't compete with this stuff that was being sewed into his soul along with the gentle joy-ride. His experience with Tab's father must have seemed to some degree dreamlike.

Oh yes, Mister Adamovich was convinced all right. To his dying day he'd believe every word Dad had told him and do his best to get other Earthans to believe them—maybe along with the Great Thoughts, maybe without.

But only Mister Adamovich would have had Mister Adamovich's experience. Not another halfway intelligent Earthan would credit for a moment the nonsense Dad had filled him up with—and insofar as they discredited his nonsense they'd discredit the Great Thoughts too. Earth would still be able to make her free choice between life and death, secure from any knowledge of the Galactic Union.

Later on Dad summed it up for me this way: "Son, the Great Thoughts can drive out any lesser thoughts—but not pure hokum."

As soon as I brought her down Dad hustled Mister Adamovich out of the saucer and out of the glade too, fast—on the grounds that we mustn't take any chances with more spying Martians or cave folk or Giant Love-Girls or any other of the mythological rabble. As they left I heard Dad starting to repeat for good measure all the stuff he'd told Mister Adamovich in the sky.

I knew what to do without Dad's high-sign. I located Tab's family saucer and we piled them all in it, still happily paralyzed, and strapped them down. When Dad got back (the Earthan's house hadn't been far) he and I piloted the two saucers back to Center without any mishaps.

I expected we'd run into all sorts of a ruckus there—in fact I was thinking that at least I'd have a good yarn to tell the other convicts on Blackgarth—but it turned out that Dad had taken care of everything there too. As I would have guessed if I hadn't been so irked at the time, his birthday greeting to Vrup had been a tip-off. It hadn't been Vrup's birthday at all and as soon as Vrup had read that stuff about the stars showing forth secrets to the whole planet he'd tumbled to what Dad was trying to tell him and had alerted the Mind Watchers and the Galactic Coordinators fast and they'd jumped on the Tour Boss and the circum-Terran police—instantaneously!

They made an example of the planet. A tight censorship was thrown around Earth and every last tourist was cleaned out of the Solar System—the Tour Boss and police too needless to say, though I never have found out if they ended up on Blackgarth.

The Tourists included Dad and me and the rest of the family, of course, so our saucer vacation was cut short. But it had certainly been exciting while it lasted.

I told Dad, we ought to be privileged to stay on because he'd so beautifully solved the problem of keeping the Earthans in the dark, but he told me to shut up about that. "Doesn't do to whip your own gong, Son," he said, "and the experts always take a dim view of the homely methods of the grunch-doctor."

Because of the unexpected load on galactic travel facilities we had to translate back in two jumps—with the stopover at Antares Three, if you please. We spent a goosey two sleeptimes there, expecting every minute to be lynched.

One of the things I remember saying to Dad while we were all talking fast to keep up our courage was: "Hey, with all this censorship we'll probably never find out what happens to Earth. Do you think they'll explode themselves, Dad?"

He shrugged his tentacles. "Son," he said, "it's a race's privilege to die if it wants to. What the Earthans do with the Earth is their problem." There was a little crackling sound like a multibrach sneaking up and Dad shot a quick look in all directions. Then he told me, "You worry about what happens to heptapussies."

PIPE DREAM

It wasn't until the mermaid turned up in his bathtub that Simón Grue seriously began to wonder what the Russians were doing on the roof next door.

The old house next door together with its spacious tar-papered roof, which held a sort of pent-shack, a cylindrical old water tank, and several chicken-wire enclosures, had always been a focus of curiosity in this region of Greenwich Village, especially to whoever happened to be renting Simon's studio, the north window-cum-skylight of which looked down upon it—if you were exceptionally tall or if, like Simon, you stood halfway up a stepladder and peered.

During the 1920's, old timers told Simon, the house had been owned by a bootlegger, who had installed a costly pipe organ and used the water tank to store hooch. Later there had been a colony of shaven-headed Buddhist monks, who had strolled about the roof in their orange and yellow robes, meditating and eating raw vegetables. There had followed a *commedia dell'arte* theatrical group, a fencing salon, a school of the organ (the bootlegger's organ was always one of the prime renting points of the house), an Arabian restaurant, several art schools and silvercraft shops of course, and an Existentialist coffee house. The last occupants had been two bony-cheeked Swedish blondes who sunbathed interminably and had built the chicken-wire enclosures to cage a large number of sinister smoke-colored dogs—Simon decided they were breeding werewolves, and one of his most successful abstractions, "Gray Hunger," had been painted to the inspiration of an eldritch howling. The dogs and their owners had departed abruptly one night in a closed van, without any of the dogs ever having been offered for sale or either of the girls having responded with anything more than a raised eyebrow to Simon's brave greetings of "Skoal!"

The Russians had taken possession about six months ago—four brothers apparently, and one sister, a beauty, who never stirred from the house but could occasionally be seen peering dreamily from a window. A white card with a boldly-inked "Stulnikov-Gurevich" had been thumbtacked to the peeling green-painted front door. Lafcadio Smits, the interior decorator, told Simon that the newcomers were clearly White Russians; he could tell it by their several bushy beards. Lester Phlegius maintained that they were Red Russians passing as White, and talked alarmingly of spying, sabotage and suitcase bombs.

Simon, who had the advantages of living on the spot and having been introduced to one of the brothers—Vasily—at a neighboring art gallery, came to believe that they were both Red and White and something more—solid, complete Slavs in any case, Double Dostoevsky Russians if one may be permitted the expression. They ordered vodka, caviar, and soda crackers by the case. They argued interminably (loudly in Russian, softly in English), they went on mysterious silent errands, they gloomed about on the roof, they made melancholy music with their deep harmonious voices and several large guitars. Once Simon thought they even had the bootlegger's organ going, but there had been a bad storm at the time and he hadn't been sure.

They were not quite as tightlipped as the Swedish girls. Gradually a curt front-sidewalk acquaintance developed and Simon came to know their names. There was Vasily, of course, who wore thick glasses, the most scholarly-looking of the lot and certainly the most bibulous—Simon came to think of Vasily as the Vodka Breather. Occasionally he could be glimpsed holding Erlenmeyer flasks, trays of culture dishes, and other pieces of biological equipment, or absent-mindedly wiping off a glass slide with his beard. When Lester Phlegius heard that, he turned pale and whispered, "Germ warfare!"

Then there was Ivan, the dourest of the four, though none of them save Vasily seemed very amiable. Simon's private names for Ivan were the Nihilst and the Bomber, since he sometimes lugged about with him a heavy globular leather case. With it and his beard—a square black one—he had more than once created a mild sensation in the narrow streets of the Village.

Next there was Mikhail, who wore a large crucifix on a silver chain around his neck and looked like a more spiritual Rasputin. However, Simon thought of him less as the Religious than as the Whistler—for his inveterate habit of whistling into his straggly beard a strange tune that obeyed no common harmonic laws. Somehow Mikhail seemed to carry a chilly breeze around with him, a perpetual cold draught, so that Simon had to check himself in order not to clutch together his coat collar whenever he heard the approach of the eerie piping.

Finally there was Lev, beardless, shorter by several inches, and certainly the most elusive of the brothers. He always moved at a scurry, frequently dipping his head, so that it was some time before Simon assured himself that he had the Stulnikov-Gurevich face. He did, unmistakably. Lev seemed to be away on trips a good deal. On his returns he was frequently accompanied by furtive but important-looking men—a different one on each occasion. There would be much bustle at such times—among other things, the shades would be drawn. Then in a few hours Lev would be off again, and his man-about-town companion too.

And of course there was the indoors-keeping sister.

Several times Simon had heard one of the brothers calling "Grushenka," so he assumed that was her name. She had the Stulnikov-Gurevich face too, though on her, almost incredibly, it was strangely attractive. She never ventured out on the roof but she often sat in the pent-shack. As far as Simon could make out, she always wore some dark Victorian costume—at least it had a high neck, long sleeves, and puffed shoulders. Pale-faced in the greenish gloom, she would stare for hours out of the pent-shack's single window, though never in Simon's direction. Occasionally she would part and close her lips, but not exactly as if she were speaking, at least aloud—he thought of calling her the Bubble Blower. The effect was as odd as Mikhail's whistling but not as unpleasant. In fact, Simon found himself studying Grushenka for ridiculously long periods of time. His mild obsession began to irk him and one day he decided henceforth to stay away altogether from his north window and the stepladder. As a result he saw little of the alterations the Russians began to make on the roof at this point, though he did notice that they lugged up among other things a length of large-diameter transparent plastic piping.

So much for the Russians, now for the mermaid. Late one night Simon started to fill his bathtub with cold water to soak his brushes and rags—he was working with a kind of calcimine at the time, experimenting with portable murals painted on large plaster-faced wooden panels. Heavily laden, he got back to the bathroom just in time to shut off the water—and to see a tiny fish of some sort splashing around in it.

He was not unduly surprised. Fish up to four or five inches in length were not unheard-of apparitions in the cold-water supply of the area, and this specimen looked as if it displaced no more than a teaspoon of water.

He made a lucky grab and the next moment he was holding in his firmly clenched right hand the bottom half of a slim wriggling creature hardly two inches long —and now Simon was surprised indeed.

To begin with, it was not greenish white nor any common fish color, but palely-pinkish, flesh-colored in fact. And it didn't seem so much a fish as a tadpole—at least its visible half had a slightly oversize head shaped like a bullet that has mushroomed a little, and two tiny writhing arms or appendages of some sort—and it felt as if it had rather large hips for a fish or even a tadpole. Equip a two-months human embryo with a finny tail, give it in addition a precocious feminine sexiness, and you'd get something of the same effect.

But all that was nothing. The trouble was that it had a face—a tiny face, of course, and rather goggly-ghostly like a planarian's, but a face nevertheless—a human-looking face, and also (here was the real trouble) a face that bore a grotesque but striking resemblance to that of Grushenka Stulnikov-Gurevich.

Simon's fingers tightened convulsively. Simultaneously the slippery creature gave a desperate wriggle. It shot into the air in a high curve and fell into the scant inch of space between the bathtub and the wall.

The next half hour was hectic in a groveling sort of way. Retrieving anything from behind Simon's ancient claw-footed bathtub was a most difficult feat. There was barely space to get an arm under it and at one point the warping of the floor boards prevented even that. Besides, there was the host of dust-shrouded objects it had previously been too much trouble to tease out—an accumulation of decades. At first Simon tried to guide himself by the faint flopping noise along the hidden base of the wall, but these soon ceased.

Being on your knees and your chest with an ear against the floor and an arm strainingly outstretched is probably not the best position to assume while weird trains of thought go shooting through your head, but sometimes it has to happen that way. First came a remembered piece of neighborhood lore that supported the possibility of a connection between the house next door and the tiny pink aquatic creature now suffering minute agonies behind the bathtub. No one knew what ancient and probably larceny-minded amateur plumber was responsible, but the oldtimers assured Simon there was a link between the water supply of the Russians' house with its aerial cistern and that of the building containing Simon's studio and several smaller apartments; at any rate they maintained that there had been a time during the period when the bootlegger was storing hooch in the water tank that several neighborhood cold-water taps were dispensing a weak but nonetheless authoritative mixture of bourbon and branch water.

So, thought Simon as he groped and strained, if the Russians were somehow responsible for this weird fishlet, there was no insuperable difficulty in understanding how it might have got here.

But that was the least of Simon's preoccupations. He scrabbled wildly and unsuccessfully for several minutes. Then realizing he would never get anywhere in this unsystematic manner, he began to remove the accumulated debris piece by piece: dark cracked ends of soap, washrags dried out in tortured attitudes, innumerable dark-dyed cigarette stumps, several pocket magazines with bleached wrinkled pages, empty and near-empty medicine bottles and pill vials, rusty hairpins, bobby pins, safety pins, crumpled toothpaste tubes (and a couple for oil paint), a gray toothbrush, a fifty-cent piece and several pennies, the mummy of a mouse, a letter from Picasso, and last of all, from the dark corner behind the bathtub's inside claw, the limp pitiful thing he was seeking.

It was even tinier than he'd thought. He carefully washed the dust and flug off it, but it was clearly dead and its resemblance to Grushenka Stulnikov-Gurevich had become problematical—indeed, Simon decided that someone seeing it now for the first time would think it a freak minnow or monstrous tadpole and nothing more, though mutation or disease had obviously been at work.

PIPE DREAM

The illusion of a miniature mermaid still existed in the tapering tail and armlike appendages, but it was faint. He tried to remember what he knew about salamanders—almost nothing, it turned out. He thought of embryos, but his mind veered away from the subject.

He wandered back into the studio carrying the thing in his hand. He climbed the stepladder by the north window and studied the house next door. What windows he could see were dark. He got a very vague impression that the roof had changed. After he had strained his eyes for some time he fancied he could see a faint path of greenish luminescence streaming between the pent-shack and the water-tank, but it was very faint indeed and might only be his vision swimming.

He climbed down the stepladder and stood for a moment weighing the tiny dead thing in his hand. It occurred to him that one of his friends at the university could dig up a zoologist to pass on his find.

But Simon's curiosity was more artistic than scientific. In the end he twisted a bit of cellophane around the thing, placed it on the ledge of his easel and went off to bed . . . and to a series of disturbingly erotic dreams.

Next day he got up late and, after breakfast on black coffee, gloomed around the studio for a while, picking things up and putting them down. He glanced frequently at the stepladder, but resisted the temptation to climb up and have another look next door. Sighing, he thumbtacked a sheet of paper to a drawing board and half-heartedly began blocking in a female figure. It was insipid and lifeless. Stabbing irritably at the heavy curve of the figure's hip, he broke his charcoal. "Damn!" he said, glaring around the room. Abandoning all pretense, he threw the charcoal on the floor and climbed the stepladder. He pressed his nose against the glass.

In daylight, the adjoining roof looked bare and grimy. There was a big transparent pipe running between the water tank and the shack, braced in two places by improvised-looking wooden scaffolding. Listening intently, Simon thought he could hear a motor going in the shack. The water looked sallow green. It reminded Simon of those futuristic algae farms where the stuff is supposed to be pumped through transparent pipes to expose it to sunlight. There seemed to be a transparent top on the water tank too—it was too high for Simon to see, but there was a gleam around the edge. Staring at the pipe again, Simon got the impression there were little things traveling in the water, but he couldn't make them out.

Climbing down in some excitement, Simon got the twist of cellophane from the ledge of the easel and stared at its contents. Wild thoughts were tumbling through his head as he got back up on the stepladder. Sunlight flashed on the greenish water pipe between the tank and the shack, but after the first glance he had no eyes for it. Grushenka Stulnikov-Gurevich had her face tragically pressed to the window of the shack. She was wearing the black dress with high neck and puffed shoulders. At that moment she looked straight at him. She lifted her hands and seemed to speak imploringly. Then she slowly sank from sight as if, it horridly occurred to Simon, into quicksand.

Simon sprang from his chair, heart beating wildly, and ran down the stairs to the street. Two or three passersby paused to study him as he alternately pounded the flaking green door of the Russians' house and leaned on the button. Also watching was the shirt-sleeved driver of a moving van, emblazoned "Stulnikov-Gurevich Enterprises," which almost filled the street in front of the house.

The door opened narrowly. A man with a square black beard frowned out of it. He topped Simon by almost a head.

"Yes?" Ivan the Bomber asked, in a deep, exasperated voice.

"I must see the lady of the house immediately," Simon cried. "Your sister, I believe. She's in danger." He surged forward.

PIPE DREAM

The butt of the Bomber's right palm took him firmly in the chest and he staggered back. The Bomber said coldly, "My sister is—ha!—taking a bath."

Simon cried, "In that case she's drowning!" and surged forward again, but the Bomber's hand stopped him short. "I'll call the police!" Simon shouted, flailing his limbs. The hand at his chest suddenly stopped pushing and began to pull. Gripped by the front of his shirt, Simon felt himself being drawn rapidly inside. "Let go! Help, a kidnapping!" he shouted to the inquisitive faces outside, before the door banged shut.

"No police!" rumbled the Bomber, assisting Simon upstairs.

"Now look here," Simon protested futilely. In the two-story-high living room to his right, the pipes of an organ gleamed golden from the shadows. At the second landing, a disheveled figure met them, glasses twinkling—Vasily the Vodka Breather. He spoke querulously in Russian to Ivan, who replied shortly, then Vasily turned and the three of them crowded up the narrow third flight to the pent-shack. This housed a small noisy machine, perhaps an aerator of some sort, for bubbles were streaming into the transparent pipe where it was connected to the machine; and under the pipe, sitting with an idiot smile on a chair of red plush and gilt, was a pale black-mustached man. An empty clear-glass bottle with a red and gold label lay on the floor at his feet. The opposite side of the room was hidden by a heavy plastic shower curtain. Grushenka Stulnikov-Gurevich was not in view.

Ivan said something explosive, picking up the bottle and staring at it. "Vodka!" he went on. "I have told you not to mix the pipe and the vodka! Now see what you have done!"

"To me it seemed hospitable," said Vasily with an apologetic gesture. "Besides, only one bottle—"

Ducking under the pipe where it crossed the pent-shack, Ivan picked up the pale man and dumped him crosswise in the chair, with his patent-leather shoes sticking up on one side and his plump hands crossed over his chest. "Let him sleep. First we must take down all the apparatus, before the capitalistic police arrive. Now what to do with this one?" He looked at Simon, and clenched one large and hairy fist.

"*Nyet-nyet-nyet*," said the Vodka Breather, and went to whisper in Ivan's ear. They both stared at Simon, who felt uncomfortable and began to back toward the door; but Ivan ducked agilely under the pipe and grasped him by the arm, pulling him effortlessly toward the roof exit. "Just come this way if you please, Mr. Gru-*ay*," said Vasily, hurrying after. As they left the shack, he picked up a kitchen chair.

Crossing the roof, Simon made a sudden effort and wrenched himself free. They caught him again at the edge of the roof, where he had run with nothing clearly in mind, but with his mouth open to yell. Suspended in the grip of the two Russians, with Ivan's meaty palm over his mouth, Simon had a momentary glimpse of the street below. A third bearded figure, Mikhail the Religious, was staring up at them from the sunny sidewalk. The melancholy face, the deep-socketed tormented eyes, and the narrow beard tangled with the dangling crucifix combined to give the effect of a Tolstoy novel's dust-jacket. As they hauled Simon away, he had the impression that a chilly breeze had sprung up and the street had darkened. In his ears was Mikhail's distant, oddly discordant whistling.

Grunting, the two brothers set Simon down on the kitchen chair and slid him across the roof until something hard but resilient touched the top of his head. It was the plastic pipe, through which, peering upward, he could see myriads of tiny polliwog-shapes flitting back and forth.

"Do us a kindness not to make noise," said Ivan, removing his palm. "My brother Vasily will now explain." He went away.

PIPE DREAM

Curiosity as much as shock kept Simon in his chair. Vasily, bobbing his head and smiling, sat down tailor-fashion on the roof in front of him. "First I must tell you, Mr. Gru-*ay*, that I am specialist in biological sciences. Here you see results of my most successful experiment." He withdrew a round clear-glass bottle from his pocket and unscrewed the top.

"Ah?" said Simon tentatively.

"Indeed yes. In my researches, Mr. Gru-*ay*, I discovered a chemical which will inhibit growth at any level of embryonic development, producing a viable organism at that point. The basic effect of this chemical is always toward survival at whatever level of development—one cell, a blastula, a worm, a fish, a four-legger. The research, which Lysenko scoffed at when I told him of it, I had no trouble in keeping secret, though at the time I was working as the unhappy collaborator of the godless soviets. But perhaps I am being too technical?"

"Not at all," Simon assured him.

"Good," Vasily said with simple satisfaction and gulped at his bottle. "Meanwhile my brother Mikhail was a religious brother at a monastery near Mount Athos, my Nihilist brother Ivan was in central Europe, while my third brother Lev, who is of commercial talents, had preceded us to the New World, where he always felt it would some day be our destiny to join one another.

"With the aid of brother Ivan, I and my sister Grushenka escaped from Russia. We picked up Mikhail from his monastery and proceeded here, where Lev had become a capitalist business magnate.

"My brothers, Ivan especially, were interested in my research. He had a theory that we could eventually produce hosts of men in this way, whole armies and political parties, all Nihilist and all of them Stulnikov-Gureviches. I assured him that this was impossible, that I could not play Cadmus, for free-swimming forms are one thing, we have the way to feed them in the aqueous medium; but to make fully developed mammals placental nourishment is necessary—that I cannot provide. Yet to please him I begin with (pardon me!) the egg of my sister, that was as good a beginning as any and perhaps it intrigued my vanity. Ivan dreamed his dreams of a Nihilist Stulnikov-Gurevich humanity—it was harmless, as I told myself."

Simon stared at him glassy-eyed. Something rather peculiar was beginning to happen inside his head—about an inch under the point where the cool water-filled plastic pipe pressed down on his scalp. Little ghostly images were darting—delightfully wispy little girl-things—smiling down at him impudently, then flirting away with a quick motion of their mermaid tails.

The sky had been growing steadily darker and now there came the growl of thunder. Against the purple-gray clouds Simon could barely make out the semi-transparent shapes of the golliwogs in the pipe over his head; but the images inside his mind were growing clearer by the minute.

"Ah, we have a storm," Vasily observed as the thunder growled again. "That reminds me of Mikhail, who is much influenced by our Finnish grandmother. He had the belief as a child that he could call up the winds by whistling for them—he even learned special wind musics from her. Later he became a Christian religious—there are great struggles in him. Mikhail objected to my researches when he heard I used the egg of my sister. He said we will produce millions of souls who are not baptized. I asked him how about the water they are in. He replied this is not the same thing, these little swimmers will wriggle in hell eternally. This worried him greatly. We tried to tell him I had not used the egg of my sister, only the egg of a fish.

"But he did not believe this, because my sister changed greatly at the time. She no longer spoke. She put on my mother's bathing costume (we are a family people) and retired to the bathtub all day long. I accepted this—at least in the water she is not violent. Mikhail said, 'See, her soul is now split into many unredeemed sub-souls, one each for the little swimmers. There is a sympathy between them—a hypnotic vibration. So long as you keep them near her, in that tank on the roof, this will be. If they were gone from there, far from there, the sub-souls would reunite and Grushenka's soul would be one again.' He begged me to stop my research, to dump it in the sea, to scatter it away, but Lev and Ivan demand I keep on. Yet Mikhail warned me that works of evil end in the whirlwind. I am torn and undecided." He gulped at his vodka.

Thunder growled louder. Simon was thinking, dreamily, that if the soul of Grushenka Stulnikov-Gurevich were split into thousands of sub-souls, vibrating hynotically in the nearby water tank, with at least one of them escaping as far as his bathtub, then it was no wonder if Grushenka had a strange attraction for him.

"But that is not yet the worst," Vasily continued. "The hypnotic vibrations of the free-swimming ones in their multitude turn out to have a stimulating effect on any male who is near. Their sub-minds induce dreams of the piquant sort. Lev says that to make money for the work we must sell these dreams to rich men. I protest, but to no avail.

"Lev is maddened for money. Now besides selling the dreams I find he plans to sell the creatures themselves, sell them one by one, but keep enough to sell the dreams too. It is a madness."

The darkness had become that of night. The thunder continued to growl and now it seemed to Simon that it had music in it. Visions swam through his mind to its rhythm—hordes of swimming pygmy souls, of unborn water babies, migrations of miniature mermaids. The pipe hanging between water tank and pent-shack became in his imagination a giant umbilicus or a canal for a monstrous multiple birth. Sitting beneath it, helpless to move, he focused his attention with increasing pleasure on the active, supple, ever more human girl-bodies that swam across his mind. Now more mermaid than tadpole, with bright smiling lips and eyes, long Lorelei-hair trailing behind them, they darted and hovered caressingly. In their wide-cheeked oval faces, he discovered without shock, there was a transcendent resemblance to the features of Grushenka Stulnikov-Gurevich—a younger, milk-skinned maiden of the steppes, with challenging eyes and figures that brushed against him with delightful shocks...

"So it is for me the great problem," Vasily's distant voice continued. "I see in my work only the pure research, the play of the mind. Lev sees money, Ivan sees dragon teeth—folded for his political cannon—Mikhail sees unshriven souls, Grushenka sees—who knows?—madness. It is indeed one great problem."

Thunder came again, crashingly this time. The door of the pent-shack opened. Framed in it stood Ivan the Bomber. "Vasily!" he roared. "Do you know what that idiot is doing now?"

For a moment Simon thought he meant God.

Then as the thunder and Ivan's voice trailed off together, Simon became aware at last of the identity of the other sound, which had been growing in volume all the time.

Simultaneously Vasily struggled to his feet.

"The organ!" he cried. "Mikhail is *playing* the Whirlwind Music! We must stop him!" Pausing only for a last pull at the bottle, he charged into the pent-shack, following Ivan.

Wind was shaking the heavy pipe over Simon's head, tossing him back and forth in the chair. Looking with an effort toward the west, Simon saw the reason: a spinning black pencil of wind that was writing its way toward them in wreckage across the intervening roofs.

The chair fell under him. Stumbling across the roof, he tugged futilely at the door to the pent-shack, then threw himself flat, clawing at the tarpaper.

There was a mounting roar. The top of the water tank went spinning off like a flying saucer. Momentarily, as if it were a giant syringe, the whirlwind dipped into the tank. Simon felt himself sliding across the roof, felt his legs lifting. He fetched up against the roof's low wall and at that moment the wind let go of him and his legs touched tarpaper again.

Gaining his feet numbly, Simon staggered into the leaning pent-shack. The pale man was nowhere to be seen, the plush chair empty. The curtain at the other side of the room had fallen with its rods, revealing a bathtub more antique that Simon's. In the tub, under the window, sat Grushenka. The lightning flares showed her with her chin level with the water, her eyes placidly staring, her mouth opening and closing.

Simon found himself putting his arms around the black clad figure. With a straining effort he lifted her out of the tub, water sloshing all over his legs, and half carried, half slid with her down the stairs.

He fetched up panting and disheveled at the top landing, his attention riveted by the lightning-illuminated scene in the two-story-high living room below. At the far end of it a dark-robed figure crouched at the console of the mighty organ, like a giant bat at the base of the portico of a black and gold temple. In the center of the room Ivan was in the act of heaving above his head his globular leather case.

Mikhail darted a look over his shoulder and sprang to one side. The projectile crashed against the organ. Mikhail picked himself up, tearing something from his neck. Ivan lunged forward with a roar. Mikhail crashed a fist against his jaw. The Bomber went down and didn't come up. Mikhail unwrapped his crucifix from his fingers and resumed playing.

With a wild cry Simon heaved himself to his feet, stumbled over Grushenka's sodden garments, and pitched headlong down the stairs.

When he came to, the house was empty and the Stulnikov moving van was gone. At the front door he was met by a poker-faced young man who identified himself as a member of the FBI. Simon showed him the globular case Ivan had thrown at the organ. It proved to contain a bowling ball.

The young gentleman listened to his story without changing expression, thanked him warmly, and shooed him out.

The Stulnikov-Gureviches disappeared for good, though not quite without a trace. Simon found this item in the next evening's paper, the first of many he accumulated yearningly in a scrapbook during the following months:

MERMAID RAIN A HOAX, SCIENTIST DECLARES

Milford, Pa.—The "mermaid rain" reported here has been declared a fraud by an eminent European biologist. Vasily Stulnikov-Gurevich, formerly Professor of Genetics at Pirc University, Latvia, passing through here on a cross-country trip, declared the miniature "mermaids" were "albino tadpoles, probably scattered about as a hoax by schoolboys."

The professor added, "I would like to know where they got them, however. There is clear evidence of mutation, due perhaps to fallout."

Dr. Stulnikov directed his party in a brief but intensive search for overlooked specimens. His charming silent sister, Grushenka Stulnikov, wearing a quaint Latvian swimming costume, explored the shallows of the Delaware.

After collecting as many specimens as possible, the professor and his assistants continued their trip in their unusual camping car. Dr. Stulnikov intends to found a biological research center "in the calm and tolerant atmosphere of the West Coast," he declared.

WHAT'S HE DOING IN THERE?

THE PROFESSOR WAS congratulating Earth's first visitor from another planet on his wisdom in getting in touch with a cultural anthropologist before contacting any other scientists (or governments, God forbid!), and in learning English from radio and TV before landing from his orbit-parked rocket, when the Martian stood up and said hesitantly, "Excuse me, please, but where is it?"

That baffled the Professor and the Martian seemed to grow anxious—at least his long mouth curved upward, and he had earlier explained that its curling downward was his smile—and he repeated, "Please, where is it?"

He was surprisingly humanoid in most respects, but his complexion was textured so like the rich dark armchair he'd just been occupying that the Professor's pinstriped gray suit, which he had eagerly consented to wear, seemed an arbitrary interruption between him and the chair—a sort of Mother Hubbard dress on a phantom conjured from its shagreen leather.

The Professor's Wife, always a perceptive hostess, came to her husband's rescue by saying with equal rapidity, "Top of the stairs, end of the hall, last door."

The Martian's mouth curled happily downward and he said, "Thank you very much," and was off.

Comprehension burst on the Professor. He caught up with his guest at the foot of the stairs.

"Here, I'll show you the way," he said.

"No, I can find it myself, thank you," the Martian assured him.

Something rather final in the Martian's tone made the Professor desist, and after watching his visitor sway up the stairs with an almost hypnotic softly jogging movement, he rejoined his wife in the study, saying wonderingly, "Who'd have thought it, by George! Function taboos as strict as our own!"

"I'm glad some of your professional visitors maintain 'em," his wife said darkly.

"But this one's from Mars, darling, and to find out he's —well, similar in an aspect of his life is as thrilling as the discovery that water is burned hydrogen. When I think of the day not far distant when I'll put his entries in the cross-cultural index . . ."

He was still rhapsodizing when the Professor's Little Son raced in.

"Pop, the Martian's gone to the bathroom!"

"Hush, dear. Manners."

"Now its perfectly natural, darling, that the boy should notice and be excited. Yes, Son, the Martian's not so very different from us."

"Oh, certainly," the Professor's Wife said with a trace of bitterness. "I don't imagine his turquoise complexion will cause any comment at all when you bring him to a faculty reception. They'll just figure he's had a hard night—and that he got that baby-elephant nose sniffing around for assistant professorships."

"Really, darling! He probably thinks of our noses as disagreeably amputated and paralyzed."

"Well, anyway, Pop, he's in the bathroom. I followed him when he squiggled upstairs."

"Now, Son, you shouldn't have done that. He's on a strange planet and it might make him nervous if he thought he was being spied on. We must show him every courtesy. By George, I can't wait to discuss these things with Ackerly-Ramsbottom! When I think of how much more this encounter has to give the anthropologist than even the physicist or astronomer . . ."

He was still going strong on his second rhapsody when he was interrupted by another high-speed entrance. It was the Professor's Coltish Daughter.

"Mom, Pop, the Martian's—"

"Hush, dear. We know."

The Professor's Coltish Daughter regained her adolescent poise, which was considerable. "Well, he's still in there," she said. "I just tried the door and it was locked."

"I'm glad it was!" the Professor said while his wife added, "Yes, you can't be sure what—" and caught herself. "Really, dear, that was very bad manners."

"I thought he'd come downstairs long ago," her daughter explained. "He's been in there an awfully long time. It must have been a half hour ago that I saw him gyre and gimbal upstairs in that real gone way he has, with Nosy here following him." The Professor's Coltish Daughter was currently soaking up both jive and *Alice*.

When the Professor checked his wristwatch, his expression grew troubled. "By George, he is taking his time! Though, of course, we don't know how much time Martians . . . I wonder."

"I listened for a while, Pop," his son volunteered. "He was running the water a lot."

"Running the water, eh? We know Mars is a water-starved planet. I suppose that in the presence of unlimited water, he might be seized by a kind of madness and . . . But he seemed so well adjusted."

Then his wife spoke, voicing all their thoughts. Her outlook on life gave her a naturally sepulchral voice.

"What's he doing in there?"

Twenty minutes and at least as many fantastic suggestions later, the Professor glanced again at his watch and nerved himself for action. Motioning his family aside, he mounted the stairs and tiptoed down the hall.

He paused only once to shake his head and mutter

under his breath, "By George, I wish I had Fenchurch or von Gottschalk here. They're a shade better than I am on intercultural contracts, especially taboo-breakings and affronts . . ."

His family followed him at a short distance.

The Professor stopped in front of the bathroom door. Everything was quiet as death.

He listened for a minute and then rapped measuredly, steadying his hand by clutching its wrist with the other. There was a faint splashing, but no other sound.

Another minute passed. The Professor rapped again. Now there was no response at all. He very gingerly tried the knob. The door was still locked.

When they had retreated to the stairs, it was the Professor's Wife who once more voiced their thoughts. This time her voice carried overtones of supernatural horror.

"What's he doing in there?"

"He may be dead or dying," the Professor's Coltish Daughter suggested briskly. "Maybe we ought to call the Fire Department, like they did for old Mrs. Frisbee."

The Professor winced. "I'm afraid you haven't visualized the complications, dear," he said gently. "No one but ourselves knows that the Martian is on Earth, or has even the slightest inkling that interplanetary travel has been achieved. Whatever we do, it will have to be on our own. But to break in on a creature engaged in —well, we don't know what primal private activity— is against all anthropological practice. Still—"

"Dying's a primal activity," his daughter said crisply.

"So's ritual bathing before mass murder," his wife added.

"Please! Still, as I was about to say, we do have the moral duty to succor him if, as you all too reasonably suggest, he has been incapacitated by a germ or virus or, more likely, by some simple environmental factor such as Earth's greater gravity."

"Tell you what, Pop—I can look in the bathroom window and see what he's doing. All I have to do is crawl out my bedroom window and along the gutter a little ways. It's safe as houses."

The Professor's question beginning with, "Son, how do you know—" died unuttered and he refused to notice the words his daughter was voicing silently at her brother. He glanced at his wife's sardonically composed face, thought once more of the Fire Department and of other and larger and even more jealous—or would it be skeptical?—government agencies, and clutched at the straw offered him.

Ten minutes later, he was quite unnecessarily assisting his son back through the bedroom window.

"Gee, Pop, I couldn't see a sign of him. That's why I took so long. Hey, Pop, don't look so scared. He's in there, sure enough. It's just that the bathtub's under the window and you have to get real close up to see into it."

"The Martian's taking a bath?"

"Yep. Got it full up and just the end of his little old schnozzle sticking out. Your suit, Pop, was hanging on the door."

The one word the Professor's Wife spoke was like a death knell.

"*Drowned!*"

"No, Ma, I don't think so. His schnozzle was opening and closing regular like."

"Maybe he's a shape-changer," the Professor's Coltish Daughter said in a burst of evil fantasy. "Maybe he softens in water and thins out after a while until he's like an eel and then he'll go exploring through the sewer pipes. Wouldn't it be funny if he went under the street and knocked on the stopper from underneath and crawled into the bathtub with President Rexford, or Mrs. President Rexford, or maybe right into the middle of one of Janey Rexford's Oh-I'm-so-sexy bubble baths?"

"Please!" The Professor put his hand to his eyebrows and kept it there, cuddling the elbow in his other hand.

"Well, have you thought of something?" the Professor's Wife asked him after a bit. "What are you going to do?"

The Professor dropped his hand and blinked his eyes hard and took a deep breath.

"Telegraph Fenchurch and Ackerly-Ramsbottom and then break in," he said in a resigned voice, into which, nevertheless, a note of hope seemed also to have come. "First, however, I'm going to wait until morning."

And he sat down cross-legged in the hall a few yards from the bathroom door and folded his arms.

So the long vigil commenced. The Professor's family shared it and he offered no objection. Other and sterner men, he told himself, might claim to be able successfully to order their children to go to bed when there was a Martian locked in the bathroom, but he would like to see them faced with the situation.

Finally dawn began to seep from the bedrooms. When the bulb in the hall had grown quite dim, the Professor unfolded his arms.

Just then, there was a loud splashing in the bathroom. The Professor's family looked toward the door. The splashing stopped and they heard the Martian moving around. Then the door opened and the Martian appeared in the Professor's gray pin-stripe suit. His mouth curled sharply downward in a broad alien smile as he saw the Professor.

"Good morning!" the Martian said happily. "I never slept better in my life, even in my own little wet bed back on Mars."

He looked around more closely and his mouth straightened. "But where did you all sleep?" he asked. "Don't tell me you stayed dry all night! You *didn't* give up your only bed to me?"

His mouth curled upward in misery. "Oh, dear," he said, "I'm afraid I've made a mistake somehow. Yet I don't understand how. Before I studied you, I didn't know what your sleeping habits would be, but that question was answered for me—in fact, it looked so reassuringly homelike—when I saw those brief TV scenes of your females ready for sleep in their little tubs. Of course, on Mars, only the fortunate can always be sure of sleeping wet, but here, with your abundance of water, I thought there would be wet beds for all."

He paused. "It's true I had some doubts last night, wondering if I'd used the right words and all, but then when you rapped 'Good night' to me, I splashed the sentiment back at you and went to sleep in a wink. But I'm afraid that somewhere I've blundered and—"

"No, no, dear chap," the Professor managed to say. He had been waving his hand in a gentle circle for some time in token that he wanted to interrupt. "Everything is quite all right. It's true we stayed up all night, but please consider that as a watch—an honor guard, by George!—which we kept to indicate our esteem."

FRIENDS AND ENEMIES

THE SUN hadn't quite risen, but now that the five men were out from under the trees it already felt hot. Far ahead, off to the left of the road, the spires of New Angeles gleamed dusky blue against the departing night. The two unarmed men gazed back wistfully at the little town, dark and asleep under its moist leafy umbrellas. The one who was thin and had hair flecked with gray looked all intellect; the other, young and with a curly mop, looked all feeling.

The fat man barring their way back to town mopped his head. The two young men flanking him with shotgun and squirtgun hadn't started to sweat yet.

The fat man stuffed the big handkerchief back in his pocket, wiped his hands on his shirt, rested his wrists lightly on the pistols holstered either side of his stomach, looked at the two unarmed men, indicated the hot road with a nod, and said, "There's your way, professors. Get going."

The thin man looked at the hand-smears on the fat man's shirt. "But you haven't even explained to me," he protested softly, "why I'm being turned out of Ozona College."

"Look here, Mr. Ellenby, I've tried to make it easy for you," the fat man said. "I'm doing it before the town wakes up. Would you rather be chased by a mob?"

"But why—?"

"Because we found out you weren't just a math teacher, Mr. Ellenby." The fat man's voice went hard. "You'd been a physicist once. *Nu*clear physicist."

The young man with the shotgun spat. Ellenby watched the spittle curl in the dust like a little brown worm. He shifted his gaze to a dead eucalyptus leaf. "I'd like to talk to the college board of regents," he said tonelessly.

"I'm the board of regents," the fat man told him. "Didn't you even know that?"

At this point the other unarmed man spoke up loudly. "But that doesn't explain my case. I've devoted my whole life to warning people against physicists and other scientists. How they'd smash us with their bombs. How they were destroying our minds with 3D and telefax and handies. How they were blaspheming against Nature, killing all imagination, crushing all beauty out of life!"

"I'd shut my mouth if I were you, Madson," the fat man said critically, "or at least lower my voice. When I mentioned a mob, I wasn't fooling. I saw them burn Cal Tech. In fact, I got a bit excited and helped."

The young man with the shotgun grinned.

"Cal Tech," Ellenby murmured, his eyes growing distant. "Cal Tech burns and Ozona stands."

"Ozona stands for the decencies of life," the fat man grated, "not alphabet bombs and pituitary gas. Its purpose is to save a town, not help kill a world."

"But why should *I* be driven out?" Madson persisted. "I'm just a poet singing the beauties of the simple life —unmarred by science."

"Not simple enough for Ozona!" the fat man snorted. "We happen to know, Mr. Poet Madson, that you've written some stories about free love. We don't want anyone telling Ozona girls it's all right to be careless."

"But those were just ideas, ideas in a story," Madson protested. "I wasn't advocating—"

"No difference," the fat man cut him short. "Talk to a woman about ideas and pretty soon she gets some." His voice became almost kindly. "Look here, if you wanted a woman without getting hitched to her, why didn't you go to shantytown?"

Madson squared his shoulders. "You've missed the whole point. I'd never do such a thing. I never have."

"Then you shouldn't have boasted," the fat man said. "And you shouldn't have fooled around with Councilman Classen's daughter."

At the name, Ellenby came out of his trance and looked sharply at Madson, who said indignantly, "I wasn't fooling around with Vera-Ellen, whatever her crazy father says. She came to my office because she has poetic ability and I wanted to encourage it."

"Yeah, so she'd encourage you," the fat man finished. "That girl's wild enough already, which I suppose is what you mean by poetic ability. And in this town, her father's word counts." He hitched up his belt. "And now, professors, it's time you started."

Madson and Ellenby looked at each other doubtfully. The young man with the squirtgun raised its acid-etched muzzle. The fat man looked hard at Madson and Ellenby. "I think I hear alarm clocks going off," he said quietly.

They watched the two men trudge a hundred yards, watched Ellenby shift the rolled-up towel under his elbow to the other side, watched Madson pause to thumb tobacco into a pipe and glance carelessly back, then shove the pipe in his pocket and go on hurriedly.

"Couple of pretty harmless coots, if you ask me," the young man with the shotgun observed.

"Sure," the fat man agreed, "but we got to remember peoples' feelings and keep Ozona straight. We don't like mobs or fear *or* girls gone wild."

The young man with the shotgun grinned. "That Vera-Ellen," he murmured, shaking his head.

"You better keep *your* mind off her too," the fat man said sourly. "She's wild enough without anybody to encourage her poetic ability or anything else. It's a good thing we gave those two their walking papers."

"They'll probably walk right into the arms of the Harvey gang," the young man with the squirtgun remarked, "especially if they try to short-cut."

"Pretty small pickings for Harvey, those two," the young man with the shotgun countered.

"Which won't please him at all."

The fat man shrugged. "Their own fault. If only they'd had sense enough to keep their mouths shut. Early in life."

"They don't seem to realize it's 1993," said the young man with the shotgun.

The fat man nodded. "Come on," he said, turning back toward the town and the coolness. "We've done our duty."

The young man with the squirtgun took a last look. "There they go, Art and Science," he observed with satisfaction. "Those two subjects always did make my head ache."

On the hot road Madson began to stride briskly. His nostrils flared. "Smell the morning air," he commanded. "It's good, good!"

Ellenby, matching his stride with longer if older legs, looked at him with mild wonder.

"Smell the hot sour grass," Madson continued. "It's things like this man was meant for, not machines and formulas. Look at the dew. Have you seen the dew in years? Look at it on that spiderweb!"

The physicist paused obediently to observe the softly twinkling strands. "Perfect catenaries," he murmured.

"What?"

"A kind of curve," Ellenby explained. "The locus of the focus of a parabola rolling on a straight line."

"Locus-focus hocus-pocus!" Madson snorted. "Reducing the wonders of Nature to chalk marks. It's disgusting."

Suddenly each tiny drop of dew turned blood-red. Ellenby turned his back on the spiderweb, whipped a crooked little brass tube from an inside pocket and squinted through it.

"What's that?" Madson asked.

"Spectroscope," Ellenby explained. "Early morning spectra of the sun are fascinating."

Madson huffed. "There you go. Analyzing. Tearing beauty apart. It's a disease." He paused. "Say, won't you hurt your eyes?"

Turning back, Ellenby shook his head. "I keep a smoked glass on it," he said. "I'm always hoping that some day I'll get a glimpse of an atomic bomb explosion."

"You mean to say you've missed all the dozens they dropped on this country? That's too bad."

"The ball of fire's quite fleeting. The opportunities haven't been as good as you think."

"But you're a physicist, aren't you? Don't you people have all sorts of lovely photographs to gloat over in your laboratories?"

"Atomic bomb spectra were never declassified," Ellenby told him wistfully. "At least not in my part of the project. I've never seen one."

"Well, you'll probably get your chance," Madson told him harshly. "If you've been reading your dirty telefax, you'll know the Hot Truce is coming to a boil. And the Angeles area will be a prime target." Ellenby nodded mutely.

They trudged on. The sun began to beat on their backs like an open fire. Ellenby turned up his collar. He watched his companion thoughtfully. Finally he said, "So you're the Madson who wrote those *Enemies of Science* stories about a world ruled by poets. It never occurred to me back at Ozona. And that nonfiction book about us— what it was called?"

"*Murderers of Imagination*," Madson growled. "And it would have been a good thing if you'd listened to my warnings instead of going on building machines and dissecting Nature and destroying all the lovely myths that make life worthwhile."

"Are you sure that Nature is so lovely and kind?"

Ellenby ventured. Madson did not deign to answer.

They passed a crossroad leading, the battered sign said, one way to Palmdale, the other to San Bernardino. They were perhaps a hundred yards beyond it when Ellenby let go a little chuckle. "I have a confession to make. When I was very young I wrote an article about how children shouldn't be taught the Santa Claus myth or any similar fictions."

Madson laughed sardonically. "A perfect member of your dry-souled tribe! Worrying about Santa Claus, when all the while something very different was about to come flying down from over the North Pole and land on our housetops."

"We did try to warn people about the intercontinental missiles," Ellenby reminded him.

"Yes, without any success. The last two reindeer—Donner and Blitzen!"

Ellenby nodded glumly, but he couldn't keep a smile off his face for long. "I wrote another article too—it was never published—about how poetry is completely pointless, how rhymes inevitably distort meanings, and so on."

Madson whirled on him with a peal of laughter. "So you even thought you were big enough to wreck poetry!" He jerked a limp, thinnish volume from his coat pocket. "You thought you could destroy this!"

Ellenby's expression changed. He reached for the book, but Madson held it away from him. Ellenby said, "That's Keats, isn't it?"

"How would you know?"

Ellenby hesitated. "Oh, I got to like some of his poetry, quite a while after I wrote the article." He paused again and looked squarely at Madson. "Also, Vera-Ellen was reading me some pieces out of that volume. I guess you'd loaned it to her."

"Vera-Ellen?" Madson's jaw dropped.

Ellenby nodded. "She had trouble with her geometry. Some conferences were necessary." He smiled. "We physicists aren't such a dry-souled tribe, you know."

Madson looked outraged. "Why, you're old enough to be her father!"

"Or her husband," Ellenby replied coolly. "Young women are often attracted to father images. But all that can't make any difference to us now."

"You're right," Madson said shortly. He shoved the poetry volume back in his pocket, flirted the sweat out of his eyes, and looked around with impatience. "Say, you're going to New Angeles, aren't you?" he asked, and when Ellenby nodded uncertainly, said, "Then let's cut across the fields. This road is taking us out of our way." And without waiting for a reply he jumped across the little ditch to the left of the road and into the yellowing wheat field. Ellenby watched him for a moment, then hitched his rolled towel further up under his arm and followed.

It was stifling in the field. The wheat seemed to paralyze any stray breezes. Their boots hissed against the dry stems. Far off they heard a lazy drumming. After a while they came to a wide, brimful irrigation ditch. They could see that some hundreds of feet ahead it was crossed by a little bridge. They followed the ditch.

Ellenby felt strangely giddy, as if he were looking at everything through a microscope. That may have been due to the tremendous size of the wheat, its spikes almost as big as corncobs, the spikelets bigger than kernels—rich orange stuff taut with flour. But then they came to a section marred by larger and larger splotches of a powdery purple blight.

The lazy drumming became louder. Ellenby was the first to see the low-swinging helicopter with its thick, trailing plume of greenish mist. He knocked Madson on the shoulder and both men started to run. Purple dust puffed. Once Ellenby stumbled and Madson stopped to jerk him to his feet. Still they would have escaped except that the copter swerved toward them. A moment later they were enveloped in sweet oily fumes.

Madson heard jeering laughter, glimpsed a grotesquely longnosed face peering down from above. Then through the cloud, Ellenby squeaked, "Don't breathe!" and Madson felt himself dragged roughly into the ditch. The water closed over him with a splash.

Puffing and blowing, he came to his feet—the water hardly reached his waist—to find himself being dragged by Ellenby toward the bridge. It was all he could do to keep his footing on the muddy bottom. By the time he got breath enough to voice his indignation, Ellenby was saying, "That's far enough. The stuff's settling away from us. Now strip and scrub yourself."

Ellenby unrolled the towel he'd held tightly clutched to his side all the while, and produced a bar of soap. In response to Madson's question he explained, "That fungicide was probably TTTR or some other relative of the nerve-gas family. They are absorbed through the skin."

Seconds later Madson was scouring his head and chest. He hesitated at his trousers, muttering, "The'll probably have me for indecent exposure. Claim I was trying to start a nudist colony as well as a free-love cult." But Ellenby's warning had been a chilly one.

Ellenby soaped Madson's back and he in turn soaped the older man's ridgy one.

"I suppose that's why he had an elephant's nose," Madson mused.

"What?"

"Man in the copter," Madson explained. "Wearing a respirator."

Ellenby nodded and made them move nearer the bridge for a change of water.

They started to scrub their clothes, rinse and wring them, and lay them on the bank to dry. They watched the copter buzzing along in the distance, but it didn't seem inclined to come near again. Madson felt impelled to say, "You know, it's your chemist friends who have introduced that viciousness into the common man's spirit, giving him horrible poisons to use against Nature. Otherwise he wouldn't have tried to douse us with that stuff."

"He just acted like an ordinary farmer to me," Ellenby replied, scrubbing vigorously.

"Think we're safe?" Madson asked.

Ellenby shrugged. "We'll discover," he said briefly.

Madson shivered, but the rhythmic job was soothing. After a bit he began to feel almost playful. Lathering his shirt, he got some fine large bubbles, held them so he could see their colors flow in the sunlight.

"Tiny perfect worlds of every hue," he murmured. "Violet, blue, green, yellow, orange, red."

"And dead black," Ellenby added.

"You would say something like that!" Madson grunted. "What did you think I was talking about?"

"Bubbles."

"Maybe some of your friends' poisons have black bubbles," Madson said bitingly. "But I was talking about these."

"So was I. Give me your pipe."

The authority in Ellenby's voice made Madson look around startledly. "Give me your pipe," Ellenby repeated firmly, holding out his hand.

Madson fished it out of the pocket of the trousers he was about to wash and handed it over. Ellenby knocked out the soggy tobacco, swished it in the water a few times, and began to soap the inside of the bowl.

Madson started to object, but, "You'd be washing it anyway," Ellenby assured him. "Now look here, Madson, I'm going to blow a bubble and I want you to watch. I want you to observe Nature for all you're worth. If poets and physicists have one thing in common it's that they're both supposed to be able to observe. Accurately."

He took a breath. "Now see, I'm going to hold the pipe mouth down and let the bubble hang from it, but with one side of the bowl tipped up a bit, so that the strain on the bubble's skin will be greatest on that side."

He blew a big bubble, held the pipe with one hand and

pointed with a finger of the other. "There's the place to watch now. There!" The bubble burst.

"What was that?" Madson asked in a new voice. "It really was black for an instant, dull like soot."

"A bubble bursts because its skin gets thinner and thinner," Ellenby said. "When it gets thin enough it shows colors, as interference eliminates different wavelengths. With yellow eliminated it shows violet, and so on. But finally, just for a moment at the place where it's going to break, the skin becomes only one molecule thick. Such a mono-molecular layer absorbs all light, hence shows as dead black."

"Everything's got a black lining, eh?"

"Black can be beautiful. Here, I'll do it again."

Madson put his hand on Ellenby's shoulder to steady himself. They were standing hip-deep in water, their bodies still flecked with suds. Their heads were inches from the new bubble. As it burst a voice floated down to them.

"Is this the Ozona Faculty Kindergarten?"

They whirled around, simultaneously crouching in the water.

"Vera-Ellen, what are you doing here?" Madson demanded.

"Watching the kiddies play," the girl on the bridge replied, running a hand through her touseled violet hair. She looked down at her slacks and jacket. "Wish I'd brought my swim suit, though I gather it wouldn't be expected."

"Vera-Ellen!" Madson said apprehensively.

"It doesn't look very inviting down there, though," she mused. "Guess I'll wait for Aqua Heaven at New Angeles."

"You're going to New Angeles?" Ellenby put in. It is not easy to be conversationally brilliant while squatting chest deep in muddy water, acutely conscious of the absence of clothes.

Vera-Ellen nodded lazily, leaning on the railing. "Going

to get me a city job. With its reduced faculty Ozona holds no more intellectual interest for me. Did you know math's going to be made part of the Home Eco department, Mr. Ellenby?"

"But how did you know that we—"

"Daughter of the man who got you run out of town ought to know what the old bully's up to. And if you're worrying that they'll come after me and find us together, I'll just head along by myself."

Madson and Ellenby both protested, though it is even harder to protest effectively than to be conversationally brilliant while squatting naked in coffee-colored water.

Vera-Ellen said, "All right, so quit playing and let's get on. You have to tell me all about New Angeles and the kind of jobs we'll get."

"But—?"

"Modest, eh? I'm afraid Pa wouldn't count it in your favor. But all right." She turned her back and sauntered to the other side of the bridge.

Madson and Ellenby cautiously climbed out of the ditch, brushed the water from their skins, and wormed into their soggy clothes.

"We've got to persuade her to go back," Madson whispered.

"Vera-Ellen?" Ellenby replied and raised his eyebrows. Madson groaned softly.

"Cheer up," Ellenby said. And he seemed in a cheerful humor himself when they climbed to the bridge. "Vera-Ellen," he said "we've been having an argument as to whether man ruined Nature or Nature ruined man to start with."

"Is this a class, Mr. Ellenby?"

"Of sorts," he told her. Behind him Madson snorted, flipping his Keats to dry the pages. They started off together.

"Well," said Vera-Ellen, "I like Nature and I like . . .

human beings. And I don't feel ruined at all. Where's the argument?"

"What about the bombs?" Madson demanded automatically. "By man our physicist here means Technology. Whereas I mean—"

"Oh, the bombs," she said with a shrug. "What sort of job do you think I should get in New Angeles?"

"Well . . ." Madson began.

"Say, I'm getting hungry," she raced on, turning to Ellenby.

"So am I," he agreed.

They looked at the road ahead. A jagged hill now hid all but the tips of the spires of New Angeles. On the top of the hill was a tremendous house with sagging roofs of cracked tiles, stucco walls dark with rain stains and green with moss yet also showing cracks, and windows of age-blued glass, some splintered, flashing in the sun, which tempted Ellenby to whip out his spectroscope.

Curving down from the house came a weedy and balding expanse that had obviously once been a well-tended lawn. A few stalwart patches of thick grass held out tenaciously.

Pale-trunked eucalyptus trees towered behind the house and to either side of the road where it curved over the hill.

In a hollow at the foot of the one-time lawn, just where it met the road, something gleamed. As Madson, Ellenby and Vera-Ellen tramped forward, they saw it was an old automobile, one of the jet antiques that were the rage around 1980—in fact, a Lunar '79. Coming closer Ellenby realized that it had custombuilt features, such as jet brakes and collision springs.

A man with an odd cap was poking a probe into the air intake, while in the back seat a woman was sitting, shadowed by a hat four feet across. At the sound of their footsteps the man whirled to his feet, quickly enough though unsteadily. He stared at them, wagging the probe. Just at that moment something that looked like an animated orange furpiece leaped from the tonneau.

"George!" the woman cried. "Widgie's got away."

The small flattish creature came on in undulating bounds. It was past the man in the cap before he could turn. It headed for Ellenby, then changed direction. Madson made an inpulsive dive for it, but it widened itself still more and sailed over him straight into Vera-Ellen's arms.

They walked toward the car. Widgie wriggled, Vera-Ellen stroked his ears. He seemed to be a flying fox of some sort. The man eyed them hostilely, raising the probe. Madson stared puzzledly at the cap. Out of his older knowledge Ellenby whispered an explanation: Chauffeur."

The woman stood in the back seat, swaying slightly. She was wearing a white swim suit and dark teleglasses under her hat. At first she seemed a somewhat ravaged thirty. Then they began to see the rest of the wrinkles.

She received Widgie from Vera-Ellen, shook him out and tucked him under her arm, where he hung limply, moving his tiny red eyes.

"Come in with me, my dear," she told Vera-Ellen. "George, put down that crazy pole. Pay no attention to George—he can't recognize gentlefolk when he sees them, especially when he's drunk. Gentlemen," she continued, waving graciously to Madson and Ellenby, "you have the thanks of Rickie Vickson." As she pronounced the name she surveyed them sharply. Her gaze settled on Ellenby. "You know me, don't you?"

"Certainly," he answered instantly. "You were my first—my favorite straight 3D star."

"Are you in 3D?" Vera-Ellen asked, a sudden gleam in her eyes.

"Was, my dear," Rickie said grandly. She ogled Ellenby through the fish-eye glasses. "Ah, straight 3D," she sighed. "Simple video-audio in depth—there was a great art-form." She began to sway again and they caught the reek of alcohol. "You know, gentlemen, it was handies that ruined my career. I had the looks and the voice, but I lacked the touch. Something in me shrank from the whole idea—be still, Widgie—and the girls with itchy fingers took over. But I'm talking too much about myself. It's hot and you wonderful gentlemen must be thirsty. Here, have a—"

The chauffeur glared at her as she reached fumblingly down into the tonneau. She caught the look and quailed slightly.

"—sandwich," she finished, coming up with a shiny can.

Madson accepted it from her, clicking the catch. The top popped four feet in the air, followed lazily by the uppermost sandwich which he caught deftly. He handed the can to Ellenby, who served himself and handed it up to Vera-Ellen. Soon all three of them were munching.

"Miss Vickson," Vera-Ellen asked between mouthfuls, "do you think I could get a job in broadcast entertainment?"

Rickie looked at her sideways, leaning away to focus. "Not with that ghastly atomglow hair," she said. "Violet is old hat this year—it's either black, blonde or bald. But give me your hand, my dear."

"Going to tell my fortune?"

"After a fashion." She held up Vera-Ellen's hand, squeezing and prodding it thoughtfully, as if she were testing the carcass of an alleged spring chicken. Then she nodded. "You'll do. Good strong hand, that's all that's needed, so you can really crunch the knuckles of the bohunks. They love it rough. Of course the technicians could step up the power when they broadcast your hand-squeeze, but the addicts don't feel it's the same thing." She looked sourly at her own delicate claws. "Yes, my dear, you'll have a chance in handies if you don't mind cuddling with two million dirty-minded bohunks—fingering them—every night and if Rickie Vickson's still got any entree at the studios." She made a face and dipped again into the tonneau, apparently to gulp something, for the chauffeur's glare was intensified.

"You're from New Angeles?" Madson asked politely when Rickie came up beaming.

"Old Angeles," she corrected. "My home's in a contaminated area. After 3D lighting I've never been afraid of hard radiations. But this time my psychic counselor told me—Widgie, I'm going to put you away in a nice little urn—that the bombs are going to miss New Angeles and fall on Old. That's why George is jetting me to the mountains. Others drink to still their fears. I do something about it—too."

"You mean you're going *away* from the studios?" Vera-Ellen demanded incredulously while Ellenby mumbled "Bombs?" through a mouthful of sandwich.

Of course," Rickie nodded. "Don't you know? Russia's touched a match to the Hot Truce. You charming gentlemen should keep up with these things."

"You see, I told you!" Madson said to Ellenby. "One more victory for science!"

"Miss Vickson, we'd better be getting on," the chauffeur interrupted, speaking for the first time. His voice was drunkenly thick. "We aren't out of the fusion fringe by a long shot and I don't like the looks of this place."

Rickie ignored him. Ellenby asked, "Was the news about Russia telefaxed?"

"Of course not." Rickie's smile was scornful. "They never tell the real truth these days. But they said to get out of our houses, and what else could that mean?"

"Miss Vickson, we better—" George began again.

"Quite, George," Rickie ordered.

George groaned faintly, shrugged his shoulders, and reached out an arm to her without looking. Rickie handed him a red, limp plastic bottle. Just as he was putting it to his lips, he jerked as if stung, vaulted into the car, and began to stamp and punch at the controls.

With a mighty *pouf* the jet took hold. Ellenby skittered away from the hot blast. The Lunar '79 jumped forward.

Things hissed and snicked through the air. From nowhere, men began to appear. With a great lurch the car gained the road, roared toward the bridge. Vera-Ellen jumped up as if to get out, then was thrown back into the tonneau. Rickie lunged forward across the seat to save the red bottle. Her four-foot hat leaped upward, hesitated, and then spun off like a flying saucer.

A man rose from the wheat near the bridge. As the car jounced across it, he leveled a rapid-fire weapon. But just as he got it trained on the car, Rickie's hat landed on him. He went over backwards, firing at the sky.

Madson and Ellenby looked around in bewilderment. There must have been a dozen men. As they stared, another bunch came hurrying down the ruined lawn from the house on the hill.

The man by the bridge got up, went over to Rickie's hat and stamped on it.

Madson and Ellenby jumped as the sky-climbing missiles from his gun pattered down around them. When they looked around again, the men from the house on the hill were closing in.

Their leader was about five feet tall, but thick. His head had been formed in a bullet mold, his features looked drop-forged.

"I'm Harvey," he told them blankly. "What you got?"

Harvey's people wore everything from evening dress to shorts. There were even two women (who drifted toward Harvey): one in a gold kimono, the other in an off-the-bosom frock of filthy white lace. Everybody was armed.

"What you got?" Harvey repeated sharply. "I know you're loaded, I saw you talking with that rich-witch in the jet." He looked them over and grabbed at Madson's side pocket. "Books, huh?" he said like a hangman, dangling the Keats by a stray page. Then he turned to Ellenby. "Come on, Skinny," he said, "shell out."

When Ellenby hesitated, two of Harvey's men grabbed

him, dumped him, and passed the contents of his pockets to their chief. When the spectroscope turned up, Harvey grinned. The eyes of his people twinkled in anticipation.

"Science gadget, huh?" he said. "Folks, there's been too much science in the world and too many words. Any minute now, more bombs are gonna fall. I do my humble bit to help 'em. I'm a great little junkman." He let the brass tube fall to the ground and lifted his foot. "Blow it a good-bye kiss, Skinny."

"Wait," Madson said abruptly, taking a step toward Harvey. "Don't do it." Then the poet's eyes grew wide and alarmed, as if he hadn't known he was going to say it.

Breaths sucked in around them. Harvey's turret head slowly turned toward Madson, its expression seemingly vacuous. "Why not?" Harvey whispered.

"Don't pay any attention to my friend," Ellenby interjected rapidly. "He just said that on account of me. Actually he hates science as much as you do. Don't—"

"Shaddup!" Harvey roared. Then his voice instantly went low again. "Ain't nobody hates science more'n me, but ain't nobody tells me so. Shoulda kept your mouth shut, Skinny. Now there's gonna be more'n gadgets stomped, more'n books tore."

Silence came except for the faint sucks of breath, the faint scuffle of shoes on grit as Harvey's people slowly moved in. Ellenby stood helplessly, yet at the same time he felt a widening and intensification of his sensory powers. He was aware of the delicately lace-edged tree shadows cast from the hill ahead by the westering sun. At the other limit of his vision the copter no longer trailed its green caterpillar; for some reason it was buzzing closer along the road. At the same time he was conscious with a feverish clarity of the page by which Harvey dangled the Keats, and without reading the words he saw the lines:

Beauty is truth, truth beauty—that is all
Ye know on earth, and all ye need to know.

Suddenly the slowly advancing faces seemed to freeze

and Ellenby was aware of something spectral and ominous about the yellowing sunlight and the whole acid-etched scene around him. It was something more than the physical threat to him and Madson—it was something that seemed to well up menacingly from the ground under his feet.

There was a sudden faint thunder and even as something inside Ellenby said, "That isn't it, that isn't what the sky's waiting for," he saw the chrome muzzle of the Lunar '79 bulleting toward them across the bridge with Vera-Ellen's violet mop above the wheel.

But even as the braking blasts gouted out redly from under the hood and the car crunched toward a stop in their midst, even as Harvey's people broke to either side and pistols popped with queerly toylike reports, the thunder multiplied until it was impossible that the Lunar '79 was causing it, until it was as the thunder of a thousand invisible jets crushing the air around them. The sky shifted, rocked. The road shook. There came a shock that numbed Ellenby's feet and sent everyone around him reeling, and a pounding, smashing sound that made any remembered noise seem puny.

The Lunar '79, which had stopped a dozen feet from Ellenby, was pitching and tossing like a silver ship in a storm. Vera-Ellen was gripping the steering wheel with one hand and motioning to him frantically with the other. In the seat beyond her Rickie Vickson was jouncing as if in a merry-go-round chariot.

Ellenby lurched as a hand clutched his shoulder and a staggering Madson howled in his ear through the tumult, "Now you've got your rotten bombs!" Between him and the car Harvey's bullet head reared up and as suddenly dropped away. Looking down, Ellenby saw that a chasm four feet wide had split the road between him and the car. Its walls were raw, smoking earth and rock. Down it Ellenby saw vanishing, in one frozen moment, Harvey and the Keats and the little brass spectroscope.

Then Ellenby realized he had grabbed Madson by the

shoulder and thrown the two of them forward and shouted "Jump!" For a moment the chasm gaped beneath them and a white little face stared upward. Then the chasm closed with a giant crunch and Ellenby's hand caught the side of the heaving car and he pitched into the back seat.

Through the diminishing thunder and shaking there came the toy roar of the car's jet and a new movement tipped him backward and he was looking toward the hill and it was getting bigger. He tried to put his feet down and felt something bulk under them. For a moment he thought it was Madson, but Madson was beside him on the seat, and then he saw it was George. He looked up and Rickie Vickson was watching him from where she was crouched in the front seat, her eyes without the teleglasses looking as foxy as Widgie's, whom she was holding close to her wrinkle-etched cheek.

"Vera-Ellen had to conk him," she explained, her gaze dipping to George. "The bum tried to betray us."

The pitching of the car had given way to a steady forward lunge. Ellenby nodded dully at Rickie and hitched himself around and looked back.

Harvey's people were scattering like ants through a dust cloud rising from the road.

The house on the hill still stood, though there were more and larger cracks in it and a nimbus of whiter dust around it.

By the bridge the copter had crashed and was flaming brightly. A tiny figure was running away from it.

Ellenby's face slowly lightened with understanding.

"We were on the San Andreas Rift," he said softly. "Madson, that wasn't the bombs at all. That wasn't Technology or Man." A smile trembled on his lips. "That was Nature. An earthquake."

Madson was the first to comment. "All right," he said, "it was Nature—Nature showing her disgust for Man."

"An idea like that is the sheerest animism," Ellenby

reacted automatically. "Now if you try analyzing—"

"Analyzing!" Madson snorted with a touch of the old fire. "You scientists are always—"

"Whoa, boys," Rickie Vickson interrupted. "If it hadn't been for that little quake to confuse things, Vera-Ellen couldn't have snatched you out no matter how pretty she tried. And I'm in no mood for arguments now. I'm not the arty type and all the science I know is what my psychic counselor tells me. Widgie, quit pounding your heart; it's all over now."

Ellenby touched her arm. "Do I understand," he asked, "that Vera-Ellen made you turn back just to save us?"

"Of course not," Rickie assured him. "Her father and his pals tried to stop us a couple of miles back. They'd been radioed by a farmer in a copter and had the road blocked. George wanted to hand you all over to Vera-Ellen's father, but we conked George—he's such a weakling—and got away. Picking you up was an afterthought."

Vera-Ellen flashed a wicked smile over her shoulder.

Ellenby realized he was feeling vastly contented. He started to lift his feet off George, then settled them more comfortably. He looked at the violet-topped new chauffeur handling the Lunar as if she'd never done anything else, and she picked that moment to flash him another half friendly, half insulting grin. He nudged Madson and said. "We'll continue our argument later—*all* our argument." Madson looked at him sharply and almost grinned too. Ellenby wondered idly what jobs they had for poets and physicists in 3D and handie studios.

Rickie Vickson's eyes widened. "Say," she said, "if they were just warning us about that little old earthquake, then Old Angeles isn't radioactive—I mean any *more* radioactive than it's ever been."

"Oh boy," Vera-Ellen crowed as the car topped the hill and the blue spires came back in sight, "New Angeles, here we come."

THE LAST LETTER

ON TENTHMONTH 1, 2457 A.D., at exactly 9 A.M. Planetary Federation Time—but with a permissible error of a millionth of a second either way—in the fifth sublevel of New-New York Robot Postal Station 68, Black Sorter gulped down ten thousand pieces of first-class mail.

This breakfast tidbit did not agree with the mail-sorting machine. It was as if a robust dog had been fed a large chunk of good red meat with a strychnine pill in it. Black Sorter's innards went *whirr-klunk*, a blue electric glow enveloped him, and he began to shake as if he might break loose from the concrete.

He desperately spat back over his shoulder a single envelope, gave a great *huff* and blew out toward the sorting tubes a medium-size snowstorm consisting of the other nine thousand, nine hundred and ninety-nine pieces of first-class mail chewed to confetti. Then, still convulsed, he snapped up a fresh ten thousand and proceeded to chomp and grind on them. Black Sorter was rugged.

The rejected envelope was tongued up by Red Subsorter, who growled deep in his throat, said a very bad word, and passed it to Yellow Rerouter, who passed it to Green Rerouter, who passed it to Brown Study, who passed it to Pink Wastebasket.

Unlike Black Sorter, Pink Wastebasket was very delicate, though highly intuitive—the machine equivalent of a White Russian countess. She was designed to scan in

3,137 codes, route special-delivery spacemail to interplanetary liners by messenger rocket, and distinguish 9s from upside-down 6s.

Pink Wastebasket haughtily inhaled the offending envelope and almost instantly turned a bright crimson and began to tremble. After a few minutes, small atomic flames started to flicker from her mid-section.

White Nursemaid Seven and Greasy Joe both received Pink Wastebasket's distress signal and got there as fast as their wheels would roll them, but the high-born machine's malady was beyond their simple skills of oil-can and electroshock.

They summoned other machine-tending-and-repairing machines, ones far more expert than themselves, but all were baffled. It was clear that Pink Wastebasket, who continued to tremble and flicker uncontrollably, was suffering from the equivalent of a major psychosis with severe psychosomatic symptoms. She spat a stream of filthy ions at Gray Psychiatrist, not recognizing her old friend.

Meanwhile, the paper blizzard from Black Sorter was piling up in great drifts between the dark pillars of the sublevel, and flurries had reached Pink Wastebasket's aristocratic area. An expedition of sturdy machines, headed by two hastily summoned snowplows, was dispatched to immobilize Black Sorter at all costs.

Pink Wastebasket, quivering like a demented hula dancer, was clearly approaching a crisis. Finally Gray Psychiatrist—after consulting with Green Surgeon, and even then with an irritated reluctance, as if he were calling in a witch-doctor—summoned a human being.

The human being walked respectfully around Pink Wastebasket several times and then gave her a nervous little poke with a rubber-handled probe.

Pink Wastebasket gently regurgitated her last snack, turned dead white, gave a last flicker and shake, and expired. Black Coroner recorded the immediate cause of death as tinkering by a human being.

THE LAST LETTER

The human being, a bald and scrawny one named Potshelter, picked up the envelope responsible for all the trouble, stared at it incredulously, opened it with trembling fingers, scanned the contents briefly, gave a great shriek and ran off at top speed, forgetting to hop on his perambulator, which followed him making anxious clucking noises.

The nearest human representative of the Solar Bureau of Investigation, a rather wooden-looking man named Krumbine, also bald, recognized Potshelter as soon as the latter burst gasping into his office, squeezing through the door while it was still dilating. The human beings whose work took them among the Top Brass, as the upper-echelon machines were sometimes referred to, formed a kind of human elite, just one big nervous family.

"Sit down, Potshelter," the SBI Man said. "Hold still a second so the chair can grab you. Hitch onto the hookah and choose a tranquilizer from the tray at your elbow. Whatever deviation you've uncovered can't be that much of a danger to the planets. I imagine that when you leave this office, the Solar Battle Fleet will still be orbiting peacefully around Luna."

"I seriously doubt that."

Potshelter gulped a large lavender pill and took a deep breath. "Krumbine, a letter turned up in the first-class mail this morning."

"Great Scott!"

"It is a letter from one person to another person."

"Good Lord!"

"The flow of advertising has been seriously interfered with. At a modest estimate, three hundred million pieces of expensive first-class advertising have already been chewed to rags and I'm not sure the Steel Helms—God bless 'em!—have the trouble in hand yet."

"Judas Priest!"

"Naturally the poor machines weren't able to cope with the letter. It was utterly outside their experience, beyond the furthest reach of their programming. It threw them into a terrible spasm. Pink Wastebasket is dead and at this very instant, if we're lucky, three police machines of the toughest blued steel are holding down Black Sorter and putting a muzzle on him."

"Great Scott! It's incredible, Potshelter. And Pink Wastebasket dead? Take another tranquilizer, Potshelter, and hand over the tray."

Krumbine received it with trembling fingers, started to pick up a big pink pill but drew back his hand from it in sudden revulsion at its color and swallowed two blue oval ones instead. The man was obviously fighting to control himself.

He said unsteadily, "I almost never take doubles, but this news you bring—Good Lord! I seem to recall a case where someone tried to send a sound-tape through the mails, but that was before my time. Incidentally, is there any possibility that this is a letter sent by one *group* of persons to another group? A hive or a therapy group or a social club? That would be bad enough, of course, but—"

"No, just one single person sending to another." Potshelter's expression set in grimly solicitous lines. "I can see you don't quite understand, Krumbine. This is not a sound-tape, but a letter written in letters. You know, letters, characters—like books."

"Don't mention books in this office!" Krumbine drew himself up angrily and then slumped back. "Excuse me, Potshelter, but I find this very difficult to face squarely. Do I understand you to say that one person has tried to use the mails to send a printed sheet of some sort to another?"

"Worse than that. A written letter."

"Written? I don't recognize the word."

"It's a way of making characters, of forming visual equivalents of sound, without using electricity. The writer, as he's called, employs a black liquid and a pointed stick called a pen. I know about this because one hobby of mine is ancient means of communication."

Krumbine frowned and shook his head. "Communication is a dangerous business, Potshelter, especially at the personal level. With you and me, it's all right, because we know what we're doing."

He picked up a third blue tranquilizer. "But with most of the hive-folk, person-to-person communication is only a morbid form of advertising, a dangerous travesty of normal newscasting—catharsis without the analyst, recitation without the teacher—a perversion of promotion employed in betraying and subverting."

The frown deepened as he put the blue pill in his mouth and chewed it. "But about this pen—do you mean the fellow glues the pointed stick to his tongue and then speaks, and the black liquid traces the vibrations on the paper? A primitive non-electrical oscilloscope? Sloppy but conceivable, and producing a record of sorts of the spoken word."

"No, no, Krumbine." Potshelter nervously popped a square orange tablet into his mouth. "It's a hand-written letter."

Krumbine watched him. "I never mix tranquilizers," he boasted absently. "Hand-written, eh? You mean that the message was imprinted on a hand? And the skin or the entire hand afterward detached and sent through the mails in the fashion of a Martian reproach? A grisly find indeed, Potshelter."

"You still don't quite grasp it, Krumbine. The fingers of the hand move the stick that applies the ink, producing a crude imitation of the printed word."

"Diabolical!" Krumbine smashed his fist down on the desk so that the four phones and two-score microphones rattled. "I tell you, Potshelter, the SBI is ready to cope with the subtlest modern deceptions, but when fiends search out and revive tricks from the pre-Atomic Cave Era, it's almost too much. But, Great Scott, I dally while the planets are in danger. What's the sender's code on this hellish letter?"

"No code," Potshelter said darkly, proferring the envelope. "The return address is—hand-written."

Krumbine blanched as his eyes slowly traced the uneven lines in the upper left-hand corner:

from RICHARD ROWE
215 West 10th St. (horizontal)
2837 Rocket Court (vertical)
Hive 37, NewNew York 319, N.Y.
Columbia, Terra

"Ugh!" Krumbine said, shivering. "Those crawling characters, those letters, as you call them, those *things* barely enough like print to be readable—they seem to be on the verge of awakening all sorts of horrid racial memories. I find myself thinking of fur-clad witch-doctors dipping long pointed sticks in bubbling black cauldrons. No wonder Pink Wastebasket couldn't take it, brave girl."

Firming himself behind his desk, he pushed a number of buttons and spoke long numbers and meaningful alphabetical syllables into several microphones. Banks of colored lights around the desk began to blink like a theatre marquee sending Morse Code, while phosphorescent arrows crawled purposely across maps and space-charts and through three-dimensional street diagrams.

"There!" he said at last. "The sender of the letter is being apprehended and will be brought directly here. We'll see what sort of man this Richard Rowe is—if we can assume he's human. Seven precautionary cordons are being drawn around his population station: three composed of machines, two of SBI agents, and two consisting of human and mechanical medical-combat teams. Same goes for the intended recipient of the letter. Meanwhile, destroyer squadron of the Solar Fleet has been detached to orbit over NewNew York."

"In case it becomes necessary to Z-Bomb?" Potshelter asked grimly.

Krumbine nodded. "With all those villains lurking just outside the Solar System in their invisible black ships, with planeticide in their hearts, we can't be too careful. One word transmitted from one spy to another and anything may happen. And we must bomb before they do, so as to contain our losses. Better one city destroyed than a traitor on the loose who may destroy many cities. One hundred years ago, three person-to-person postcards went through the mails—just three postcards, Potshelter! —and *pft* went Schenectady, Hoboken, Cicero and Walla Walla. Here, as long as you're mixing them, try one of these oval blues—I find them best for steady swallowing."

Bells jangled. Krumbine grabbed up two phones, holding one to each ear. Potshelter automatically picked up a third. The ringing continued. Krumbine started to wedge one of his phones under his chin, nodded sharply at Potshelter and then toward a cluster of microphones at the end of the table. Potshelter picked up a fourth phone from behind them. The ringing stopped.

The two men listened, looking doped, Krumbine with an eye fixed on the sweep second hand of the large wall clock. When it had made one revolution, he cradled his phones. Potshlter followed suit.

"I do like the simplicity of the new on-the-hour Puffyloaf phono commercial," the latter remarked thoughtfully. "The Bread That's Lighter Than Air. Nice."

Krumbine nodded. "I hear they've had to add mass to the leadfoil wrapping to keep the loaves from floating off the shelves. Fact."

He cleared his throat. "Too bad we can't listen to more phono-commercials, but even when there isn't a crisis on the agenda, I find I have to budget my listening time. On minute per hour strikes a reasonable balance between duty and self-indulgence."

The nearest wall began to sing:

> Mister J. Augustus Krumbine,
> We all think you're fine, fine, fine, fine.
> Now out of the skyey blue
> Come some telegrams for you.

The wall opened to a small heart shape toward the center and a sheaf of pale yellow envelopes arced out and plopped on the middle of the desk. Krumbine started to leaf through them, scanning the little transparent windows.

"Hm, Electronic Soap . . . Better Homes and Landing Platforms . . . Psycho-Blinkers . . . Your Girl Next Door . . . Poppy-Woppies . . . Poppy Woopsies . . ."

He started to open an envelope, then, after a quick look around and an apologetic smile at Potshelter, dumped them all on the disposal hopper, which gargled briefly.

"After all, there *is* a crisis this morning," he said in a defensive voice.

Potshelter nodded absently. "I can remember back before personalized delivery and rhyming robots," he observed. "But how I'd miss them now—so much more distingué than the hives with their non-personalized radio, TV and stereo advertising. For that matter, I believe there are some backward areas on Terra where the great advertising potential of telephones and telegrams hasn't been fully realized and they are still used in part for personal communication. Now me, I've never in my life sent or received a message except on my walky-talky." He patted his breast pocket.

Krumbine nodded, but he was a trifle shocked and inclined to revise his estimate of Potshelter's social status. Krumbine conducted his own social correspondence solely by telepathy. He shared with three other SBI officials a private telepath—a charming albino girl named Agnes.

"Yes, and it's a very handsome walky-talky," he assured Potshelter a little falsely. "Suits you. I like the upswept antenna." He drummed on the desk and swal-

THE LAST LETTER

lowed another blue tranquilizer. "Dammit, what's happened to those machines? They ought to have the two spies here by now. Did you notice that the second—the intended recipient of the letter, I mean—seems to be female? Another good Terran name, too, Jane Dough. Hive in Upper Manhattan." He began to tap the envelope sharply against the desk. "Dammit, where *are* they?"

"Excuse me," Potshelter said hesitantly, "But I'm wondering why you haven't read the message inside the envelope."

Krumbine looked at him blankly. "Great Scott, I assumed that at least *it* was in some secret code, of course. Normally I'd have asked you to have Pink Wastebasket try her skill on it, but . . ." His eyes widened and his voice sank. "You don't mean to tell me that it's—"

Potshelter nodded grimly. "Hand-written, too. Yes."

Krumbine winced. "I keep trying to forget that aspect of the case." He dug out the message with shaking fingers, fumbled it open and read:

Dear Jane,

It must surprise you that I know your name, for our hives are widely separated. Do you recall day before yesterday when your guided tour of Grand Central Spaceport got stalled because the guide blew a fuse? I was the young man with hair in the tour behind yours. You were a little frightened and a groupmistress was reassuring you. The machine spoke your name.

Since then I have been unable to forget you. When I go to sleep, I dream of your face looking up sadly at the mistress's kindly photocells. I don't know how to get in touch with you, but my grandfather has told me stories his grandfather told him about young men writing what he calls love-letters to young ladies. So I am writing you a love-letter.

I work in a first-class advertising house and I will

slip this love-letter into an outgoing ten-thousand-pack and hope.

Do not be frightened of me, Jane. I am no caveman except for my hair. I am not insane. I am emotionally disturbed, but in a way that no machine has ever described to me. I want only your happiness.
Sincerely,
Richard Rowe

Krumbine slumped back in his chair, which braced itself manfully against him, and looked long and thoughtfully at Potshelter. "Well, if that's a code, it's certainly a fiendishly subtle one. You'd think he was talking to his Girl Next Door."

Potshelter nodded wonderingly. "I only read as far as where they were planning to blow up Grand Central Spaceport and all the guides in it."

"Judas Priest, I think I have it!" Krumbine shot up. "It's a pilot advertisement—Boy Next Door—or that kind of thing—printed to look like hand-written, which would make all the difference. And the pilot copy got mailed by accident—which would mean there is no real Richard Rowe."

At that instant, the door dilated and two blue detective engines hustled a struggling young man into the office. He was slim, rather handsome, had a bushy head of hair that had somehow survived evolution and radioactive fallout, and across the chest and back of his paper singlet was neatly stamped, "RICHARD ROWE."

When he saw the two men, he stopped struggling and straightened up. "Excuse me, gentlemen," he said, "but these police machines must have made a mistake. I've committed no crime."

Then his gaze fell on the hand-addressed envelope on Krumbine's desk and he turned pale.

Krumbine laughed harshly. "No crime! No, not at all. Merely using the mails to communicate. Ha!"

THE LAST LETTER

The young man shrank back. "I'm sorry, sir."

"Sorry, he says! Do you realize that your insane prank has resulted in the destruction of perhaps a half-billion pieces of first-class advertising?—in the strangulation of a postal station and the paralysis of Lower Manhattan?—in the mobilization of SBI reserves, the de-mothballing of two divisions of G. I. machines and the redeployment of the Solar Battle Fleet? Good Lord, boy, why did you do it?"

Richard Rowe continued to shrink but he squared his shoulders. "I'm sorry, sir, but I just had to. I just had to get in touch with Jane Dough."

"A girl from another hive? A girl you'd merely gazed at because a guide happened to blow a fuse?" Krumbine stood up, shaking an angry finger. "Great Scott, boy, where was Your Girl Next Door?"

Richard Rowe stared bravely at the finger, which made him look a trifle cross-eyed. "She died, sir, both of them."

"But there should be at least six."

"I know, sir, but of the other four, two have been shipped to the Adirondacks on vacation and two recently got married and haven't been replaced."

Potshelter, a faraway look in his eyes, said softly, "I think I'm beginning to understand—"

But Krumbine thundered on at Richard Rowe with, "Good Lord, I can see you've had your troubles, boy. It isn't often we have these shortages of Girls Next Door, so that temporarily a boy can't marry the Girl Next Door, as he always should. But, Judas Priest, why didn't you take your troubles to your psychiatrist, your groupmaster, your socializer, your Queen Mother?"

"My psychiatrist is being overhauled, sir, and his replacement short-circuits every time he hears the word 'trouble.' My groupmaster and socializer are on vacation duty in the Adirondacks. My Queen Mother is busy replacing Girls Next Door."

"Yes, it all fits," Potshelter proclaimed excitedly. "Don't you see, Krumbine? Except for a set of mis-

229

chances that would only occur once in a billion billion times, the letter would never have been conceived or sent."

"You may have something there," Krumbine concurred "But in any case, boy, why did you—er—written this letter to this particular girl? What is there about Jane Dough that made you do it?"

"Well, you see, sir, she's—"

Just then, the door re-dilated and a blue matron machine conducted a young woman into the office. She was slim and she had a head of hair that would have graced a museum beauty, while across the back and—well, "chest" is an inadequate word—of her paper chemise, "JANE DOUGH" was silk-screened in the palest pink.

Krumbine did not repeat his last question. He had to admit to himself that it had been answered fully. Potshelter whistled respectfully. The blue detective engines gave hard-boiled grunts. Even the blue matron machine seemed awed by the girl's beauty.

But she had eyes only for Richard Rowe. "My Grand Central man," she breathed in amazement. "The man I've dreamed of ever since. My man with hair." She noticed the way he was looking at her and she breathed harder. "Oh, darling, what have you done?"

"I tried to send you a letter."

"A letter? For me? Oh, darling!"

Krumbine cleared his throat. "Potshelter, I'm going to wind this up fast. Miss Dough could you transfer to this young man's hive?"

"Oh, yes, sir! Mine has an over-plus of Girls Next Door."

"Good. Mr. Rowe, there's a sky-pilot two levels up—look for the usual white collar just below the photocells. Marry this girl and take her home to your hive. If your Queen Mother objects refer her to—er—Potshelter here."

He cut short the young people's thanks. "Just one

thing," he said, wagging a finger at Rowe. "Don't written any more letters."

"Why ever would I?" Richard answered. "Already my action is beginning to seem like a mad dream."

"Not to me, dear," Jane corrected him. "Oh, sir, could I have the letter he sent me? Not to do anything with. Not to show anyone. Just to keep."

"Well, I don't know—" Krumbine began.

"Oh, *please*, sir!"

"Well, I don't know why not, I was going to say. Here you are, miss. Just see that this husband of yours never writtens another."

He turned back as the contracting door shut the young couple from view.

"You were right, Potshelter," he said briskly. "It was one of those combinations of mischances that come up only once in a billion billion times. But we're going to have to issue recommendations for new procedures and safeguards that will reduce the possibilities to one in a trillion trillion. It will undoubtedly up the Terran income tax a healthy percentage, but we can't have something like this happening again. Every boy must marry the Girl Next Door! And the first-class mails must not be interfered with! The advertising must go through!"

"I'd almost like to see it happen again," Potshelter murmured dreamily, "if there were another Jane Dough in it."

Outside, Richard and Jane had halted to allow a small cortege of machines to pass. First came a squad of police machines with Black Sorter in their midst, unmuzzled and docile enough, though still gnashing his teeth softly. Then—stretched out horizontally and borne on the shoulders of Gray Psychiatrist, Black Coroner, White Nursemaid Seven and Greasy Joe—there passed the slim form of Pink Wastebasket, snow-white in death. The machines were keening softly, mournfully.

Round about the black pillars, little mecho-mops were

scurrying like mice, cleaning up the last of the first-class-mail bits of confetti.

Richard winced at this evidence of his aberration, but Jane squeezed his hand comfortingly, which produced in him a truly amazing sensation that changed his whole appearance.

"I know how you feel, darling," she told him. "But don't worry about it. Just think, dear, I'll always be able to tell your friends' wives something no other woman in the world can boast of: that my husband once wrote me a letter!"

ENDFRAY OF THE OFAY

ALERTED BY THEIR WATCHMEN, who were mostly Seminoles, the Red-Necked Ofays of the Okefinokee Reservation came hurtling out of their soggy holes and nests with such violence that the alligators and water moccasins went hurtling back into theirs. Reptiles can take only so much exictement.

With hoarse cackles of happiness, the emaciated whites and their Red Indian fellow-reservationists floundered about snatching at the little transparent packets of hominy grits, chitterlings, and moonshine originally intended for the poor Black trash of Appalachia, but now miraculously diverted and falling like manna from the sweaty southern sky.

Along with the hillbilly ambrosia and nectar, a faint cry haunting as the flight of the flamingo lingered in those same dismal hot heavens: "Compliments of the Endfray of the Ofay!"

The Red-Necked Ofays paused in their snatching to lift a ragged cheer.

This was not the first exploit of the mysterious marauder who had thus far left no clue to his identity except a cry from the sky. Most folks now attributed to him the signs, "Whitey lives!" which a month ago had begun to appear scrawled big in shiversomely daring spots, such as the front wall of the Black House in

Memphis. Then a week ago a boisterous party of Luxor Blacks on a sweep-and-annoy excursion through the Bayous Reservation had had their persons and swamp buggies deluged with Yazoo mud "Courtesy of the Endfray of the Ofay!" Many intellectual and fashionable Blacks had secretly approved this literally dirty trick, since the chivvying and terrorizing of helpless Ofays was beginning to be considered uncouth behavior. Then only yesterday a 17-year-old white concubine of the Caliph of Harlem had been kidnapped by the Endfray and levitated back to her tribe in the Great Barrens Reservation. Reactionary and moralistic Blacks, long detesting the Caliph for his contempt of the strict rules against miscegenation, had openly praised the act. In fact, only the rescued and windblown white girl had been completely unhappy about the whole business. But no Blacks could be expected to approve the food drop, which not only upset the national economy, but also violated the even stricter laws against interfering, by helping the weak, with the divine principle of survival of the fittest.

The Black wardens of the Okefinokee melted with their furious and frightened messages the wires to Memphis, Cairo, Thebes, Luxor (once Vicksburg and Natchez) and the other great Government cities of the American Nile.

Within ten seconds two squadrons of Black Angels based on Karnak had scrambled and another was screaming down through the stratosphere.

At her palatial HQ in Memphis, Her Serene Darkness noted the disturbance and ordered that samples of the food packets be recovered and rushed to her. She did not, nevertheless, shift one black iota of her essential concentration off the great war that was being fought between North America and Africa to Make the World Safe for Black Supremacy, by determining which Blacks really were supreme.

Ten seconds more and all three squadrons of Black

ENDFRAY OF THE OFAY

Angels were reversing course west as quickly as their already great velocity would permit, and then shifting into overdrive.

Word had come that there had been another drop of mysteriously diverted viands—this time on the Death Valley Reservation of the Bearded and Beaded Ofays.

Once again there had come that weird cry from the sky: "Compliments of the Endfray of the Ofay!"

Along with the packets of fruit and saffron-tinted, precooked rice and vegtables, there were falling foam-packaged Tibetan prayer wheels, smuggled no man might say how through the Nirvana Screen.

The starving descendants of ancient hippies, beats, cultists and movie moguls had come boiling up out of the furnace-hot mouths of *their* caves and holes. Even outside the reservations, holes were a popular residence in those exciting times when Black atom bombs were in the air and when all mankind was preoccupied, to a degree at least equal to his interest in space, with Earth's molten, slow-churning mantle, rich in mohole-minable radioactivies and also a source of strange and mighty powers when properly tickled by CDEF (Coleman-Dufresne Electrogravitomagnetic Fields) or by magic spells. For in the new world sorcery and science walked arm in arm, sometimes so closely that none might tell which was which, or who was holding the other up. And the density and darkness of Earth's interior suited the Black Age. Russia, which ever since Dostoevsky Day had shifted her fundamentally introspective and peasant interests from the sky to the East European plains and Siberian steppes, had used CDEF (and possibly some Tungu chants) to carry by slow convection and concentrate vast subcritical masses of fissionable radioactives underneath all the world's continents. Increased CDEF tickling would produce unimaginably destructive earthquakes— the so-called mantle bombs that were the USSR's doomsday answer to aggression. Africa and North America utilized the same methods to enrich the radioactives they took from their mohole mines. Australia had employed CDEF and bone-pointing Aboriginal magic to accelerate continental drift, so that the great down-under island, shoving Tasmania before it, was now separated from Antarctica by only a narrow strait. Australia enjoyed a Canadian climate and was hemmed by extremely rich fisheries. While the great Buddhist hegemony of Sino-India had used CDEF (possibly) and yoga and zen (certainly) to create the Nirvana Screen.

In response to the echoing cry from the dry sky, the Beaded and Bearded Ofays touched fingertips to foreheads and briefly meditated their gratitude.

In the fringes of her awareness, Her Serene Darkness noted this food-drop also, and she gave the same order.

Over the Pacific, a tiny westward-speeding vehicle reversed course instantaneously, and so of course without circling, to return momentarily to a point over Death Valley and shout down, "The Endfray thanks you for your prayers."

The Ofays below rejoiced, while by the psionic grapevine that tenuously links unfortunates, a little hope was kindled in the Swarthy Ofays of the Chihuahua Reservation, the Stunted Ofays of the Jersey Flats, the Giant Ofays of the Panhandle Reservation, the Long-Haired Ofays of the Tules, and even in the Wild or Unfenced Honkies of the Rocky Mountains, the Black Hills, and the Badlands.

The Endfray's linear loop wasted enough time to let the Black Angels zero in on him, her, it or them, with their radars and telescopes. With hardly a millisecond's delay, they aimed and activated their deadly lasers, rocket bombs and constriction fields.

The Endfray went zigzagging west again just in time. His evasive tactics were masterly. He seemed able to anticipate each move of his pursuers. Mini-atomics burst into searing violet spheres about him, red laser-needles lanced past him, space itself was squeezed and wrenched, but he bobbed along unharmed like a Ping-pong ball in a tornado.

For an instant one Black Angel telescoped him clearly. The fleeing vehicle was incredibly tiny, the size and shape of a chunky dwarf's spacesuit, snow white in hue, and across it went the red letters "Endfray of the Ofay." There were no jets or antennae. It flashed out of sight perhaps a microsecond before a laser pierced the space it had occupied.

Yet despite or perhaps because of the Endfray's ingenious doublings and dartings, the Black Angels were gaining on him. He veered south, but Australia sent up a line of warning star rockets. He veered north, but when he neared the moored, melancholy black balloons marking the Russian border, they moaned, "nyet, nyet," at him and he once more reversed course and sought the Equator.

The blue of the sky ahead became grainy and glittering like a holograph. It extended down to sea level, blotting out Borneo and the western shore of Celebes.

Without hesitation the Endfray plunged, at precisely 120 degrees east longitude, into the Nirvana Screen.

Chanting their fatalistic death chants, the pilots of the Black Angels sent their slim ebon ships after him.

Without perceptible passage of time, pursued and pursuers emerged over the Indian Ocean at 60 degrees east longitude.

The same thing would have happened in reverse if they had been traveling east, or at 45 degrees north latitude and the Equator if they had been traveling along a north-south vector. It was the Orient's master mystery, greater than the rope trick. Truth to tell, no one outside knew for sure whether India and China still existed inside the Nirvana Screen, or not. Explanations ran the gamut from spacewarp to mass hypnosis and the Nigerian null-spell. While what the superscientific and-or superpsychic Buddists of the Fourth Dimensional Path might do if they ever came out, chilled even Earth's blackest blood.

Africa loomed, the continent that was the home of the

biggest animals, the biggest magics and the biggest bombs in the world. The Endfray climbed steeply. Already at greater altitude, the Black Angels rode the hypotenuse of a collision course.

Ninety miles from intercept, magnibombs mashed the stratosphere everywhere around the Endfray and coalesced into one massive incandescence.

Veering off with hardly nanoseconds to spare, the Black Angels' wing commander bounced home his message off the most convenient orbital relay: "Target destroyed by African antispacecraft fire."

But before it was received at Memphis, there was dropping on the Fierce Fuzzy, or Bluecoated Ofays of the Chicago Craters Reservation, a shower of packeted food —wienerschnitzel, corned beef and cabbage, Irish whisky, beer—and foam-crated roller skates, the latter diverted from a shipment intended for the great gladiatorial ring at Cairo. While down the slants of rain from the dismal sky there resounded, "Compliments of the Endfray of the Ofay!"

No one knew why the Chicago Craters Ofays were called fuzzy, or simply referred to as "the fuzz," since all of them were totally bald from residual radioactivity. It was one of recent history's many mysteries, about which thought was discouraged. But anyone could figure out that roller skates would be an excellent means of transportation on crater glass. And by now everyone, Black or White, knew that the Endfray was an impudent and unbearable affront to absolute authority.

Her Serene Darkness made a decision and took her mind completely off the war. She could safely do this because her uncles were good generals and because her psionic intelligence organization was the world's best, with vast powers of telepathy, clairvoyance, clairaudience, telekinesis and teleportation, from the orbiting espers each shuteyed in her capsule to the Blacks in Blackness: whole psionic families which had lived for generations in deep-buried, absolutely anechoic, aoptical psi-spy-proof environments, their only connections with the upper world being inbound nutrient-pipes and oxypipes and quartzcable bound waste-pipes and report lines. Psionic Intelligence's chief task was to spot and course-chart bombs lobbed over from Africa and up from Argentina and Brazil, where Africa had an enormous beachhead, and then either turn them back by telekinesing their controls, or else guide atomic interceptors to them. Her Darkness was certain that her espers were the world's finest because she had been their working chief before taking over her largely conscious, nonpsionic imperial duties.

Now like an arboreal black leopard—slim, flashing-eyed and dangerous—she gazed down the Watusi-Hottentot gap between her and her pages.

"Summon me my psychiawitches and sorceresps," she commanded.

The patter of springing bare feet faded from the tesselated floor, which was a great, diagrammatic map of Earth and the spaces around. Turning her beautiful, small head on her slender, long neck, Her Darkness gazed out between the narrow pillars of Vermont marble fretted with California gold at the rippling blue Mississip, and she meditated.

A page entered and knelt to her, lifting a golden tray on which gleamed glassy packets, samples from the Endfray's food-drops. She silently indicated where to set it.

A tall, glossy warrior in HQ harness folded his arms in the Communications doorway and intoned, "Acapulco, Halifax and Port of Spain have sustained medium to severe damage from nuclear near-misses. Our rockets intercepted, but not in good time. Orbital warnings on the three African attacks were late and inadequate."

"What from the Blacks in Blackness?" Her Serenity inquired.

"No warning whatever from that quarter."

She nodded dismissal and returned to her meditations. Yet it seemed hardly picoseconds before the Presence

Pavilion was once more full and silent, except for the faint susurrus of the most respectful breathing and the pounding of frightened hearts.

Slowly, one by one, Her Darkness gave her assembled psychiawitches and sorceresps the leopard look which her populace expected of her and loved, especially when they did not have to face it.

Those gathered in the pavilion were almost as tall as she and even more gorgeously clad, but they crouched away from her and ducked their heads like terrified children.

Then she asked in a voice that set them shivering "why is our newest and insolentest enemy uncaught by you, nay, unreported even," and without waiting for an answer commanded, "Read me the mind of the Endfray. Ice it and slice it, dice it and rice it. Skewer him in space, nail him in time. Sound him from his lowest note to the top of his compass. Tell me his source, his nature and his fate."

Instantly a sorceresp of the Seventh Rank babbled, "He is a dwarf white trained and equipped in a secret laboratory in a branch of the Carlsbad Caverns underlying the White Sands Reservation of the Bulge-Brained Ofays. His aim, unquestionably, is the fomenting of an Ofay revolt, a Honky insurrection. He is now hovering seventeen miles above Aswan-St. Paul."

Without intervening pause, the Second Psychiawitch chittered, "He is an African agent of Pygmy extraction, a marauder skilled in teleportation and telepathy. His means of aerial locomotion is a deceit; he uses sloweddown teleportation, not speeded-up field flight. Under cover of the magnibomb blast, he landed unharmed in the territory of our hateful enemies and is now making report to His Terrible Tenebrosity in his shelterpalace beneath Mogadishu."

"The Endfray is not one, but many," another took up. "He is radioactive atoms over the Somali coast. He also speeds east intact over Old Cleveland on the Dead Sea. Another of these duplicates—"

"By Bast and by Ptah, the Endfray is extraterrestrial," yet another cut in. "A seven-tentacled amphibian from the fourth planet of pulsing Altair, he is the forerunner of an invasion which—"

"By Serapis and Harpocrates, she is an Indian witch, sister to Kali, able to penetrate the Nirvana Screen and let others through. She—"

"The Endfray is a group-minded nation of Black Martian Ants. Only such tiny creatures could survive the changes of momentum that—"

"The Endfray is a fantasm! That's why no material weapon can—"

"That'll be enough!" interposed Her Serene Darkness. "When I want improvisations, I'll summon me my artists." The faint, jeering notes of an electronic calliope on a distant pleasure barge seemed an overtone of her scornful contralto voice. "Facts I desire. Where is the Endfray? Take scent and search!" And picking up the gold tray, she scattered its contents across the room in one sweep.

The soaring, transparent foodpackets were snatched, sniffed, fingered, held to ear and forehead, passed hand to hand. There were faint growlings and eager whimperings as the assembly transformed into a pack.

Her Serenity directed, "Each search that part of earth or space on which she stands," referring to the diagrammatic floor map. "Let not one oozy sea cranny or fissure of damp clay cave be overlooked, and forget not the far side of the moon. Except you . . . and you," she added, beckoning the First Psychiawitch and also the sorceresp of the Seventh Rank who had been first to answer. "The rest, to work!"

"How many minutes have we for our task?" the Second Psychiawitch ventured. The eyes of most of the others had already closed or gone blank as the minds behind them clairvoyantly scanned.

"I give you each one hundred seconds." Then, turning to the Seventh-Rank sorceresp, "You spoke of an Ofay revolt. Where? When?"

"One is planned, Your Darkness. It will begin in Los Alamos and be timed to coincide with an all-out African assault ordered by His Terrible Tenebrosity."

"Ridiculous!" the First Psychiawitch interjected in a whisper. "Not even His Idiocy would be so stupid as to think the reservation Ofays might be roused to helpful revolution, or the wild Honkies organized for any purpose. Nor would even His Vileness stoop to use such foul and tawdry means."

In the Communications doorway there appeared a warrior, impassive but white-eyed. Her Serenity showed him her finger. He intoned, "The Blacks in Blackness report that Africa has launched from Casablanca a vehicle with a two-hundred-million-pound first-stage thrust. Window clouds surround it. Its course bends west."

"Two hundred million?"

"Aye. Ten times that of any known Afric or Americ launching vehicle."

"It is the revolt-sign!" the Seventh-Rank sorceresp wailed.

"From its size, it's more likely itself our death-sign, if our interceptors let it get over our land," the First Psychiawitch remarked coolly.

"Silence," Her Darkness said, not unkindly. Then, to the room, "The hundred seconds are up. Where is the Endfray?"

In the hundred and seventy-odd faces, eyes opened and/or came alive with spirit, looking toward Her Serenity with a professional confidence which, as the seconds passed and not one of them spoke, transformed, again into fear.

"Has any one of you not completed search?" Her Darkness inquired. "Or failed to make it as thorough as I commanded?"

Heads rotated from side to side. Lips formed, "No."

"Then the Endfray is nowhere," the First Psychiawitch whispered in a voice that was not meant to carry, but did.

One cried, "It is as I said. He is a fantasm, invisible to psionic search."

"No, it is as *I* said!" another took up. "He is from Altair, and returned there in the twinkling of a self-teleportive thought. We have not searched Altair, only space out to Pluto."

"When the possible seems to fail, only weak brains grasp at the impossible," Her Serenity interposed. "Stellar teleportation takes perceptible time and leaves perceptible clues, as you well know. While fantasms make no teleportive food-drops and leave no psychic scent. No, to solve our problem we must use an apothegm of Sherlock Holmes."

Eyes grew puzzled, while the First Psychiawitch murmured, "Who is that?"

"Sherlock Holmes was a Cryptoblack of vast deductive intelligence, who lived in—" Her Darkness rapidly starred herself, moving fingertips to the seven cardinal points— "the Tabooed Times."

Everyone else copied Her Darkness and starred herself at once, to ward off any ill hap which might come from mention of a forbidden area of the continuum.

Her Serenity continued, "The Sherlockian apothegm I have in mind is this: when all other explanations are proven false, then the least likely explanation must be the true one. You have not searched *all* of habitable Earth and Solar space."

The psychiatrist standing on Memphis said hesitantly, "But, begging Your Serenity's pardon, I have searched every closet of your secret quarters, including the apartments housing your harem and your laboratories of magic and the vault guarding your secret fortune."

"It is well that you have," Her Darkness replied, smiling most dangerously. "But those are not the sole forbidden or esp-proof volumes of Earth."

"You are thinking of the mantle and core?" one asked.

"I said, 'habitable,'" Her Darkness snapped. "Can you not guess the other spot I have in mind?"

A sorceresp standing just south of Louisville cried out, "I scent the Endfray over Bowling Green! His vector, southwest by west. He speeds. Already he overpasses Clarksville."

The psychiawitch standing between her and the one on Memphis took up with, "And now I catch his scent in turn. He comes on fast. He is over Paris, Milan, Bells, Brownsville, Covington—"

"And now—" the one on Memphis began.

The air screamed. The gold-chased pillars shook, and the purple silken awning snapped and flapped as something white flashed through the pavilion, tumbling by its blast everyone but Her Serenity.

The scream, which had abruptly dropped in pitch as the disturbance went by, and then faded somewhat, now rose again in pitch and volume.

"He returns to buzz us once more," the First Psychiawitch gasped from the floor.

Her Dark Serenity—hair unspiraled and straight on end, eyes like a mad tiger's, fists clenched, knees bent, slender feet a-stamp—incanted rapidly,

"Null Kull, null Rull,
Null time, null space,
Null motion and null Grace.
By Hanged Man, Spades, and Lovers
Be winged-clogged, all that hovers.
Paralysis know, and fear—"

The screaming knifed. The pillars began to shake. Something white—

"—And drop down here!"

ENDFRAY OF THE OFAY

Silence returned with a roar. Something white lay on the tesselated floor—a squat and rigid spacesuit like a white oil drum with stubby cylindrical arms and legs, but windowless and without sign of head.

Her Serenity drew and expelled three gasping but controlled breaths. Her hair recurled with faintest rustlings. Those around craned, leaned in, and peered, though without rising fully from the floor where they had been sent sprawling.

Holding out her right hand prone, Her Serenity commanded, "Arise!"

Like the reversed motion picture of a rigid fall, the white spacesuit swung erect as if its heels were hinged to the floor.

"Emerge!" Her Serenity continued.

The suit did not open, but out of it, as if walking through a white wall, there stepped a handsome black boy who looked nine years old. He wore a loincloth. Though his eyes were shut tight, his face was animated, and he smiled as he looked up.

"My Empress—" he began.

Her slender hands, snaking forward to capture him, clamped tight on air.

A chuckle came from the far end of the pavilion, where the black boy had rematerialized midway between awning and floor. Heads switched around to watch him where he stood on air.

Two sorceresps pointed at him, the one a wand, the other a yellow thighbone.

Three warriors appeared at the Force door, bearing silvery, cone-nosed hand weapons. Her Darkness snapped her fingers.

Still shut-eyed, the black boy chuckled again. The three warriors swayed like ticked bowling pins, arms tight to sides, legs tight together, bound by the constriction fields their weapons had projected backfiring on them. And the pointed wand and thighbone hung limp as cooked spaghetti from the hands of the sorceresps.

"Any more games?" the black boy inquired hopefully. If he'd been chubbier, he'd have seemed like a wingless cupid.

"Who are you?" Her Darkness demanded far more coolly than she felt.

"The Endfray, of course, Empress," he replied, looking at her as directly as if his eyes had been open. "At your service, providing—I humbly beg your pardon—the service suits me."

"Yet you have helped the Honkies, aided the Ofays—why?" Her Darkness asked automatically. She was still half in shock.

The Endfray's grin widened and he quirked his face. Finally, "Just for fun," he said. "No, that's not true. Fact is, you see, I like stories of wars and battles, and—"

"As any young Black should," Her Serenity interrupted approvingly. She was regaining her sense of command, and her mind was beginning to work again.

At her feet the First Psychiawitch took fire from her and cried out, "Indeed yes! Brave battles! Complete courage! Stark strength! Merciless might! Violence and victory!"

The Endfray hung his head. His expression became an odd mixture of embarrassment and defiance. "But you see, Empress, I always like the losing side best. Being with the winners is no fun. But siding with the losers, when all the odds are against them—And you got to admit, it's hard to imagine a losinger side than the Ofays."

"Accommodation! Tomism!

"Honky-love!" the Second Psychiawitch cried scandalized.

"Don't you know the first sign of high intelligence is the faculty of violence?" the First Psychiawitch demanded.

"Inside the Nirvana Screen, they think it's the ability to sit still," the Endfray countered.

ENDFRAY OF THE OFAY

"Strength is virtue. Weakness is sin," the Leading Sorceresp chanted.

"But you've got to remember we were the losingest once, we were the weak ones, we——" the Endfray continued stubbornly, but his voice was drowned in cries of horror at his unprefaced and unstarred reference to the Tabooed Times.

The warrior appearing at the Communications doorway did not stand on ceremony, but roared over the din, "Our psionic trackers have lost touch with the African super-missile south of the Azores! The Blacks in Blackness have broken off their reports."

There was shocked silence, in which the Endfray's voice sounded out clearly. His grin was gone. "Yes," he said, "and now, big as a metal moon, it's approaching Bermuda. Our interceptors rise to destroy it. Countermissiles shoot from it and become balls of white flame. Our interceptors puff into nothingness. It still comes on."

The Leading Sorceresp pointed a shaking arm at him. "He is an African agent," she screeched, "sent to disrupt our counsels at this moment of crisis."

"That's not true, Empress," the Endfray protested. "I've stuck with America because *we* are the losingest side of this war. We are the weak ones. Africa's going to win, unless I——"

Once again his voice was lost, this time in a din of outrage that broke off only when Her Dark Serenity threw up her arms and cried, "Fools! Have you not yet guessed who the Endfray is? Have you not yet solved the Sherlockian riddle? The only spot you haven't psionically searched is psi-proof Mammoth Cave, immemorial home of the Blacks in Blackness and just by Bowling Green. He is clearly one of them, and their best tracker too, highest product of our breeding for psionicity. When he was out on his mad mission to the Ofays, three bombs got through. When he returned home and you could not find him, we got reports on the launching of the African super-missile. When he started here, those reports stopped. And did it not occur to you that he keeps his eyes shut because he has never before been in an environment of optical light? You are all idiots! Endfray, how goes it?"

"The big one zoomed in over Savannah and Macon. Its last counter-missiles blasted those of our coastal and backup defenses. Ten seconds ago it was about to break up over Birmingham and shower all the cities of the Nile with a hundred hydrogen heads."

"Was?"

"Of course, 'was,' Empress. While all these here were squawking, I jiggered its controls and put it into a permanent 93-minute circular orbit around Terra. I'm going to keep it there too. I'm sorry, Empress, but in spite of you being very bright and right about me, I don't trust you with that big a bomb. Or His Terrible Tenebrosity, of course. War's romantic, but destruction's too realistic."

Her Darkness turned on him. "You have your nerve!"

His embarrassment returned. "I *told* you I'm sorry, Empress."

She paused and turned toward the Communications doorway, where a warrior had appeared. "The super-missile still speeds west," he rapped out. "Twenty of our interceptors have risen from Colorado Springs and thirty from Frisco to destroy it."

"Imbeciles! Would you break it up, to do destruction, while it is still over our continent?"

"Don't worry, Empress," the Endfray said.

A second warrior appeared behind the first. "Our fifty interceptors have escaped control and formed themselves into two goose wings slanting back from the super-missile. Their radar blips are unmistakable."

The Endfray grinned. "And now, my Empress, I've got to be going. That flock needs looking after."

A third warrior appeared behind the second. "A bliplet, tiny but unmistakable, has added itself to the fifty blips and one superblip."

"We know," Her Dark Serenity said a shade wearily, waving her hand in dismissal. Then, to the First Psychiawitch, who was at last pushing herself up from the floor, "What exactly, Sister, means the word Endfray?"

"O Your Dread Serenity," the other replied, "now that the taboos are lifting, it comes to me. I take it to be a word of Swine Roman, or Pig Latin if you prefer, a secret language of the Evil Days when Satan-Dis-Ahriman ruled. It was formed from English by putting the last part of the word first and then adding a long A. Even as Ofay means foe, Endfray means friend."

"Friend of the Foe," Her Darkness intoned tiredly. "I might have deduced all from his name alone." Her eyebrows lifted. "Or Ender of the Fray. Frayender."

"However you name him, he appears to have a lost-cause fixation and a comics-book mentality," the First Psychiawitch intellectualized.

"Stop," Her Serenity protested, raising a listless palm. "We've heard enough about Honkies for today. Dismiss all."

Russia noted the super-bomb orbiting with its entourage and set off a warning earthquake that quivered all Antarctica. Australia in turn dropped in the Bering Sea a warning bomb that upset a sealer and sent small tsunami foaming over the beaches of Kamchatka.

But that night the Ofays in their reservations went to sleep for the first time in a century with hope and even a little confidence in their hearts. Someone cared.

Next day North America and Africa agreed to a bombing halt. It was madness to continue a war which only built up the Endfray's orbiting armory. They diverted all their research—scientific, psionic and sorcerous—to a hunt for a means of knocking the Endfray out of the high sky. But secretly Her Dark Serenity decided that he would make her ideal successor. She pondered plans to win him over. So did His Terrible Tenebrosity.

The Endfray turned his major attention to the plight

of the Untouchables behind the Nirvana Screen. There was a cause even more lost than that of the Ofrays.

And he still had, for a lost-cause ace in the hole, the Boers and other white trash of the Blancostans and concentration camps of Rhodesia and South Africa.

CYCLOPS

As THE *Flea* fell out of Moon's shadow into sunlight, its frame and skin began to squeak and ping from the sudden heat, like an old aluminum house at dawn. To the three crewmen of the *Flea* it was a welcome relief to the silence of free fall, although only five minutes had passed since *brennschluss*. This was starting out to be an eerie jump. The stars through the big curved spacescreen looked like spiders' eyes in a vast black nest.

Of course Pyne or Allison or Ness might have spoken or hummed or even jingled in a close-cupped hand some coins or lunar curio-nuggets. But there are times in space when such deliberate sounds only intensify the silence, like whispering in a haunted house. Everywhere you see double stars like eyes and you almost think that the spiders are at last going to spring.

The sun's fierce ion-lashing rays, striking *Flea* from behind, didn't make the tiniest highlight, only some faintly milky patches where the screen was dust-peppered. It may have been only these false nebulas which determined the remarks Ness ventured, now that the ship herself had cleared her throat with her pongings and creakings, like some crusty four-star captain indicating speech was permitted. Ness himself wasn't clear as to what had touched off his thoughts.

"I wonder if there was Life before Life" he said. "I mean in the soup of a stellar-planetary system forming from the original whirlpool. There'd be all the needful elements in the dust, I'd think. And then suppose the heat of an older star—a close double—or of a premature atomic flickering in the central mass struck out and bred those elements. That could have happened here, you know. Pluto may be the cinder of a white dwarf."

Allison shook his head, though his gaze shifted toward the great nebula beside Orion's sword. "You'd never get the right ecospheric conditions," he answered drily "or adequate concentrations of matter."

"But suppose you did," Pyne granted in his large easy voice. "What then, Ness? What are you driving at?"

"Well, it would be a different life from ours," Ness replied haltingly, wondering himself what he was driving at and why. "Born more than halfway between Earth and space, you might say. In a tenuous space marsh. Not planet-bound. A primal life. The Old Life, if we're the New. A different life with different powers."

"The old Is-There-Life-in-the-Vacuum-of-Space buzz?" Pyne chuckled loudly but unmockingly. "They haven't found any in the crevices of the moon, even now when we're digging 'em deep. Any, that is, we mightn't have brought ourselves."

"Ostwald thought that life came to Earth from outside, didn't he?" Ness asked. "Some of the old boys made smart guesses."

"He was thinking of bacterial spores driven by light pressure," Allison explained. "Nobody believes that any more." He paused. "Of course there is viral life in the stratosphere of Venus."

"I was thinking of something bigger," Ness said.

"A space squid with a tungsten gut and a sweet tooth for monatomic hydrogen? A living spaceship from a phylum Linnaeus knew only in nightmares?" Pyne laughed. "You were a kid in the Yukon, Ness. Some winter mornings you wouldn't see smoke coming from the cabin on the next ridge but one, and you'd wonder if your neighbors and their little girl had been eaten by wolves.

Now the *Outward Bound* misses her wireless contact with Moon Central and we're routined to check up and get the same feeling. You're a sensitive guy, Ness. And come to think of it, I'm thinking of something in your records."

"Irregular ESP," Ness said distastefully. "The psychers saw some coincidences where I didn't. It's a great gag." His lips shut firmly.

"Oh, sure," Pyne agreed carelessly. He looked at Ness a moment longer, then frowned at the stars.

The ship was utterly quiet again, its temperature change complete. A few motes of dust danced in the sunlit nose around the three unoccupied seats. The two small goldfish revolved in their bubbly greenish globe bracketed to the ship's back where the men tried to relax, floating uneasily. The atmosphere of a long-deserted church had returned. The stars in their twos and fours in Taurus dead ahead still looked like spiders' eyes.

Ness thought, *Pyne's right, of course. He knows my background. The imagination of the lonely. Idiot psychers, to make me doubt even my thoughts are mine. Idiot pseudosensitivity. I shouldn't find anything eerie in this jump from a dead world to an unborn ship circling it. The* Outward Bound, *our first starship is being built in orbit around the moon simply because, now that the lunar mines and smelters and rolling mills are working, it's a lot cheaper to lift material from Luna than from Earth. Not to create shiver effects. This is the fifth time* Outward Bound *missed her wireless contact. Three times it turned out to be nothing but a tongue of the solar storm licking out between the starship and Luna. And once, their oversight—big laugh. Every time we checked the construction team was as snug in their living globe as bugs in a blanket. We've been afraid of a secret strike by the Russians or the Congo, but that's moonshine.*

The false nebulas and dust motes vanished. The *Flea*

had fallen out of the sunlight into Earth's shadow. She began to clear her throat in reverse. Once again the simple stimulus pulled aside a curtain in Ness' mind.

"I like your vacuum octopuses, Pyne," he mused. "I even think living beings born in young stardust could travel across interstellar space. Existing in weak gravity or none at all, they'd live longer, like sea creatures. They'd have tissues to resist airlessness and cold. Deep-sea creatures are built to oppose positive pressure; they'd be built to oppose negative. Their mouths and other orifices would be double, like airlocks. And once launched on their courses in the light-webbed intersteller dark, they'd hibernate or go into complete deep-freeze. A thousand years, a million, what would it matter? Time would stop for them until they were warmed by their target star."

Allison stared at him. "You're seriously suggesting an animal with the velocity of a rocket?"

Ness thought, *Somebody is*. He said, "They'd be a sort of squid. Pyne's idea. Maybe like a ramjet they'd gather and eject the dust they drive through. Maybe communities of them would help one member gather speed, like step rockets."

"Like bloody acrobats," Pyne muttered. "Squid pyramids."

"Living speeding cones breaking away at the bottom," Ness agreed. "But they wouldn't need tremendous velocities. They'd have time. They'd go in Hohman-type minimum-energy orbits from star to star. They'd take off in the general direction their own stellar system was moving and slowly catch up with another star moving in the same general direction. For instance, any being—or any slow starship or traveling planet, for that matter—would always be coming toward our sun from Lepus, or thereabouts."

"That piddling constellation under Orion's feet? Why from there?" Pyne demanded.

"Because that's at the opposite end of the starfields from Hercules, the constellation toward which Sol moves at about 12 miles a second. Anything slow catching up with Sol would come from Lepus. If it were going 30 miles a second—stars average about 20—and if it caught up with Earth when Earth was starting to swing ahead of the sun, then Earth's 18 miles a second and Sol's 12 would add up to the newcomer's 30. It could go into orbit around Earth or Moon with no braking at all."

"But traveling at 30 miles per second, interstellar trips would take what they call forever," Pyne objected.

Ness shook his head. "Only 25,000 years to Alpha Centaurus and a million and a third to the Pleiades. Time spans like that are trifles to the creatures I have in mind."

"Double or triple those estimates for overtaking time," Pyne insisted.

Allison snorted, "Some creatures! Well, since anything goes in this bull session, I suppose they'd know what course to take between the stars by magic."

"No magic," Ness answered softly. "Creatures with such life spans, adding memory to memory, would see the stars moving, like that goldfish watching the slow swing of crumbs in his globe. Their eye would be like a great wide-angle astronomical telescope. They'd center it on their target star, allowing for its drift, and sleep their way to it, frozen like death."

"With no course corrections for a million years?" Pyne's voice was simply curious.

Ness frowned, his eyes narrowing sleepily. "Maybe a little of their eye would stay alive, warmed by the focused sunlight. The retina and a few tracks in the nervous system. Three of their squid-like jets—"

"What would motivate such creatures?" Allison asked.

"Curiosity, adventure, desire for warmth if their protoflickered out," Ness replied, then added softly, "hunger."

The pilot's board buzzed.

"*Outward Bound's* only a half hour away," Pyne said.

"We'll suit up now and you two will arm the ship. Space-to-space rockets, jet grenades directed outward and set to fire from the board—the works."

Allison said, "You don't believe—" and stopped.

"I believe in danger," Pyne said, "and maybe just a little in Ness' psychers."

"I don't," Ness protested.

"Then you shouldn't have told us your dreams," Pyne said. His mouth laughed, but his eyes didn't, as, reaching for his suit, he glanced out at the arachnid-eyed stars.

One short deceleration burst, a longer one, a tiny correction nudge, and the *Flea* hung beside the *Outward Bound*. The three men sat side by side now, strapped in the nose. Pyne in the pilot's seat, Allison to his left with the firing board for the new-mounted artillery, Ness to Pyne's right with the hot mike to Moon Central.

In decelerating, the *Flea* had come around so that they faced the moon again. It hung in the right end of the screen, its cratered bulk near full phase. In the other end was the dark globe or the construction team's quarters, rotating very slowly, its portholes ominously black. Between these spheres, one inky, one more than half alight, there stretched against the starfields the vast long empty skeleton of the starship, three-quarters sheathed.

But no space-suited figures crawled on it anywhere, nor any of the eight-armed manipulation vehicles called spiders. Several skin sections drifted loose, reflecting moonlight.

The effect was dismal, as of a building project abandoned for millennia, not one that had been busy with workers and that had talked to Moon Central only a quarter day ago.

Then into the right end of the spacescreen there came gently bobbing, pressed to the transparency of the screen, a human skull. All three men saw it at once and for the moment could only stare at the ivory-hued jawless irregular sphere with its great black orbits and triangular nasal opening.

The sharpest horror of the thing lay in its movements. Either the *Flea* had stopped so very close to it that it had been attracted at once by the moonship's miniscule gravity, or else it had been traveling very slowly toward the moonship. But in either case it must also have been rotating slowly, to account for the way it now rocked back and forth against the spacescreen, the cheekbones stopping and reversing each roll, as if it were slowly shaking its head or else peering into the cabin first with one eye, then the other, through each of which, from time to time, a star glittered. This made them notice the great holes blasted or eaten from the skull's top and back. A few inches behind it drifted a human femur.

Ness thought, *it's nuzzling the screen. No, it's librating like the moon. Why should a skull look so much more essentially human and feelingful than a face? Our common denominator? Rock mated to life. Intelligence shaped in stone. The earliest of all sculptures. Craggy mountains . . . and the moon.*

Allison thought, *this is quite impossible—unless the construction team's doctor kept a skeleton. Dead flesh doesn't vanish in space, whether the man dies by accident, sickness, or a blaster. The place for bones is Earth, where there are beasts and birds to rip the flesh away, and maggots and beetles to tidy up, and microbes and water to leach out the last taint of color. Space is where everything lasts, safe from oxygen, acids, everything but the tiny hammers of radiation and the lone wandering ions and dust grains. Yet this skull isn't even faintly pink. It's been sucked dry.*

Pyne thought, *it's a danger sign* and forgot it. He scanned swiftly, searchingly.

There could be any number of hiders inside the partially sheathed starship, but he saw none. He saw bones, then another skull, tiny as a tooth in the distance. It was beginning to look as if there weren't a survivor.

Then something changed in the edge of his vision and he swung to the left.

The dark construction sphere, in rotating, had become deformed. The side swinging into view was crushed inward as if by some unimaginably great judo chop. An opening yards long, feet high, had been torn in the globe's equator. Only darkness inside—

No. Now moonlight began to show something long and straight and pale and divided into sections like a white tape-measure stretched out straight, only longer and much wider. The pale band widened and narrowed rhythmically.

And now, just above the band's center, behind it in the darkness of the smashed globe, a pale dark-centered circle big as a man's chest appeared. It brightened in the moonlight, brightened, and then when that eye—for Pyne was sure suddenly it was a single great eye—when that eye became its brightest, gazing directly at *Flea*, it began to move toward him, slowly at first, then very swiftly, and the white band came with it. As the whole launched out of the construction globe, he saw that it was a round flat object about eight yards in diameter and a yard in thickness, with single eye and great white toothwall in front and with a dozen jets behind.

Pyne would never have noted its circularity except that his fingers had automatically fired *Flea's* jets to take the little ship upward out of the path of the crushing stroke. Now the creature's dull gray flesh was passing under the *Flea*—straight into its fiery jets—when two gray striated tentacles whipped upward from beside the great eye, like steel cables snapped under tension. They struck the *Flea* ringingly, grooving its double skin where they clutched, whitening the spacescreen where one gripped.

A strong vibration went through the ship, the suits, the men. Then the *Flea* was flipped over, so that all three of them were staring straight down at the creature.

At that instant Allison called, "Mask!" and fired all the forward rockets. Their explosion a scant ten yards away battered the *Flea*—explosion front almost as harsh as shock wave—and almost blinded the three men despite the polarization "Mask" of their face plates. Yet the explosions didn't snap or shake loose the tentacles, and when the men saw again, there was the creature with four holes gaping in it, each a yard across, and all still bathed by the fiery tongues of the *Flea's* jets.

Then the creature drew itself up through the yellow flames and enfolded the *Flea*.

Allison fired the dozen jet grenades unlaunched; recoiling pressures raised inward blisters which broke to let in brief fires. Then the *Flea* was swinging and spinning, its sides buckling. Allison fired what was left, Pyne turned the jets to full power—and suddenly the convulsions were over.

What still clung against the spacescreen was the forward rags of the creature, its tatters of skin thick as armor plate, its inner vessels like heavy piping, and among them still a few bones. There were the stumps of the gripping tentacles and the great white mouth below them—a mouth which they saw now was double, with one toothplate in front and one behind. The forward set were still shutting and opening feebly, grating against the spacescreen. It made Ness think of the rocking of the skull.

And there was the eye. Its cornea and lens had been blasted away, baring the black retina. On this were permanent white markings in a pattern all of them slowly recognized: the constellation Hercules and around it Draco and Corona Borealis and a part of Ophiuchus and Lyra with great Vega. In the center was a white round bigger than all the rest—a star that didn't fit, unless it were Sol as seen from the orbit of Saturn. That, Pyne decided, was where the creature had awakened. The white markings would be a sort of scar tissue—the markings of light focused there for eons. Most of the lightscars were not dots but lines recording the movements of the stars over about the last quarter million years.

He said grudgingly, "That's your alien, all right, Ness."

Ness nodded. "One of them," he said softly.

MYSTERIOUS DOINGS IN THE
METROPOLITAN MUSEUM

THE TOP HALF of the blade of grass growing in a railed plot beside the Metropolitan Museum of Art in Manhattan said "Beetles! You'd think they were the Kings of the World, the way they carry on!"

The bottom half of the blade of grass replied, "Maybe they are. The distinguished writer of supernatural horror stories H. P. Lovecraft said in *The Shadow Out of Time* there would be a 'hardy Coleopterous species immediately following mankind,' to quote his exact words. Other experts say all insects, or spiders, or rats will inherit the Earth, but old H.P.L. said hardy coleopts."

"Pedant!" the top half mocked. " 'Coleopterous species'!" Why not just say 'beetles' or just 'bugs'? Means the same thing."

"You favor long words as much as I do," the bottom half replied imperturbably, "but you also like to start arguments and employ a salty, clipped manner of speech which is really not your own—more like that of a deathwatch beetle."

"I call a spade a spade," the top half retorted. "And speaking of what spades delve into (a curt keening signifying the loamy integument of Mother Earth), I hope we're not mashed into it by gunboats the next second or so. Or by beetle-crushers, to coin a felicitous expression."

Bottom explained condescendingly, "The president and general secretary of the Coleopt Convention have a trusty corps of early-warning beetles stationed about to detect the approach of gunboats. A coleopterous Dewline."

Top snorted, "Trusty! I bet they're all goofing off and having lunch at Schrafft's."

"I have a feeling it's going to be a great con," bottom said.

"I have a feeling it's going to be a lousy, fouled-up con," top said. "Everybody will get conned. The Lousicon —how's that for a name?"

"Lousy. Lice have their own cons. They belong to the orders *Psocoptera, Anoplura,* and *Mallophaga,* not to the godlike, shining order *Coleoptera.*"

"Scholiast! Paranoid!"

The top and bottom halves of the blade of grass broke off their polemics, panting.

The beetles of all Terra, but especially the United States, were indeed having their every-two-years world convention, their Biannual Bug Thing, in the large, railed-off grass plot in Central Park, close by the Metropolitan Museum of Art, improbable as that may seem and just as the grassblade with the split personality had said.

Now, you may think it quite impossible for a vast bunch of beetles, ranging in size from nearly microscopic ones to unicorn beetles two and one-half inches long, to hold a grand convention in a dense urban area without men becoming aware of it. If so, you have seriously underestimated the strength and sagacity of the coleopterous tribe and overestimated the sensitivity and eye for detail of Homo sapiens—Sap for short.

These beetles had taken security measures to awe the CIA and NKVD, had those fumbling human organizations been aware of them. There was indeed a Beetle Dewline to warn against the approach of gunboats— which are, of course, the elephantine, leather-armored feet of those beetle-ignoring, city-befuddled giants, men.

MYSTERIOUS DOINGS IN THE METROPOLITAN MUSEUM

In case such veritable battleships loomed nigh, all accredited beetles had their directives to dive down to the grassroots and harbor there until the all-clear sounded on their ESP sets.

And should such a beetle-crusher chance to alight on a beetle or beetles, well, in case you didn't know it, beetles are dymaxion-built ovoids such as even Buckminster Fuller and Frank Lloyd Wright never dreamed of, crush-resistant to a fabulous degree and able to endure such saturation shoe-bombings without getting the least crack in their resplendent carapaces.

So cast aside doubts and fears. The beetles were having their world convention exactly as and where I've told you. There were bright-green ground beetles, metallic wood-boring beetles, yellow soldier beetles, gorgeous ladybird beetles, and handsome and pleasing fungus beetles just as brilliantly red, charcoal—gray blister beetles, cryptic flower beetles of the scarab family with yellow hieroglyphs imprinted on their shining green backs, immigrant and affluent Japanese beetles, snout beetles, huge darksome stag and horn beetles, dogbane beetles like fire opals, and even that hyper-hieroglyphed rune-bearing yellow-on-blue beetle wonder of the family *Chrysomelidae* and subfamily *Chrysomelinae Calligrapha serpentina*. All of them milling about in happy camaraderie, passing drinks and bons mots, as beetles will. Scuttling, hopping, footing the light fantastic, and even in sheer exuberance lifting their armored carapaces to take short flights of joy on their retractable membranous silken wings like glowing lace on the lingerie of Viennese baronesses.

And not just U.S. beetles, but coleopts from all over the world—slant-eyed Asian beetles in golden robes, North African beetles in burnished burnooses, South African beetles wild as fire ants with great Afro hairdos, smug English beetles, suave Continental bugs, and brilliantly clad billionaire Brazilian beetles and fireflies constantly dancing the carioca and sniffing ether and generously spraying it at other beetles in intoxicant mists. Oh, a grandsome lot.

Not that there weren't flies in the benign ointment of all this delightful coleopterous sociability. Already the New York City cockroaches were out in force, picketing the convention because they hadn't been invited. Round and round the sacred grass plot they tramped, chanting labor-slogans in thick accents and hurling coarse working-class epithets.

"But of course we couldn't have invited them even if we'd wanted to," explained the Convention's general secretary, a dapper click beetle, in fact an eyed elater of infinite subtlety and resource in debate and tactics. As the book says, "If the eyed elater falls on its back, it lies quietly for perhaps a minute. Then, with a loud click, it flips into the air. If it is lucky, it lands on its feet and runs away; otherwise it tries again." And the general secretary had a million other dodges as good or better. He said now, "But we couldn't have invited them even if we'd wanted to, because cockroaches aren't true beetles at all, aren't *Coleoptera*; they belong to the order *Orthoptera,* the family *Blattidae—blat* to them! Moreover, many of them are mere German (German-Jewish, maybe?) Croton bugs, dwarfish in stature compared to American cockroaches, who all once belonged to the Confederate Army."

In seconds the plausible slander was known by insect grapevine to the cockroaches. Turning the accusation to their own Wobbly purposes, they began rudely to chant in unison as they marched, "Blat, blat, go the *Blattidae*!"

Also, several important delegations of beetles had not yet arrived, including those from Bangladesh, Switzerland, Iceland and Egypt.

But despite all these hold-ups and disturbances, the first session of the Great Coleopt Congress got off to a splendid start. The president, a portly Colorado potato beetle resembling Grover Cleveland, rapped for order. Whereupon row upon row of rainbow-hued beetles rose to their feet amidst the greenery and sonorously sang—drowning out even the gutteral *blats* of the crude cockroaches—the chief beetle anthem:

"Beetles are not dirty bugs
Spiders, scorpions or slugs.
Heroes of the insect realms,
They sport winged burnished helms.
They are shining and divine.
They are kindly and just fine.
Beetles do not bite or sting.
They love almost everything."

They sang it to the melody of the Ode to Joy in the last movement of Beethoven's Ninth.

The session left many beetle wives, larval children, husbands and other nonvoting members at loose ends. But provision had been made for them. Guided by a well-informed though somewhat stuffy scribe beetle, they entered the Metropolitan Museum for a conducted tour designed for both entertainment and cultural enrichment.

While the scribe beetle pointed out notable items of interest and spoke his educational but somewhat long-winded pieces, they scuttled all over the place, feeling out the forms of great statues by crawling over them and reveling inside the many silvery suits of medieval armor.

Most gunboats didn't notice them at all. Those who did were not in the least disturbed. Practically all gunboats —though they dread spiders and centipedes and loath cockroaches—like true beetles, as witness the good reputation of the ladybug, renowned in song and story for her admirable mother love and fire-fighting ability. These gunboats assumed that the beetles were merely some new educational feature of the famed museum, or else an artistry of living arabesques.

When the touring beetles came to the Egyptian Rooms, they began to quiet down, entranced by art most congenial to coleopts by reason of its antiquity and dry yet vivid percision. They delighted in the tiny, toy-like tomb ornaments and traced out the colorful murals and even tried to decipher the cartouches and other hieroglyphs by walking along their lines, corners and curves. The absence of the Egyptian delegation was much regretted. They would have been able to answer many questions, although the scribe beetle waxed eloquent and performed prodigies of impromptu scholarship.

But when they entered the room with the sign reading SCARABS, their awe and admiration knew no bounds. They scuttled softer than mice in feather slippers. They drew up silently in front of the glass cases and gazed with wonder and instinctive reverence at the rank on rank of jewel-like beetle forms within. Even the scribe beetle had nothing to say.

Meanwhile, back at the talkative grassblade, the top half, who was in fact a purple boy tiger beetle named Speedy, said "Well, they're all off to a great start, I don't think. This promises to be the most fouled-up convention in history."

"Don't belittle," reproved the bottom half, who was in reality a girl American burying beetle named Big Yank. "The convention is doing fine—orderly sessions, educational junkets, what more could you ask?"

"Blat, blat, go the *Blattida*e!" Speedy commented sneeringly. "The con's going to hell in a beetle basket. Take that sneaky click beetle who's general secretary —he's up to no good, you can be sure. An insidious insect, if I ever knew one. An eyed elater—who'd he ever elate? And that potato bug who's president—a bleedin' plutocrat. As for that educational junket inside the museum, you just watch what happens!"

"You really do have an evil imagination," Big Yank responded serenely.

Despite their constant exchange of persiflage, the boy and girl beetles were inseparable pals who'd had many an exciting adventure together. Speedy was half an inch long, a darting purple beauty most agile and difficult for studious gunboats to catch. Big Yank was an inch long, gleaming black of carapace with cloudy red markings. Though quick to undermine and bury small dead animals to be home and food for her larvae, Big Yank was not in the least morbid in outlook.

Although their sex was different and their companionship intimate, Speedy and Big Yank had never considered having larvae together. Their friendship was of a more manly or girlish character and very firm-footed, all twelve of them.

"You really think something *outré* is going to happen inside the museum?" Big Yank mused.

"It's a dead certainty," Speedy assured her.

In the Scarab room silent awe had given way to whispered speculation. Exactly what and or who were those gemlike beetle forms arranged with little white cards inside the glass-walled cases? Even the scribe-beetle guide found himself wondering.

It was a highly imaginative twelve-spotted cucumber beetle of jade-green who came up with the intriguing notion that the scarabs were living beetles rendered absolutely immobile by hypnosis or drugs and imprisoned behind walls of thick glass by the inscrutable gunboats, who were forever doing horrendous things to beetles and other insects. Gunboats were the nefarious giants, bigger than Godzilla, of beetle legend. Anything otherwise nasty and inexplicable could be attributed to them.

The mood of speculation now changed to one of lively concern. How horrid to think of living, breathing beetles doped and brainwashed into the semblance of death and jailed in glass by gunboats for some vile purpose! Something must be done about it.

The junketing party changed its plans in a flash, and they all scuttled swifter than centipedes back to the convention, which was deep into such matters as Folk Remedies for DDT, Marine Platforms to Refuel Transoceanic

Beetle Flights, and Should There Be a Cease Fire Between Beetles and *Blattidae*? (who still went "Blat, blat!").

The news brought by the junketters tabled all that and electrified the convention. The general secretary eyed elater was on his back three times running and then on his feet again—click, click, click, click, click, *click!* The president Colorado potato beetle goggled his enormous eyes. It was decided by unanimous vote that the imprisoned beetles must be rescued at once. Within seconds Operation Succor was under way.

A task force of scout, spy, and tech beetles was swiftly told off and dispatched into the museum to evaluate and lay out the operation. They confirmed the observations and deductions of the junketters and decided that a rare sort of beetle which secretes fluoric acid would be vital to the caper.

A special subgroup of these investigators traced out by walking along them the characters of the word Scarab. Their report was as follows:

"First you got a Snake character, see?" (That was the s.)

"Then you get a Hoop Snake with a Gap." (That was the c.)

"Then Two Snakes Who Meet in the Night and have Sexual Congress." (That was the A.)

"Next a Crooked Hoop Snake Raping an Upright or Square Snake." (The R.)

"Then a repeat of Two Snakes Who Meet in the Night, et cetera." (The second A.)

"Lastly Two Crazy Hoop Snakes Raping a Square Snake." (The B.)

"Why all this emphasis on snakes and sex we are not certain.

"We suggest the Egyptian delegation be consulted as soon as it arrives."

Operation Succor was carried out that night.

It was a complete success.

Secreted fluoric acid ate small round holes in the thick

MYSTERIOUS DOINGS IN THE METROPOLITAN MUSEUM

glass of all the cases. Through these, every last scarab in the Egyptian Rooms was toted by carrying beetles —mostly dung beetles—down into deep beetle bunkers far below Manhattan and armored against the inroads of cockroaches.

Endless atempts to bring the drugged and hypnotized beetles back to consciousness and movement were made. All failed.

Undaunted, the beetles decided simply to venerate the rescued scarabs. A whole new beetle cult sprang up around them.

The Egyptian delegation arrived, gorgeous as pharaohs, and knew at once what had happened. However, they decided to keep this knowledge secret for the greater good of all beetledom. They genuflected dutifully before the scarabs just as did the beetles not in the know.

The cockroaches had their own theories, but merely kept up their picketing and their chanting of "Blat, blat, go the *Blattidae*."

Because of their theories, however, one fanatical Egyptian beetle went bats and decided that the scarabs were indeed alive though drugged and that the whole thing was part of a World Cockroach Plot carried out by commando Israeli beetles and their fellow travelers. His wild mouthings were not believed.

Human beings were utterly puzzled by the whole business. The curator of the Met and the chief of the New York detectives investigating the burglary stared at the empty cases in stupid wonder.

"Godammit," the detective chief said. "When you look at all those little holes, you'd swear the whole job had been done by beetles."

The curator smiled sourly.

Speedy said, "Hey, this skyrockets us beetles to the position of leading international jewel thieves."

For once Big Yank had to agree. "It's just too bad the

general public, human and coleopterous, will never know," she said wistfully. Then, brightening, "Hey, how about you and me having another adventure?"

"Suits," said Speedy.

THE BAIT

FAFHRD THE NORTHERNER was dreaming of a great mound of gold.

The Gray Mouser the Southern, ever cleverer in his forever competitive fashion, was dreaming of a heap of diamonds. He hadn't tossed out all of the yellowish ones yet, but he guessed that already his glistening pile must be worth more than Fafhrd's glowing one.

How he knew in his dream what Fafhrd was dreaming was a mystery to all beings in Newhon, except perhaps Sheelba of the Eyeless Face and Ninguable of the Seven Eyes, respectively the Mouser's and Fafhrd's sorcerer-mentors. Maybe, a vast, black basement mind shared by two was involved.

Simultaneously they awoke, Fafhrd a shade more slowly, and sat up in bed.

Standing midway between the feet of their cots was an object that fixed their attention. It weighed about eighty pounds, was about four feet eight inches tall, had long straight black hair pendent from head, had ivory-white skin, and was as exquisitely formed as a slim chesspiece of the King of Kings carved from a single moonstone. It looked thirteen, but the lips smiled a cool self-infatuated seventeen, while the gleaming deep eye-pools were first blue melt of the Ice Age. Naturally, she was naked.

"She's mine!" the Gray Mouser said, always quick from the scabbard.

"No, she's mine!" Fafhrd said almost simultaneously, but conceding by that initial "No" that the Mouser had been first, or at least he had expected the Mouser to be first.

"I belong to myself and to no one else, save two or three virile demidevils," the small naked girl said, though giving them each in turn a most nymphish lascivious look.

"I'll fight you for her," the Mouser proposed.

"And I you," Fafhrd confirmed, slowly drawing Graywand from its sheath beside his cot.

The Mouser likewise slipped Scalpel from its rat-skin container.

The two heroes rose from their cots.

At this moment, two personages appeared a little be-behind the girl—from thin air, to all appearances. Both were at least nine feet tall. They had to bend, not to bump the ceiling. Cobwebs tickled their pointed ears. The one on the Mouser's side was black as wrought iron. He swiftly drew a sword that looked forged from the same material.

At the same time, the other newcomer—bone-white, this one—produced a silver-seeming sword, likely steel plated within.

The nine-footer opposing the Mouser aimed a skull-splitting blow at the top of his head. The Mouser parried in prime and his opponent's weapon shrieked off to the left. Whereupon, smartly swinging his rapier widdershins, the Mouser slashed off the black fiend's head, which struck the floor with a horrid clank.

The white afreet opposing Fafhrd trusted to a downward thrust. But the Northerner, catching his blade in a counter-clockwise bind, thrust him through, the silvery sword missing Fafhrd's right temple by the thinness of a hair.

With a petulant stamp of her naked heel, the nymphet vanished into thin air, or perhaps Limbo.

The Mouser made to wipe off his blade on the cot-

THE BAIT

clothes, but discovered there was no need. He shrugged. "What a misfortune for you, comrade," he said in a voice of mocking woe. "Now you will not be able to enjoy the delicious chit as she disports herself on your heap of gold."

Fafhrd moved to cleanse Graywand on *his* sheets, only to note that it too was altogether unbloodied. He frowned. "Too bad for you, best of friends," he sympathized. "Now you won't be able to possess her as she writhes with girlish abandon on your couch of diamonds, their glitter striking opalescent tones from her pale flesh."

"Mauger that effeminate artistic garbage, how did you know that I was dreaming diamonds?" the Mouser demanded.

"How did I?" Fafhrd asked himself wonderingly. At last he begged the question with, "The same way, I suppose, that you knew I was dreaming of gold."

The two excessively long corpses chose that moment to vanish, and the severed head with them.

Fafhrd said sagely, "Mouser, I begin to believe that supernatural forces were involved in this morning's haps."

"Or else hallucinations, oh great philosopher," the Mouser countered somewhat peevishly.

"Not so," Fafhrd corrected, "for see, they've left their weapons behind."

"True enough," the Mouser conceded, rapaciously eyeing the wrought iron and tin plated blades on the floor. "Those will fetch a fancy price on Curio Court."

The Great Gong of Lankhmar, sounding distantly through the walls, boomed out the twelve funeral strokes of noon, when burial parties plunge spade into earth.

"An after-omen," Fafhrd pronounced. "Now we know the source of the supernal force. The Shadowland, terminus of all funerals."

"Yes," the Mouser agreed. "Prince Death, that eager boy, has had another go at us."

Fafhrd splashed cool water onto his face from a great bowl set against the wall. "Ah well," he spoke through the splashes, "Twas a pretty bait at least. Truly, there's nothing like a nubile girl, enjoyed or merely glimpsed naked, to give one an appetite for breakfast."

"Indeed yes," the Mouser replied, as he tightly shut his eyes and briskly rubbed his face with a palm full of white brandy. "She was just the sort of immature dish to kindle your satyrish taste for maids newly budded."

In the silence that came as the splashing stopped, Fafhrd inquired innocently, *"Whose* satyrish taste?"

THE LOTUS EATERS

I ALWAYS STRONGLY DISAPPROVED of castrating male cats or spraying female ones—I believed that such operations diminished strength, invaded individuality, and were an insult to any being's right to procreate—until I started to take care of a house and three neutered cats in Summerland in Southern California. It was a lovely house on the dry, steep hillside.

Soon I began to have an understanding of my three eunuchs.

My wife spent most of her time in bed. She was ill and had an addiction for alcohol and books and soft fireside lights.

I fed the three cats: Braggi, a big, soft, sloppy male, red of hair and eye; Fanusi, a small beige female with the habits of a flapper; and the Grand Duchess, white with black spots, snaky and strong, who looked like some creature who should be riding point (though on what steed I don't know) before a troop of western cavalry.

Braggi was a lover. He would come over and just suddenly flop on my shoes—a great big gesture of affection.

Fanusi was a neurotic, despite her basic flapper behavior. Even while wooing you, she was nervous and apt to run off.

The Grand Duchess never lost her cool, though she was the smallest—yet hardiest—of the three.

The thing that most startled me about them, after about a week, was that they were all killers. They would bring in dead mice, rats even, birds and gophers, not eating them, but tossing them at my feet. I expected they were devoted exponents of blood sports. In fact, I noticed that the Grand Duchess had a regular hunting trail she took each day, waiting for a few minutes at each kill spot.

I wondered how they got enough to eat, since they apparently didn't eat their kills—merely displayed them to me, while their mistress, who owned the house, when strictly giving them into my trust, assured me that they each took only two teaspoons of canned cat food a day. A statement I immediately wondered about.

Soon I found the solution, through my wife, who understands people better than I do. Each of the three had a regular route to four sympathetic houses in the near neighborhood, where they got good victuals off the human tables.

Then I became more aware of the quite large garden on the downhill side of the house my wife and I were taking care of—along with the three desexed hunting cats. (Heck—desexed!) They even indulged often in sex play with each other—neutering isn't nearly such a disaster to sexual activity as many people think. Those three felines enjoyed each other.

I got still more interested in the garden downside of the house, from which the cries of the cats would sometimes come in the evenings like the soft coughs of lions.

The garden was a jungle. No, worse than a jungle. More like chaos.

So I started in on the worst stuff first. This happened to be a weed that had black spikes looking like early bamboo phonograph needles, but with tiny black burrs on the ends of them. They stuck on my socks and trousers very determinedly. But I kept getting rid of them, through the help of my wife.

Then I tackled a weed with small, brown, circular

burrs. They weren't so troublesome to deal with. The back garden began to look like something I could conquer.

I started to cut out all sorts of dead wood. There were bushes that bore red berries in the center of the garden. When I'd sawed all of their gray, dry, dead underwood away, I discovered a simple cement fountain underneath. I imagine the mistress and master of the house we were tending—along with their three cats—could hardly have known about the fountain, since for five years they had merely ground-hosed the garden from above a half hour every afternoon, their only attention to that area. I never did find out how that fountain worked.

My wife had a mild heart attack about that time, but we found her a doctor who did her good, and both she and I kept up our lonely ways of life, she in her bedroom, I at my typewriter in my study, and always for a strenuous, sweaty hour or three in the back garden.

I cleaned the lower surface out—now that the nastiest weeds were taken care of—first with a machete, then with a hand mower.

Then I began to get at the trees and the high border vegetation. This meant much more deadwood—too much for our garbage cans. I would load up my car with big corrugated cardboard boxes filled with my dead gray vegetable refuse and take it to the city dump, a huge dark valley behind the sea hills, but circled always with screaming sea birds. It gave me a strange feeling to do this, as if I were burying my wife—or one or all of the three cats she and I were tending.

At about this time Braggi started visiting me in the downhill garden while I worked. He would watch me closely, and when I sat down on the crude fountain edge to rest and wipe my face, he would topple against my ankles in affection. I would stroke him.

My wife read her books and drank her highballs in our bedroom. When she looked down at me from the wide window, it was companionably, affectionately, and concernedly. I would wave at her.

I was fascinated by the things my afternoon cuttings were uncovering. Working at the dead gray underbranches of two tall avocado trees, I discovered a complete hemispherical "pleasure dome," as in the poem by Coleridge, a dome walled overhead with huge green leaves and large green dropping fruit. My wife and I had a tremendous salad that night.

During later days, we gave away a number of these lovely, grainy-skinned fruits to briefly visiting friends.

At about this time the two "altered" female cats—the neurotic Fanusi and the stately Grand Duchess—began to look in on me and Braggi from a distance occassionally as I worked in the garden.

Then I attacked the fifteen-foot hedge of the whole garden—all green and vigorous with clumps of small yellow strange berries. I was amazed at my discoveries as I cut down this fierce stuff—three small evergreens growing sidewise in their attempt to get out of their huge green prison and reach the sun; two lovely branches of enormous, softly yellow roses just in bloom; and a small orange tree with tiny fruit.

That night my wife and I had a beautiful centerpiece at our dining table and lovely screwdrivers. I had a great feeling of triumph at having conquered the garden.

But later that night it was horrible. I awakened from a light sleep, and slipping out of the king-size bed very quietly, so as not to awaken my wife, I put on a dressing gown and stole down to the back garden.

Everything I had cut down was growing at a supernatural velocity, though I don't know what god or goddess had the power at that point.

For a moment I stood astounded—long enough to note Braggi, Fanusi, and the Grand Duchess watching me from the hillside, silhouetted by the moonlight.

It seemed clear that all the vegetation—grasses, weeds, shrubs, vines, and trees—was determined to encircle and strangle to death me and my wife and the house.

I realized I had not a green thumb, to give life, but a

gray thumb, to give death, though this left me with the paradox that in trying to bring the garden to life—to free it—I had infuriated it against me.

I rushed uphill and upstairs. My wife roused instantly. I grabbed a bottle for her. Without packing, we raced out to our car past threatening growing hedges and weeds which stung our legs. We jumped into the auto and started it, opening the back door and yelling, "Fanusi! Grand Duchess! Braggi! Pile in!"

To my relief and utter amazement they did—Fanusi almost in fits, Braggi loving as usual (in fact, snuggling up to my wife), the Duchess staring back over her white blackspotted shoulder in a proud way at the vegetation which appeared to be pursuing us.

Days later I sent some letters.

Three months afterward I heard from the couple who owned the house.

The chief points were that they were grateful to us for taking on their three cats—which had been a bother to them for a long time—but no offer to redeem their pets. And why had I left the back garden in such a rank state after promising tô clear it? And yet taken away all the ripe avocados?

In view of which my plea for a little extra care-taking fee was ridiculous.

My wife and I looked at each other, while Braggi, Fanusi, and the Grand Duchess looked up at us from their appointed places before the flickering, red, streaming, mysterious fireplace, and smiled their Cheshire smiles.

WAIF

I WAS SITTING at my typewriter at Venice, California, in my *tiny,* bedraggled house at eight o'clock in the morning. Through the window, which was finely filmed by smoke, dust, and grease and imprinted by our cat Selim's nose, I saw a medium heavy fog that made nearby buildings dim low rectangles, the street a wide, cottony path; I knew there was a white line down the middle, but I couldn't see it.

Everything was still as death.

Which was good and proper for my wife in the other room. Estelle gets her deep sleep in the mornings, after restless or wakeful nights. She has terrors in darkness and then grows calm with the dawn.

Even the ocean, two blocks away, couldn't be heard. Though its surf, light or loud, is never anything but a lovely embroidery on what silence there may be.

Beside me, a wisp of steam still rose from a half cup of black coffee and there smoldered a half cigarette, and from it rose a lazier curve of smoke.

The silence continued, unusual even for Venice and almost beginning that sort of tension where the ticking of a distant clock becomes artillery and one begins to listen for one's heart.

Most outsiders, even the rest of those in Los Angeles, think of Venice as a wild and dangerous place, noisy with blacks and chicanos and their protestings, rackety with beatniks and hippies and their street music and riots and arrests, wailing with winos, screaming bloody murder with street fights and rapes, screeching with the punished tires of lawless, chain-draped motorcycle gangs or those of dope pushers' cars fleeing pursuing police. Could be, but the sounds I've chiefly heard in my many years here have been soft conversation, the distant strumming of a guitar, the occasional screech of a sea gull, the faint thud of oil wells in back yards and on the beach, and the almost unhearable thrum of the tires of squad cars softly cruising along wide Ocean Front Walk, forbidden even to bicycles, between the low buildings and the sand.

Maybe the socially nasty sounds are kept away from me, by chance or my unconscious, but my notion is that Venice is dying and its silence that of the deathbed— or that of the death cell, an area of Los Angeles doomed by the forces that want to mash it flat and replace it with towering high-rise apartments and vast areas of asphalted parking space, the entire link between past and future gone, the present somehow completely vanished, and forgotten forever the fairy city of canals built in 1905 by Abbott Kinney, who hasn't now even a gravestone of his own, but only one empty street a half block long bearing his last name.

These were death thoughts, I realized, or fog thoughts, as I sat with motionless hands before my typewriter.

Yet sea fog was the reason the forces wanted Venice. It meant that nine times out of ten the west wind was blowing back the smog of Los Angeles and replacing it with relatively pure marine air. Which made the land here potentially more profitable than that, say of the San Fernando Valley, darling of suburbs in the 1930's but now a soup plate of smog.

I drained half the coffee remaining in my cup, took the last drag of my cigarette, stubbed it out, and looked once more at the fog. It was thicker, if anything, completely shrouding the higher outlines of the Home for the Wanted, a progressive orphanage founded anonymously by Abbott Kinney and still continued by Los Angeles, largely on the basis of private contributions.

The silence continued intense. I listened for my wife's breathing in the other room and didn't hear a thing. It was strange that a car hadn't come by in the last few minutes—or was it only seconds? Anyhow, I began to get that feeling of being the last man in the world, which isn't at all bad when you know your wife is sleeping peacefully nearby. But what if she should be dead?

I shook my head to clear it and my fingers to supple them. I lit another cigarette. I lifted my hands.

And now I was—perhaps—going to shatter the continuing intense silence with the staccato blat of my typewriter. But that was the one sound which wouldn't waken my wife. She would know it meant I was happy and working, and that would only make her sleep deeper.

I hesitated. It was hard to decide what to start on. In my mind were thunderings and explosions, about an article on the generation gap and one on pollution, and several short stories, and this and that and everything, in fact, the entire universe or universes. But all this cannonade stirred not a grain of dust nor a delicate curl of cigarette smoke. As they say, "Silent as thought."

But then my mind grew deathly silent, too. Something—Estelle close beyond the flimsy wall, old guilts, the fog silent and beautiful as the stars—made me think of our daughter Lynn, dead at the age of twelve—eleven years ago—of an obscure heart ailment. For the thousandth time I told myself that if Lynn had lived, Estelle would still have an occupation, or at least a concern, or perhaps gone naturally on to another occupation, instead of feeding on me alone, which made me feed on her, and she giving way to grief, then boredom, and finally terror, so that she never felt safe except with two bolts, a chain, and the lock on the front and only door. Perhaps I should have taken her away from Venice, but I'm a slow mover.

These thoughts, too, made me start to remember an old guilt I tried to fight down, not even to know about.

At my ear, at last breaking the silence, a soft girlish voice said, "Hey, mister, I've found your cat."

I jerked around, spilling the dregs of my coffee on the floor and losing my cigarette. After fumble-finding the latter, I slowly looked up.

She wasn't at my ear, but halfway to the front doorway. She was a slim girl about eleven or twelve years old. She had low black shoes, black stockings or pantyhose, a pale gray mini dress. Gently clutched to her tummy was our cat Selim, who managed to remain dignified even in this situation—a grave, thoughtful-eyed male who looked both sleek and battle-scarred.

My first reaction was that the girl was my dead daughter Lynn come back. But then I saw that her hair was black, not brown, her face thinner and more tapering, her eyes violet and larger and coolly inspecting, not green and shyly peering, her mouth wider than Lynn's.

She smiled and said, "He was 'way down the street."

My second reaction was sexual attraction. Her smile made her seem years older. Her figure and dress fitted that, too, especially her long, black-sleeved legs. The twin swellings at her bosom might be small, developing breasts—or else a foam-rubber-padded brassiere perhaps provided by a mother who thought her daughter couldn't become erotically attractive early enough.

What was I doing with a desire like this when my wife was sleeping on the other side of the wall?

For that matter, considering the laws of the land, what legal thing could I do with some girl at most a year or so over twelve?

And what was I thinking of having any aggressive intentions at all toward a girl who returned me my cat?

But how could I have such intentions in any case?— for now she seemed to me simply a creature of the fog, despite her smile. A waif in shades of gray, something from another realm, despite her human speech and appearance? Something impalpable, untouchable. But with what a sweet visage.

And then I got the fourth of my reactions, but stronger —that this girl was not dead Lynn or some strayed nymphet, but someone I had known and known and known —to an unendurable degree. But that was only a shadow memory. Yet somehow the girl halfway between me and the door now seemed dangerous—a sinister figure from another planet.

She let down Selim onto the floor. He strode dignifiedly toward the farther end of the room, where his eating, drinking, and toilet facilities were.

My fears vanished. Now that Selim was gone, I saw that my little girl was wearing around her slim middle a black plastic belt carrying a black plastic toy pistol in a black plastic holster.

She was a Girl Adventurer, out on mornings as well as evenings. Probably going to school right now.

Taking an easy step toward me, she said, "Selim was more than two blocks away when I found him, Mr. Andre."

Her voice was not reproachful, only factual.

I did not tell her Selim was a free cat and could rove as many blocks as he pleased. "Thanks for finding him," I said. "How did you know my name is Andre—and his Selim, for that matter?"

She said, "I've heard you calling him Selim. And your wife calling you. I live with the Fosters, three houses up. They're not my real Poppa and Momma. My Momma died when I was born and my Poppa went away. I was brought up in the Home for the Wanted. Then they put me with the Fosters two months ago."

"Did the Fosters give you that charming dress?"

She smiled. "I made it. They taught me a little sewing at the Home and I went on from there."

I was suddenly struck with mild guilt or uneasiness at passing even mild compliments to a sub-adolescent girl child alone with me. Estelle is forever warning me against such situations. Mostly I think she's silly, but sometimes I think she's half right, considering the society in which we spend our days, with its queer mixture of freedom and puritanism, its tendency to translate all body contacts and privacies into sexual ones.

"You'd better get on to school, hadn't you?" I said lamely, "or you'll be late."

Her eyes twinkled and she laughed softly. "It doesn't matter. They still haven't decided whether to put me into fourth grade or jump me to seventh. I read in the little library."

"Uh, kiddo—" I started. It didn't sound right. "What's your name, if I may ask?" Which sounded much too grown-up, I told myself. Or did it?

"They call me Sophy."

"Well, Sophy, what did they teach you at the Home besides sewing?"

"I helped look after the little kids. When I got a chance, I'd sneak away to the beach and look at the ocean and make up things. On clear nights I'd go up on the roof and look at the stars and imagine what sort of worlds are up there. Worlds of cats with no people, worlds where spaceships are buses you take every hour to some other planet, worlds ruled by children who never grow up, worlds of flowers, water worlds with wise porpoises, worlds where wishes always work, worlds—"

I might have listened to her all morning, except I heard Estelle move in the bedroom and cringed at the row she might make.

So I interrupted softly, "That's nice, Sophy, but now I've got to get to work and you've got to get to school." I turned to my typewriter and made a big thing of poising my hands over the keys.

"Can I come again?" Her low voice was receding.

I nodded briefly and clattered out, "Now is the time for all good men to come to the aid of the party" and "The quick brown fox jumped over the lazy dog."

When I looked up, the girl was gone and Selim had

come from his end of the room and was peering around.

I opened the bedroom door in slow motion, artful to avoid its two creaks. Estelle was still sleeping. She had just changed position. I closed the door the same way.

Then I moved to the front door and felt a little shiver as I saw that all the bolts and chains were locked.

The shiver didn't last long. Beside the door the tall, narrow window was open, with only an easy three-foot drop to the lawn, which wouldn't show footprints in any case. An unconventional entry, but then, an unconventional girl.

So I stopped thinking of Sophy whisking off through the roof to the stars, but skipping to school instead through the thinning fog.

As if to emphasize the point, Selim gave me a look I judged to be contemptuous and sprang out the window without even touching its sill.

Still, Sophy stayed on my mind all day, or more precisely on the top of my subconscious. I was concerned at the depth of my first reactions to her, especially in the sexual area.

That afternoon I spent some time at the Santa Monica Library, boning up on the Roman Republic for a novel I might set there. When I got home, Estelle and Sophy were having tea and thin sandwiches together. Estelle is English.

I wasn't really surprised at Sophy coming back so soon, but I was at how well she and Estelle seemed to be getting along. Veddy ladylike, both of them.

Sophy stood up, nodded slightly toward me, and gave me the ghost of a curtsy. Veddy British, indeed. From another century.

At that moment a hell peculiar to the owners of cats and dogs broke loose.

Black hair on end so he looked three times his size, Selim bounded in through the tall, open window, closely followed by a huge, tall, skinny brown dog, jaws agape, who looked a mix of hound, police dog, and Mexican hairless.

They circled the room twice like hairy comets, one of them mangy—Estelle clutching her tea service, me slow to react as usual—and shot into the bedroom.

Sophy, moving coolly, was at the bedroom door ahead of me. Through the yips and snarls I heard a sharp little click. Then all sounds ceased. I looked around quickly. Selim was standing on the tousled bed, still like a green-eyed porcupine in battle array. But the big brown dog was nowhere.

"He went out that way," Sophy told me, pointing at the bedroom window. "You should have seen him scramble."

The window was open less than a foot at the bottom. Still he had been a very scrawny dog, despite his height.

"I bet people have shot at him before and he knows guns soon as he spots them," Sophy said. She presented her little black plastic pistol sidewise, close to my face. I saw it didn't even have a hole in the muzzle, which was flat, unbroken plastic like the rest. "I clicked it and he beat it." She returned the toy to its black holster. Then she advanced to pick up Selim

"Don't," I said. "You can't handle him when he's like that. He once gave me a bite a half inch deep when I tried."

"Andre had to have tetanus shots," Estelle supplemented over my shoulder. "Don't try."

Sophy picked up the bristling Selim. There were no bites, scratches, growls, yowls, or squirmings. She sat down on the edge of a chair in the living room with Selim on her lap. In a couple of minutes his hair was down and he was purring. We mostly stared at her and didn't speak.

She put him down with a final caress and stood up.

She said, "Well, I must be going now or the Fosters will be wondering. Thanks so much for the tea, Mrs. de Leon."

And she went out the door to the street. No windows or mysterious vanishings.

About an hour later Estelle remarked, "You know, Andre, Sophy reminds me of how Lynn was when she died. Or how Lynn would have been."

I nodded after a bit. "About the same age."

"She's very interested in you," Estelle went on matter-of-factly. "She already knew you were a writer. She wanted to know if you turned out science fiction and fantasy. She was a little disappointed when I told her, no, historical novels and articles on social stuff and anthropology."

"You used a big word like that?"

"She took it in her stride." Estelle smiled a slightly crooked smile. "You know, she looks a little like you."

I suppressed a guffaw. Estelle becomes resentful when her slightest opinion is questioned or, still worse, ridiculed, even obliquely.

The smile grew crookeder. "What's more, she has a crush on you."

I smiled, but once more I did the suppression bit, this time of a groan. Estelle believes that every female from eighteen months to eighty years plus has a crush on me. Even if she makes friends with them all by herself, I steal them away from her as soon as I see them.

I never disagree unless I lose my temper. One doesn't question the absolutes of someone one loves, whatever shape the love or the absolutes may take.

After dinner Estelle resumed, but on a different tack.

"Sophy told me she hasn't been adopted by the Fosters. They just get a little money from the Home for taking care of her." She paused and looked sidewise at me without the crooked smile—indeed, she seemed wistful, tentative.

"Do you think, Andre, we could possibly adopt her? She'd be like Lynn, come again. Maybe she was even conceived the moment Lynn was dying. Oh, I know you would be the main attraction, even though she does like playing high tea. But I could sop up the overflow, and she would give me something to occupy myself."

The mixture of selfishness and tolerance in that almost cool little speech stopped me. Also, I felt a sudden mysterious twinge of guilt different from any of my other feelings about Sophy, even that disturbing sexual angle. Offhand, I guessed it referred to something I'd sunk so deep and heavy-weighted into my subconscious that even its shadow hadn't obtruded into my conscious mind. Though completely masked, it bothered me sharply.

To Estelle I temporized, "That'll take a lot of thinking about. After all, we're middle-aged, have been for a few years."

Estelle said, "Sophy told me the Fosters are each of them seventy or more. As for Sophy, I'd do the taking care of."

"Still, it would take a lot of thinking." That strange new pinpoint of unknown guilt was still thrusting into me.

"Think about something and you don't do it," Estelle said quickly, giving me a look of cynical contempt. "But think about it anyhow. Nice to have a slim, pre-nubile maiden around the house, eh?" she added with a slight smile as mirthless as a madam's.

"And nice for you to have a doll to dress up and play with," I was tempted to add, but of course didn't.

Later that evening I strolled down to the empty beach to look at the small white breakers coming in through the black like troops of children's ghosts. Overcast hid all the stars. Venice's old street lights were unobtrusive, there was no sound but the gentle yet always shiversome surf and the west wind cool and steady and humming faintly like a seashell held to my ear.

Trudging home, a shade tired from footing it through the loose sand, I noticed Norman Saylor sitting on his front steps a few doors from ours smoking a smelly pipe. At his lazy wave I joined him and half in self-protection lit a harsh cigarette myself.

Norman is in his sixties, a retired professor of sociology

and anthropology. Very bright, almost a great mind in his day, but uncompetitive and lazy. I think he does a lecture now and then and even writes an occasional paper and still gets it reputably published, but mostly he just rails genially at the world he helped to create in his revolutionary, actively anti-establishment days and loafs around and wanders the beach and re-explores his books. His library is a bit bigger than his house, but somehow he keeps the volumes from coming out the windows or completely blocking the doors. Naturally he is a godsend to me when I get hung up on knotty points in my articles—or my novels, too, for that matter. And most fortunately he doesn't think being a godsend amounts to a hill of beans.

He fetched us a couple of tall, big, stiff highballs and pretty soon I was telling him the works about Sophy.

"That sex-attraction angle is interesting," he interrupted once. "From the silent way Sophy came and went, and from her air of cool command—something I guess at from the things you say and don't say—she might be your Anima."

"Anima?" I said. "That's some idea of Jung's, isn't it? One of the Archetypes. The female . . ." I trailed off, my own ideas and knowledge uncertain.

"Uh-huh," Norman responded. "Each man's female self, existing in the subconscious a level or so below what Jung calls the Shadow—another Archetype. She appears to a man in dreams and sometimes in fantasies and hallucinations and sometimes she merely makes her lovely and—yes—terrible presence felt to him. She is generally a beautiful woman, though she can appear as a hag. She's really more goddess than woman, inspiring a man's creativity and other urges: imperious, fierce, idealistic yet utterly realistic, sometimes whimsical, and merciless toward a man who fails her, meaning a man who is cowardly or flinches from producing the best that's in him.

"For of course, as you know very well, she's no real

woman or goddess, but a man's concept of what such a goddesswoman would be. Someone to inspire him, someone to adore. An essence of femininity forever pulling him out and away, first from his mother, then from his wife—though both his wife and mother have entered greatly into her make-up. And she's always linked with the wild and the mysterious and the infinitely distant."

"That's odd," I said. "While I was alone with Sophy this morning, I distinctly got the notion that she hadn't come by door or window, but straight from the stars. By transporter maybe, like the *Enterprise*. Ridiculous, isn't it?"

At that moment Norman took a deep draw on his new-filled pipe, and by its glow I saw his usually sardonic lips curl upward in a brief, but genuine, grin.

"Another odd thing, to use your first adjective, not your second," he said. "It happens—maybe you know it —that Jung was very much interested in space flight and other worlds, something that made more conservative psychoanalysts consider him (privately, of course) an eminent crackpot, a somewhat flawed bigwig, high in their hierarchy—one of the big three with Freud and Adler—but not (in some areas) taken seriously. Jung even dug flying saucers, though he appears to have thought of them as significant mental projections rather than actual vehicles.

"He even read and valued science fiction. He thought —and stated in his books for his colleagues to read and maybe shake their heads at—that the best fictional representations of the Anima where She in H. Rider Haggard's book, L'Atlantide in the Frenchman's novel of that name, and Selene in William Solane's *To Walk the Night*. You'll recall Selene came from the stars and had to kill her two Earth husbands against her will before she went back to the stars."

"Very interesting," I commented somewhat noncommittally. I'd heard most of that part of his talk before, but one doesn't voice such things if one hopes to keep friends.

At the same time I felt a little shiver. Venice does get dark once you're a little bit off the infrequent boulevards, and there weren't even the garish lights of a small liquor store in sight. Twice I felt impelled to look up for stars while fearing to see them, silly as that may sound, but the sky was still completely overcast. Good to be sitting by Norman with a little of my drink left.

He went on. "Jung says that a young man usually has a mature, or somewhat more than mature, woman for an Anima. For a middle-aged man she takes the form of a girl *Playboy* might feature or someone a little older —no bunny, though, but a young goddess. While an elderly man is apt to have a little girl for an Anima, perhaps accounting for child molestation by the proto-senile. I hardly think of you as middle-aged, Andre, so Sophy seems a little young for your Anima."

"I don't know," I said. "Sometimes I feel awfully old."

He chuckled. "Well, now you've got a nymphet Anima, halfway between child and young goddess. Just remember, young or old, she's equally powerful."

He fetched us another highball and we chatted of other things.

After a bit I said suddenly, "My God, it's late. Estelle will be frightened. Probably already is."

As I eased his little yard-gate shut, Norman called after me softly but with his customary raillery, "Hey, Andre, don't take seriously any of that guff I told you about the Anima. Jung was never much of anything but a prose poet, and a very ponderous one."

Late next afternoon Sophy paid us another visit. Estelle invited her to stay to dinner. Sophy said the Fosters wouldn't mind, and she was so certain and mature about it that we didn't check with the Fosters, something I'm sure we'd have done in the case of any other child.

It was a lovely meal. Estelle outdid herself—tender steak-and-kidney pie with crispy crust that almost melted in your mouth, peas and tiny new potatoes, mixed salad, chocolate pudding with whipped cream. There were no apparent constraints among the three of us. We were like three congenial adults, yet Sophy remained a child—paradoxical, but true.

"I wish we could always do this," Estelle said at last, settling back with a cigarette and broaching the matter closest to her heart.

I nodded before I realized I'd done so. Dammit, I'd better watch out or I'd be committing myself to the adoption project.

Sophy said, "It *has* been nice. Like three cats having dinner."

"I don't know about that," I said, "I've known some cats were hellers. No table manners at all."

"I mean civilized cats," Sophy explained.

"The cats you told me lived up in the sky?" I asked.

"On a cat-size planet circling a sun," she corrected me with gentle pedantry.

Estelle said, her eyes dreamy with brandy and unfulfillment, "I'd like to live in the sky forever. Just lie on a cloud and float and dream."

"I don't think you're a sky person, Mrs. de Leon," Sophy observed, so obviously absorbed in thought no one could have taken offense. "You like a room better than room."

This child-epigram went unnoticed because both Estelle and I realized how true it was. At any rate Estelle's eyes flickered toward the other room, where she did spend much of her time in bed with a book and a bottle.

She rallied by asking Sophy, "Didn't you ever have a favorite room?"

"Oh, yes, the little one in the Home on the third floor near the ladder to the roof. It made it easy to go up and look at the stars."

That made it easy to talk about Sophy's early childhood. It turned out her mother hadn't died exactly when she was born, but when she was about three, though her father had been out of the picture from the start.

"I don't remember him myself at all, but I do remember a lot about my mother, though the psychologist from the Home told me I was just imagining, especially when I told him she taught me things about the stars."

"What sort of things?" I asked.

"Anyhow, she must have taught me pretty well," Sophy parried, "to be able to stand up to a psychologist when I wasn't quite four. Oh, she taught me about cats, how to stroke them and other animals, including people." She gave me a mischievous grin. "She taught me how space and time didn't mean anything. And she taught me how to keep cool and never to back down in the real clutches and how to—" she hesitated an instant—"love."

Her eyes were directed at me and her gaze was sinking deeper and deeper into mine as she said that last word. There wasn't the least thing trite or saccharine about it the way she said it. The way her gaze pierced me, I felt I was being possessed. Totally. I was afraid. Of course all this was a moment's fantasy.

"And she taught me love is forever and fierce," she finished, so softly it might have been ESP, or else more of my own fantasy, fortified by Norman Saylor's "guff" about the Anima.

But once again there came to me that odd sense of unidentifiable guilt, of something I'd buried very deep and still couldn't dig up—if it were wise to try.

Apparently Estelle hadn't noticed the interchange between Sophy and me, which was a happy wonder, as it would have provided fine ammunition for her theory of "Every female has a crush on you." Her wistful eyes looked through a wall.

"Excuse me, Sophy," she said, "but I'm afraid your mother was wrong about time." She ran a thin hand lightly across her graying hair. "We all grow old."

Sophy said, "But if it were that way, how could we ever wait long enough for the important things?" She added stoutly, "My mother told me to try to live at least a thousand years."

Estelle asked, not unkindly, "Did she tell you how?"

Sophy shook her head and quickly went on, for once a little brittlely, "My mother also left me some presents—"

Estelle glanced at the window and interrupted with "Well, whatever time means elsewhere, I'm afraid it's real here, or we have to act as if it were. It's getting late. It's been a nice party, but the Fosters will be getting worried. Andre, would you see Sophy home?"

One of the things Estelle always insists on, if it's after dark or merely the onset of twilight, is that I see any single woman home, be she a snooty fifty or a lissome eighteen, cleaning woman or scholar or life guard. I suppose it's a nice thing, really, a touch of the old courtesy—even when Estelle's mood changed and she berated me about the crush the lady had on me—and maybe I on her—when I got back from escort duty.

As soon as we got outside, Sophy and I saw it wasn't dark at all and that the sun or at least part of it was still above the horizon. So it seemed the most natural thing in the world for us to stroll hand in hand past the Fosters' down to the beach.

The Pacific was living up to her name. The tide was going out. We stood side by side on the wet, firm sand looking toward Japan. There was still a narrow, orange-yellow slice of sun above the distant water. There wasn't any spectacular sunset, just a low reddish glow in the west, because there wasn't a single cloud in the sky.

The sun went under. As usual I watched for the green flash some people can see under ideal atmospheric conditions at the instant the last silver of sun vanishes. As usual, I didn't spot it. I explained about it to Sophy with a chuckle at my failure. She nodded.

And then it seemed the most natural thing in the world for us to stroll down the beach. At first we wandered separately, then once more hand in hand. Bright Venus winked on in the west, then golden Jupiter overhead, then icy-diamond Sirius, lower than Venus in the southeast, and somewhat above her the compact rectangle of yellow-red Betelgeuse and the other three big stars that are the chief ones of Orion, the Hunter.

Sophy said, "Andre, how would you like to go to the stars, just with me?"

"That'd be fun," I said, giving her hand a gentle squeeze.

"When we got to my planet," she said, "we could settle down and have cats. And babies."

Once again Norman's "guff" came to my mind. There was something eerie about the darkened beach now and perhaps about Sophy, too. I tried to make my grip on her hand light and neutral.

"You're a little young to be thinking about babies," I told her with a jocularity that didn't register in my voice. At the same time I was remembering that Anne of Austria had been betrothed to Louis XIII at eleven.

"Young and old mean different things different places," Sophy said. "Someone who's supposed to be a child on one planet may be a grownup on another."

Thinking of just Earth's many sharp intercultural differences, I couldn't but agree. I said, "Of course, Estelle would have to come along on the trip."

"No," Sophy said. "She doesn't like space. She'd never agree to it. And Mother told me you have to travel very light when you journey between stars. And besides—"

"You know, Sophie," I interrupted, "Estelle is a pretty sweet person, really, even if she's a little narrow-minded and vindictive."

Sophy said, "Yes, I liked playing high tea and other games with her. That's what makes it harder."

I went on quickly, "So I guess I'll just have to stay home on Earth and look after Estelle." My voice again failed to register the lightness and jocularity I intended.

"You're right, too, about Estelle needing to be looked after," Sophy agreed soberly. "I don't think she could make it even on Earth without you. So you'll just have to do something about her."

"And there isn't anything to do about her, so I'll just have to stay on Earth," I said, this time managing to register a tone of finality. I added gently, "A pity."

"It's more than a pity, Andre," Sophy said. "It's a tragedy. It's always a tragedy when true love is foiled."

That stopped me dead on the firm sand.

Sophy said, "A lot of people think kids can't know anything about tragedy. Andre, I've never told you or anyone the whole story about my Momma and Poppa. They were on an inspection-exploration ship checking up on Earth. They were on the team that came down. I wasn't born then, hadn't even been conceived—Momma told me all about it afterwards. They dug Earth, came to love it, and decided to stay, pretending to be Earth folk, until the next inspection ship came around. Permission was granted."

Sophy sighed in an infinitely world-weary way. "Things happened just as you'd expect. For a couple of years they scurried around and enjoyed themselves. Then they both got bored. People were so stupid and brutal here— even the nicest and sweetest of them, even Einstein and Gandhi, I guess, though I don't even see myself how that could be. And the next inspection ship might be five hundred years.

"Anyway, one night Poppa was away and Momma got so bored she went out to bars and got drunk and let an Earth man give her a baby. That was me."

A shiver went down my neck. I was still just standing. "Sophy," I asked, "did your mother have brown hair?"

I could not see Sophy's face, for it was long ago full dark, with only the tiny white breakers to see, and the feeble, low lights of Venice across the sand, and the stars above. But I could sense her eyes closed in thought, her faint frown.

"I don't know," she admitted at last. "Why can't I remember? But whatever the color was, there was a narrow silver streak running back from the middle of her forehead."

That did it for me. That was quite enough. I had found my hidden guilt. I suppose there are tens of thousands of women with such silverstreaks in their hair. No matter. The mind recognizes logic, chance, and coincidence. But the feelings don't. For the feelings, the most improbable, airy possibility can be fully as real as a fact proven, witnessed, and sealed.

Because eleven years ago, you see, after six months of Lynn's last sickness, with Estelle tending her night and day as the child slowly and steadily weakened, and the doctors no help at all, and me spelling Estelle part of the nights and then going off to my editorial job in the mornings, I got fed up with it all. I took off one night and roamed the bars and forgot my troubles and felt my usual brilliant self, only more so. I met a beautiful babe, and bantered with her, and laid her—delicious—and left her.

A beautiful babe with a silver streak down the middle of her hair. I didn't remember the color of the rest of it.

And then when I had got home, Lynn was dead. I don't think Estelle has ever forgiven me for being away that night. She never questioned me about it, but I think she guessed. It was then that life stopped meaning much for her.

Still motionless there on the beach, I grew chilled as ice, although my heart was throbbing painfully. My hand went limp and Sophy's dropped out of it.

Why, Sophy might have been conceived the instant Lynn died.

My daughter's hand . . .

Sophy went on as if she hadn't noticed my reactions. "Momma didn't tell Poppa what had happend, but after a while he could see she was pregnant with me. They had terrible fights, mostly with words. Maybe being all alone in a strange world took away their control. After one bad quarrel, Poppa turned his gun on himself and vanished himself." She paused. " Momma told me all about it after I could understand a little of it. She thought I ought to know everything, good or bad. She planned that we'd wait for the next inspection ship, which might take less, very much less, than five hundred of your years, for our people have ways, which often work, of sensing if one of us is in distress on an alien planet. And then they reroute a ship for rescue if they reasonably can.

"But Momma let herself get too sad and too guilty about Poppa and me. She was the wisest woman in this world, but she couldn't save herself. I guess you can say she died of a broken heart."

I couldn't make any comment whatever, just went on standing there paralyzed.

"Well, anyhow," Sophy went on, suddenly brisk, *"there's"* where we're going on our trip."

She had something of the Anima authority, all right. I followed her slim, ghostly finger to the center of Orion, where the belt and the sword now blazed, the whole of the constellation bespangled with tinier stars—the gaudiest and most gorgeous sight in the entire sky.

Then I realized for the first time it was pitch-dark, and through all my infinitely more serious wondering and fears, there stabbed the trivial but sharp concern that Sophy and I were out way after hours and God knows what the Fosters and Estelle would be thinking or doing.

Sophy found my hand and gripped it reassuringly. "Don't worry, Andre," she said. "Don't worry about the Fosters or Estelle. Things will work out. And especially don't worry about you and me, and how we feel toward each other. On my planet it's perfectly all right for a daughter and widowed father to marry, if they both want to."

For me, that was another dose of paralysis, though I'll always remember the feeling of Sophy's slim little hand around mine.

I don't know how long that moment lasted. But before I could do anything, Sophy had let go of my hand to point once more at Orion and say in a voice closer to excitement than I'd ever heard it, "The sign! *They've* sent a ship for us. Hurry. *They* may be here tomorrow. We've got to get ready."

Then the faint scuff of her light, running feet across the dry sand.

I want to be very careful what I put down now, especially since I can't be sure whether what I saw, or thought I saw, came before what Sophy said, or afterwards, or somewhere during.

I looked up at Orion, and in the sword was a bright scarlet asterisk, consisting of eight narrow, straight lines radiating from the center, the whole appearance occupying about the diameter of the moon.

It instantly vanished.

Then I was running after Sophy, as usual making hard work in the dry sand.

I caught up with her finally in our street. We didn't talk about what had happened. I didn't have the breath to do so.

Lights were on in the Fosters' home and mine and both front doors stood open. But there were voices coming from mine. We headed toward it. I was gritting my teeth in cringing anticipation. I don't know about Sophy.

It could hardly have been worse. Estelle was playing it cool, leaning back in an armchair, and puffing a cigarette in her best eyebrow-raised, lady-of-the-manor style.

The two Fosters, whom I now saw for the first time, were pacing about everywhere. Or maybe stumbling and tottering would be better words. He was a senile hulk of a man, looking like a big upright log that had been bleaching on the beach for ten years. She was a scrunched-over little buzzard of a woman, forever darting her shiny black eyes around and backing most of her husband's imbecile plays. They both landed on me at once.

"What the hell were you doing, mister, out until all

hours with Sophy?" the Hulk demanded.

"Yes, mister, what were you doing out with a little girl hours after dark?" the Buzzard supplemented.

I noticed that after one look at Sophy neither of the Fosters gave her another glance, or said a word to her, or laid a hand on her in love or anger. She stepped between them, took a place a yard behind them, and stood there as cool and unconcerned as I'd ever seen her.

"I was—" I began impatiently, and then hesitated.

Estelle cut in neatly, in a voice both imperious and plaintive, "Andre, these two crude persons pushed their way in. I would have sent for the police to put them out, except police are crude, too. Do something about them."

The Hulk blustered, "Mister, I'd have sent for the police long ago myself except out of consideration for your missus. Now I think I ought to ask them to haul her in, too."

The Buzzard bravely seconded, "Haul in the both of you. I'll have you know, we get *paid* for taking care of Sophy. Money from the Home and from the County, too."

"Shut up about that, Myra," the Hulk said.

Estelle remarked airily and speculatively, "Support money from two sources, eh? Is each aware of the other? I wonder how that would sound in court. Or your vile accusations against a distinguished author, even if you are playing footsie with some of the cruder members of the local Cossack post."

The Hulk said something unprintable, or rather (these days) not worth printing, about how writers and other hippies were darkening the skies of Los Angeles (apparently industrial fumes and automobile exhausts had nothing to do with it) and ought to be all shipped back to the Bronx, or Poland, or San Francisco, or somewhere.

As usual in a crisis, I'd said nothing much.

Quite an evening.

After a while the Hulk and the Buzzard went stumbling off, still complaining and breathing threats and warnings, with Sophy stepping lightly two paces in the rear. I wasn't a bit worried about anything they might do to her. She obviously had the good old Anima whiphand of them.

But I *was* worried about a lot of other things—things which of course I couldn't hint of to Estelle. For a wonder she didn't nag me about "Sophy's crush," just kidded me a bit about the perils of taking nymphets for walks after dark and the astonishing degree to which most older Americans and married couples worried about the molestation of their darling daughters by middle-aged men, even if the latter were the most trusted of old friends.

Still, I had to take three pills to get to sleep.

Despite the pills, the reflex of habit woke me at dawn. Estelle was sleeping like a log. Nonetheless, I was very slow and cautious about slipping from between the sheets. The springs didn't creak. I sat on the edge of the bed and wormed my feet into thick woolen socks with thin, pliant leather soles stitched to them. Venice mornings are chilly.

Then I picked up my bathrobe and edged my way to the kitchen without knocking anything over. I started heating a half pot of stale coffee, then put on my thick robe over my pajamas. As soon as the coffee was barely hot, I downed a cup of it with a shudder and a grimace, heated the rest hotter, and bore a steaming cup of it to my icy, stern typewriter, lit my first cigarette, and sat down and stared at the cryptic, silent, loveless keyboard.

My mind was still quite fuzzy with the three barbiturates I'd had. There wasn't a consequential thought in it, for which I was grateful.

My trance lasted five seconds or fifteen minutes, I don't know how long, when I thought I heard the faintest of scuffs, turned my head, and saw Sophy crossing the living room without seeing me. She was dressed exactly as when I'd first met her, except that now she held her little black plastic pistol in her hand. She vanished into the bedroom.

Drugged or not, I was up and after her like a silent flash.

All I remember glimpsing by the way was Selim backed up against the far wall. His fur was bristled out as much as when the dog had chased him. Only now his eyes weren't furious, but terrified.

I saw into the bedroom. Sophy was leaning grave-faced over the bed and had the muzzle of the plastic pistol an inch from Estelle's temple.

All I could remember was how there had been a click and the big dog had been gone.

I hurled myself silently forward so I landed half on the bed. My hand closed around Sophy's hand and the plastic pistol and reversed the aim of the latter.

There was a click.

Then Sophy wasn't there at all, and I was just holding the black plastic pistol, which was so tiny my big hand concealed it completely, and Estelle had reared up from the flesh-scented warm sheets. Face puffed with sleep, hair stringy as Medusa's, eyes blazing with the fierceness of a fury's (or an Anima's?), she was yelling, "What do you mean waking me up like this? Have you finally gone crazy as I've always told you you would?"

Later that day I hid the little toylike pistol where I thought no one would ever find it.

Estelle and I had a little trouble over Sophy, but really not much. The Fosters came over and gave us another hard time. Then the local police dropped in and asked some questions, but Estelle was on her good behavior and they didn't seem very interested. I guessed the Fosters had set them on and they didn't think much of the Fosters. Paranoids, especially elderly ones, can be a bore to the police.

And a languid young man came over from the Home for the Wanted and most politely asked us a few questions and took a few notes and thanked us courteously and went his languid way. We said a couple of nice things about Abbott Kinney, but I don't think he'd ever heard of the man.

Next morning I looked for the gun—or "toy"—where I'd hidden it. It was gone.

Maybe *they*—the Ones of the Red Sign—tracked it down and took it away with them, off this planet.

At least I hope so. I would hate to think of it falling into the hands of any Earth child—or any Earth adult, for that matter.

And sometimes I hope it "disappeared" Sophy back to her own planet. But from the way she talked about what happened to Poppa, I very much doubt that.

In the midst of Life we are in Death.

Yet in the midst of Death we are in Life.

MYTHS MY GREAT-GRANDDAUGHTER TAUGHT ME

ONE AFTERNOON I woke in the patio feeling sun-toasted and relaxed, my mind very clear but with the glisten of dreams still on it. I ran my hand through my beard and decided to chop it off, which didn't make sense as it felt silky and looked a beautiful silver-gray—when who should come around the corner of the house but my great-granddaughter with her chin tucked down against her chest and her big eyes boring into me as they always do when she's prepared to confound me.

One skinny arm hugged to her side a weatherbeaten gray book showing faintly on the cover a gold-stamped design of three curved horns interlocking. I knew that detail because I'd noticed the same warped-covered book lying around the house several times lately, but never bothered to check what it was, though I'd been meaning to.

She stopped in front of me and untucked her chin and pushed a strand of long pale hair back from her cheek and even yawned fakily, but I knew that was just to get me off guard.

Then she suddenly shot at me, "G'gramps" (she pronounces it guh-GRAMPS) "G'gramps," she shot at me, "why do the frost Giants always talk Russian?"

"Well, I guess they have some pretty tall people in Russia," I temporized, "and they certainly have some pretty chilly winters, as Napoleon and Hitler learned to their sorrow. Hey, how do you know these Frost Giants talk Russian?"

"Because they write B for V and P for R," she explained impatiently, "and for G they make a little gibbet."

"That's not talking, that's writing," I started to object, but she pursed her lips and bored her eyes into me again and asked suspiciously, "G'gramps, do you *know* Norse mythology?"

"You ought to say *dig*," I told her. "Why don't you talk cute beatnik like all the other brainy little eight-year-olds with authors for fathers, or fathers once or twice removed? Why, I've known writers to make vast fortunes just copying down what their cute teenage beatnik daughters say over the phone."

She cut me off with "G'gramps, beatnik went out twenty years ago."

"I'm very glad to hear that," I said. "But now about this Norse jazz, it's all very wild and doomful and warlike, and they have nine worlds, I think, but I remember Jotunheim, where the Frost Giants live, and Asgard—that's where our boys live—"

"Oh, so you admit they're our boys?" she interrupted.

"Well, I mean they're the heroes, sort of. They're the Aesir—"

"How do you spell that? AEC? As in Atomic Energy Commission?"

"No, AES," I told her, "though I suppose you could have C-cedilla."

"Or AE could stand for American Empire," she suggested.

"Look I'm telling this," I told her. "There are these Aesir—Odin, Thor and Company—and they live in Asgard boozing it up and being athletic. Leading off from Asgard is the bridge Bifrost (you say that Beef Roast and not By Frost) with Heimdall to guard it—"

"The launching orbit," she interrupted excitedly. "Bi-

MYTHS MY GREAT-GRANDDAUGHTER TAUGHT ME

frost is the launching orbit and Heimdall is the big radar station that guards against missiles from Jotunheim and the other countries."

"That's too science-fictiony," I objected, "though I do seem to remember that Heimdall could see for a hundred miles in every direction and even hear the grass grow—"

"Sonar too," she said. "Radar and hyper-sonar."

I chuckled in my throat at that, it was rather cute, though there was a little chill in the back of my neck, just behind the chuckle, because it has always seemed to me that there is something frighteningly for-our-times in this Norse notion of embattled worlds with magic weapons poised against each other and then just going ahead and destroying each other at Ragnarok.

"Go on," she prompted. "Tell me some more about Asgard. Tell me any story you remember."

"Well, it's been a long time," I objected, scratching my chin through my silky silver beard. "I forget what led up to it, but there was one about the dwarfs having a contest to see who could make the most wonderful gifts for the gods."

"They're the scientists," she said sharply, nodding her head. "The dwarfs are the scientists and the engineers."

"Have it your own way," I told her. "Well, these gifts for the Aesir—who were the gods, of course—"

"They would naturally think that," she agreed smoothly.

I blinked at her, but went on, "These gifts included the spear Gungnir, which would hit whatever mark it was thrown at no matter how bad the aim of the thrower."

I thought I heard her say, "Self-correcting homing missile," but I went on, "And the boat Skidbladnir—you know, it's funny but I always read that as skin-bladder—anyhow, the boat Skidbladnir, which a person could fold up and fit in his pocket—"

"Pocket battleship," she said instantly. "It says just that."

"And the boar Gold Bristle that flew forever, shedding

light"—I was determined to finish off my list.

"Atomic spaceship," she said. "Or maybe photonic."

"And Thor's hammer Mjolnir."

"Another missile, of course. Don't they actually have one called Thor?"

"And the gold ring Draupnir, that dropped eight rings like itself every ninth night—"

"That could be atomic transmutation," she said thoughtfully, "or maybe just the capitalist economic system as it dreams of itself."

"Now look here," I said rather loudly, for I wanted to end this nonsense before it got any more nightmarish, "you use awfully big words and subtle concepts, even for a little girl who's outgrown beatnik."

"I'm your own great-granddaughter, aren't I?" she countered.

Nobody could protest that comeback, so I just said, "You sure are, honey, but you're looking pretty scrawny with all this intellection." Really, there was something that had begun to bother me about her skinniness and the anxious intensity of her lemurlike gaze. "Why don't you go inside and ask your g'gramma for a big peanut-butter sandwich and a glass of milk?"

"Later maybe," she said. "Right now I want you to tell me every last thing you remember about the Nine Worlds." She came over and leaned straight-armed on my couch and bored with the big eyes again.

"That's asking too much," I protested, "especially with this science-fiction angle you've added. You seem to know more about it than I do, so why don't you tell me the answers? Why do the Frost Giants always talk Russian?"

She leaned two inches closer and whispered, "Because the Frost Giants *are* Russians, see?"

"Well," I said, trying to get back into the spirit of it all, "I have to admit that the Russians do talk guttural and ho-ho-ho harshly and lumber around in fur coats and pound on tables and knock themselves out with monster construction projects and act obtuse but menacing, just like the Frost Giants."

"That's right," she told me, nodding. "Khrushchev was the giant Skyrmir, I'm pretty sure. Jotunheim and Asgard are Russia and America, all set to shoot missiles at each other across England and Europe, which must be Midgard, of course—though sometimes I think the English are the Vanir."

"Say, have you been reading all this crazy stuff in that gray book?" I asked her uneasily. "I remember now: three interlocking horns are Odin's symbol. Let me see it."

"Later maybe," she said, twisting the side with the book clamped to it away from my hand and then backing off a couple of steps. "Right now we've got to dig some important things out of your memory. G'gramps, there's a tradition that Odin wondered all over Midgard, and some of the Nine Worlds too, in disguise. Do you know who Odin might be, like Skyrmir being Khrushchev or Lenin being Hresvelgr or Balder Abraham Lincoln?"

"William O. Douglas?" I suggested wildly, making another attempt to play the game. "He traveled all over the world to see things for himself and he wrote a lot of books about it."

"I don't think so," she said, shaking her head, "but maybe it's not so important to know that. After all, Odin was one of the good guys. For that matter, all the Aesir were pretty good, at least they were brave and well-intentioned, but there was one of them who wasn't . . ." She hesitated and for some reason, I shivered. "Loki wasn't," she said and hesitated again, and as she said "Loki" and stared at me with those big eyes, the patio seemed to waver for a moment behind her and the sun grew dim. "Loki was always causing trouble. He was one of the Aesir, they adopted him, but he was always working the worst mischief he could. G'gramps, who was Loki?"

"Now let's stop all this right now," I commanded, "or we'll be getting to Ragnarok." I laughed and reached out to tousle her hair, but really I was a little frightened. You see, ever since I first ran across the Norse myths in third grade I've never believed for a second in that fakey tacked-on happy ending about the sons of Odin and Thor establishing a new world after the other gods and the giants were dead. It's always been clear to me that Ragnarok must lie in the future, a horror overhanging us all, a doom toward which the universe is relentlessly working—any other solution would be dramatically wrong. And right now I didn't want a little girl to glimpse the dread and despair that had gripped the heart of a third-grader and never quite let go.

I must have done a poor job of concealment, though, for what she said, backing out of reach again, was, "But G'gramps, don't you see that we've *got* to get to Ragnarok?—that that's what all this is leading up to? It all fits. The Midgard serpent, coiled around the world under the seas and never coming up till the end, is atomic submarines. The Fenris wolf, his jaws scraping earth and the stars, is spaceflight—and missiles! And Surtur, who came from Muspelheim and ended the war with a fireweapon that destroyed everything—he must have been the top general of a country, not America or Russia, that started throwing atomic bombs. But G'gramps, which country was Muspelheim? Who was Surtur? And who was the one who tricked them all into it?—who was Loki?"

Now she was the one who was advancing, her big eyes pleading but fierce, and I was the one who was backing off a little across my couch. She seemed to have changed, or maybe it was just that I now saw for the first time that her cheeks were starved-sunken and her dress was ragged and her skinny legs were scarred.

"Who was Loki, G'gramps" she repeated. "If you knew, you could stop him. We can't remember, we've got amnesia for that part. We sent back the book and the myths, so you'd know what was coming and figure out the rest, and stop it from happening, but that didn't do any good, so we had to try to come back ourselves. G'gramps, *please*—"

She reached out her hand brushing my beard, and shook my shoulder. Her fingers were ice.

"*G'gramps, who was Loki?*"

"Stop it, I don't know!" I cried out, flinching away from her. "*I don't even know your name!*"

At that shadow and a strong vibration passed across everything and when I opened my eyes again, she was gone.

My beard was gone too, though I had to rub my chin several times to convince myself of that.

Then I remembered that I never had a beard, certainly not a silver one. I also remembered that I don't have a great-granddaughter. I have one grandchild, a girl, but she's only two.

Oh, one other thing: my wife and a couple of friends remember seeing that gray weathered book with the Odin symbol around the house, but none of them ever looked into it. And now we can't find it anywhere.

So there you are, that's the entire experience, just as it happened. No, wait a moment, I have one slight correction to make—a correction that keeps me wondering.

I don't have a great-granddaughter . . . yet.

CATCH THAT ZEPPELIN!

THIS YEAR on a trip to New York City to visit my son who is a social historian at a leading municipal university there, I had a very unsettling experience. At black moments, of which at my age I have quite a few, it still makes me distrust profoundly those absolute boundaries in Space and Time which are our sole protection against Chaos, and fear that my mind—no, my entire individual existence—may at any moment at all and without any warning whatsoever be blown by a sudden gust of Cosmic Wind to an entirely different spot in a Universe of Infinite Possibilities. Or, rather, into another Universe altogether. And that my mind and individuality will be changed to fit.

But at other moments, which are still in the majority, I believe that my unsettling experience was only one of those remarkably vivid waking dreams to which old people become increasingly susceptible, generally waking dreams about the past, and especially waking dreams about a past in which at some crucial point one made an entirely different and braver choice than one actually did, or in which the whole world made such a decision with a completely different future resulting. Golden glowing might-have-beens nag increasingly at the minds of some older people.

In line with this interpretation I must admit that my whole unsettling experience was structured very much like a dream. It began with startling flashes of a changed world. It continued into a longer period when I completely accepted the changed world and delighted in it and, despite fleeting quivers of uneasiness, wished I could bask in its glow forever. And it ended in horrors, or nightmares, which I hate to mention, let alone discuss, until I must.

Opposing this dream notion, there are times when I am completely convinced that what happened to me in Manhattan and in a certain famous building there was no dream at all, but absolutely real, and that I did indeed visit another Time Stream.

Finally, I must point out that what I am about to tell you I am necessarily describing in retrospect, highly aware of several transitions involved and, whether I want to or not, commenting on them and making deductions that never once occurred to me at the time.

No, at the time it happened to me—and now at this moment of writing I am convinced that it did happen and was absolutely real—one instant simply succeeded another in the most natural way possible. I questioned nothing.

As to why it all happened to me, and what particular mechanism was involved, well, I am convinced that every man or woman has rare brief moments of extreme sensitivity, or rather vulnerability, when his mind and entire being may be blown by the Change Winds to Somewhere Else. And then, by what I call the Law of the conservation of Reality, blown back again.

I was walking down Broadway somewhere near 34th Street. It was a chilly day, sunny despite the smog —a bracing day—and I suddenly began to stride along more briskly than is my cautious habit, throwing my feet ahead of me with a faint suggestion of the goose step. I also threw back my shoulders and took deep breaths, ignoring the fumes which tickled my nostrils. Beside me, traffic growled and snarled, rising at times

CATCH THAT ZEPPELIN!

to a machine-gun rata-tat-tat. While pedestrians were scuttling about with that desperate ratlike urgency characteristic of all big American cities, but which reaches its ultimate in New York, I cheerfully ignored that too. I even smiled at the sight of a ragged bum and a fur-coated gray-haired society lady both independently dodging across the street through the hurtling traffic with a cool practiced skill one sees only in America's biggest metropolis.

Just then I noticed a dark, wide shadow athwart the street ahead of me. It could not be that of a cloud, for it did not move. I craned my neck sharply and looked straight up like the veriest yokel, a regular *Hans-Kopf-in-die-Luft* (Hans-Head-in-the-Air, a German figure of comedy).

My gaze had to climb up the giddy 102 stories of the tallest building in the world, the Empire State. My gaze was strangely accompanied by the vision of a gigantic, long-fanged ape making the same ascent with a beautiful girl in one paw—oh, yes, I was recollecting the charming American fantasy-film *King Kong*, or as they name it in Sweden, *Kong King*.

And then my gaze clambered higher still, up the 222-foot sturdy tower, to the top of which was moored the nose of the vast, breath-takingly beautiful, streamlined, silvery shape which was making the shadow.

Now here is a most important point. I was not at the time in the least startled by what I saw. I knew at once that it was simply the bow section of the German Zeppelin *Ostwald*, named for the great German pioneer of physical chemistry and electrochemistry, and queen of the mighty passenger and light-freight fleet of luxury airliners working out of Berlin, Baden-Baden, and Bremerhaven. That matchless Armada of Peace, each titanic airship named for a world-famous German scientist—the *Mach*, the *Nernst*, the *Humboldt*, the *Fritz Haber*, the French-named *Antoine Henri Becquerel*, the American-named *Edison*, the Polish-named *Sklodowska*, the

American-Polish *T. Sklodowska Edison*, and even the Jewish-named *Einstein!* The great humanitarian navy in which I held a not unimportant position as international sales consultant and *Fachman*—I mean expert. My chest swelled with justified pride at this *edel*—nobel—achievement of *der Vaterland*.

I knew also without any mind-searching or surprise that the length of the *Ostwald* was more than one half the 1,472-foot height of the Empire State Building plus its mooring tower, thick enough to hold an elevator. And my heart swelled again with the thought that the Berlin *Zeppelinturm* (dirigible tower) was only a few meters less high. Germany, I told myself, need not strain for mere numerical records—her sweeping scientific and technical achievements speak for themselves to the entire planet.

All this literally took little more than a second, and I never broke my snappy stride. As my gaze descended, I cheerfully hummed under my breath *Deutschland, Deutschland uber Alles*.

The Broadway I saw was utterly transformed, though at the time this seemed every bit as natural as the serene presence of the *Ostwald* high overhead, vast ellipsoid held aloft by helium. Silvery electric trucks and buses and private cars innumerable purred along far more evenly and quietly, and almost as swiftly, as had the noisy, stenchful, jerky gasoline-powered vehicles only moments before, though to me now the latter were completely forgotten. About two blocks ahead, an occasional gleaming electric car smoothly swung into the wide silver arch of a quick-battery-change station, while others emerged from under the arch to rejoin the almost dreamlike stream of traffic.

The air I gratefully inhaled was fresh and clean, without trace of smog.

The somewhat fewer pedestrians around me still moved quite swiftly, but with a dignity and courtesy largely absent before, with the numerous blackamoors among them quite as well dressed and exuding the same quiet confidence as the Caucasians.

The only slightly jarring note was struck by a tall, pale, rather emaciated man in black dress and with unmistakably Hebraic features. His somber clothing was somewhat shabby, though well kept, and his thin shoulders were hunched. I got the impression he had been looking closely at me, and then instantly glanced away as my eyes sought his. For some reason I recalled what my son had told me about the City College of New York —CCNY— being referred to surreptitiously and jokingly as Christian College Now Yiddish. I couldn't help chuckling a bit at that witticism, though I am glad to say it was a genial little guffaw rather than a malicious snicker. Germany in her well-known tolerance and noble-mindedness has completely outgrown her old, disfiguring anti-Semitism—after all, we must admit in all fairness that perhaps a third of our great men are Jews or carry Jewish genes, Haber and Einstein among them—despite what dark and, yes, wicked memories may lurk in the subconscious minds of oldsters like myself and occasionally briefly surface into awareness like submarines bent on ship murder.

My happily self-satisfied mood immediately reasserted itself, and with a smart, almost military gesture I brushed to either side with a thumbnail the short, horizontal black mustache which decorates my upper lip, and I automatically swept back into place the thick comma of black hair (I confess I dye it) which tends to fall down across my forehead.

I stole another glance up at the *Ostwald*, which made me think of the matchless amenities of that wondrous deluxe airliner: the softly purring motors that powered its propellers—electric motors, naturally, energized by banks of lightweight TSE batteries and as safe as its helium; the Grand Corridor running the length of the passenger deck from the Bow Observatory to the stern's like-windowed Games Room, which becomes the Grand Ballroom at night; the other peerless rooms letting off that corridor—the *Gesellschaftsraum der Kapitan* (Captain's Lounge) with its dark woodwork, manly cigar smoke and *Damentische* (Tables for Ladies), the Premier Dining Room with its linen napery and silver-plated aluminum dining service, the Ladies' Retiring Room always set out profusely with fresh flowers, the Schwartzwald bar, the gambling casino with its roulette, baccarat, chemmy, blackjack (*vingt-et-un*), its tables for skat and bridge and dominoes and sixty-six, its chess tables presided over by the delightfully eccentric world's champion Nimzowitch, who would defeat you blindfold, but always brilliantly, simultaneously or one at a time, in charmingly baroque brief games for only two gold pieces per person per game (one gold piece to nutsy Nimzy, one to the DLG), and the supremely luxurious staterooms with costly veneers of mahogany over balsa; the hosts of attentive stewards, either as short and skinny as jockeys or else actual dwarfs, both types chosen to save weight; and the titanium elevator rising through the countless bags of helium to the two-decked Zenith Observatory, the sun deck windscreened but roofless to let in the ever-changing clouds, the mysterious fog, the rays of the stars and good old Sol, and all the heavens. Ah, where else on land or sea could you buy such high living?

I called to mind in detail the single cabin which was always mine when I sailed on the *Ostwald*—*meine Stammkabine*. I visualized the Grand Corridor thronged with wealthy passengers in evening dress, the handsome officers, the unobtrusive ever-attentive stewards, the gleam of white shirt fronts, the glow of bare shoulders, the muted dazzle of jewels, the music of conversations like string quartets, the lilting low laughter that traveled along.

Exactly on time I did a neat *"Links, marschieren!"* ("To the left, march!") and passed through the impressive portals of the Empire State and across its towering

CATCH THAT ZEPPELIN!

lobby to the mutedly silver-doored bank of elevators. On my way I noted the silver-glowing date: 6 May 1937 and the time of day: 1:07 P.M. Good!—since the *Ostwald* did not cast off until the tick of three P.M., I would be left plenty of time for a leisurely lunch and good talk with my son, if he had remembered to meet me—and there was actually no doubt of that, since he is the most considerate and orderly minded of sons, a real German mentality, though I say it myself.

I headed for the express bank, enjoying my passage through the clusters of high-class people who thronged the lobby without any unseemly crowding, and placed myself before the doors designated "Dirigible Departure Lounge" and in briefer German *"Zum Zeppelin."*

The elevator hostess was an attractive Japanese girl in skirt of dull silver with the DLG, Double Eagle and Dirigible insignia of the German Airship Union emblazoned in small on the left breast of her mutedly silver jacket. I noted with unvoiced approval that she appeared to have an excellent command of both German and English and was uniformly courteous to the passengers in her smiling but unemotional Nipponese fashion, which is so like our German scientific precision of speech, though without the latter's warm underlying passion. How good that our two federations, at opposite sides of the globe, have strong commercial and behavioral ties!

My fellow passengers in the lift, chiefly Americans and Germans, were of the finest type, very well dressed— except that just as the doors were about to close, there pressed in my doleful a Jew in black. He seemed ill at ease, perhaps because of his shabby clothing. I was surprised, but made a point of being particularly polite towards him, giving him a slight bow and brief but friendly smile, while flashing my eyes. Jews have as much right to the acme of luxury travel as any other people on the planet, if they have the money—and most of them do.

During our uninterrupted and infinitely smooth passage upward, I touched my outside left breast pocket to reassure myself that my ticket—first class on the *Ostwald!* —and my papers were there. But actually I got far more reassurance and even secret joy from the feel and thought of the documents in my tightly zippered inside left breast pocket: the signed preliminary agreements that would launch America herself into the manufacture of passenger zeppelins. Modern Germany is always generous in sharing her great technical achievements with responsible sister nations, supremely confident that the genius of her scientists and engineers will continue to keep her well ahead of all other lands; and after all, the genius of two Americans, father and son, had made vital though indirect contributions to the development of safe airship travel (and not forgetting the part played by the Polish-born wife of the one and mother of the other).

The obtaining of those documents had been the chief and official reason for my trip to New York City, though I had been able to combine it most pleasurably with a long overdue visit with my son, the social historian, and with his charming wife.

These happy reflections were cut short by the jarless arrival of our elevator at its lofty terminus on the 100th floor. The journey old love-smitten King Kong had made only after exhausting exertion we had accomplished effortlessly. The silvery doors spread wide. My fellow passengers hung back for a moment in awe and perhaps a little trepidation at the thought of the awesome journey ahead of them, and I—seasoned airship traveler that I am—was the first to step out, favoring with a smile and nod of approval my pert yet cool Japanese fellow employee of the lower echelons.

Hardly sparing a glance toward the great, fleckless window confronting the doors and showing a matchless view of Manhattan from an elevation of 1,250 feet minus two stories, I briskly turned, not right to the portals of the Departure Lounge and tower elevator, but left to those

CATCH THAT ZEPPELIN!

of the superb German restaurant *Krahenest* (Crow's Nest).

I passed between the flanking three-foot-high bronze statuettes of Thomas Edison and Marie Sklodowska Edison niched in one wall and those of Count von Zeppelin and Thomas Sklodowska Edison facing them from the other, and entered the select precincts of the finest German dining place outside the Fatherland. I paused while my eyes traveled searchingly around the room with its restful, dark wood paneling deeply carved with beautiful representations of the Black Forest and its grotesque supernatural denizens—kobolds, elves, gnomes, dryads (tastefully sexy) and the like. They interested me since I am what Americans call a Sunday painter, though almost my sole subject matter is zeppelins seen against blue sky and airy, soaring clouds.

The *Oberkellner* came hurrying toward me with menu tucked under his left elbow and saying, *"Mein Herr!* Charmed to see you once more! I have a perfect table-for-one with porthole looking out across the Hudson."

But just then a youthful figure rose springily from behind a table set against the far wall, and a dear and familiar voice rang out to me with *"Hier, Papa!"*

"Nein, Herr Ober," I smilingly told the head waiter as I walked past him, *"heute hab ich ein Gesellshafter. Mein Sohn."*

I confidently made my way between tables occupied by well-dressed folk, both white and black.

My son wrung my hand with fierce family affection, though we had last parted only that morning. He insisted that I take the wide, dark, leather-upholstered seat against the wall, which gave me a fine view of the entire restaurant, while he took the facing chair.

"Because during this meal I wish to look only on you, Papa." he assured me with manly tenderness. "And we have at least an hour and a half together, Papa —I have checked your luggage through, and it is likely already aboard the *Ostwald*." Thoughtful, dependable boy!

"And now, Papa, what shall it be?" he continued after we had settled ourselves. I see that today's special is *Sauerbraten mit Spatzel* and sweet-sour red cabbage. But there is also *Paprikahuhn* and—"

"Leave the chicken to flaunt her paprika in lonely red splendor today," I interrupted him. "Sauerbraten sounds fine."

Ordered by my Herr Ober, the aged wine waiter had already approached our table. I was about to give him directions when my son took upon himself that task with an authority and a hostfulness that warmed my heart. He scanned the wine menu rapidly but thoroughly.

"The Zinfandel 1933," he ordered with decision, though glancing my way to see if I concurred with his judgment. I smiled and nodded.

"And perhaps *ein Tropfchen Schnapps* to begin with?" he suggested.

"A brandy?—yes!" I replied. "And not just a drop, either. Make it a double. It is not every day I lunch with that distinguished scholar, my son."

"Oh, Papa," he protested, dropping his eyes and almost blushing. Then firmly to the bent-backed, white-haired wine waiter, "*Schnapps also. Doppel.*" The old waiter nodded his approval and hurried off.

We gazed fondly at each other for a few blissful seconds. Then I said, "Now tell me more fully about your achievements as a social historian on an exchange professorship in the New World. I know we have spoken about this several times, but only rather briefly and generally when various of your friends were present, or at least your lovely wife. Now I would like a more leisurely man-to-man account of your great work. Incidentally, do you find the scholarly apparatus—books, *und so weiter* (et cetera)—of the Municipal Universities of New York City adequate to your needs after having enjoyed those of Baden-Baden University and the institutions of high

CATCH THAT ZEPPELIN!

learning in the German Federation?"

"In some respects they are lacking," he admitted. "However, for my purposes they have proved completely adequate." Then once more he dropped his eyes and almost blushed. "But, Papa, you praise my small efforts far too highly." He lowered his voice. "They do not compare with the victory for international industrial relations you yourself have won in a fortnight."

"All in a day's work for the DLG," I said self-deprecatingly, though once again lightly touching my left chest to establish contact with those important documents safely sowed in my inside left breast pocket. "But now, no more polite fencing!" I went on briskly. "Tell me all about those 'small efforts,' as you modestly refer to them."

His eyes met mine. "Well, Papa," he began in suddenly matter-of-fact fashion, "all my work these last two years has been increasingly dominated by a firm awareness of the fragility of the underpinnings of the good world-society we enjoy today. If certain historically minute key-events, or cusps, in only the past one hundred years had been decided differently—if another course had been chosen than the one that was—then the whole world might now be plunged in wars and worse horrors then we ever dream of. It is a chilling insight, but it bulks continually larger in my entire work, my every paper."

I felt the thrilling touch of inspiration. At that moment the wine waiter arrived with our double brandies in small goblets of cut glass. I wove the interruption into the fabric of my inspiration. "Let us drink then to what you name your chilling insight," I said. "*Prosit!*"

The bite and spreading warmth of the excellent *schnapps* quickened my inspiration further. "I believe I understand exactly what you're getting at . . ." I told my son. I set down my half-emptied goblet and pointed at something over my son's shoulder.

He turned his head around, and after one glance back at my pointing finger, which intentionally waggled a tiny

325

bit from side to side, he realized that I was not indicating the entry of the *Krahenest*, but the four sizable bronze statuettes flanking it.

"For instance," I said, "if Thomas Edison and Marie Sklodowska had not married, and especially if they had not had their supergenius son, then Edison's knowledge of electricity and hers of radium and other radioactives might never have been joined. There might never have been developed the fabulous T. S. Edison battery, which is the prime mover of all today's surface and air traffic. Those pioneering electric trucks introduced by the *Saturday Evening Post* in Philadelphia might have remained an expensive freak. And the gas helium night never have been produced industrially to supplement earth's meager subterranean supply."

My son's eyes brightened with the flame of pure scholarship. "Papa," he said eagerly, "you are a genius yourself! You have precisely hit on what is perhaps the most important of those cusp-events I referred to. I am at this moment finishing the necessary research for a long paper on it. Do you know, Papa, that I have firmly established by researching Parisian records that there was in 1894 a close personal relationship between Marie Sklodowska and her fellow radium researcher Pierre Curie, and that she might well have become Madame Curie—or perhaps Madame Becquerel, for he too was in that work—if the dashing and brilliant Edison had not most opportunely arrived in Paris in December 1894 to sweep her off her feet and carry her off to the New World to even greater achievements?

"And just think, Papa," he went on, his eyes aflame, "what might have happened if their son's battery had not been invented—the most difficult technical achievement, hedged by all sorts of seemingly scientific impossibilities, in the entire millennium-long history of industry. Why, Henry Ford might have manufactured automobiles powered by steam or by exploding natural gas or conceivably even vaporized liquid gasoline, rather than the

CATCH THAT ZEPPELIN!

mass-produced electric cars which have been such a boon to mankind everywhere—not our smokeless cars, but cars spouting all sorts of noxious fumes to pollute the environment."

Cars powered by the danger-fraught combustion of vaporized liquid gasoline!—it almost made me shudder and certainly it was a fantastic thought, yet not altogether beyond the bounds of possibility, I had to admit.

Just then I noticed my gloomy, black-clad Jew sitting only two tables away from us, though how he had got himself into the exclusive *Krahenest* was a wonder. Strange that I had missed his entry—probably immediately after my own, while I had eyes only for my son. His presence somehow threw a dark though only momentary shadow over my bright mood. Let him get some good German food inside him and some fine German wine, I thought generously—it will fill that empty belly of his and even put a bit of a good German smile into those sunken Yiddish cheeks! I combed my little mustache with my thumbnail and swept the errant lock of hair off my forehead.

Meanwhile my son was saying, "Also, Father, if electric transport had not been developed, and if during the last decade relations between Germany and the United States had not been so good, then we might never have gotten from the wells in Texas the supply of natural helium our Zeppelins desperately needed during the brief but vital period before we had put the artificial creation of helium onto an industrial footing. My researchers at Washington have revealed that there was a strong movement in the U.S. military to ban the sale of helium to any other nation, Germany in particular. Only the powerful influence of Edison, Ford, and a few other key Americans, instantly brought to bear, prevented that stupid injction. Yet if it had gone through, Germany might have been forced to use hydrogen instead of helium to float her passenger dirigibles. That was another crucial cusp."

"A hydrogen-supported Zeppelin!—ridiculous! Such an airship would be a floating bomb, ready to be touched off by the slightest spark," I protested.

"Not ridiculous, Father," my son calmly contradicted me, shaking his head. "Pardon me for trespassing in your field, but there is an inescapable imperative about certain industrial developments. If there is not a safe road of advance, then a dangerous one will invariably be taken. You must admit, Father, that the development of commercial airships was in its early stages a most perilous venture. During the 1920's there were the dreadful wrecks of the American dirigibles *Roma, Shenandoah*, which broke in two, *Akron,* and *Macon,* the British *R-38,* which also broke apart in the air, and *R-101*, the French *Dixmude,* which disappeared in the Mediterranean, Mussolini's *Italia,* which crashed trying to reach the North Pole, and the Russian *Maxim Gorky,* struck down by a plane, with a total loss of no fewer than 340 crew members for the nine accidents. If that had been followed by the explosions of two or three hydrogen Zeppelins, world industry might well have abandoned forever the attempt to create passenger airships and turned instead to the development of large propeller-driven, heavier-than-air craft."

Monster airplanes, in danger every moment of crash from engine failure, competing with good old unsinkable Zeppelins?—impossible, at least at first thought. I shook my head, but not with as much conviction as I might have wished. My son's suggestion was really a valid one.

Besides, he had all his facts at his fingertips and was complete master of his subject, as I also had to allow. Those nine fearful airship disasters he mentioned had indeed occurred, as I knew well, and might have tipped the scale in favor of long-distance passenger and troop-carrying airplanes, had it not been for helium, the T.S. Edison battery, and German genius.

Fortunately I was able to dump from my mind these uncomfortable speculations and immerse myself in ad-

CATCH THAT ZEPPELIN!

miration of my son's multisided scholarship. That boy was a wonder!—a real chip off the old block, and, yes, a bit more.

"And now, Dolfy," he went on, using my nickname (I did not mind), "may I turn to an entirely different topic? Or rather to a very different example of my hypothesis of historical cusps?"

I nodded mutely. My mouth was busily full with fine *Sauerbraten* and those lovely, tiny German dumplings, while my nostrils enjoyed the unique aroma of sweet-sour red cabbage. I had been so engrossed in my son's revelations that I had not consciously noted our luncheon being served. I swallowed, took a slug of the good, red Zinfandel, and said, "Please go on."

"It's about the consequences of the American Civil War, Father," he said surprisingly. "Did you know that in the decade after that bloody conflict, there was a very real danger that the whole cause of Negro freedom and rights—for which the war was fought, whatever they say—might well have been completely smashed? The fine work of Abraham Lincoln, Thaddeus Stevens, Charles Sumner, the Freedmen's Bureau, and the Union League Clubs put to naught? And even the Ku Klux Klan underground allowed free reign rather than being sternly repressed? Yes, Father, my thoroughgoing researchings have convinced me such things might easily have happened, resulting in some sort of re-enslavement of the Blacks, with the whole war to be refought at an indefinite future date, or at any rate Reconstruction brought to a dead halt for many decades—with what disastrous effects on the American character, turning its deep simple faith in freedom to hypocrisy, it is impossible to exaggerate. I have published a sizable paper on this subject in the *Journal of Civil War Studies*."

I nodded somberly. Quite a bit of this new subject matter of his was *terra incognita* to me; yet I knew enough of American history to realize he had made a cogent point. More than ever before, I was impressed by his multifaceted learning—he was indubitably a figure in the great tradition of German scholarship, a profound thinker, broad and deep. How fortunate to be his father. Not for the first time, but perhaps with the greatest sincerity yet, I thanked God and the Laws of Nature that I had early moved my family from Braunau, Ausria, where I had been born in 1889, to Baden-Baden, where he had grown up in the ambience of the great new university on the edge of the Black Forest and only 150 kilometers from Count Zeppelin's dirigible factory in Wurttemberg, at Friedrichshafen on Lake Constance.

I raised my glass of *Kirschwasser* to him in a solemn, silent toast—we had somehow got to that stage in our meal—and downed a sip of the potent, fiery, white, cherry Brandy.

He leaned toward me and said, "I might as well tell you, Dolf, that my big book, at once popular and scholarly, my *Meisterwerk*, to be titled *If Things Had Gone Wrong*, or perhaps *If Things Had Turned for the Worse*, will deal solely—though illuminated by dozens of diverse examples—with my theory of historical cusps, a highly speculative concept but firmly footed in fact." He glanced at his wristwatch, muttered, "Yes, there's still time for it. So now—" His face grew grave, his voice clear though small—"I will venture to tell you about one more cusp, the most disputable and yet most crucial of them all." He paused. "I warn you, dear Dolf, that this cusp may cause you pain."

"I doubt that," I told him indulgently. "Anyhow, go ahead."

"Very well. In November of 1918, when the British had broken the Hindenburg Line and the weary German army was defiantly dug in along the Rhine, and just before the Allies, under Marshal Foch, launched the final crushing drive which would cut a bloody swath across the heartland to Berlin—"

I understood his warning at once. Memories flamed in my mind like the sudden blinding flares of the battlefield with their deafening thunder. The company I had commanded had been among the most desperately defiant of those he mentioned, heroically nerved for a last-ditch resistance. And then Foch had delivered that last vast blow, and we had fallen back and back and back before the overwhelming numbers of our enemies with their field guns and tanks and armored cars innumerable and above all their huge aerial armadas of De Haviland and Handley-Page and other big bombers escorted by insect-buzzing fleets of Spads and other fighters shooting to bits our last Fokkers and Pfalzes and visiting on Germany a destruction greater far than our Zeps had worked on England. Back, back, back, endlessly reeling and regrouping, across the devastated German countryside, a dozen times decimated yet still defiant until the end came at last amid the ruins of Berlin, and the most bold among us had to admit we were beaten and we surrendered unconditionally—

These vivid, fiery recollections came to me almost instantaneously.

I heard my son continuing, "At that cusp moment in November, 1918, Dolf, there existed a very strong possibility—I have established this beyond question—that an immediate armistice would be offered and signed, and the war ended inconclusively. President Wilson was wavering, the French were very tired, and so on.

"And if that had happened in actuality—harken closely to me now, Dolf—then the German temper entering the decade of the 1920's would have been entirely different. She would have felt she had not been really licked, and there would inevitably have been a secret recrudescence of pan-German militarism. German scientific humanism would not have won its total victory over the Germany of the—yes!—Huns.

"As for the Allies, self-tricked out of the complete victory which lay within their grasp, they would in the long run have treated Germany far less generously than they did after their lust for revenge had been sated by that last drive to Berlin. The League of Nations would not have become the strong instrument for world peace that it is today; it might well have been repudiated by America and certainly secretly detested by Germany. Old wounds would not have healed because, paradoxically, they would not have been deep enough.

"There, I've said my say. I hope it hasn't bothered you too badly, Dolf."

I let out a gusty sigh. Then my wincing frown was replaced by a brow serene. I said very deliberately, "Not one bit, my son, though you have certainly touched my own old wounds to the quick. Yet I feel in my bones that your interpretation is completely valid. Rumors of an armistice were indeed running like wildfire through our troops in that black autumn of 1918. And I know only too well that if there had been an armistice at that time, then officers like myself would have believed that the German soldier had never really been defeated, only betrayed by his leaders and by red incendiaries, and we would have begun to conspire endlessly for a resumption of the war under happier circumstances. My son, let us drink to your amazing cusps."

Our tiny glasses touched with a delicate ting, and the last drops went down of biting, faintly bitter *Kirschwasser*. I buttered a thin slice of pumpernickel and nibbled it—always good to finish off a meal with bread. I was suddenly filled with an immeasurable content. It was a golden moment, which I would have been happy to have go on forever, while I listened to my son's wise words and fed my satisfaction in him. Yes, indeed, it was a golden nugget of pause in the terrible rush of time—the enriching conversation, the peerless food and drink, the darkly pleasant surroundings—

At that moment I chanced to look at my discordant Jew two tables away. For some weird reason he was glaring at me with naked hate, though he instantly dropped his gaze—

But even that strange and disquieting event did not

CATCH THAT ZEPPELIN!

disrupt my mood of golden tranquillity, which I sought to prolong by saying in summation, "My dear son, this has been the most exciting though eerie lunch I have ever enjoyed. Your remarkable cusps have opened to me a fabulous world in which I can nevertheless utterly believe. A horridly fascinating world of sizzling hydrogen Zeppelins, of countless evil-smelling gasoline cars built by Ford instead of his electrics, of re-enslaved American blackamoors, of Madame Becquerels or Curies, a world without the T.E. Edison battery and even T.S. himself, a world in which German scientists are sinister pariahs instead of tolerant, humanitarian, great-souled leaders of world thought, a world in which a mateless old Edison tinkers forever at a powerful storage battery he cannot perfect, a world in which Woodrow Wilson doesn't insist on Germany being admitted at once to the League of Nations, a world of festering hatreds reeling toward a second and worse world war. Oh, altogether an incredible world, yet one in which you have momentarily made me believe, to the extent that I do actually have the fear that time will suddenly shift gears and we will be plunged ino that bad dream world, and our real world will become a dream—"

I suddenly chanced to see the face of my watch—

At the same time my son looked at his own left wrist—

"Dolf," he said, springing up in agitation, "I do hope that with my stupid chatter I haven't made you miss—"

I had sprung up too—

"No, no, my son," I heard myself say in a fluttering voice, "but it's true I have little time in which to catch the *Ostwald. Auf Wiedersehn, mein Sohn, auf Wiedersehn!*"

And with that I was hastening, indeed almost running, or else sweeping through the air like a ghost—leaving him behind to settle our reckoning—across a room that seemed to waver with my feverish agitation, alternately darkening and brightening like an electric bulb with its fine tungsten filament about to fly to powder and wink out forever—

Inside my head a voice was saying in calm yet death-knell tones, "The lights of Europe are going out. I do not think they will be rekindled in my generation—"

Suddenly the only important thing in the world for me was to catch the *Ostwald,* get aboard her before she unmoored. That and only that would reassure me that I was in my rightful world. I would touch and feel the *Ostwald,* not just talk about her—

As I dashed between the four bronze figures, they seemed to hunch down and become deformed, while their faces became those of grotesque, aged witches—four evil kobolds leering up at me with a horrid knowledge bright in their eyes—

While behind me I glimpsed in pursuit a tall, black, white-faced figure, skeletally lean—

The strangely short corridor ahead of me had a blank end—the Departure Lounge wasn't there—

I instantly jerked open the narrow door to the stairs and darted nimbly up them as if I were a young man again and not 48 years old—

On the third sharp turn I risked a glance behind and down—

Hardly a flight behind me, taking great pursuing leaps, was my dreadful Jew—

I tore open the door to the 102nd floor. There at last, only a few feet away, was the silver door I sought of the final elevator and softly glowing above it the words, *"Zum Zeppelin."* At last I would be shot aloft to the *Ostwald* and reality.

But the sign began to blink as the *Krahenest* had, while across the door was pasted askew a white cardboard sign which read "Out of Order."

I threw myself at the door and scrabbled at it, squeezing my eyes several times to make my vision come clear. When I finally fully opened them, the cardboard sign was gone.

CATCH THAT ZEPPELIN!

But the silver door was gone too, and the words above it forever. I was scrabbling at seamless pale plaster.

There was a touch on my elbow. I spun around.

"Excuse me, sir, but you seem troubled," my Jew said solicitously. "Is there anything I can do?"

I shook my head, but whether in negation or rejection or to clear it, I don't know. "I'm looking for the *Ostwald*," I gasped, only now realizing I'd winded myself on the stairs. "For the zeppelin," I explained when he looked puzzled.

I may be wrong, but it seemed to me that a look of secret glee flashed deep in his eyes, though his general sympathetic expression remained unchanged.

"Oh, the zeppelin," he said in a voice that seemed to me to have become sugary in its solicitude. "You must mean the *Hindenburg*."

Hindenburg?—I asked myself. There was no zeppelin named *Hindenburg*. Or was there? Could it be that I was mistaken about such a simple and, one would think, immutable matter? My mind had been getting very foggy the last minute or two. Desperately I tried to assure myself that I was indeed myself and in my right world. My lips worked and I muttered to myself, *Bin Adolf Hitler, Zeppelin Fachman* . . .

"But the *Hindenburg* doesn't land here, in any case," my Jew was telling me, "though I think some vague intention once was voiced about topping the Empire State with a mooring mast for dirigibles. Perhaps you saw some news story and assumed—"

His face fell, or he made it seem to fall. The sugary solicitude in his voice became unendurable as he told me, "But apparently you can't have heard today's tragic news. Oh, I do hope you weren't seeking the *Hindenburg* so as to meet some beloved family member or close friend. Brace yourself, sir. Only hours ago, coming in for her landing at Lakehurst, New Jersey, the *Hindenburg* caught fire and burned up entirely in a matter of seconds. Thirty or forty at least of her passengers and crew were burned alive. Oh, steady yourself, sir."

"But the *Hindenburg*—I mean the *Ostwald!*—couldn't burn like that," I protested. "She's a helium zeppelin."

He shook his head. "Oh, no. I'm no scientist, but I know the *Hindenburg* was filled with hydrogen—a wholly typical bit of reckless German risk-running. At least we've never sold helium to the Nazis, thank God."

I stared at him, wavering my face from side to side in feeble denial. While he stared back at me with obviously a new thought in mind.

"Excuse me once again," he said, "but I believe I heard you start to say something about Adolf Hitler. I suppose you know that you bear a certain resemblance to that execrable dictator. If I were you, sir, I'd shave my mustache."

I felt a wave of fury at this inexplicable remark with all its baffling references, yet withal a remark delivered in the unmistakable tones of an insult. And then all my surrounding momentarily reddened and flickered and I felt a tremendous wrench in the inmost core of my being, the sort of wrench one might experience in transiting timelessly from one universe into another parallel to it. Briefly I became a man still named Adolf Hitler, same as the Nazi dictator and almost the same age, a German-American born in Chicago, who had never visited Germany or spoken German, whose friends teased him about his chance resemblance to the other Hitler, and who used stubbornly to say. "No, I won't change my name! Let that *Fuehrer* bastard across the Atlantic change his! Ever hear about the British Winston Churchill writing the American Winston Churchill, who wrote *The Crisis* and other novels, and suggesting he change his name to avoid confusion, since the Englishman had done some writing too? The American wrote back it was a good idea, but since he was three years older, he was senior and so the Britisher should change *his* name. That's exactly how I feel about that son of a bitch Hitler."

CATCH THAT ZEPPELIN!

The Jew still stared at me sneeringly. I started to tell him off, but then I was lost in a second weird, wrenching transition. The first had been directly from one parallel universe to another. The second was also in time—I aged 14 or 15 years in a single infinite instant while transiting from 1937 (where I had been born in 1889 and was 48) to 1973 (where I had been born in 1910 and was 63). My name changed back to my truly own (but what is that?). And I no longer looked one bit like Adolf Hitler the Nazi dictator (or dirigible expert?), and I had a married son who was a sort of social historian in a New York City municipal university, and he had many brilliant theories, but none of historical cusps.

And the Jew—I mean the tall, thin man in black with possibly Semitic features—was gone. I looked around and around but there was no one there.

I touched my outside left breast pocket, then my hand darted tremblingly underneath. There was no zipper on the pocket inside and no precious documents, only a couple of grimy envelopes with notes I'd scribbled on them in pencil.

I don't know how I got out of the Empire State Building. Presumably by elevator. Though all my memory holds for that period is a persistent image of King Kong tumbling down from its top like a ridiculous yet poignantly pitiable giant teddy bear.

I do recollect walking in a sort of trance for what seemed hours through a Manhattan stinking with monoxide and carcinogens innumerable, half waking from time to time (usually while crossing streets that snarled, not purred) and then relapsing into trance. There were big dogs.

When I at last fully came to myself, I was walking down a twilit Hudson Street at the north end of Greenwich Village. My gaze was fixed on a distant and unremarkable pale-gray square of a building top. I guessed it must be that of the World Trade Center, 1,350 feet tall.

And then it was blotted out by the grinning face of my son, the professor.

"Justin!" I said.

"Fritz!" he said. "We'd begun to worry a bit. Where did you get off to, anyhow? Not that it's a damn bit of my business. If you had an assignation with a go-go girl, you needn't tell me."

"Thanks," I said, "I do feel tired, I must admit, and somewhat cold. But no, I was just looking at some of my old stamping grounds," I told him, "and taking longer than I realized. Manhattan's changed during my years on the West Coast, but not all that much."

"It's getting chilly," he said. "Let's stop in at that place ahead with the black front. It's the White Horse. Dylan Thomas used to drink there. He's supposed to have scribbled a poem on the wall of the can, only they painted it over. But it has the authentic sawdust."

"Good," I said, "only we'll make mine coffee, not ale. Or if I can't get coffee, then cola."

I am not really a *Prosit!*-type person.

LAST

"TIME TRAVELING is finished," the blotchily transparent man whispered, no longer struggling against the embrace of the even more ghostly machine.

"Why?" Last questioned gently.

"Because there's nowhere to go."

"The Black Wall?" Last said.

The trapped man nodded so that the fine sand of the valley's floor wavered through him. "Not one day's distance in the past," he answered faintly, "And not one hour's in the future. Time is being squeezed to nothingness. . . . " His gnat voice failed and sand showed through him.

Last, now fully meriting his name, stood up knowing that the long-expected moment had come. His face was the end of all faces—evolution's simplest, most expressive, and most enigmatic. In the soot-black sky a half dozen stars glowed redly, fewer than when he had knelt. Underfoot the dark sand lay like a soft cloak, covering not a rocky planetary core but what had once been the most strongly built of all artificial planets.

Last felt very tired and completely used. He knew that every atom in his body, like every atom in the narrowing cosmos, had been marked and manipulated by the consciousness and striving, one of whose names is man.

The valley around him was crowded with time machines, silvery and irregularly dim, stretching shattered across more moments than the present, wrecked against the Black Wall they had gone to explore, which was closing in from the beginning and the end.

Last had also visited the valley of the space machines, pillared with the ships whose final, almost instantaneous transits across the twists and turns of the folded dimensions had found no life surviving anywhere else in the cosmos and at the ends of it only the inward-rushing Black Wall. He had peered into the valley of the metal brains, whose sparkling minds had traveled the infinities of possibility and found no more answers. He had wandered slowly through the elvish valley of the espers, the perfectly telepathic beings whose thoughts had journeyed throughout the great inner universe of consciousness and will, discovering nothing but deep-worn tracks. Now all the valleys were silent.

Last, feeling everything around him concentrating to a womb, said clearly, "Black Wall, I will not wail at you, I have accepted your challenge, I have helped to make the universe a single great white word standing out against your nothingness, Oh Wall."

And his face broke into a tender, bold, whimsical smile as the red stars went out like coals and time contracted to a single moment and thought closed in on itself and it was the end.

CLIFFORD D. SIMAK

10624	City	$1.75
77220	So Bright the Vision	$1.50
81002	Time and Again	$1.75
82442	The Trouble With Tycho	$1.50

Available wherever paperbacks are sold or use this coupon.

ace books, (Dept. MM) Box 576, Times Square Station
New York. N.Y. 10036

Please send me titles checked above.

I enclose $.............. Add 35c handling fee per copy.

Name ....

Address ....

City.................... State............. Zip........

34C

FRITZ LEIBER

06218	The Big Time $1.25
30301	Green Millennium $1.25
53330	Mindspider $1.50
76110	Ships to the Stars $1.50
79152	Swords Against Death $1.25
79173	Swords and Deviltry $1.50
79162	Swords Against Wizardry $1.25
79182	Swords in the Mist $1.25
79222	The Swords of Lankhmar $1.25
95146	You're All Alone 95¢

Available wherever paperbacks are sold or use this coupon.

ace books, (Dept. MM) Box 576, Times Square Station
New York, N.Y. 10036

Please send me titles checked above.
I enclose $.................Add 35¢ handling fee per copy.

Name ....

Address ....

City.................... State............. Zip.........

6H